The Road is Open

A Novel

Michael Burns Haggerty

NFB
<<<>>>
Buffalo, NY

ISBN: 978-0692369074

Printed in the United States of America.

Haggerty, Michael Burns. The Road is Open/ 1st Edition

1. Fiction 2. Travel Log. 3. Haggerty
1. No Frills Buffalo   2. New Author

NFB
119 Dorchester Road
Buffalo, NY 14213

For more information visit
Nofrillsbuffalo.com

This book is affectionately dedicated to my Maria

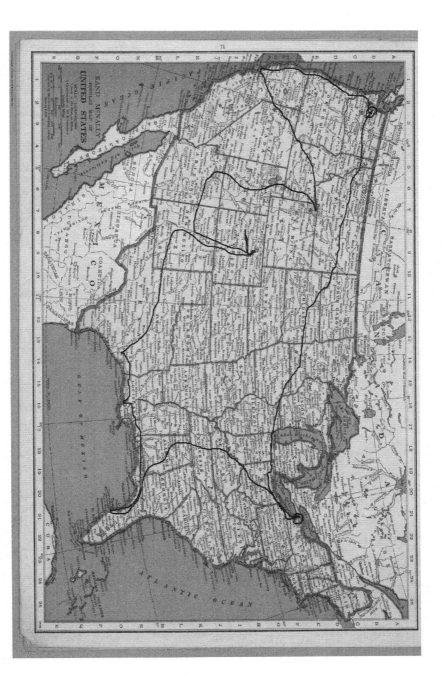

RAND McNALLY
POPULAR MAP OF
UNITED STATES

Chapter 1

Early Morning

It was early morning and I was in that semi-consciousness between being asleep and awake and coming out of a senseless dream. In the cloudy distance I heard a persistent tapping growing louder and louder. I suddenly realized something was smacking against the window above my head. I planted my feet onto the worn carpet of my bedroom floor and looked out the window. There, on the grass below, stood Michael with the clothesline pole in both of his hands thrashing it relentlessly against my window. The clothesline had dropped to the ground and my Grandmother's big white cotton underwear lay scattered on the grass below. He peered straight up at me with big brown determined eyes. I lifted the glass and looked out.

"Prop that line back up! You're getting all those clothes dirty," I said.

"Let me in," he said.

I stumbled down the stairs, in my underwear, toward the back door, and past my chubby, blind grandmother leaning over the kitchen sink washing dishes and reminding me it was inappropriate to have my shirt off. I don't know how she knew I didn't have a shirt on, being blind and all, but somehow she knew. She waddled in my direction and hung close to me, putting her tiny wet hands on each side of my waist and taking little shuffling steps behind me to the back hallway to see who was at the door.

"Where are your manners?" she asked.

I unlatched the back screen and let Michael in.

"Hey Granny," he said climbing the stairs, leaning down, and planting a big wet kiss on her soft fleshy cheek. He had an armful of underwear in his hands and pushed them into her arms.

"Are these yours?"

"Jesus, Mary and Joseph!" she said wiping the mess from her face and clutching the pile of underwear. "What are you doing here so early?"

"I'm taking your boy away to see this big land of ours."

"Let's go upstairs," I said.

Michael stopped suddenly, cocked his head and sniffed the aroma of cooked bacon coming from the kitchen and sitting in the same spot it did every morning: on the stove on a plate and on a napkin soaking up grease. He grabbed a couple curled strips and threw them down in one bite.

"Love it," he said following me up the stairs.

"Keep it down up there," my Grandmother warned. "It's the crack of dawn and everyone's still sleeping!"

"Ah Granny, I love it when you talk dirty to me," he teased.

She looked away blushing and shuffled back into the kitchen to her dishes. Brown spotted hands and big doughy arms slid into the sink. The soapy water was warm and soothing. Elvis Presley crooned *Love me Tender* from the portable radio. Granny hummed along gently, lost somewhere inside of the song.

Michael was wild with excitement. His dark eyes were opened wide and he spoke quickly, waving his hands in animated frenzy.

"We're going," he said.

"What do you mean we're going?"

"I mean, I want to get out of here. I want to go somewhere. I'm sick of sitting on my ass in this town and doing nothing. Summer's coming and I want to get out of Buffalo and see what's out there."

"What do you mean see what's out there? Where do you want to go? What do you have in mind?"

"Backpacks," he said. "We get backpacks, a roadmap, and head to the 90 West and we figure it out. We'll go wherever we want to."

"I've got a job; it's early in the morning. You're out of your mind."

"You have a job? You're working in a scented candle factory. You come home every day smelling like some kind of two-cent cheap whore. What do you do? You're on an assembly line watching candles go by all day long. Come on, man, that's bullshit and you know it. You hate that job. It's summer; we have an opportunity to do something really great, so let's do it."

I leaned against the headboard, took out a cigarette, lit it, and watched the smoke curl aimlessly towards the ceiling. I had to go to work in a couple of hours. Michael sat at the foot of the bed. His piercing eyes intently focused on me, urging me to think hard about the possibility of getting a backpack and heading for the road. I'd seen that look countless times. I knew he wouldn't let up. I knew he had no one else he could, or would, want to ask.

I also knew his brother George was living somewhere near Seattle. At least that's what Michael thought. George. He split from Buffalo about five years ago after their old man took himself out. Saved up a couple of bucks, got a beat up rusted old car and bolted west. George told the family, "I'm headin' out. Been hangin' in this frigid dump long enough. Gonna see what's out West."

Except for one letter where he scribbled that he was working in a bookstore in Seattle and never coming back, no one had heard from him. There was a lot of talk that he drank too much and he had some sort of depression thing going on. I always thought he was a bit distant and odd. Never did talk much. Brooded sullenly, at least when I saw him. I also remember he used to beat us up a lot. Said we were annoying. I never felt particularly close to George. I think Michael understood him more than most. I guess, looking back, Michael wanted to rescue him from himself and maybe offer George a road home.

I also knew Michael wanted to find him and tell him his mother was dead. She died a couple of months ago trying to get down an old set of crystal salt and pepper shakers tucked away in the back of a cupboard. They were given to her years earlier as a wedding gift. She never used them, but one sunny Saturday morning she and Michael were having a breakfast of fried eggs and bacon on a toasted English muffin and she pointed to a chair tucked under the kitchen table and said, "Mikey, drag that chair out for me; I want to see if those crystal shakers are up in the cupboard." She got up on the chair and it slid across the smooth linoleum floor. She slammed down hard on her back. She didn't move or say a word. She just lay there with her eyes pointed wide-open toward the ceiling and not making a sound. Michael stopped chewing his muffin and watched her quietly for a moment until the blood flowed in rivulets from both sides of her mouth leaving a big dark red pool expanding onto the yellow linoleum floor. Her rib pierced into her heart and she was gone just like that.

I first met Michael on the front steps of Herbert Hoover Middle School, just outside of Buffalo, NY, on a stifling hot summer day in nineteen sixty-eight. The granite steps sparkled in the sunlight. We were both entering the third grade that coming September. He was roller-skating with his younger sister Colleen and her friend Betty. Betty had once wet her pants sitting in the noisy school cafeteria while munching on a jelly sandwich. Her nickname *Betty wet-her-pants* stuck and dogged her into high school. I lived directly across the street from the school. I can't remember specifically what I was doing at the school on that day, probably just getting away from the insanity of my home and finding refuge by sitting peacefully on the school's great stone steps.

They rolled toward me. All three on shiny silver roller-skates with red wheels. The kind that fit on your sneakers and you tighten with a key. Michael's key hung from a warn shoelace tied around his neck. I don't believe the girls had a key. I can't remember how the conversation went exactly, but I do recall mentioning something about Betty and her famous accident. Colleen replied that I'd better shut my damn mouth or else she would get her brother to take care of me. Not one to back down, Michael confirmed that he would indeed beat the piss out of me if I didn't take back the nasty remark. I did. After sizing one another up for a moment, Michael seemed content with my apology and we headed to his house with his sister and Betty rolling a comfortable distance behind us.

Looking back, I can pinpoint that as being the precise moment we became friends. I remember feeling excited that this dark, black-haired boy lived around the corner from me. When we got to his house and into his kitchen he climbed up on a yellow and chrome chair, reached into the cupboard, and pulled out a package of root beer Fizzies. We plopped a couple of tablets into two glasses of water and watched the fizz erupt quickly over the tall glasses. Then we chugged the sweet drink, letting the foam escape our mouths and run down our chins. From then on we considered ourselves best friends.

In the spring of the next year, we moved from the house across the street from the school to an Irish neighborhood on the north side of Buffalo. We never lost touch. Michael spent weekends at my new house. The kids were a lot tougher in that neighborhood and the crazy mick ruffians I hung with never quite knew how to deal with this animated fast talking dark skinned boy. He was loud and boisterous and his voice was raspy. He sounded like a miniature Louis Armstrong. He didn't look like the rest of us. Dark, bold Greek blood flowed through him. To the Irish kids it appeared as if he was abandoned from some far off Mediterranean island. His eyes were intense and coffee brown. His lips hung like thick slabs on a dark face and his deep black hair was cut so that the back hung over his collar. His bangs draped carelessly, with a disheveled part, showing a smooth, strong forehead. The girls in my neighborhood found him interesting and they watched him and whispered and giggled among themselves. This angered the boys and every once in awhile one would take a chivalrous stand and sucker punch him or challenge him on the spot to a down and dirty fight. In a fury, Michael would rip apart anyone one who raised a hand toward him. Having older brothers who slapped him around relentlessly worked to his advantage, as I never saw Michael back down from a fight or lose one for that matter. Perhaps it was his strength or his fiery desire to lose at nothing that earned him respect in our neighborhood. Over time Michael became, almost, an honorary North Buffalo Celt.

"I've got close to three hundred bucks saved up," he said. "That's enough to get started. We can work along the way at labor pools and make enough money to keep moving. They're in every city."

There was no way I was going to get out of this. His mind was set. He was insistent. It didn't matter that I had a job and a girlfriend. It didn't matter that I wasn't up for sleeping in the dirt for the next couple of months. It did not matter if I felt that hitchhiking around the United States without any direction or destination was not a particularly bright idea. We could get into trouble. Where would we stay? How would this ever work? It simply did not matter. He would pursue this tenaciously until I buckled under the pressure.

I stretched out on the bed and said reluctantly, "I can probably manage around three hundred dollars. I know they have backpacks at *Twin Fair*. I've seen them there. They're orange and cost around thirty-five bucks. I've got a sleeping bag somewhere around here."

Chapter 2

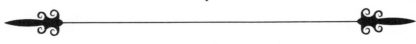

Day One

We left on Sunday July 16, 1978 at two o'clock in the afternoon. The air hung hot and breezy. Michael's older brother Nick and younger sister Colleen grabbed the beat up olive-green family Ford and took us to the entrance ramp of US I-90. It sits off Main Street in Amherst a few miles west of Buffalo. Colleen kissed us both and gave Michael a long tearful and tight hug. Nick said, "Good luck running into George," but figured that was a long shot.

"George wants nothin' more to do with us," he said giving us each an awkward hug and a pat on the back.

They jumped back into the old Ford and we watched Nick merge into traffic and head back into the city. A hollow pit sunk deep in my stomach. We stood under a sign warning us that pedestrians were not allowed onto the interstate. At that moment the both of us felt pretty ill at ease and filled with trepidation.

I had a brand new bright orange backpack with a blue nylon sleeping bag tied onto the bottom rack. On top of the pack I carried a lightweight nylon tent, and strapped to the front of my pack was a new Rand McNally road map of the United States. Packed tightly inside were five t-shirts, two pairs of shorts, one pair of Levi 501 button denim blue jeans, five pairs of underwear, five pairs of white socks, a rain poncho, a denim jacket, a canteen, a mess kit, a can opener, a flashlight, a box of Blue Tip matches, a roll of toilet paper and a small maroon nylon bag filled with soap, shampoo, a toothbrush, toothpaste, and three of those plastic disposable razors. I packed a writing journal, three ballpoint pens, and a copy of *The New American Poetry 1945-1960* loaded with raw writers like Ginsberg, Snyder, Ferlinghetti, Creeley, Kerouac, and my favorite, Gregory Corso, who wrote the sad and humorous poem *Marriage*. I kept twenty dollars in my pocket and hidden in my shoe was my remaining fortune of two hundred and eighty dollars. I figured I had packed pretty well. Michael packed about the same. He had a small hatchet and a copy of Ernest Hemingway's *The Short Stories: The First Forty-Nine.* We swapped the books and read the poetry and the stories over and over. I particularly enjoyed Hemingway's *The Battler* and *The Killers.*

After a few minutes of throwing our thumbs into the air, two girls in a blue Ford Mustang heading for Cleveland pulled over and offered us a ride. They were returning to the interstate after getting gas at the Mobil station. We bolted towards Cleveland with the windows rolled down. The driver sat low in her seat smoking cigarettes and kept the throttle at seventy. She focused ahead and rarely looked back at the two of us crammed into the back seat nervously clutching our packs. She was a tough chick with a wide forehead and a pleasant face. We were cruising. The other girl turned in her seat facing us and talked incessantly about the great time they had in New York: the Big Apple, SOHO, The Village, Central Park, subways.

"It's not scary and surprisingly the people were very friendly," she said. "I guess we had always heard that New Yorkers were rude, but they really weren't. They were very nice. We're going back to Cleveland, packing our shit up, and heading back to New York. Who cares if we have jobs or not… we'll figure it out."

The driver confirmed the plan with an enthusiastic nod and smile. She kept her eyes on the road and smoked. Her hair whipped in the wind behind her. They were cute girls, all smiles. A little over three hours later they dropped us off at a truck stop just this side of Cleveland.

"You'll have better luck here than trying to get a ride from the ramp," the girl in the passenger seat said. "Maybe a trucker will hook you up."

Close enough. We got a lift on the back end of a tow truck pulling an old beater towards Columbus. It felt good rushing down the highway with our backs pressed against the driver's cabin, our legs stretched out before us, and passing through gentle rolling hills dotted with barns sitting next to fields of cattle. The sun was taking its time setting over our shoulders. The tow truck dropped us off at an exit ramp somewhere between Cleveland and Columbus. About a quarter mile up the road was a McDonalds. We hiked over and got a Big Mac, an order of fries and a Coke. Cost us a little over two bucks apiece. We both knew that soon we would stick to mostly canned foods: Spaghetti-Os, beans, bread, cheap stuff that we could pack and eat whenever. After dinner we hiked back to the Interstate and hung on the ramp for about an hour waiting for a lift further south. We leaned against the guardrail. Michael held three rocks and was focusing intently on learning to juggle. Over and over, with his right hand, he threw one rock straight up and then the other as the first was returning. The other rock he held idly with his left hand. He was waiting to perfect this motion before adding the third rock.

It was almost dark. The sun disappeared and the horizon glowed in fiery orange streaks. The day faded in a sweet-scented silence. We could smell the fresh grassy fields. Traffic was sparse. An old-timer, with a large nose and thick hairy nostrils, driving a faded red pick-up pulled over. The pick-up truck had a white roof. We threw our packs in the back and sat in the cab with him. He drove steadily into the approaching darkness and spoke of FDR and the Depression and riding the rails to California to look for work in the canneries and orchards. Good days and honest times.

"Not like that anymore," he said spitting a stream of brown chew into a can nestled between his legs.

A little later he dropped us off and pointed a crooked finger toward a field below the ramp.

"You can sleep there. No one will bother you," he said. The old man told us it was a comfortable field and we would sleep well.

Chapter 3

Columbus to Louisville

It was blazing hot. The sun suspended fiercely above. I hadn't felt the morning sun scorch like that in a long time. I peeled out of my sleeping bag and felt the heavy, sticky wetness in the air. Michael slept uneasily. He rolled and tossed awkwardly in the dirt and grass. Close by, I heard the whine of an eighteen-wheeler's tires cruising on the highway. I pulled the Rand McNally from my pack and studied it. I figured we were just west of Buckeye Lake, not too far from Columbus. Michael stirred, groaned, and dragged himself out of his sleeping bag.

"Jesus, it's hot," he said.

I studied his face. It was loaded with bright red dots scattered under his eyes, across his cheeks, and down to his chin.

"Do I have anything on my face?" I asked.

"No, why do you ask?"

"Just wondering," I said.

We rolled our bags, and brushed our teeth using water from the canteens to rinse our mouths. Michael grimaced while dragging a comb through his thick hair. Mine went through easier. We both put on a clean pair of underwear and put the dirty ones in a plastic bag in our packs. When our bags got full we would have to hit a laundry.

As soon as we made it to the entrance ramp, a car stopped and gave us a lift. I hopped up front and Michael settled in the back seat. The driver's name was Jerry. He told us he was a forklift operator heading for work. He drank coffee from a thermos and had a big black metal lunch box at his side. Monday morning. He let us off in a dreary industrial section on the outskirts of Columbus. The smell of oil and grime filled the air. He pointed across the road to a diner and told us that was the best place to eat breakfast. Food was cheap and there was none better. We contemplated our funds for a moment, still aware of last night's extravaganza at McDonalds. That thought passed quickly and we agreed we would shop later, but now it really did not matter. It was early and a good breakfast seemed like the perfect idea.

It was clear that this diner was the popular spot for workers in this part of town. The place was packed. The counter was lined with black and white workers slamming down eggs with sausage or bacon or ham. They drank from big heavy coffee mugs. A waitress moved in choreographed discipline, feverishly filling each waiting mug propped in front of her. She poured from the coffeepot with one hand and had a fist full or orders in the other. Behind her two cooks tossed big heavy white plates full of breakfasts in the pick-up window. They were piling on fast. She threw orders back at them and grabbed the plates from the window. She spun, twisted, and twirled, lining plates up her arms and slinging them back at the workers. It was all very much under control. Most every table was filled in the dining area. Luckily we were able to snag a seat and order two of the morning specials: two eggs, fried ham, hash browns, toast, and all the coffee we needed for only ninety-nine cents.

After we ordered, Michael went into the bathroom to wash-up. I drank black coffee and read the menu to pass time. The menu was extensive: breakfasts, meat loaf, club sandwiches, open-faced turkey sandwiches with homemade gravy and thick fries, burgers, pork chops, fried chicken. It read beautifully. I realized that I was pretty hungry and breakfast would be good. Michael returned with an irritated look.

"What, you haven't seen my face?"

I did kind of forget about it. It didn't really matter much. I guess he was self-conscience now that he knew about that rash-thing.

"I didn't want to alarm you."

"Great," he said sliding his fingertips over his cheeks. "What's all over my face? Jesus, how could you not tell me?"

"Maybe you slept on an ant hill or something. It'll go away."

The waitress hurried over, dropped off our breakfasts, poured more coffee, and asked if everything was okay.

"Everything's great," he answered and she quickly moved to the next table. He was still concerned. "You think it's a rash or something? Maybe it's the heat. Maybe it's a heat rash. I didn't see any ants and I didn't feel anything either. I would have felt if a bunch of ants were crawling over my face…don't you think? Does it just go away or do I need to get some cream or something? That pink cream, what's it called?"

"Calamine lotion," I said. "You know, it looks a lot better than it did when you first woke up; a lot better."

"You could have mentioned something."

"And worry you? Not a chance."

"You're an ass," he said.

"Works for me," I said.

We had no real deadlines to meet so we lingered at our table, looking over the map, and planning our trip. My brother Kevin and his buddy, who also happened to be named Kevin except everyone knows him as McShay, were getting ready to hit the road. Somehow we had to figure out where and when to meet them. Our plan before we left was sketchy. I told my brother I would call him from wherever we were on the morning of the twenty-fifth, and then we could figure out a meeting place. Probably in Colorado. Our friend Johnny had a brother living in Englewood, Colorado. Johnny was heading out there for the summer, so the bunch of us could all meet and then head into the mountains and camp. They had a sister named

Michelle. She moved up to Breckenridge and we were planning on hanging with her once we got out that way. No big deal. It was a pretty easy plan.

Michael calmed down. Breakfast did him good. After we ate he sipped coffee, lit a Marlboro and smoked. The workers rose from their seats, steadily paid their checks, and shuffled out sharing lots of "see ya tomorrows." Tables opened. The lull between breakfast and lunch gave the waitress relief. She moved at a less frantic pace now. She cleared and wiped the empty tables. Her arms were thin and muscular. Her legs were too. She wore her hair up in some sort of bun and carried a pen behind her ear.

"Once we get through Columbus we can pick up Highway 71 and take it south through Cincinnati and on into Louisville," I said tracing the route on the map with my finger.

"I want to go to New Orleans," Michael said.

"We're heading in the right direction. Louisville, Nashville, Birmingham, Montgomery, then New Orleans," I said as he watched my finger glide down the page traveling south through the eastern United States.

Neither one of us had ever been out of New York. We'd both been to Canada, but for us that didn't count. From Buffalo you cross the Peace Bridge that extends over the Niagara River and you're in Canada. We used to ride our bikes to the bridge and go fishing. We must have done it a million times. We'd ride over the Peace Bridge stopping right at the center where the Canadian and American Flags meet. We'd hop off our bikes and watch the tumultuous Niagara River flow dangerously below us. The ride from the center of the bridge towards customs was one long fast downhill coast all the way. In those days getting through customs was fast. The custom's officer would simply ask us our name and where we were heading. It was short and sweet. Once we got on the Canadian side, we'd ride to our spot at the big rocks where the mouth of the Niagara meets Lake Erie. We'd cast our lines into the fast moving Niagara and catch a bunch of sheep head, a strong boney fish that hardly anybody eats except maybe the old black guys who fish along the banks. Every once in a while we'd hit on bass or perch and sometimes even a pike or a muskie. Crossing the border was easy then. It's pretty tough nowadays with all the trouble at the border. I haven't seen anyone take a bike over the bridge in years.

A couple of black dudes heading into downtown Columbus offered us a ride. They told us we were crazy to be hitchhiking all that way. When we told them we were going all over the country they let out a big ol' laugh and the driver said *whooo-weee* and shook his head in good-natured disbelief. His thick lips and big white teeth opened revealing a hearty smile. The other was a skinny dude with a big 'fro and a couple of long hairs dangling from his chin.

"You boys is nuts," the skinny one chuckled.

They dropped us off in downtown Columbus. We walked the streets and found a small grocery store and figured on getting just enough supplies to last us a couple of days. No need weighing ourselves down. One loaf of bread, a half pound of bologna, a small jar of mustard, two cans of Libby's pork and beans, two cans of Spaghetti-O's, and a couple of single bags of chips would cover us for now.

After about a half an hour we had walked out of Columbus and on the Highway 71 south ramp towards Cincinnati. An elderly woman picked us up and got us all the way through Cincinnati to a place called Independence, Kentucky. She hardly spoke along the way, so it was pretty quiet and that was fine with me. Michael dozed in the back seat, his head tilted back and his mouth open. The woman was heading to Independence to visit her daughter who was divorcing her husband and needed her mama as she put it. She had a long neck and a wide face and soft cropped hair. She reminded me of the woman who used to play Jane Hathaway on *The Beverly Hillbillies* or maybe someone out of a Willa Cather novel. She had that down-home prairie look to her. It was a quiet ride and a couple of hours later she let us off on the interstate just outside of Independence, Kentucky.

Our luck was good. We were barely settled on the side of the road when this longhaired kid with his beagle pulled over and asked us what we were doing.

"We're on the road hitching across the country taking it all in and heading towards Louisville," Michael answered.

"Well, hell, y'all need to see a bit of Kentucky, then. I'm headin' up to Doe Run Lake. Not too far from here. Nice fishin' and swimmin' too. Y'all want to hop in and check it out?"

"What the hell," I said and before long we were off the highway and tearing up a dirt road in a thick green forest kicking gravel behind us and leaving big plumes of dust rising into the air. Purple and blue and white wild flowers lined the road.

"My name's Austin. Austin McCracken. I'm thinkin' bout doing the same, gittin' on the road and maybe headin' towards Big Sur. You ever read about Big Sur? Way out there in California. Hippies, concerts, and real nice people from what I gather."

He had the face of a boy, but he had this beard that was thick and long like an Amish dude might wear. He was shirtless and wore a string of brown wooden beads around his neck. He drove fast. He liked to talk.

"It's nice and all here, but there ain't a thing to do," he said. " People get stuck here. Don't go nowhere. They just ain't thinkin' about places like Big Sur or California or any place, really. Why, I know old folks who never left Independence let alone Kentucky. They just don't care. They say why bother? There ain't nothing out there worth seein' anyhow. I just say no way man. There's plenty out there. You boys gonna head to Big Sur?"

Michael was awake now and enjoying this wild ride kicking up dirt and blazing through the forest.

"We've got no real plans. Big Sur sounds just as good as anywhere," he said.

"Better!" Austin said. "I'm told there's not a better lookin' place in the world than Big Sur. Got them Santa Lucia Mountains coming out of the Pacific. Nice steep roads looking down. I've seen pictures and I've seen that movie too. The one of the big concert with Crosby, Stills, Nash and Neil Young. Real green woods and old hippies just hidin' back in them real nice quiet green woods. You know Kerouac wrote about it. Lived in a cabin all by himself out there, but he was nuts and didn't appreciate the beauty. Started going crazy and had to high tail it outta there. You boys smoke?"

"Sure thing," Michael said eager to hit off of the pipe. I was never really too thrilled with the pot thing. It made me too uncomfortable. Threw a haze over everything. I know a whole bunch of people who can smoke and just carry on like nothings changed in their heads. I guess it just kind of mellows them out. Not me, it makes me all nervous and unsure of everything and then real hungry.

Michael and Austin sucked hard on the pipe. Their eyes glazed and their smiles broadened. I was content just being with this whacked-out hippie-kid and heading to a lake at the end of this old gravel Kentucky road.

Once we made it to the lake the beagle jumped out of the window and bolted into the water. The water was calm. Trees hovered thick and close to the bank casting shadows and giving the water a greenish hue. The embankment slanted slightly. There was no sand on the shore, only dirt and flat stones. Good for skipping. A few old-timers scattered themselves along the bank and cast for trout. Some wore chest waders and wandered into the water searching for a hole where they might have luck finding a trout hiding in the coolness of the deeper water. Some squatted peacefully on the shore with their poles in hand. The lake was silent except for the rhythmic sound of humming cicadas and the occasional whirr and plunk from a casting rod.

"It's quiet up here. Nobody much comes here 'cept them old fishermen. They sit for hours and pull in some big ol' trout, the speckled kind. They know the deal, ain't got no cares in the world," Austin said.

We hiked along the bank of the lake until we found a hidden inlet. I stripped down to my shorts, walked into the lake and swam out. The water was clean, cool and deep. I floated with my feet pointing towards the sky and my head tilted back. All sound ceased. The sun baked my forehead. It dried immediately. I rolled into the water and swam underneath with my eyes open. The sun created translucent rays in the water. I swam slowly back to shore. Michael threw me a bottle of soap.

"Use this," he said. "It's biodegradable, can't hurt the water."

We washed ourselves and brushed our teeth, spitting the toothpaste into the lake. Austin and his beagle wandered further down the bank of the lake. I sat on the embankment looking over the water and letting the sun warm me. Michael lay on the flat stones to dry himself. He placed his hands behind his head with his elbows pointing on either side of him. His skin was deep coffee brown. He drifted to sleep. Time stood still. After a while Michael shook his head and stretched.

"I must have fallen asleep. Where's that dude?"

"Over there," I said pointing. "He's walking back towards us. He's been playing fetch with that beagle for about half an hour."

"I'm starving. That pot made me hungry."

I caught Austin's attention and waved him over. The beagle ran on ahead. It was having a pretty good day.

"Them ol' boys is catchin' some prize trout up yonder past that bend," he said.

Michael walked to the car, grabbed his pack and brought out some stuff to make a sandwich.

"You guys hungry?"

We each took bread, slathered on mustard, piled on the bologna and threw some chips on the sandwich to give it a nice crunch. Michael and Austin ate earnestly. Austin shared a couple of bites with the beagle. The cicadas hummed louder under the oppressive Kentucky sun. A trout jumped slapping itself back into the lake leaving ringlets of outward moving water where it landed.

"So, where you boys headin' today?" Austin asked.

Michael answered with a mouth full of sandwich, "We expect to make our way into Louisville. We looked at the map this morning and figured that's a good destination for one day. Shit, I could stay here for a few days, though. It's pretty nice."

"Yeah, it is a nice place and all, but hell you boys is off to see some pretty nice shit. Damn, I gotta get me a road partner and head on out. Independence just don't cut it, boy."

Once we had the place cleaned up, Austin took us on out from the seclusion of the lake and dropped us on the seventy-one south ramp. He gave us a hearty good-bye and said he had a great time showing us around. He promised that he would be in Big Sur at some point and said we should look him up. He hopped in his car and peeled away kicking gravel onto our packs and shins. I watched him heading down the road with the beagle in the front seat sticking his head out the window, and wondered if this kid would ever leave Kentucky.

Chapter 4

Tasos Theotikos

Tasos Theotikos was born in nineteen twenty-seven on the Greek island of Sifnos in the western half of the Cyclades on the Aegean Sea. Living in the capital town of Apollonia, nestled in the rugged green hills and looking over the endless deep turquoise sea, Tasos spent his early years with his four brothers and three sisters living in a two room white-washed house under the strict jurisdiction of his father Kostas, a fisherman, and his tired mother Aspasia. Kostas would wake before sunrise; climb aboard his skiff and in the cool darkness, row with the other fishermen, out into the bay. His skiff was flat bottomed with a pointed bow and a flat stern. The hull was painted white, the interior light blue, and accented with a ring of red trim. Each morning Kostas rowed effortlessly to his spot away from the others, cast his net, and brought in his daily haul. Years of fishing had dried his skin into deep brown-furrowed leather. His arms were large and powerful. His moustache was black, thick, and course to the touch. When the fish were plentiful and he reached a surplus, Kostas would trade for olive oil or wheat or Ouzo or anything he needed, as there was always plenty of trading activity in the bay late in the day when the fishermen rowed in from under the big blood-orange sky. Later, after a meal of fire roasted fish, lamb, chicken or goat, Kostas would hike the worn path leading to the kafenion where he and the other men of the town spoke of their luck at fishing while sitting at little white tables sipping Ouzo and thick black coffee.

It was this simple life that Tasos found undesirable and drove him to leave Sifnos. His opportunity came when Kostas' older brother Dmitri was forced to leave the island quickly and under mysterious circumstances. Dmitri was dim-witted and often made dangerous choices that produced consequences he could not fully understand. It was clear to Kostas that the current situation involving Dmitri and the thirteen year old daughter of a local fisherman could not be settled in a manner that would preserve Dmitri's current living situation. The town would protest. They would not put up with Dimitri and would look to lock him up somewhere for many years. Tasos saw this as an opportunity and insisted on taking his uncle from the island and finding safe harbor for him. When this was accomplished, he would write his father telling him of their whereabouts. Tasos had no real fondness for Dmitri. He just saw this as a way to leave the confines of Sifnos and the stifling existence that was sure to follow.

In those days it was easy to gain passage from island to island. It was not uncommon to climb aboard a neighbor's sturdy wooden skiff and venture from one island to another. There was much trading between the islands and the waterways were always busy with travelers. Three days later sixteen year old Tasos and his confused thirty-seven year old uncle Dmitri had made passage to Corfu where they found a safe haven in the outskirts of the little town of Agios Georgios on the Northern shore of the island.

Under warm bright skies, the pair spent hours swimming and diving deep into the warm blue waters of the Ionian Sea fitted with crude spears whittled from sticks to catch the camouflaged octopi hiding in the rocky bottom. Dmitri could hold his breath for an eternity, and his slender body allowed him to plunge deep into the water and scale the rocks until he found an octopus hidden in a crevice. Usually the octopus was furrowed deep in the smallest cranny, hidden except for its dull eye watching the strange intruder. Dmitri looked into the eye under the water, and aimed the stick towards his prey, stabbing into its head and yanking it out from the rock. Tasos was impressed with Dmitri's talent. In Sifnos the beaches were much sandier than the rocky terrain of Corfu, yet in a very short time Dmitri learned to navigate the waters effortlessly. It was apparent that Dimitri had a natural gift for retrieving the fruits from the sea, and soon small crowds gathered as he proudly pulled each octopus from the water. To prepare for cooking Dmitri took his knife and cut into the body, releasing the ink. Then he beat the octopus onto the rocks until it was tenderized. This needed to be done immediately so that the meat did not become tough. Later in the day, before the sun landed on the Western horizon, Dmitri found more luck away from the rocks and on the sandy beach netting sardines. He had found some discarded fishing nets and pieced them together until he had a suitable net for trolling. Waist deep in the water, Dmitri would throw the net in front of him with graceful elegance, and with a steady sweep against the current, he would pull in dozens of the small, silvery, sweet sardines.

During the starlit evenings Tasos and Dmitri built small fires on a hill under the cypress trees, sat on blankets, and looked into the vast blackness that was the Ionian Sea. The sea slapped endlessly upon the rocks and the briny freshness of the air soothed and comforted them. They cooked the octopus tentacles delicately on a stick over the fire. The octopus transformed from a purplish translucency to a white, firm, sweet, delicious meal. The sardines were prepared in the same manner and eaten whole. They bit the heads off and then the bodies, bones and all.

Sometimes early in the evenings, after a productive day, Tasos and Dmitri ventured through a wooded valley to the small hill village of Pagi carrying enough octopi to sell in the streets. Along the way they crossed through a wonderful orchard of wide thick-rooted olive trees. The two moved steadily through the orchard picking their fill and eating the deliciously salty and pungent olives, spitting the pits back to the ground. Over time, those who lived in the village came to expect the young man and the simple gentle stranger, who had become famous for his diving skills, and offered them pleasantries when they encountered one another. With the money earned, Tasos bought bread from the tiny bakery located on a narrow street in the village, and fresh goat's milk from a farmer they had become acquainted with during their walks into Pagi. A scrawny large-nosed man, often the topic of village gossip, sold them hand pressed wine.

Sometimes when they passed the kafenion, the townsmen would offer them a seat at their table and give them a small glass of Ouzo, and a good coffee. Dmitri, who remained silent, sat casually fingering his komboloi, or worry-beads as they are known here, and let the anise flavored Ouzo slide gently down his throat. The Ouzo had a calming effect on Dmitri, and he was quite content with this new life. In fact he hardly thought of Sifnos where he had spent most of his years.

Tasos, still, was not so content. Constant companionship with Dmitri was dull and stifling. Often, while the two sat under the cypress trees at night cooking octopus and sardines, he would gaze sordidly at Dmitri, gently lit by the fire, squatting, contently biting the heads off of sardines and washing the mouthfuls down with deep ruby colored wine from the bottle. It was during those moments he pondered leaving Dmitri to the villagers of Pagi. Someone would take him in, he figured. On the other hand, Tasos was a dutiful son, and he had promised his father to care for him and keep him safe. Leaving Dmitri to fend for himself was not an option.

In those days when Tasos and Dmitri spent their time quietly diving deep into the blue Ionian Sea and cooking under the big cypress trees, all of Greece was not enjoying the same tranquility. In fact, there was much turmoil as Greece had not been able to escape the Great World War. She battled the Italians and the Germans relentlessly. First, three years earlier, in nineteen-forty, the Greek Army fought off Mussolini's invasion from Albania. The Italian army weakened and retreated from the hard-fighting Greeks. Next, Germany gathered her troops and attacked. Although, Hitler was met with strong resistance in Crete, losing almost seven thousand troops, the crush was successful and the Greek Government was exiled. Germany's occupation caused division among the Greek people: those who subserviently bowed down to the newly formed German rule and those who *had the guts and bravery to fight. Those who were brave enough fought the Resistance and formed groups resulting in civil outbreaks. By nineteen forty-three Greece was devastated. Civil war had broken out, the economy and infrastructure was all but deleted, and casualties were plentiful. It was not a good time. Tasos and Dmitri knew little of the magnitude of the situation, only what they heard from the men who nervously fingered their kombolois in the kafenion.*

       One villager, Aggelos Vlahos, reflected upon moving his small fishing business from Greece to America where he had a brother living in Tarpon Springs on the western coast of Florida. His brother, Spiro, wrote often telling him of the Greek community, the fine weather, and the lucrative business of sponge diving. Spiro had made it in America. His wealth included: a share in the sponge industry, a fleet of three active boats, and a strong crew of Greek transplants. He owned a tiny café where he spit-roasted lamb, steak, and chicken and served souvlaki with patates. He also served fourno, mousaka, pastitsio, rice pudding, and baklava to the Greeks and the Americans living along the docks and in the town. Spiro urged Aggelos for years to leave Pagi and enjoy the wealth of American life. Aggelos, content with his life on Corfu with his wife Georgia, never thought any further about leaving. In the recess of his mind it was just a romantic possibility. This changed when Georgia suddenly fell ill and died. He buried her in the family plot on a green hill that looked over the village and contemplated his life. He had no children. His only remaining family lived thousands of miles away in Tarpon Springs, Florida. His meager wages from fishing had grown into an adequate fortune as he was frugal, lived simply, and had no vices that could destroy him financially. It was this situation and these thoughts that Aggelos pondered aloud at a table in the kafenion with his new friends Dmitri, who sat silently aloof fingering his komboloi and drinking a short coffee, and Tasos who sat next to him, erect, elbows on the table, leaning and listening intently with an eager curiosity to Aggelos' predicament. Tasos listened to the array of thoughts moving within Aggelos' mind:" Should I go? How long would it take? This war is too big, the entire world is involved. Can I bear to leave my Georgia? Shall I sell my boat?"

Tasos saw this as his passage to a wonderful adventure and spoke highly and convincingly of the fruits America had to offer. Tactfully, he presented Aggelos the virtues of exploration, of setting forth to reach new opportunities. The War would end and America would survive. This was the time to take advantage of a situation and become a strong man in spite of it. He reassured Aggelos that there was no other choice, really, than beginning anew, in America, with Spiro.

After much discussion and correspondence with Spiro, it was settled. Aggelos would sail to America to a port in Savannah, Georgia. He would take a train into Tampa, Florida, meet Spiro, and head to Tarpon Springs. Aggelos would bring along a quiet man named Dmitri who had quickly earned a reputation as being the finest and most dependable diver in all of Corfu, and he would pay passage for a sixteen year old Greek named Tasos Theotikos, a romantic and an adventurer who had given up his homeland and was left alone in this world to care for his simple uncle.

Chapter 5

The Cop Outside of Louisville

They were moving in on me quickly. I tried to outrun them. My legs stiffened and I knew in a moment it would be over. The gigantic long-haired bearded one, who was gaining on me the fastest, stopped suddenly, lowered himself to one knee, pulled his rifle onto his shoulder, peered into the scope and calmly aimed toward the back of my head. My legs ceased. They could carry me no further. My heart beat wildly. I was scared and frustrated. With all of my power, I tried to out run this man knowing it was over for me. I waited for the explosion and awoke suddenly. Michael stirred. Our sleeping bags were wet with dew. His rash was gone.

After Austin dropped us on the highway, we took a few rides to the outskirts of Louisville, settled in a field, ate some more bologna and potato chip sandwiches, wrote in our journals, read, and then fell asleep. The ride was pleasant, taking us down a lightly traveled two-lane highway through green rolling hills with miles and miles of white wooden fences. Sleek thoroughbreds galloped gracefully or grazed peacefully upon the bright green grasses of Kentucky. This was horse country; Kentucky Derby land. Prized, pampered horses pranced in abundance in proud Kentucky fashion living better than most Kentuckians themselves; living better than you and me, at least.

On this morning our first ride came from two guys in a Ford Pinto with Levi Strauss interior. They were heading into Louisville and passing a bottle of red wine between them. They took swigs from the bottle. These two were funny. Laughed the entire drive, except we never knew exactly what they were laughing about. They never said. They just kept passing that bottle back and forth snickering like they pulled off some great caper. Maybe they did. Both looked guilty of something. We ignored them. They dropped us off in Louisville.

Louisville. Nice looking city, sits on the Ohio River. Michael saw a sign that read 65 South Nashville. "This way," he said. We had some walking ahead of us. I followed. He led us over a long bridge that crossed the Ohio River. Louisville was at our backs. I found a tattered magazine on the bridge on the pavement between the street and the sidewalk. *Pain Was Her Pleasure.* It looked interesting. We walked over the bridge and I read aloud to Michael. *I stuck my slippery schwanz up her slimey schmoo; slap me crimson red you filthy slut; the crop slapped against her pulsating pelt unleashing a river of orgasmic goo.* It went on like that. No pictures, just stories, like in an old dime store novel. Michael felt that writing that stuff would be a good way to make a living. Then he thought you probably couldn't make all that much money, though. He figured it couldn't rest on most book shelves. That's why it lay tattered in the road unclaimed, blowing through the streets of Louisville getting picked up, read, and thrown back to the streets over and over again.

We headed down a slight incline to where the bridge ends and the highway begins. Out of nowhere, a cop in a black and white patrol car clicked on his PA and told us to get off the highway and onto the ramp. Silently, like a snake, he slid next to us, pointed towards the ramp, and with a forceful authoritative movement of his pointer finger, he instructed us to get moving. He sped away as quickly and silently as he arrived.

We continued walking and facing ahead while I kept my thumb out. Neither one of us saw him return on the other side of the highway. We were engrossed with *Pain Was Her Pleasure.* Again, like a silent snake he slithered next to us, and abruptly indicated his presence by tripping the siren.

Red lights flashed. I dropped *Pain Was Her Pleasure*. He told us to get in. He told us to give him fifteen bucks or spend a day in jail. He told us hitch-hiking on Kentucky highways was illegal. *Did we want to go to jail?* Michael was pissed. I gave him the look: shut up and be cool. The cop told us he would take us ten miles up the highway to a better ramp where there was less traffic. Cars could pull over easier. Along the way he gave us ten of the fifteen dollars back. He said this was for being good. We talked about our trip. He told us about his tour of duty in Vietnam. He told us about Kentucky. He told us about being a cop and all the fucked up people he deals with and how at times he just can not figure out all of the shit that goes on in this fuckin' world. He asked us if we were hungry, took us for breakfast at a diner where we ate eggs, sausage with gravy, and grits with butter and salt and pepper. We drank black coffee. He took us to the ramp as promised and gave us our five bucks back. He told us good luck, and then he sped away.

Chapter 6

Louisville to Nashville

Michael was getting better at juggling. He had three good rocks saved since Columbus. All rounded and about the same size. The third rock was in proper rotation now. He demonstrated and gave me a step-by-step tutorial.

"Watch me. It's easy. Take one rock in your right hand. Throw it up and catch it with your left hand. Now, take this rock in your left hand and throw it up and catch it in your right hand. Keep doing that until it becomes comfortable."

We propped our packs together and stood on the ramp. Big puffy white clouds drifted slowly across the sky. It was two hours since the cop dropped us here. There wasn't much around except for a truck stop about a quarter mile off the highway. We could see it in the distance and figured that's where we would eventually snag our ride. Someone would pull into the truck stop, eat lunch, fill up with gasoline, hop back into their car, approach the ramp, see us, pick us up, and we'd be heading towards Nashville. Just like that.

After three hours I was ready for the second level of instructions.

"OK, throw the rock in your right hand up and as its coming down towards your left hand throw the rock in your left hand up and catch it with your right. Keep doing that until you get a smooth rhythm going. Keep both rocks around the same height just a little over your head. Once you can do that, the third rock is easy."

It was getting hotter. The day dragged on. This spot was cursed.

"We need to make a sign," I said.

I tore a sheet from my journal and wrote in big bold letters NASHVILLE.

"I'll hold it. You keep practicing," Michael said.

Another hour passed and I had this two-rock juggling down pretty well. Now it was time for the third rock. Once mastered, I would be a juggler. Another trick up my sleeve.

"This is the easy part," Michael said. "Now, you've basically got the juggling down. Hold two rocks in your right hand. Throw one rock from your right hand to your left. Before it goes into your left hand throw the rock from your left hand to your right. And, before that rock goes into your right hand, throw that to your left hand and keep it going. That's it. That's all there is to it."

I concentrated, getting the flow, working through the movements, the rotations, the height, feeling each rock move from one hand to another. Looking straight ahead and letting the rocks arc in perfect unison.

"This is pretty cool," I said suddenly grasping the technique. I was juggling. Like a clown or one of those shirtless bearded guys who go to the park on Sunday afternoons wearing those baggy pants and juggle while a small crowd gathers and watches in awe.

Later, I learned that it did not matter what I juggled or what size it was. Once I had the fundamental understanding of the juggling motion, I could juggle anything. Three lemons? Absolutely. An olive, a basketball, and an orange? No problem. A bottle, a battery, and a dead mouse? With ease. It was that simple. This could go anywhere for anyone. Bowling pins, chainsaws, it really didn't matter once you learned the technique.

And there we stood, quietly on the entrance ramp of Interstate 65 South, under the bright scorching Kentucky sun, intently juggling. Lost in our world until a '56 Caddy with Tennessee plates pulled over and asked if either one of us had a license.

The driver looked beat. He introduced himself as Blain. Wore white shoes and white linen bell-bottomed pants. His shirt was shiny turquoise and around his neck a silk lime green scarf hung casually to one side. His hands were soft and manicured and the nails on his little fingers were long and brushed with a deep red glossy polish. His hair was bleach-blonde. It hung just above his collar. He slid into the passenger seat and I got behind the great big white steering wheel of this gleaming red Sedan De Ville with a white roof, white wall tires, and all the room in the world. Two Yorkshire Terriers with little pink bows on the tops of their heads rested themselves comfortably on his lap. In the back seat, two backpackers who couldn't have been more that sixteen greeted us with shy smiles. Michael squeezed in next to them and we were off.

"I've been driving since Cleveland. Heading into Nashville," Blain said taking a slug from a silver flask. "The girls and I need a break from driving."

He stroked each of the *girls* perched facing him on either knee. Cute little doggies. Pink collars. Little pink tongues panting furiously.

I stretched my legs and my arms and contentedly navigated this big red boat down the highway knowing that we were making up for the lost time on the ramp outside of Louisville. We would make Nashville in about three or four hours.

Chapter 7

Nashville

Nashville. I glided the big red Caddy onto Lower Broadway and pulled over in front of *Tootsie's Orchid Lounge*. We hopped out, grabbed our packs, thanked Blain, and nodded farewell to the two kids sitting peacefully in the back seat.

Tootsie's Orchid Lounge stood nestled among a row of low red brick buildings with hanging neon signs offering barbeque, live music, Budweiser and Pabst Blue-Ribbon. The façade was painted purple and two big windows gave us a view inside the bar. We figured a cold PBR would be our perfect companion right about now. Inside was dark, smoky, and sour smelling. On a small stage by the front window a pretty girl with tight blue jeans, cowboy boots and a cowboy hat crooned Patsy Cline songs. Her hair was red and delicate and her face was pale and smooth. The band could have been a group of diesel mechanics: blue jeans, flannel shirts, and cowboy boots. All three of them were scruffy looking and playing tender, liquid and caressing songs. The bass player gently plucked a battered stand-up while, using an old pair of wire brushes, the drummer stirred evenly on his snare, and an old timer with a long gray beard and a Cat Diesel cap strummed delicately on his tattered sunburst acoustic. Sweet Tennessee. We sat on tall stools, leaned our backs against the bar, and watched the band. The PBR's came at us cold and in cans. Michael lit a Marlboro.

A good looking brunette waitress, with big warm brown eyes, and carrying a tray load of empty beer cans wandered over, eyed our backpacks, and asked where we were from.

"Buffalo," I replied.

She kept her hair cropped short and had on tight Levis and pointed black cowboy boots. She had on sleeveless tank top that had Jack Daniel's written on it and wore a big horseshoe belt buckle.

"You boys came a long way. What brings y'all down here?"

"Adventure," Michael said. "We decided to go on a hitch-hiking adventure!"

"Y'all hitchhiked here?" she said. "That's a long way. How'd you end up in Tootsie's?"

"Well, an old queen in a '56 Caddy dropped us at your doorstep and told us you were the nicest person we'd meet in Tennessee. So, we didn't argue," he told her.

"Shoot, that's nice. I'm gonna get the Polaroid and take a picture of y'all and put it up on the wall. We don't see too many folks from Buffalo down here."

I did not believe there was any more space left on the walls. Hundreds, possibly thousands of Polaroids, show posters, license plates, dollar bills, black and white photos of honky-tonk cowboys and syrupy voiced ladies who've stomped and crooned in *Tootsies* for years, hung on every bit of wall. Thousands of signatures and notes written in black marker invaded any remaining open space.

"I like it here," Michael said. "It's nice. I like the music. We should see about getting a room and hanging for the night."

"We really don't have too much money," I said.

"Fuck it. When we run out we'll work. Every city has a labor pool, you know."

"Maybe that waitress knows where we can stay."

She came back with two cold cans of Pabst Blue Ribbon. Big droplets of water slid down the sides.

"These are for y'all. They're ice cold. They even got some frosty tops."

"That is one nice gesture," Michael said. "What's your name?"

"I'm Dawn. Here, hold this tray," she said placing the tray on my lap. "Now scoot together and let me snap your picture."

I moved closer to Michael. He put his arm around my neck. We looked into the camera. I felt a chill from the icy can in my hand. Dawn snapped the picture and we were temporarily blinded by the flash.

"This will only take a few minutes, and then we'll see how it looks," she said.

"So, if we want to stay in Nashville for the night, where can we find a cheap room?" I asked.

"I know of one or two, but you'd better secure a room before dark or the hookers will take 'em."

"Nice place," Michael said.

"It's a room with a door that locks. It's not bad. You can put your stuff there. Nobody will bother you."

"Hell, we've been sleeping in fields. It'll feel good to take a hot shower and clean up before we head out," I said.

We drank the PBR's, smoked some Marlboros, listened to the sweet band, and watched the steady flow of Nashville wander in, drench themselves in beer, slug back tiny shots of brown whiskey, and shuffle to the music on the worn wooden floor. There was energy in this place.

The rest of the evening moved quickly. Dawn slipped me a note with the name of a hotel on it. Said she got off in a couple of hours. Stop back if we want. Have a safe trip if not.

The room was small with one double bed. It was surprisingly clean.

"Think I'll take that shower now," Michael said.

"I'm right after you," I said.

<<<>>>

On the streets of Nashville darkness was falling on Lower
Broadway. Our first stop was a barbeque joint where we feasted on slow-
cooked chicken, pan fried corn, baked beans, cornbread, and more of those
PBR's. Our mood was cheerful and we laughed hard at nothing in particular.

Back at *Tootsie's* the soft sounds of Patsy Cline were replaced by a
grizzled honky-tonk band playing aggressive country rockabilly and belting
sing-alongs to songs like *Mama Don't Let Your Babies Grow Up To Be
Cowboys* and *She's a Good Hearted Woman.* Tootsie's was packed tight.
Shoulder to shoulder. The crowd, in a wave of drunken unison,
enthusiastically stomped furiously when the fiddle player leaned from the
center of the stage into the crowd and made that thing scream in brilliant
high-pitched lightning speed. They clapped, stomped, and whistled in
approval, raising their beers high over their heads and saluting the band. A
thick cloud of smoke hung in the air. Dawn was off of her shift and sipped
from a can of Budweiser. She was happy to see us.

"Why, I'm glad you came back," she said.

Michael was on fire. He moved excitedly throughout the bar
meeting new friends, telling stories of Buffalo and being on the road, and
explaining that he was Greek and not Mexican. He settled in with a busty go-
go dancer who was having a couple of drinks before her show later in the
evening. They bought each other shots of whiskey, smoked Marlboros,
danced closely like lovers on the floor in front of the band, held hands and
kissed.

Dawn perched herself on a stool next to me, crossed her legs,
sipped her Budweiser, and told me her life story. I listened quietly and
watched the band play.

Michael bolted back with the go-go dancer. Sweat trickled down the
sides of his red face.

"It is hot dancin' up there, but damn, this girl moves," he said spinning her in an awkward twirl.

She pulled out of the spin with grace. He introduced her as Tammie. Said she was a dirty little Southern girl for a nasty Northern boy.

He took me aside and leaned into me, "Look, I'm hanging out with her, gonna head to her show. It's at some joint around the corner from here. How 'bout if I just catch up with you later tonight. We both have keys. We can meet back at the room if we have to, or you can meet me at the club, whatever."

"Yeah, sure, I'll hang here for awhile. Go on, have fun."

Michael and the go-go dancer left. Dawn suggested we leave *Tootsies* and take a walk up Lower Broadway. I was hot from being inside and some fresh air was appreciated. Outside was clear and a slight warm breeze moved through the streets. A big fat yellow moon hung noticeably low in the sky. We walked past the go-go club. Dawn said it was a pretty clean place.

"More like a burlesque with a fun crowd and live music. Girls hide behind big feathers while they dance provocatively on stage. Don't take it all off. It's tasteful," she said. "Later they break into a sixties go-go revival. Swingin' band. Not like those strip clubs where the girls are skanks and the crowd is filled with old married guys slipping dollar bills in the girls' panties just to sneak a peek at their coochie."

Lower Broadway was jumpin'. We strolled past loud rusty honky-tonks. Country music blasted from open doors. We passed diners, barbeque joints, liquor stores, souvenir shops and a bunch of record stores. We stopped inside a store with a big neon sign of a guitar looming over the front door that read *Ernest Tubb Record Shop*. It shined in the Nashville sky. Inside folks rummaged through thousands of records from every country artist, I believe, that ever recorded a piece of music. Dawn rifled through rows of records explaining who the greatest artists were: Tubbs, Roy Acuff,

Little Jimmy Dickens, Flat & Scruggs, Kitty Wells, Hank Williams, Hank Snow, Jimmy Rodgers and her favorite, Porter Wagoner.

"I never heard of some of these people. I never heard of Porter Wagoner," I said.

"Why, Porter Wagoner is the sweetest voice in country. There ain't nobody that sings as sweet and gentle as Porter," she said.

I held the record in my hand. I liked the song title *Eat, Drink and be Merry (Tomorrow You'll Cry)*. Dawn told me I couldn't leave Nashville without Porter Wagoner. She found a cassette with songs like *Dig That Crazy Moon* and *A Satisfied Mind* and bought it for me. It was a collection of early recordings.

"You put this on when you get a chance. Sit down and listen to it closely. You listen to it over and over until he becomes part of you. Once Porter gets inside, he'll never leave you."

"I'll do that," I said.

Once we were back on the street, we stopped at a liquor store and got a bottle of red wine and headed back to the hotel. Dawn went into the shower and I stretched out on the bed. It *is* pretty clean, I thought. Dawn came back from the shower wrapped in a big white towel. Her hair was short and wet and combed back. Her forehead was smooth and wide. I could smell the freshness of her skin as she slipped into the bed and under the covers. I got undressed and slid next to her. It was quiet. The window was open. A gentle fragrant breeze cascaded into the room from the warm Nashville night. The big moon cast a tender light. In the distance the melodious notes of a fiddle climbed steadily faster like an old locomotive entering a tunnel and chugging towards a lonely mountaintop.

Chapter 8

Alabama

Barreling South down US 31 on this thick, hot and humid morning, we sat tightly in an ancient rusted gold Ford pick-up with this crazy old coot named Saul who spun one bull-shit story after another. With a Budweiser in his hand and a twelve pack on the passenger side floor, this skinny wild-eyed old timer picked us up outside of Athens, Alabama after we'd been dropped off by an ancient black pig farmer in bib overalls. He let us share space on the back of his pick-up with a couple of smelly, grunting thick-whiskered pigs.

The muffler must have dropped off of this old Ford. The pipes were louder than hell and we pretty much had to yell if we wanted to hear one another.

"I kin git you down to Birmingham," he said in a high-pitched whine. "I got my little lady waitin' on me down there."

Saul pulled a shabby black wallet from his back pocket and took out a worn and tattered photo.

"That, there is my girlfriend," he said. "Right here, take a look at her. She's my baby. I'm headed to Birmingham to see her now."

A wholesome country girl in a tight red checkered button shirt tied above her waist and red painted lips posed against a wooden fence. She had long shiny brown hair, large breasts straining upwards, and a pleasant smile. It was one of those photos that come with the wallet when you purchase it. I wasn't sure what this guy was up to, but we were on the road and we were moving and that was all that mattered.

"My Granddaddy fought in the Civil War," he continued. "Took two slugs from a musket. One in each leg. Pulled them outta his leg hisself and put 'em back in his own musket and shot the damn Yankee bastards who shot him first."

Saul was a dank, skinny old timer wearing a rotten smelling unbuttoned sleeveless shirt with a grimy blue Texaco cap cocked comfortably on his head. Black and grey whiskers spotted his face, and thick bushy nose hairs shot from his nostrils. He had no teeth as far as I could tell. He sat comfortably hunch-shouldered behind the steering wheel balancing an unfiltered Lucky Strike in his left hand and a Budweiser in his right. Driving down the road shooting the shit. His eyes were pale blue. Bright and alive as a rascally schoolboy. He had one of those big Adam's apples that rode up and down his throat when he spoke. I sat in the middle, between him and Michael, taking in his sour stench of motor oil, tobacco and sweat.

"You see that scar on my arm? I got that when I went huntin' mountain lion in West Virginia with my brother. I was just sittin' there by the fire a little past midnight... just cookin' some squirrel by the fire after a long day's hunt. It was one of those hot nights in the mountains when the skies stay lit by a big bright moon. Shone like a spotlight all night long. It come out of the sky millions of miles I am told. A meteor came out of the sky and sunk right here into my arm."

"No shit," Michael said. "Is that a fact?"

"Hell yes, truer than hungry flies on a cow carcass," Saul confirmed.

We continued south on the highway and drank the Budweiser's and Saul told us a bunch of stuff about hunting and how good squirrel tastes if you cook it good and long and slowly in a stew with plenty of onions and carrots and parsnips and potatoes.

"Got more flavor than rabbit," he said.

Saul did like he said. He got us into Birmingham and made pretty good time too. He dropped us off in the business section downtown among a bunch of tall buildings. Businessmen and women wearing tight business suits walked with purpose from one building to another.

"Ya'll have a safe journey, boys," he said with a toothless smile and before we could yell loud enough he was pulling away shifting gears and merging into the Birmingham traffic with our back packs in the bed of his pick-up. I noticed for the first time that the old pick-up was kind of cocked to one side.

"Hey! What the fuck!" Michael yelled. "That old fuck's got our packs!"

It took a moment to settle in. Our back packs were gone and old Saul probably didn't even realize he had them. He couldn't hear us yelling for him to pull over with those damn loud pipes. He probably wouldn't figure out he had our stuff till who knows when.

I felt the sun slap heavy against the back of my neck. "Was your money in your pack?" Michael asked.

"No," I said. "It's in my shoe and in my belt."

"Mine too," he said. "At least we've got that."

I wasn't feeling well. Something had been bugging me since Columbus and it was coming to a head right about now. I was feverish and needed to sleep. We sat in a place called Linn Park at a big fountain shooting water high into the sky in front of city hall. The sound of the water was soothing. The air was hot, heavy, and damp. I was drenched in sweat. Michael went to a small grocery about a block away and came back with two bottles of grape Crush and some peanuts. A few feet in the distance a man with a handle-bar moustache sat behind his easel and stroked diligently on his canvas, presumably capturing the white abstract water climbing into the Birmingham afternoon with the great white façade of city hall in the background. The park was busy. Workers relaxed leisurely around the fountain sipping soda or engaging in conversation. Everything stood still.

"You look like shit," Michael said. "We need to find a room."

I was beginning to see the pattern of getting rooms as a direct hit on our funds. We had been on the road for a couple of days and already our money was running out and now we didn't have anything more than the clothes on our backs.

"We can't keep spending our money on rooms," I said.

"What the hell do you suggest?" he said. "You want sleep in some alley? All of our stuff is gone. Our sleeping bags are gone. You got a better plan?"

"Our books are gone too and so is the map," I said.

"No shit," Michael said. "What the hell does that have to do with anything?"

"We need a new map and I want those books," I said. "We need a tooth brush and tooth paste too."

"Fuck it," Michael said. "We don't have a lot of choices. We'll work after tomorrow. We've got enough to get into Florida. Let's get a room for today, relax for a bit, and tomorrow we'll get to Florida and find work and be a little more careful spending money."

"I guess we don't have a whole lotta choices," I said.

"Not too many," Michael said.

The room was on the fifteenth floor. It had a big window that looked onto downtown Birmingham. I could see the water from the fountain at Linn Park climbing upward. The white churning water looked small from here. I put the air-conditioner on high, took off my clothes, and slid into bed. It was firm and the sheets were crisp, white and clean smelling. I slept soundly. I was wiped out. When I woke, Michael was sitting on the edge of my bed with a couple of burgers, fries, and iced Cokes in paper cups. He had turned on the television and was watching The Flintstones. It was the episode where Fred caused a mix-up by sending a clown to perform for the boys down at the Water Buffalo Lodge and dancing girls to Pebbles' birthday party. It should have been the other way around. Wilma was furious, and the boys weren't too thrilled, either. They all wanted Fred's head.

The burgers looked and smelled good: greasy with onions, cheese, lettuce and mayonnaise. The fries were heavily salted with lots of ketchup on them.

Michael motioned for me to grab a burger. His cheeks were puffed as he crammed more fries in his mouth. He always ate really fast.

"Eat up, while it's hot," he said. "Dude you've been sleeping for like six hours. It's nine o'clock already." He focused back on Fred. Wilma and Betty were both giving Fred a bunch of shit.

I was famished. I drank the Coke in one long gulp. It was ice cold and beautiful. I stayed in bed, under the covers, devouring the burger and the fries. I felt much better.

"I needed to sleep. I don't think I have a fever any more," I said, beginning to wake out of my funk.

We got out of the room and took a walk into the sweltering Alabama night. The transformation between day and night was absurd. Gone were the secretaries and the business people moving from one building to another. Gone was the flow of traffic moving hurriedly throughout the streets. Whores, drunks, pimps, careful shady white men with a degenerate purpose blended into the steamy pavement. Black and white whores with big dangling jewelry and wearing painted-tight hot pants, tube tops, and high heels, told us to get off the fuckin' streets. *Go home you little pricks.* The night was hot and sticky. There was nowhere to go but back to the hotel, in the room, on the bed, and watching the television. We stopped in a small store, bought two bottles of Coke and headed back. At 1:00 the next day a maid furiously pounded on our door telling us in a thick Spanish accent that check-out was at 11:00 am.

Chapter 9

Florida

"Some of you are Hell-bound drunks. Hell-bound drug addicts. Worthless to society. But, God has a plan! He has a plan for y'all. Each and every one of you miserable wretches and lost souls, God is here! In here with you! In your stinking booze marinated bodies! God is with you and he loves each and every one of y'all. Remember what Luke says: *Be careful, or your hearts will be weighed down with dissipation, drunkenness and the anxieties of life, and that day will close on you unexpectedly like a trap. For it will come upon all those who live on the face of the whole earth. Be always on the watch, and pray that you may be able to escape all that is about to happen, and that you may be able to stand before the Son of Man.*"

Dressed in grey pants, a wrinkled white shirt, sleeves rolled to his elbow, and a pair of scuffed black shoes, Reverend Snyder perspired heavily and pranced fanatically about the alter, red faced, raising his bible high into the air crooning and hanging onto each syllable, "Ye must be born again. Come to me and join Jesus! Come up here, y'all and accept your Lord and Savior Jesus Christ." To his right, obediently off to the side, stood his wife, in a long, drab, home-made, grey dress. The heavy material ending just above her ankles revealing black thick soled shoes tied with big bulky laces. They were practical. Her hair was pulled back and tied neatly into a bun. No jewelry or make-up donned this plain lady; she was the closest thing to a pioneer woman that I had ever seen. Later, I would come to know her as Sis

Snyder. She stood firmly, in a trance, her head tilted towards her husband, lips moving rapidly in prayer with closed eyes as the Reverend jutted his arm to the sky holding the Bible high, illustrating its power, building his sermon into a crescendo: "Come to the Lord! Now is the time! Come now! Come to God's alter! Come to Jesus! Be brave and join him in his love!"

Silence. A deep phlegm-laden cough echoed in the sanctuary. Someone cleared mucus from his throat. The homeless, the wanderers, the drunkards, men who lost it all or never had it, those with dull bleary eyes and yellow tobacco stained fingers stood silently and unmoving. A sour stench of collective body odor wafted throughout the room. To avoid eye contact with the Reverend, some inspected their dirty fingernails or simply lowered their heads as if they were, themselves, deep in prayer. Reverend Snyder gazed across the room waiting pathetically for a lost soul to join him at the altar. The room held its breath. The men waited in awkward silence for the preacher to finish so they could eat a hot meal.

Reverend Snyder exhaled slowly, lowered his arm, and let the Bible fall delicately and disappointedly to his side. "Supper will be ready in a few minutes, boys. Y'all wait out front and we'll call you in."

Reverend Snyder addressed each of us as we shuffled out from the sanctuary, "Jesus loves you. God is good to all who love him."

An old timer responded, "You gave one hell of a great sermon, preacher. Thought you were gonna get one of us up with you this time."

The men, in usual fashion, assembled on the front sidewalk of the Tampa Rescue Mission until they were called by Sis Snyder into the small dining hall for the evening meal. These were men who spent their adult lives sleeping in parks, in back alleys, and under highway bridges. Anywhere they could rest their tired bodies. Men who asked for spare change. Men who walked great distances, rode the rails, and waited behind restaurants for dishwashers to unload scraps of food into the dumpsters so they could eat. These were men beaten down by the hot sun, their skin as shriveled as beef jerky. These were men who gave blood for a few bucks and held the money tightly in their hands while hurrying to the corner store to buy a bottle of MD 20/20 or Thunderbird or Night Train. Some of the hard core drunks managed to get a bottle of Rebel Yell to hold them over for a bit. They rolled Bugler or Drum tobacco into tight little cigarettes and smoked them down till they were but a nub on their stained fingers. These were men with vacant eyes, sun bleached hair, and long forgotten dreams. They were homeless, hungry, troubled, and if Reverend Snyder had his druthers he would win all of their lost souls and have them accept Christ as their personal Lord and Savior and they would all live together for eternity in God's Promised Land.

We first heard about the Mission, as it was known around here, from a wanderer who called himself Tucson. Found him stretched casually on a bench at a bus stop on a Tampa corner smoking a tightly rolled Bugler. It was a silent, hot, scorching afternoon. He sported cowboy boots, tight Levi jeans and a white western short-sleeved shirt with yellow stains at the armpits and white pearl snaps. His straw Stetson was worn and soiled. His missing teeth accented a long pointed chin.

We were burned out and had a tough time getting into Florida. The stretch of road between Birmingham and Tampa was long, and we found little luck catching rides. We crawled through Alabama in a series of short rides, mostly on the back of pick-ups. It took us three days of standing on the side of the road, juggling, and sleeping in fields to get outside of Tallahassee. At a truck stop on the outskirts of Tallahassee, we met a trucker heading for Tampa. I guess we figured anywhere was better than nowhere, so off we went slapping pavement high in the big cab of that eighteen-wheeler, listening to Waylon Jennings, Merle Haggard, Willie Nelson, and switching off napping in the little sleep compartment. The trucker drove intently, and didn't talk much. That was fine with us, we were just glad to be moving and heading somewhere new. After the driver dropped us off in Tampa, we figured we'd better check out our surroundings and look for a beach somewhere.

Tucson spotted us and introduced himself by bumming a cigarette from Michael. We told him about our back packs and he said that was about the worse damn luck any road-dog could have. To him we were ok. We were road-dogs. We'd been places. Tucson was going to take care of us by showing us a few things like where to get a place to sleep, a hot meal, and where we could find day labor and get back on our feet.

"I've been on the road five years," he said pulling a flask from his shirt pocket and taking a swig. "Tampa don't like back-packers or wanderers. All kinds of bums come down here and cause trouble. Weather's so nice they can sleep wherever they want, so you see 'em in every back alley, under every fuckin' bridge and casin' out every mother fucker who walks in this town. It's not that they're so bad, it's 'cause the weather's so nice there's too many of 'em. Tampa police don't like backpackers or wanderers. And you don't want to get your asses locked up in the Tampa slammer. I'm just telling you like it is."

So, Tucson told us how it was and he told us about the Mission saying it might be a good place for us to hang for a bit, make a few bucks, and move on. He explained that the Reverend was a pretty good dude.

"A little fucked-up wavin' that Bible and all," he said. "But a pretty good guy, anyway."

Tucson led us towards the Mission through the quiet bucolic neighborhoods of Tampa. He told us of his life in Arizona and the stretch of jail time he did with his cousin for stealing a car and setting it on fire in the desert just because his cousin was crazy and liked to do that kind of shit.

"One minute I'm sittin' in a car with my cousin drinkin' beer and watchin' a beautiful sunset, and the next thing I know that crazy fucker is pulling out a gas can and lighting the damn car on fire. I asked him how the fuck are we gonna get outta here now? We were in the flat land and that damn Sherriff saw that car a blazin' miles away. Next thing I knew I was in the desert slammer with my cousin and a bunch of crazy drunken yahoos for three months."

At the Mission, Reverend Snyder sat on his front porch reading the Bible to his wife, Sis Snyder. A sweaty glass of iced-tea melted on a card table at his side. It must have been about a hundred degrees in the shade.

"Afternoon, Tucson," the Reverend said. Both the Reverend and Sis Snyder nodded at Michael and me.

"Afternoon Reverend, Sis Snyder," he replied. "Sure is a hot one."

"Been workin'?" the Reverend inquired.

"Been lookin'," he said. "I met these two boys downtown. They're from up North… been hitchin' since Buffalo. They're travelin' around the country. I told em' 'bout the cops here in Tampa. They ain't got much tolerance for backpackin'. Ain't that right Reverend?"

"Well, you got that right, Tucson. They ain't got much tolerance for that," The Reverend answered looking us over. "If you're backpackin', how come I don't see no packs?"

"They were stolen from us in Birmingham," Michael said. "At least they were still in the back of the pick-up when the guy pulled out."

I told him about our books and our map being gone too.

"That is an unfortunate mishap," the Reverend said. "*Store up for yourselves treasures in Heaven, where moth and rust do not destroy, and where thieves do not break in and steal,* Matthew said that."

He looked us up and down closely. I suppose we looked pretty harmless to him and Sis Snyder. "So what's goin' on up there in Buffalo?"

Michael leaned toward the Reverend, "We've been hitching for a couple of weeks now. We're planning to head west eventually, Colorado, The Grand Canyon, California probably."

"I ain't never been up to New York," the Reverend said. "I ain't never been out of Florida. I stay right down here where the Lord needs me and do what the Lord tells me, and he tells me to help the lost souls. Plenty of them down here. How 'bout you? You boys alive with Christ?"

"Well, I'm Greek and Jimmy here is Catholic, but I suppose we're okay with it all," Michael answered.

53

Reverend Snyder looked us over more carefully, lifted the sweaty glass, and took a long slow swallow. "This here's my wife. We call her Sis, Sis Snyder." Sis nodded. She didn't say anything, nor did she extend her hand in our direction. She simply acknowledged us with a pleasant nod. "Sis, why don't you go on in and get these boys a cold glass of iced tea."

Sis Snyder bowed slightly towards the Reverend and silently excused herself. I figured she wasn't much of a talker.

Tucson rolled a tight one, lit it, took his Stetson off, wiped his forehead with the back of his hand, and perched the Stetson gingerly back on top.

"You boys are welcome to stay here for a bit if you'd like. We have rules though. No drinking. You don't come here smellin' of booze, and no smoking inside. We have a couple of bunks open, so if you want to stay, work around town, make a few bucks and get back on your feet, well… that's fine with me."

"That would be real helpful," I said. "We appreciate it."

Sis Snyder silently returned carrying three glasses of iced tea on a tray. She served them to us and we drank them quickly. The tea was cold and sweet with pieces of lemon mixed in with the ice. It was very good.

And that is how we landed at the Mission and met Reverend Snyder and watched him transform from a quiet, reflective, shy, blue-eyed peaceful thinker to a hell raising fire and brimstone preacher. His balance between tranquility and fanaticism was remarkable. When he was not on the alter preaching his demeanor was aloof, shy. He appeared preoccupied.

We stayed at the Mission for close to a week. Each evening at 6:30, after sitting on the hard wooden benches and receiving mandatory spiritual support from Reverend Snyder in the chapel, we sat down with the vacant men and ate plates of food prepared by Sis Snyder and the other women who volunteered in the kitchen. Most of the volunteers were old ladies who were tired of sitting through long hot afternoons, bored with their ancient husbands. They needed to get out of their houses. These were the old timers who got away from places like Michigan and New York and Pennsylvania to live out their lives in the warm pleasant weather miles away from the bitter, gray, darkness of the Northeast. They couldn't wait to throw a meal together for their husbands, and then politely excuse themselves and head toward the Mission for the quiet companionship of Sis Snyder. The husbands encouraged them to *find something to do*, as they needed just as much of a break from their own dullness of longevity. Others were local high school students putting in required hours for community service, and others were local Bible thumpers from nearby churches who enjoyed serving their community and helping the down-trodden in the name of the Lord.

Dinner hour at the Mission: Dull men with unshaven faces shuffle in single file after chapel and head to the buffet line. The busy old ladies and awkward school kids serve spaghetti or baked chicken and corn, whatever Sis Snyder cooked up for the night, from big bowls brought from the kitchen. Plates of stacked white bread sit at the end of the table. Sometimes a big pot of beef barley or chicken noodle soup steams warmly on the table. Usually there's a bowl of Saltine crackers next to the soup. Each man has a big glass of iced tea or Kool-Aid, or lemon-aid made from powder. The hard cores spike their drinks with rock-gut whiskey when no one is looking. Full mouths grind rapidly. Men lean into their plates chewing seriously and eagerly, like wolves tearing at a carcass. Reverend Snyder sits alone at a small table each night. He pulls up a seat, leans into his plate taking enormous mouthfuls of food and passes around to anyone who was interested an old photo of him in, as he calls it, his lost days. The picture shows a bloated, long haired man with eyes barely open. He looks stoned, like one of those dudes in the rock group *Kansas* on a bad day, or some wasted biker dude, or one of those guys spinning freely in a circle at Woodstock without a care in the world. Reverend Snyder shares his thoughts and reflects on his past life as a useless lost soul.

"Boys, I was a lost soul there. I look at that photo and I ask myself: Who is that man? What is missing? I lived my life with only one goal, to get as drunk and high as I could. I was good for nothin' and nobody." And after a long pause while looking at that stranger in the picture, Reverend Snyder lifts his eyes towards the men, "Jesus saves, yes he does. Jesus loves, yes he does."

Afterwards the men file out, thank Sis Snyder and her helpers, and hang around the front yard smoking tightly rolled cigarettes. Some wander a little way down the street and pull out tiny bottles of cheap brown booze taking a long hard swallow, shuddering slightly as it burns its way down.

Wake-up is at 6:00 AM. Pots of coffee and donated donuts line the table in the dining area. Some of the old timers grab a coffee and a donut and then wander out into the blazing Florida sun to find shade and sleep. Some go downtown to sell their blood, and some panhandle on one of the busy Tampa corners until police move them along and out of site. Some of the other younger ones head downtown to the labor pool to find work. It's pretty simple. Around seven o'clock a group of men gather in front of the temporary labor agency in downtown Tampa. They call it the labor pool. When the door is unlocked, those who decide to go into the agency take a seat on one of the wooden folding chairs lined up in a small room facing a counter. A thin bald man with thick black-framed glasses and a pointy nose sits nervously behind the counter shuffling job orders from one pile to another. He carefully looks at each order and periodically surveys the room scanning the men and making a mental note as to who is best suited to fit a particular job. This takes about ten minutes. Once his paperwork is in the proper place, he offers the available jobs. Some of the men sitting in the room have proven themselves to be good workers and don't cause any trouble. They get the jobs. Others are lazy or have difficulty taking orders and their tempers flare on job sites. Others are just plain drunk all of the time and pretty much worthless. They sit with their arms folded and their heads down in a semi-conscience state. For them it's just routine, something to do before hitting the streets. Unfortunately the latter fill up the majority. Those who are able, and want to work, and do not get picked at the agency, go back out to the corner and wait for contractors cruising by in dusty pick-up trucks offering day labor to anyone willing or not too drunk to work. This is all done quickly. Soon these men are heading towards construction sites, warehouses, manufacturing plants, hospitals, restaurants, or any other place that needs a quick labor fix.

Michael and I lucked out. We were new, appeared eager, and after being sized up by the bald guy, were given the job of unloading railroad cars in some old warehouse district on the outskirts of downtown. Our foreman was a blonde stuttering Florida born guy named Dave. He wore a pair of navy blue pants, shiny black shoes, and a short sleeved plaid shirt with three pens clipped securely in a pocket protector. A typical sentence from Dave sounded something like this: "We need to unload this car cuz, cuz, cuz, cuz, another one's coming" or "Hurry up cuz, cuz, cuz, it's lunchtime." You would size him up as a good guy. A hard worker really excited about his job at the loading docks where an endless supply of trains arrived constantly. We found out quickly he was a dependable go-to guy. We called him Cuzley.

The warehouse was massive. Dave sat proudly on his fork-lift diligently jotting stuff down on a clipboard. Rows and rows of boxes were stacked high in the sky on pallets that loomed over us as far as we could see. We hopped on the lift and Dave tore through the warehouse until we reached the back where the loading docks perched over a set of endless train tracks.

This was the Florida the tourists would not see. The sun burned relentlessly and the smell of oil, cinders, and railroad wood wafted through the loading dock. Dave pulled the big lever and opened the train car. It was packed tightly with large boxes. From one end of the car to the other and from floor to ceiling boxes were crammed. Not a space was wasted.

Dave took a step backwards, and placed his hands on his hips, bending slightly back. "You boy's are lucky cuz, cuz, cuz, today you're unloading snot rags... you know tissue. Cuz, cuz, cuz, cuz, those boxes are light as all hell."

Michael jumped up and pulled out a huge box with ease. "This is going to be all right," he said tossing the box in my direction.

"Take it easy cuz, cuz, we gotta system we gotta follow." He pointed to me and motioned for me to get up into the car. "You grab them boxes and toss them to your buddy there and he's gonna place them on these here pallets cuz, cuz, cuz, I gotta fork-lift them over to another part of the warehouse... cuz, cuz,cuz, cuz, okay?"

We worked non-stop at a frantic pace. Dave maneuvered that fork-lift in and out, and up and down through the massive warehouse in brilliant ballet movement. He was enthusiastically engaged in the work and was feeling pretty damn good as he "had some real workers here for a change." We pulled, stacked, and moved the boxes at a steady pace. That train car was wide open and swept clean about an hour before quittin' time. There wasn't much to do now except sit back on the docks, with our feet dangling over the train tracks and listen to Dave tell us his story. Michael juggled pieces of cinder while Dave told us how he graduated from some high school in Tampa and got a job unloading trains right here on the docks. After a couple of years he got promoted to run a fork-lift and now he was the floor manager in charge of the entire warehouse. He was getting married to a girl named Diane, who worked in an office at a travel agency, in a couple of weeks and they were going to take four days off from work and honeymoon up in Savannah, Georgia because he loved the way that Spanish moss looked hanging over the black wrought iron fences that line the streets up there. He didn't care about any beach or any sun. He had enough of that right here where he lived.

At the end of the day Dave slapped thirty-five bucks in our palms and said we could finish out the week if we wanted. That would be close to one hundred bucks apiece; we told him we'd be right back tomorrow bright and early.

That evening the men, as usual, gathered in front of the mission smoking and sharing stories of their wanderings. Tucson told us he met some hot-bitch Yankee from Pennsylvania vacationing down here and she took him to her hotel room and fucked him for hours. We didn't believe a word and imagined most of his day was probably spent sitting in the shade, under some tree, slugging a bottle of brown. The crew entered the chapel for Reverend Snyder's nightly invite to the kingdom of Heaven. He stood at the entrance to the chapel with Sis Snyder by his side greeting the men with a wide smile as they shuffled past.

"How did my Yankees do today?" he asked extending his hand. His countenance was one of warmth and general concern.

Michael clasped his hand, "We worked like dogs today, Reverend. We got down and dirty in one of your fine Tampa railroad docks and worked till our muscles ached."

"Very good; I like that." He paused for a moment, looked towards the sky, and in the recess of his great memory pulled out a quote from Proverbs: *Have you beheld a man skillful in his work? Before kings is where he will station himself; he will not station himself before commonplace men.*

Michael looked at Sis Snyder and gave her wink. Her face flushed in spotty patches. "Well, Reverend, that gives me all the incentive I need to do it all over again tomorrow."

The next couple of days at the warehouse were not as easy as the first. We unloaded lawnmowers, pallets of concrete mix, boxes of motor oil, and on our last day the train was packed tightly with car batteries. Dave loved every minute of the hard work. The tighter the train was packed the better he felt.

"It's too bad you have to go cuz, cuz, cuz, cuz, you're really good workers. You can always come back and work here if you want."

We'd keep that offer in our back pockets. The next day was Sunday. We had money in our pockets and the road on our minds. New Orleans, Bourbon Street, black magic, file gumbo, all beckoned. It was decided. Monday morning we would make our way across the panhandle and head into Louisiana. But, first, Sunday would be devoted to fishing. A day to sit in the sun, relax, and enjoy the peace and tranquility of a hot Florida day.

Chapter 10

The Pier

We walked down the pier with our fishing poles in our hands. Michael carried a bucket of live herring for bait. He was hoping to catch something big. By the time we reached the end, the water was deep. Spread before us spanned the eternal blue-green sea. In the distance an infinite spectacle of white caps broke, but they were very small. Behind us, on the shore, stretched endless white and pink buildings surrounded by palm trees. Some stood tall and thin, others were thick and low to the ground.

We positioned ourselves at the far right corner of the pier. The sun hovered directly above locking firmly onto a cloudless sky. Michael decided to cast into the deeper water. He pulled a herring from the bucket securing its head firmly on the hook. Its silver back glistened in the sunlight. With fine precision he held the pole behind him, and with a long arching motion he sent the rig flying far into the sea. When the rig plopped into the water he let it settle, and then cocked the reel so no more line would escape. He trolled gently back towards the pier. The line was taut and if he got a hit the pole would bend quickly with great force. He knew he might have luck landing a grouper or a snapper. There were plenty of them in these waters. And, he knew he could reel in kingfish, cobia, tuna, amberjack, Spanish mackerel, dolphin, shark, barracuda, mahi-mahi, tarpon, or any number of exotic fish. This excited him. He was used to trolling for northern pike or muskie along the Niagara River or going out into Lake Erie for perch and small-mouth bass. Great fishing, but nothing compared to what we could pull out here. The Gulf was unpredictable; anything could bite. I pulled out a herring and placed it in the palm of my hand, its shiny white belly before me. I slid the hook firmly in front of the anal fin and down through its body. I cast my pole letting the rig pop into the water and find its way down. I cocked the reel and the line drifted and tightened from the weight of the sinker and the current. I did not reel in. I chose instead to sit back and watch those around us pulling in their catches. There was a slight warm breeze. The simple fragrance of clean fresh salty air was lazily pleasing.

To our left a shirtless, sun-bleached, leather-faced man stood hunched over the railing dropping his line beneath him and pointing his pole directly towards the water. He wore a straw hat with a wide brim. He fished quietly and earnestly, methodically swaying his pole back and forth in a hypnotic rhythmic motion. Fishing a little further down stood a man burned terribly by the sun, presumably a Northerner, probably on vacation or down to visit an elderly parent. I wasn't sure, but I figured it had to be something like that. And so it was, we were on this wonderful pier that stretched far into the Gulf, quietly and patiently waiting to land a big fish. To have those around us clamor with excitement when one of us pulled in a beauty.

Sitting on a bench with my legs up on the railing, I could hear the Northerner strike up a conversation with the old man wearing the straw hat.

"Boy, I sure would love to hook into a large tarpon," the Northerner said with enthusiasm.

"No you wouldn't," the old man quickly replied.

"Why not?"

"Because if you hook into a two-hundred pound tarpon standing on this pier, he's gonna hurt you."

"I'll bet it'll take a couple of hours just to reel him in," he said trying to sound as if he knew something about tarpon.

"No it wouldn't," the old man said. "But I guarantee you that bastard will hurt you. You hook a two-hundred pound fish that size, he's three times his weight in the water. That bastard is strong and mad. With no leverage, he'll break your back."

"Well, hell, if you ever brought him in there would be plenty of good meat on 'em."

"They're sport fish," the old man said. "Meat's no good; too many bones."

The Northerner dropped his rig into the water trying, in poor imitation, to mimic the smooth technique of the old man. The sun was high in the sky. It reflected in the water like many bright stars on a clear night. Far out on the horizon a ship headed south. Scattered among us brown pelicans sat nestled on the railing or near the edge of the pier lazily waiting for hand-outs. It was quiet and each of us was lost in our own thoughts enjoying the tranquility of this sizzling Florida afternoon. Michael was deep in his own rhythmic trance maneuvering and pulling in his line slowly and deliberately.

Very close to the pier I saw the fin of a porpoise then nothing. A moment later I saw the whole animal black and shiny from the sun and water. It rose up and cut back down in a series of poetic movements. The Northerner's eyes excitedly followed the movement as well.

"Nice dolphin," he said to the old man.

"That's not a dolphin," the old man snapped.

"Like hell it isn't."

"Like hell nothing. That's a porpoise not a dolphin; there's a difference, a tremendous difference."

"Well, I thought they were the same; a dolphin is the same as a porpoise and a porpoise is the same as a dolphin. They're the same thing."

"Well, they're not," the old man insisted.

"Well, I thought they were."

"Well, they're not."

I couldn't help but thinking what a bastard that old man was. He wouldn't give that Northerner a break.

We had been fishing for about an hour and the two men quit talking. It was a slow day and none of us had much luck. It was very hot. I never got a bite. Michael reeled in a couple of small catfish and the Northerner pulled in one catfish and a couple mullet. The mullets were olive green with blue tints on their backs. Their silvery sides blended into a creamy white belly. He threw the catfish back and tossed the mullets to the tramping pelicans. They swallowed them whole quickly raising their heads to the sky and letting the fish slide down their throats. This awakened the seagulls who circled the pelicans sending out high piercing shrieks in anticipation of a dropped morsel.

The old man was displeased with the actions of the Northerner. "You know when you give one pelican a fish, you rile up the whole of them and the gulls too…causes too much commotion. Y'all should leave things as they are."

"Sorry," the Northerner said.

"Things are different here. It's a different kind of fishin' than up North. You fish up there?" the old man asked.

"Yep, mostly trout in the streams. I use light hooks usually number sixes. Catch 'em best with salmon eggs."

"Well I reckon you can at least snag a trout."

"What?"

"Nothin'."

"Do you enjoy eating snook?" the Northerner asked.

"They're the tastiest fish to eat down here. Most Northerners don't know that, sweet as hell."

"I should try it sometime."

The old man stared coldly at the Northerner with dull, cruel shark eyes. He crouched into a pugnacious stance continuing to provoke the poor bastard.

"Don't talk to me you damn-bastard!"

"Ease up," the Northerner said.

"Your pale skin will burn and blister in this sun!"

Just then the Northerner felt a tremendous jerk on his pole, then another, then a very powerful tug. He raised his arms and held both hands tightly on the foam handle. The pole arched downward and he was losing it.

"Give him some line!" the old man shouted.

The line spun out whirring and drawing the attention those fishing nearby. The pelicans lifted their heads with eager anticipation. The gulls hovered excitedly overhead. The fish bolted towards the bottom. Then he came up fast and broke the surface. I could see his long lean body, his translucent green dorsal fin. A thin black stripe ran across his body from head to tail. He crashed down and again headed for deep water.

"You got a snook!" the old man yelled. "Pound for pound he's the toughest fish to catch! Bring him in you pale bastard! He's thirty pounds I'm sure!"

The Northerner did all he could to work with the fish and reel him in. He let up giving the fish line and began reeling in. He could feel its strength and tried to keep control of the fish cutting sharply in the water. The snook was trying, with all his power, to rid himself of the hook. Fifteen minutes passed and the snook was tired and almost up.

"Bring him in easy you Northern ass, you pale scum."

The fish was now only a few yards below us on the surface. He was tired and being led easily to the pier. Once the fish was directly underneath the Northerner lifted the fish half way out of the water. A crowd had gathered and was impressed by the size of the snook. In an instant, the fish turned slightly and the hook slipped easily from his mouth freeing him back into the deep water.

"You worthless Northern scum!" the old man screamed. "You snotty bastard! I hate you, you bastard!"

The Northerner stepped backwards and avoided a punch that would have hit hard. At that moment, from out of nowhere, a well muscled man reached up and under the old man stilling him with a half-nelson.

"Come on now," the man said. "Fishing is over for today."

"How'd I do?" the old man asked suddenly speaking in the tone of a little boy.

"Pretty good, Jerry. You did all right."

"Did I catch many fish?"

"You caught a whole bunch, Jerry," the man said letting go of the old man and helping him gather his fishing tackle. "I threw them back for you. You know we like to leave them here."

"We're they big?"

"Very."

"Good."

"I'm sorry," the man said to the Northerner. "I was watching. He usually doesn't get like that, at least not in a long time. He's pretty cracked up. We let him out once in a while to get some fresh air and see if he remembers."

"That's okay."

"I probably shouldn't have let it go that far."

"Again, it's okay."

The old man neatly packed his tackle and stood calmly waiting for instructions from the man.

A pelican lifted his head to the sky, fluttered his wings, and settled back into slumber.

"Take care," the man said.

"You too," replied the Northerner.

"It was nice meeting you," the old man said to the Northerner. "You're a very nice gentleman. It was a pleasure. Goodbye."

The old man and the well muscled man walked down the pier towards the shore. The old man focused ahead while the other craned his neck to notice the catches brought in by other fishermen. The Northerner looked at me, shook his head, then cast out a short distance letting his line drop until it became taut and slowly reeled it back in. He caught a few more mullet and a few more catfish using this strategy. He threw them all back.

The sun was setting behind the shore now and the water had turned a deeper blue. Michael and I grabbed our tackle and packed it neatly. Michael dumped the fish from the bait bucket into the water. We walked to the shore passing underneath a big sign that read: *The gods do not subtract from the allotted span of men's lives the hours spent in fishing.*

Chapter 11

Northwest Florida

Right before we were ready to say good-by to the Reverend and Sis Snyder, he called us into his office and presented us with two backpacks.

"Found these at the thrift shop and they ain't bad lookin'," he said. "Sis Snyder insisted we get them for you boys, said you'd be needin' 'em."

"That's real nice," Michael said shaking the Reverend's hand. "We sure can use them and we sure appreciate it."

"Why don't you go to the thrift shop?" Sis said. "They got clothes and books and maps and such. You can get all you need."

We did just that and got pretty lucky replacing our books and getting ourselves some decent clothes. We even got us a couple of old sleeping bags which we figured would do us just fine. We had to get a new Rand McNalley at a gas station and as far as we were concerned, were ready to move on.

We had good luck catching rides out of Tampa and up Interstate 75. After a couple of hours we made it to Interstate 10, just outside of Live Oaks, Florida and headed west. It was cloudy and humid. Thick air hung low to the ground. Traffic was sparse. I leaned against the guardrail and read Hemingway's *Indian Camp*, a beautiful and sad story about growing up. Michael stood nearby silently juggling rocks and throwing his thumb out when a possible ride approached. We didn't talk very much. After a couple of hours two cars pulled over at the same time. In the excitement of finally getting a ride, I grabbed my pack and ran up the road to an orange Dodge Charger with chrome exhaust pipes. Inside sat a young couple heading to Greensboro. I waved Michael towards me, knowing he'd be glad that we caught a decent lift. He was fifty yards in the other direction waving intently for me to come to him. I waved back earnestly, signaling that my ride would get us a long way. He waved back just as pronounced. I knew he wouldn't let up. I thanked the couple and ran back towards Michael and his ride.

Michael jumped in the back. I slid my pack in the back seat next to him and hopped up front. In an instant we were in this car barreling down the highway with the speedometer breaking a hundred miles an hour and swerving from one lane to another. The driver reeked of booze and was scaring the piss out of me. I looked back and saw a strange grin on Michael's face and realized he was thoroughly enjoying the adventure. The silent driver gazed ahead. He tore into Interstate 10. The road was straight and wide open. There was little traffic. The driver's eyes never left the road. He never looked at either one of us. He didn't say a word. He drove faster and faster and continued to swerve from one side to the other, every now and then catching gravel on the shoulder of the road. I said, "You're out of the lane; get back on the road!" He ignored my pleas and moved along, fixated on driving, his knuckles clutched tightly on the steering wheel. He was on another fucking planet. Michael was amused at my reaction. He knew I was scared and he loved it. He thought it was the funniest situation. He loved this. I was praying, "Please, just get me out of this fucking mess."

After a few more miles, the driver pulled off of the interstate taking the ramp at about 70 miles an hour and screeching rubber as we slid around the curve. He pulled into the gravel parking lot of some old crab shack and bar and said, "Wait here while I get a drink." Dust rose from under his car. I jumped out, ripped my pack from the back seat and hurried the hell back onto the highway.

"Wait up!" Michael hollered. "Slow down, man."

I moved deliberately and stubbornly away from him and toward the entrance ramp to Interstate 10. When I found a good spot, I threw my pack against the guardrail and waited.

Michael walked toward me in a hearty guffaw. His mouth opened wide. No sound came out, just a wide open mouth hanging in the hot wetness of a Florida afternoon.

"What?" he managed to say.

"What?" I said. "Are you fucking nuts? That guy was hammered. He could have killed us. Are you out of your mind?"

"You should have seen your face. You were hilarious."

"Yeah, I hate that shit. You're just…" I couldn't spit any words out. He really pissed me off and I suddenly realized his purpose for taking this trip. This wasn't a soul searching road trip for him. He wasn't out to discover America or whatever I thought the whole point of this trip was. He wanted adventure, danger, a shot of life's adrenalin. If we had the opportunity to tie a rope around our ankles and jump off a bridge he'd do it. If I told him to shoot an apple off of my head, he'd do that too. Whatever it took to satisfy that curiosity, that adventure, to negotiate face to face an audacious danger, Michael was willing to enter that realm and I was along for the ride.

After all that nonsense, we were still only a couple of miles outside of Live Oaks, and it was a long way to New Orleans. Our first lift came from a young black dude who took us across Interstate 10 to Oakdale, a city west of Tallahassee. The ride was long and dull. Interstate 10 through northwest Florida between Tallahassee and Pensacola is an endless monotony of four straight lanes cutting through rows and rows of endless pines, mile after mile. Long stretches without exits are common. Only a sluggish ripple of hills breaks up the dullness a bit. The road is sparsely populated. The towns are small and few.

The black dude dropped us off at a tiny Hopperesque diner with a tattered sign hanging over the front door that read *Home of the World's Best Fried Chicken.* A bell was attached to the door. It jingled as we entered. It was quiet inside. Two ceiling fans stirred the hot, dead air. A horsefly buzzed angrily throughout the room. An old black man sat alone at the counter spooning sugar into a tall mug of coffee. He sat bent over a huge piece of apple pie; a bunch of napkins lay scattered in front of him. He looked in our direction, nodded, and went back to spooning the sugar steadily into his coffee. I could smell grease from the fryer. Two teenage girls wearing skimpy shorts and halter-tops sat in casual conversation at a booth. They whispered to one another while drinking Cokes and sharing a basket of fries. Behind the counter, next to the register, a tired woman in a white waitress uniform filled an endless supply of salt and pepper shakers lined at the counter with the tops off. She used a paper funnel to fill each one. Behind the counter, and in the kitchen, an old wire-thin black man, with gray kinky hair, prepped his workstation by chopping potatoes and throwing them in a big oiled skillet with onions. The pan sizzled when the potatoes hit the skillet. He wore a Miami Dolphins cap and silently looked down at his work. This was the quiet time between lunch and dinner. We grabbed a booth in the front of the restaurant. It looked out over the gravel parking lot. Our packs rested against the seat and under the table. The interstate stretched long and lonely in the distance. The big horsefly landed on our table roving aimlessly over the yellowed linoleum.

The waitress wiped her brow with the back of her hand, put the shakers aside, and walked towards our booth. She carried a pungent, stale scent of cigarette tobacco with her. The two girls looked up from their Cokes and watched her approach us. Michael caught the eye of the pretty little one in the yellow halter, and winked at her. They smiled bashfully, lowered their heads, and concentrated on the basket of fries before them.

There were no menus. Over the counter, on a big sign, was a list of items: Fried Chicken in a Basket $2.99. Hamburger $1.49, Cheeseburger $1.59, Fries .79, Coffee, Coke, the usual stuff.

"What can I get for y'all?"

Michael looked towards the sign, "How's that chicken in the basket?"

"Best around, but it ain't gonna be ready for 'bout half hour. We cook it fresh."

"Sure… that's okay," he looked at me, "You care?"

"No. I'm good." I ordered the same along with an iced Coke.

The waitress looked at our packs, "Where you boys headin'?"

"We're hoping to get into New Orleans in the next day or so," Michael said.

"Good times over there," she reflected. She walked back to the counter. "Two in the basket, Jess." She poured coffee for the old timer working through the pie, and then pulled out a long slender cigarette from her apron, lit it, and returned to the salt and pepper shakers.

Michael grabbed a Marlboro from a side pocket in his back pack and lit it.

"Doesn't look like much goes on around here," he said.

"Not much," I agreed taking the Rand McNally from my pack and spreading it before us. "We still have a way to go before we get to New Orleans. It looks like we'll be sleeping in a field around here unless we get a night ride out."

"We need to find a truck stop and get a ride. I don't want to sleep in some field," Michael said.

The waitress returned with two iced Cokes. They came in tall sweaty glasses that said Coca-Cola on the sides. She set them before us and laid our silverware down. The fan whirred; the air was thick and heavy. A white Chevy Nova with a black top pulled into the parking lot. It could be a ride out of here, I thought. Two men got out of the car and headed towards the door. The bell jingled when two men entered. The one carefully closed the door. It appeared the jingle annoyed him.

The first man was short with bowed legs, and a thick head of wavy hair. His eyes were mismatched. His left eye almost permanently shut. He wore about a week's worth of stubble on his face. The second was tall and stupid looking with a large wide forehead and deep almond brown eyes. They wore blue jeans and western shirts. The tall one kept his unbuttoned. The stupid looking man glanced pensively at us, then at the waitress, and then at the two girls who had lost their smiles and fidgeted with the straws in their Cokes.

The short one asked the waitress how far town was from here.

"'bout two miles up the road," she answered.

"That's good," the man said. He looked at the stupid one fixated on the two girls. "Hey, ain't that good?"

"Yeah, boy," the tall one said.

The short man pointed to the kitchen. "Who's the fella with the Dolphin's cap?"

"That's Jess. He does the cookin'. Famous for makin' the best chicken anywhere around."

"Is that right?"

The waitress could not look into the short man's eyes. She turned slightly away and asked if he and his friend would like to sit at the counter or would they prefer a booth.

The man at the counter with the pie coughed and rose from his seat. The short one took a step forward and leaned into him.

"You just sit back down there, old feller. You ain't goin nowhere right now."

"Hey, what's goin' on?" the waitress asked.

"You just lean against that counter and tell that old Jess to get his ass out here pronto," the short one said.

Jess dragged a dead leg reluctantly from the back of the pick-up counter and showed himself. He stood before the men scared and trying to look dignified. The stupid one sat in the booth next to the pretty girl in the yellow halter and leaned into her. He whispered into her ear. She trembled and peed right there in the booth. When the stupid one felt the warm liquid

73

penetrating his pants he smiled and stood up. Then he looked at Michael and me.

The waitress spoke clearly. "Look, this here is a little place. We ain't got hardly nothing in the register. Take what's in there and leave us be."

The short one with the eyes that could not look straight grabbed her forcefully by the arm and dragged her to the counter.

"You shut your damn trap and sit your ass down right here," he looked towards Jess, "You too, boy, sit your ass down next to her."

The short one needed to think for a moment while the stupid one stood slack-jawed waiting for directions. The short one looked at us.

"You two dumb asses; git up here, now."

The stupid one ushered us to the counter. Through his open shirt, I noticed the chocolate brown handle of a pistol resting in his pants and on his hip. The two girls were moved to the counter. They moved carefully towards us, and the stupid one took the palm of his hand and rested it on the girl with the yellow halter's ass feeling the wetness from her shorts. He looked at his hand and caressed his palm with his fingers. He cupped his hand to his nose and took in the scent.

So there we were. All sitting in a row at the counter, all silent except for the faint whimpering of the two girls and the buzz of that damn angry horsefly.

The short one got behind the counter and faced us. The stupid one lurched menacingly from behind. We were sandwiched. The short one pointed to the waitress.

"Move your ass over and open that thing."

She moved quickly to the register. She punched a key and the drawer opened with a thud and the ring of a bell.

"Ain't but seventy-five dollars in here," she said.

She pulled the small wad out carefully and handed it to the short one. The stupid one hung behind us still. He was eyeballing the girl in the yellow halter.

"That ain't shit," the short one said. "What kind of place is this that ain't got money in the register?"

"We don't get much business till dinner time," the waitress said. "I guess you're better off robbin' us after the dinner shift," she said.

"Shut your mouth!" the short one said.

The short one glanced at the stupid one. For a moment he stood thinking. The stupid one lumbered directly behind the frightened girl in the yellow halter. He rested his hands firmly on each of her shoulders, and leaned into her ear.

"Why don't you get up and show me what the back of that kitchen looks like," he whispered.

Michael nudged me with his leg and shot a glance downward. He was holding a small hatchet he had taken out of his pack before we were brought up to the counter. He shot his eyes toward the big stupid one and then his eyes directed me to take care of the short one with the screwed up eyes. The stupid one lifted the girl from the counter to her feet. She was trembling and could barely stand. She whimpered, "No... please."

"Come on, now," he said guiding her away from the counter and towards the back.

The short one with the mismatched eyes smiled and I could see that his teeth were black and brown with big spaces between them. I noticed, on the counter, a large glass cylinder filled with sugar and for a moment everything stood still. Silence. Then, in one great and powerful motion, Michael pulled the hatchet from under the counter, cocked his arm like a pitcher releasing a fast ball, and hurled the hatchet at the tall stupid one with the blade tearing at the muscle under his left shoulder. He turned and in an instant Michael lowered his head and rammed the stupid one into the ground removing his pistol from his waist and shoving it hard into his mouth. At that moment, I lunged over the counter grabbed the sugar container and smashed it against the side of the short one's head. He dropped to the ground, and like an insane ally cat, the waitress pounced on the short one and slammed his head repeatedly onto the tile floor screaming "You bastard, you fucking bastard!" The two girls high-tailed out of the restaurant and for a moment everything remained silent.

Michael cocked the hammer on the pistol and forced it further into the stupid one's mouth. Blood flowed down his chin and he choked on broken teeth.

Old Jess' hands shook and he pulled a set of keys from his pocket. "Put them in the walk-in cooler," he said. "It's got a lock on it."

The short one was out cold. The waitress dragged him by his feet into the walk-in cooler. Michael told the stupid one to get up. The stupid one told Michael to fuck-off and said he wasn't "gettin' in any cooler." Michael shot him in the foot and kicked him inside. Old Jess slammed the door shut and nervously locked the outside with a Master lock.

"Jesus Christ," Michael said. "Who are those guys?"

The waitress hurried toward the phone and frantically dialed a number.

"Get down to the diner pronto, Sheriff. Bring some boys with you 'cause we got two crazy fuckers locked in the cooler and one's been shot in the foot!"

Sirens cut into the hot afternoon. The sheriff showed up about fifteen minutes before the ambulance arrived. The ambulance had to come quite a distance from the hospital. The two girls came back once they figured it was safe and then, joined by the waitress, they told the sheriff the whole story.

The sheriff looked at Michael and me. He was a fat man with dark sunglasses and a big hat.

"Well, goddamn. I do believe we got us a couple of super-heroes."

And that's how we were treated, like a couple of super-heroes. And for the next five days we held up right there in Oakdale so the sheriff and the district attorney and guys from the FBI and all the curious town folks could get the facts straight and figure out what needed to be done with the legal system and all. The sheriff put us up in a creaky old hotel room right in the middle of town and the owner of the diner who was home napping when it all went down told us to "Order up boys any time, cause it's all on the house," and the two pretty girls came to our room with a bottle of sweet apple wine and we sat on the worn floor of this old beat up room, with the rays of the sun slanting in from an open window, cross-legged and playing poker and rummy and Michael showed them card tricks, and the pretty one who wore the yellow halter that day sat close to Michael so their shoulders touched and he held her hand gently and made her laugh often. Both girls smiled and smelled like fresh cut wheat.

The FBI let us know that these two were a traveling pair of serial killers. The short one with the half closed eye was admitting to killing hundreds throughout the South. Said he had bodies buried everywhere. Said he'd been traveling with the stupid one for quite sometime now and they'd done a whole bunch of killin'. Newspaper reporters from all over the country came too. They took pictures of the diner. They took a picture with Old Jess and the waitress standing in front of the walk-in cooler. Old Jess holding up the padlock like you would hold up a big fat prize catfish. They even tried to interview the old man who muttered into his coffee cup. There wasn't much luck in that.

Chapter 12

New Orleans

We got caught in the back of a jeep riding into New Orleans below slate skies and getting drenched under dark torrential Louisiana rains. The couple in front took us about a hundred miles and dropped us off on Bourbon Street.

The rain stopped. The air was thick and stifling. A sour stench of garbage wafted uneasily on the street. A thin, shirtless black boy wearing suspenders and dirty blue pants tap-danced on the sidewalk under a scrolled wrought iron terrace. He looked like a little man and his grin showed off big bright white teeth. He had a skinny black dog with him. The dog looked like it hadn't eaten in a week. A small crowd formed a tight circle around the dancing boy and dropped coins into a cap he had placed before him on the sidewalk. He was very good and his Cheshire smile never left his mug. A few yards from the gathering hung a tattered sign that read *Fritzel's European Jazz Pub*.

"This looks as good as anywhere," Michael said.

The bar was dark and crowded with worn paint faded brick walls. In a corner, perched on stools, two fat men, with rolling chins, in gray pants and white shirts and sleeves rolled up past their elbows sweated profusely and blew furiously into their dull beat-up clarinets. They were accompanied by a tall, skinny, slick-haired piano player hunched over a battered upright piano and pounding heavily on the keys. His hands were lightening and his hips writhed to the rhythm. They played classic boogie-woogie ragtime jazz. It was afternoon and the place moved and swung. It was juicy. Whistles and cheers from the audience, mostly tourists. We sat at a table and ordered two beers and two whiskeys. They came quickly.

Michael took the whiskey down in one fast smooth motion.

"I like it here," he said. "We'll get a room and check this scene out."

We had another and then another and left pretty high. We found a room with a terrace looking over a floral courtyard and a rust tiled floor. In the center of the courtyard a statue of a little boy peed into a pond filled with big orange koi. Inside, the room was clean and bright with big white shuttered windows that climbed to the ceiling, shiny hardwood floors, and one very large and ornate bed with a dark wooden scrolled headboard. The furniture was a mismatched collection in the style of Early American and smelled of clean lemon wax. On the walls hung portraits of French peasant girls and over the bed a ceiling fan quietly moved the thick air.

We emptied our backpacks letting our clothes air out and dry. They lay scattered neatly around the room. We placed our books and journals on the night stands next to the bed. Michael's journal was over stuffed with poems and stories he had written. It was a good thing he had it in his lap when old Saul pulled away. Inside, folded in half on well-worn paper, was a story simply titled *My Dad*. I thought of the Hemingway story *My Old Man* and decided *My Dad* was a friendlier title.

"Can I read this?" I asked.

"Sure, I'm going to take a shower, and then we'll go out and get some dinner. Check out the town," he said.

I lit a cigarette, stretched-out on the bed, propped both pillows behind me, and re-read the title. I tried to remember Michael's dad. A dark skinned slight built Greek named Tasos Theotikos. He came from Greece to Florida and later moved to Buffalo where he married Michael's mother. They had four children. Three boys and a girl. Michael was the third child.

His dad worked in restaurants, first owning a small breakfast diner. Later he was a maître at an exclusive supper club in downtown Buffalo called the Park Lane. His accent was thick. He was always seen wearing creased black pants and a starched white shirt. His shoes always carried a brilliant shine.

Inside the bathroom the water ran. I stretched out and read his story.

She had been angry with him as usual. He entered the restaurant nervous and unsteady. His hands shook. He needed to perform a task to get his mind off the constant dull aching pain in his head. The waiters had not arrived. This was good. He had no desire to see anyone just yet. It was ten o'clock and the others would not arrive to begin lunch set up until at least ten-thirty. He had this calculated. By the time they strolled in he would appear composed. Any task would do, but as usual, he chose to polish the wine glasses. He filled a coffee pot with boiling water, retrieved a clean white linen napkin from a side stand and steamed each glass wiping away water spots left from the dish washing machine. Occasionally, he came upon a glass with thick lipstick prints along the perimeter. He thought that was rather sexy and he tried to imagine the woman who left her prints. His nervousness faded. The twitch under his left eye ceased. He placed each polished smooth wine glass on every table at each place setting directly over the knife.

Knowing him was to know a slight man with ambition. His face was angelic. Thin, tight, blood red lips placed themselves finely on a porcelain androgynous face. He had dark eyes and a delicate nose. His hair was fine, the color of midnight. Being slight was not to his disadvantage. In fact, his presence suggested quite the opposite. His manner was intense. He spoke of politics, literature, film, art, anything that could create interesting discussion with great enthusiasm and intensity, often raving to secure his opinion. His weakness was not his slightness, but his suffering of false ambition. He was cursed with having too many ideas. His ideas were unfounded…incomplete. Whether it was his steadfast aim towards ambition or the tremendous frustration of never achieving his goals that led to his demise can only be speculated.

He wrote pages of poetry and left each poem unfinished. He outlined short stories and plays in precise detail, never writing a paragraph. Ideas ran fast and brilliant. Never able to catch one, put it down, own it. Without completion, ambition was a cruel trick, something mocking, taunting, torturing. It tore at the core of him.

"Why do I have these ideas without being able to complete anything?" he pondered. "It's a trick!"

The notion of suffering from false ambition drove him into long periods of depression. This along with the abuse from his wife weakened his esteem. In turn, he was boyishly fragile. Fortunately, his uneasiness faded in the restaurant. At least it went unnoticed. In fact, he was looked upon by his co-workers as easy going, calm and mostly in good humor.

The restaurant was spacious and presented a cheerful atmosphere. Blonde wood floors, tan walls, and high ceilings supported massive crystal chandeliers. Bold, colorful, dramatic paintings similar to the paintings of Mark Rothko hung on bright white walls. A giant picture window separated the restaurant from stately Delaware Avenue. On this day sunlight slanted warmly through the window, illuminating water spots on the glasses and silverware. He had things to do. He would polish them all.

His co-workers showed up a little past ten-thirty carrying freshly pressed black pants and crisp white shirts. Immediately they fell into the routine of setting up the dining room. Silverware was polished and placed at each setting, salt shakers were filled and wiped, chairs and tables were positioned and straightened into uniformity, flowers were watered, candles were replaced and lit and the host began the routine of assigning reservations to the tables. This was accomplished while sipping coffee and engaging in conversation. He was happy during this time. She was not around to intimidate him and that made it easier to think clearly. Ambition developed and new ideas came. When a co-worker inquired about the fresh bloody scratches on the back of his neck and face, Tasos waved his hand nonchalantly.

"My damn reckless cat, he jumps on me in the middle of the night and scratches the hell out of me," he said.

"I'd get rid of that cat in a hurry," replied the co-worker.

Indeed. Lying had become easier. Bruises were dismissed as clumsiness. Scratches were the result of overly zealous cats. Black eyes could easily be explained as bumping into doors or walls in the middle of the dark night when he used the bathroom. Lying for her had become a part of his everyday existence. He wore visible bruises and shrugged them off while inside he froze.

After lunch was served, he had a break until dinner.

I listened to Michael whistling happily in the shower. I took another Marlboro from the night stand, lit it, got off the bed and leaned over the balcony watching and listening to the little boy pee into the koi pond. A couple sat at a wrought iron table on the far side of the courtyard. She wore a white cotton sun dress and her legs were crossed and tanned and shapely. They shared a bottle of white wine. The bottle and glasses glistened. The sun had broken through the clouds softly lighting the courtyard and the air was hot and wet. I smoked the Marlboro and then snubbed it out in an ashtray on the night stand next to the bed. I lay back on the bed, propped the pillows again and continued to read.

He entered through the big wrought iron gates of Forest Lawn Cemetery. The grass had been recently cut. It was the first cut of the season and the scent was fresh and lively and long overdue. Cherry blossoms were in full bloom. Tulips and daffodils surrounded many of the gravestones still tended to by relatives or friends. Other headstones were faded and tilted or knocked down completely from years of forgotten upkeep. The eternal had simply out-rested all living connections. Big noble mausoleums donned with pillars, and stained glass renditions of the heavenly world honoring some of

Buffalo's most prominent citizens overshadowed the rows and rows of smaller stones bearing the names of families, men, women, and children.

He wandered down a steep grassy embankment stopping here and there to look at the names and dates on the scattered gravestones. He could not help but wonder at the significance of these stones. The dead with their last material possessions: Looming Celtic crosses bearing proud Irish names. Statues of saints and angels peered serenely over the bucolic gardens. Thousands of headstones of all shapes and sizes protruded in every direction across the scattered hills of Forest Lawn. He questioned the grand mausoleums especially. Were these reflections of a person's gaudy avarice, or were these simply tributes to societies most appreciated and dedicated servants?

Advancing from the embankment, he found himself suddenly upon the serenity of tiny Mirror Lake. There he was greeted by a wonderful silence. Out of the glass smooth water, The Graces danced with splendor and merriment. Aglaia, Euphrosyne and Thalia invited him to join in their festivities. They went unnoticed. All was silent save the splashing and fighting of the senseless ducks that lived on the little lake. In the distance the sound of the lawnmower faded.

The seclusion of this refuge seduced him. He allowed his thoughts to carry him through stages of his life. Each image entered with precise clarity. Everything was exposed leaving him hollow and disgusted. Resting comfortably on the soft grass, his arms crossed behind his head, he stared at the big white puffy clouds overhead and wrestled with these thoughts. They ran wild. Laughing, spitting, assaulting and torturing his very fibers within. He tried to think of pleasant thoughts, but the cumbersome banality of his life shamed him. His self-proclaimed uselessness destroyed any chance of allowing wisdom to place ambition into a position of positive gratification.

After a brief courtship filled with romantic infatuation, he married. His wife soon became a hindrance to his emotional state. He married out of the desperation that many people suffer with, to quell loneliness. Although he preferred solitude, he craved companionship. His thoughts when entering marriage were idealistic. He had hoped to spend his early mornings writing and in the evenings he and his wife would stroll down the neighborhood streets in the silence of married couples who have found serenity in the idleness of conversation. Together they would take in the beauty of the large Victorian homes and the big ancient elms. Later they would dine at a loud and crowded restaurant where many conversed boisterously over bottles of red wine and big plates of pasta. She would applaud his efforts writing and he would bask under the praise of his most revered critic. Later they would return to their apartment and go to the big quilted bed.

They had children and he loved them deeply. He was gentle with them. With his wife, though, their relationship failed miserably. His ability to produce his thoughts on paper never existed and the romance of sharing ideas and ambitions as a writer with his love was never fulfilled. She despised him. Their infrequent strolls through the neighborhood resulted in a cold uncomfortable silence. He had nothing to say. He could not explain what he had not yet found.

In some strange and torturing way he had many ideas that were easy and clear. The more he considered these ideas the more he wanted to put them to paper, and then they vanished. What a cruel trick! Soon the quick brilliant ideas vanished into the great abyss of forgotten abstract thought and he became depressed and quite impossible. Rather than comforting him, his wife turned repulsive and aggressive. She became infuriated and chastised his dreamy existence, often raging into tantrums and inflicting violent punches on her husband in the quiet of their cramped apartment. He did not respond. He took each blow silently and after she was finished he was broken.

The sound of the lawnmower returned. It moved closer. In the middle of the tiny lake he watched as one duck continued to chase another and repeatedly bite its neck. The weaker duck tried earnestly to fend off his attacker, but was not strong or quick enough. He tried to join the others swimming contently together, but could not escape his angry neck biting foe.

The comfort of this warm spring day caused him to fall asleep on the soft grassy hill at the side of the lake. When he awoke he noticed a praying mantis perched on the tip of his shoe, its arms folded toward him and its head cocking from one side to the other. The big black eyes locked firmly on Tasos. He shuddered and realized his incompleteness as a man whose thoughts and ideas go unnoticed. The pain cut into him far too deeply to ignore.

Later, when the waiters arrived back to the restaurant, they noticed the dining room had been completely set for the dinner crowd. Lights were dimmed, candles flickered on each table and each glass was steamed and polished and placed at each setting. An extra rack of glasses had been polished and placed in the waiter's station in the alcove just next to the dining room. Billie Holiday crooned from the speakers overhead. In a short while the doors to the restaurant would open and service would begin. A waiter noticed him slumped forward with his head pressed to the table and a delicate steady stream of deep red blood flowing from the left side of his forehead and even with his eye. To the left of the fork on the table lay a small smooth handled snub nosed revolver. To the right, just above the knife, lay a shattered wine glass.

Michael came out from the shower wrapped from the waist down in a white towel. He looked dark from the sun. He took a Marlboro from the night stand, lit it, and sat at the foot of the bed. Smoke swirled toward the ceiling fan.

"I remember when your dad died," I said. "I didn't know it happened like that."

Michael shifted uneasily and crossed his legs. He took a long pull from his cigarette.

"That was a long time ago," he said. "I remember it like it was yesterday, but it was a long time ago. He was a nice man. I never saw him angry. The story is unfair to my mother, though. She didn't understand him. Thought he was a lazy dreamer. She had kids and she was busy and she wanted things. She always yelled at him. Said our house was a tiny box that suffocated her. She called him foolish. She loved him, but she just did not understand that part of him. My mom was practical. My dad was a romantic. She never understood what he needed."

"It's a good story," I said.

"I don't think my brother George got over it," he said. "I guess that's why he left. I don't think he forgave my mother for hounding the old man. He's the oldest. He remembers more. I suppose it got too hard for him, but I understood her. I did."

"And that's what you need to talk to him about?" I said.

"No, it's because he left and he has to come back," he said. "He can't stay away forever."

"He might want that."

"He can't just stay gone. It's not fair and I won't let him," Michael said.

We left the room and found our way to the bar in the crammed noise of the *Acme Oyster House.* We ate raw oysters on the half shell and we had red beans with rice and smoked sausage. Michael poured hot sauce over the rice and beans. The oysters were cold and firm and tasted sweet and briny. We doused each oyster with a shot of Tabasco, chewed them slightly and slid them down in wonderful sensation. We drank ice cold PBR's and watched a crew of black guys behind the bar with wide smiles, red shirts and red baseball caps, shucking dozens and dozens of oysters in rapid fire. Every time they threw an iced platter on the bar a waitress would scoop them up, slam them out, and another would return.

The Oyster House filled quickly. Two girls in tight blue jeans with high heels and low cut tight white shirts grabbed the stools next to us. They ordered two beers using thick accents and telling the bartender they were from Switzerland. Their lipstick was red and their perfume was strong. I thought they were trying to look American. They were out of our league. One of the girls noticed me sliding and oyster down my throat.

"Those things look disgusting," she said laughing.

"Ah, but they taste wonderful," Michael responded. "Here, let me show you."

He gently took her arm and placed the little fork in her hand, "Like this. Put a drop of Tabasco on the oyster. Now, jab that baby with your fork." He guided her arm toward her mouth, "Chew only twice and then swallow."

She ate the oyster. "Hey, that is good. I think it is good."

"You can eat them with lemon, or horseradish, or cocktail sauce, or with nothing on them at all. Any way you like," he said.

We ordered more oysters and spicy boiled crawfish and more beers and to our surprise and delight the girls stayed with us for a long time. Their names were Ursel and Sandra and they were on holiday in America. They had been to Miami and now New Orleans and in a couple of days they would fly to New York and then go home. They told us they loved it here and I thought of all of the things here in America they would miss in-between, but it didn't really matter much to them. And, I figured, they were really experiencing three uniquely flavored cities.

The girls laughed loudly and boisterously and crossed their legs while sitting at the bar while sliding down raw oysters and sucking the meat from crawfish shells and smoking American cigarettes and drinking American beer and saying American phrases like *that's cool* or *hell yeah* and even outdated ones like *I can dig it* and *right on.* They kept right up with us drinking the PBR's and the place was warm and friendly and we were having a whole lot of fun.

Sandra jumped from her stool and stood in front of me. She was a head taller. Her heels were high. She placed a hand on either side of my shoulders and emphasizing the long o and shaking like Charo said, "Let's boogie-woogie!" Ursel stood, just as tall, "Yes, let's boogie-woogie!" We left the Oyster House, took our beers in plastic cups and slid into fast moving, hot Bourbon Street.

The streets were filled. A warm breeze cascaded through the decadent wrought iron city. Neon lights flashed from music clubs, bars, restaurants, gift shops, and strip-clubs. All kept their doors open inviting anyone willing to enter, but the real fun was on the street. Drunken middle-aged housewives roamed in packs arm-in-arm, drinks in hand, laughing, shouting, bold, daring, and leaving behind husbands, dirty laundry, snotty kids, and folksy mid-western morals. Middle aged men, in an effort to capture their vitality, prowled Bourbon Street searching for that break from loneliness, that chance to revive their burnt-out passion for dreams and lose the realization that their lives have halted to a gloomy existence of monotony. Work, eat, sleep and watch love, ambition, and dreams fall into a bleak black abyss. The swarm of people swelled and ebbed and flowed with college kids, junkies, vagabonds, soldiers, cross-dressers, gays, Europeans, Asians, and groups of elderly tourists, who carefully clutched on to one another and watched in curious and cautious disbelief. All roamed the streets freely.

Sandra jumped on my back. "Give me a ride," she said.

Ursel hopped on Michael's back and we bumped our way through the Quarter in a game of chicken with these two lovely creatures. "Let's boogie-woogie," they shouted in delight. Roaming towards us in shimmering gowns and high heels, a group of cross-dressing men surrounded us and beckoned us to watch their show at a club on the other side of the street. We hit more clubs, drank more beers, Irish danced, square danced, slow danced closely and tightly, and somehow we ended up crammed in a twenty-five cent booth watching dirty filthy porn with the girls laughing so hard they were snorting in our ears.

It was fun. At four-thirty in the morning we walked, arm in arm, with the girls to their hotel. We sat down on the front steps and finished the last few swallows of warm PBR's. They sat close to us and we kissed and they promised to write when they got back to Switzerland. We couldn't have been happier.

Chapter 13

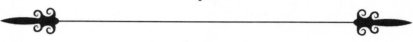

Houston

We took the secondary road from New Orleans to Lafayette and passed through Cajun towns like Des Allemands, Amelia, Morgan City, Patterson and Broussard. Our first ride came from an intellectual hippie with a thick head of curly hair and a far-away stare. He wore round-rimmed glasses and had a deep voracious laugh. He laughed often; said his name was O'Donnell but everyone called him O.D. Said he would get us up to a big truck stop near Lafayette where we would be sure to catch a ride towards Houston. First, though, he needed to stop and pick some crazy mushrooms he heard about in a cow pasture up the road.

In his beat up nineteen sixty-five dull yellow convertible Rambler with a big white steering wheel, we took to the road in a smooth steady glide. O.D. pulled off the paved road and onto a dirt road lined with wooden fences. After about a quarter of a mile of a bumpy dirt and gravel, he pulled over. We hopped out and watched the dirt rising from the road settle. It was hot. The air was wet and thick. Big puffy clouds hung low in a dreary sky. They hovered suspended in the air hardly moving. It was quiet except for the occasional high pitched moan from a cow or the abrupt hollow clank from a cow bell. The grass smelled sweet. Crickets chirped. Flies buzzed and hummed and attacked soft, flat piles of cow shit. The cows stood in the distance under a clump of trees contently chomping grass in the shade. They ignored us.

O.D. slung a worn green canvas bag loosely over his shoulder, "You got to look in the cow shit for these mushrooms. They got a smooth yellowish top. They're kind of bell shaped and they got a thick bluish stalk. Spread out and let's see what we can find."

We wandered the field in different directions and I searched through the dung-pies. Some were flat and wide and petrified. They lie scattered on the ground like dried brown lava. Other piles were brown and yellow and moist and fresh. I found a couple of these mushrooms and wondered why the cows did not eat them. That was a thought. I ended up moving closer towards the cows. They grazed disinterested. Some lay under the trees watching me, their ears fluttering flies away.

O.D. whistled us back. Michael and I showed him our gatherings.

"Cool, man."

He took our mushrooms, examined each one quickly and put the good ones in his green canvas bag.

"These are crazy, man. I didn't think we'd find so many. Glad I picked y'all up," he laughed.

"So, what happens when you eat these things?" I asked.

"You get a good high, man," he laughed. "A good clean high; nice and mellow. Here, y'all take some for later. You boys will have a good time on this shit."

O.D. dropped us at one of those giant truck plazas on Highway 10 right outside of Lafayette. Dozens of big cross country trucks idled on the huge black-top parking lot. They churned and rumbled and smelled of oil and diesel. Cars lined themselves and waited their turns at the self-serve gas pumps.

We entered the restaurant. The restaurant was crowded. A plump girl wearing an apron and a stained waitress uniform led us to a table. We passed a tall cylinder case loaded with a bunch of cream pies all with about a foot of whipped cream piled on them. It was a kick-ass truck stop and they had some fine Louisiana home cookin' and we ate a big plate of red beans and rice with spicy steamed crawdads or what they call mudbugs. They were damn good and we ate voraciously with sheer pleasure until we could eat no more. After dinner we went into the bathroom to wash our faces and brush our teeth. Then we slung our packs over our shoulders and headed to the exit ramp. We found a spot at the foot of the ramp hoping a trucker would see us and whistle us over. Once the trucks got onto the ramp, and started shifting into higher gears, it was unlikely they would stop and give us a lift. We propped our packs against the rail.

Michael pulled a couple of mushrooms from his pocket.

"What do you think?" he said.

"They look like shit."

"I'm going to try 'em."

We downed them one at a time. The pungent taste was awful. We sat on the guardrail for close to an hour reading the map as darkness settled onto the Louisiana sky. Michael juggled three smooth rocks. They were perfect for juggling. The mushrooms were duds. Nothing happened.

"We probably shouldn't have eaten them on a full stomach. I think I read somewhere you shouldn't do that," Michael said.

"It really doesn't matter to me. What are we going to do, sit at the side of a guardrail tripping?"

"It is pretty stupid," Michael agreed.

It was getting dark. Truck after truck passed us by. Their gears grinding forward, powerfully crawling up the ramp, picking up speed, churning, bellowing, approaching the vast, dim, wide open highway to the towns, cities, and loading docks of America.

Our ride came finally from a squirrely dude with a thin black moustache pasted above a lipless mouth. He wore sunglasses and I figured him to be well over six feet tall. His seat was pushed as far back as it could go. He was wearing shorts and his legs were long and thin. We tossed our packs in the back and, as usual, I hopped up front and Michael lounged in the back. I never could figure out why Michael insisted on sitting in the back. He was the one who could capture the attention of anyone. His stories, his jokes, his easy going wit and knowledge and conversation kept everyone easy. He could captivate anyone. I was uncomfortable being put in the spot as the one who had to carry on conversations during these rides. I preferred not to talk. Michael usually drifted easily to sleep while I had to stay awake and keep drivers company through miles and miles of open road.

This guy told us he would get us to Houston. He told us a whole bunch of lies too. He bragged about the women he fucked, his love of whiskey, and his job with the Secret Service. Said he could outrun a jackrabbit. He told us how much he loved his car. I asked him what kind of car it was. He said he did not know. I noticed there was no key in the ignition. He spoke of Vietnam and being in the Special Forces and *kill or be killed* and his love of rice and bamboo and young Vietnamese girls who would do anything for you. *Fuckie, fuckie anytime anywhere.* Said the world was a fucking evil hell-hole where nobody gives a shit about anybody else. "You gotta look out for yourself because nobody else will. Women are all whores." As we rode towards the flickering lights of Houston, he explained a series of grisly murders that took place in the last couple of months in horrendous bloody detail. He said Houston, like most cities, was a shithole. I listened as Michael slept with his head tilted back and his mouth wide open.

The car pulled over on a residential street in the north end of Houston at 3:30 in the morning. I never even asked the driver his name. We grabbed our packs and got out of his car. We were groggy.

"Welcome to Houston," he said and sped into the darkness.

Michael stood on the cracked sidewalk half asleep. His bangs hung carelessly over his forehead. He was trying to wake up.

"What time is it? Where are we?"

"I don't know. North Houston, I guess."

He pulled his bangs away from his forehead and surveyed the neighborhood. It was quiet. The houses were small wooden bungalows lined on wide streets with crumbling sidewalks and big trees with thick trunks and huge branches that met high over the streets forming archways. Most of the lights were off inside of the houses.

"Where the hell are we going to sleep?" he said.

"Let's look for a park. Maybe we can hide in some trees."

We walked quietly into the still thick night. A little way up the street we came upon a tiny, skinny, little girl sitting squat legged under a big tree on the sidewalk. She leaned forward with her forehead touching the sidewalk as if she was blending in and trying to disappear. When we got closer, she slithered further into the cracks.

"Hey," Michael said. "What are you doing out so late?"

She gazed toward us cowering. Her cheeks were raw and crimson. Her eyes were big, round and deep brown and her greasy hair was long and brown and stringy. She looked like a scared mouse or maybe a chipmunk.

"I'm hidin' from my Mama's boyfriend," she faintly said. "He's a mean bastard and he's drunk and he's got it in for me."

She slunk further into the cracks of the sidewalk trying to disappear. We weren't quite sure what to do.

"Is he looking for you?" I asked.

"He's looking for me now and when he finds me he's gonna beat me good 'cause I've been disobedient."

She wore a tight sleeveless shirt and there wasn't much to her. Her arms were long and skinny and bruised with black and yellow marks. Her legs were bare and thin and she had no shoes on. Her toes were long and delicate.

"You can't just sit here on the sidewalk in the middle of the night," Michael said. "Can we take you somewhere? Do you have any friends? Should we go to the police?"

"The police?" she laughed. "What them police gonna do? They know him. They don't do shit."

"Well, you can't just stay out here on the sidewalk all night. That's no good," Michael said.

From down the street a set of headlights slowly moved in our direction. The car rumbled low and guttural. Like a hot rod. The girl slithered behind the big round tree trunk and hid.

"That's him," she whispered.

We both stood on the sidewalk awkwardly as he approached. He stopped and leaned toward the passenger side. He was a skinny little fuck with a sleeveless shirt and a bunch of dull green homemade tattoos running up his arm. He hadn't shaved in days. A cigarette dangled from his lower lip.

"Ya'all seen a brown-haired little girl walkin' around here?" he asked.

"It's pretty quiet. I haven't seen anyone," I answered.

"What are you boys up to so late?"

I told him our story and he seemed content.

"You see a little brown-eyed girl 'bout thirteen years old, her name is Becca, you see that little Becca, ya'all tell her to get her ass home."

"Will do," I said and we watched him continue slowly down the street.

"He looks like a real prick," Michael said.

The girl came out from behind the tree. She slid back into the sidewalk.

"I ain't goin' back till he settles down," she said. "He'll forget about it in the mornin'."

"We can't just sit here," Michael said. "Where can we find a place to sleep?"

"There's a church right down the block," the girl said. "There's a bunch of bushes in the back, ain't nobody gonna go there. You can roll out your bags there for a bit."

"What about you?" I asked.

"I'm just gonna stay put for a while. He's done this before. It ain't no big deal. He'll calm down and pass out on the couch. I'll climb in my mama's window and I'll sleep in my mama's bed with her. Then I'll get up and get ready for school."

"You take care of yourself," Michael said. "We're going to head to that church and crash in the back. If you need any help, you just come to us and we'll help you out."

"Sure will," the girl said and moved cautiously down the sleepy tree lined street to her home.

Chapter 14

Labor Pool

It was hot. Big time hot. Texas hot. We peeled our sleeping bags off our sweating bodies and opened up a can of fruit cocktail and ate the warm fruit and drank the sweet syrup. We brushed our teeth using water from our canteens. The water was warm and dull. The girl was right. There were a lot of bushes to hide in and nobody came around.

We put on clean underwear, socks and shirts, combed our hair, rolled up our sleeping bags and attached them to our backpacks. We made sure all of the zippers were closed, put the packs firmly on our backs, tightened the waistbands, and headed out onto the street to look for a bus that would lead us into downtown Houston.

Walking along the crumbling sidewalks, we listened to cicadas humming loudly in the trees above. The trees hovered overhead blocking the scorching sun. The girl was long gone. I imagined her sitting at a desk in school trying to look wide-eyed and wondered if some teacher was giving her shit for not doing homework. I could only imagine.

We left the neighborhood and moved onto a wide treeless boulevard where we found a bus stop and were told by a short, chubby Mexican with a thin mustache that a bus would be coming soon and heading downtown. "Should be here in a couple of minutes," he said. He was a painter and wore a clean white t-shirt and white canvas painter's pants. His shoes were black and covered with paint. He carried a metal black lunchbox with him. When we got on the bus, he took a seat and pulled a Spanish newspaper from under his arm and read it thoroughly. The bus carried mostly Mexican workers heading into Houston. We found two seats in the back and planned out the next couple of days.

We needed to work. New Orleans pretty much tapped our funds and a couple of days working would get us back on the road for a while. We had been living foolishly since leaving Buffalo. We were almost broke. It was time to get it together.

We arrived in downtown Houston and walked under the big sky scrapers for a bit and inquired about finding day labor. Soon we were sitting on tattered folding chairs in the dingy waiting room of a downtown labor pool. Close to twenty other men sat on chairs reading newspapers and smoking. A cloud of cigarette smoke hung in the morning air. Most were Mexicans. Some napped. One old drunkard slid off of his seat and hit the ground. The room filled with muffled laughter. The frustrated man behind the counter shook his head in disgust and sent another man from the back to pick the old timer up and put him on the street. As he dragged him out the man's face turned red and he addressed his audience angrily.

"What I tell you about sleeping off a drunk in here? If you're drunk you're out for good," he said.

They paid little attention to him. A couple of them continued to laugh. We waited for hours. No jobs came in. We sat on the wooden chairs and lunched on a can of spaghetti with miniature meatballs. The room smelled of stale tobacco. I read Hemingway's *Soldiers Home* about Krebs who came back home from World War I and had given up on girls, working, praying, everything. He just didn't give a shit anymore. I also read *Indian Camp* where the boy in the story watched his doctor father give an Indian squaw a cesarean section using a jackknife and fishing line. She had been in labor for long time and something needed to be done. I read the newspaper and an auto trader cover to cover. Michael wrote in his journal and dozed every once in a while. The others in the room slept, smoked, and snuck hits from tiny whiskey bottles. No jobs were coming in.

It was July 25, 1978. I figured I'd better make a call home and give my brother Kevin a date to meet us in Colorado. That was our plan from the beginning.

Michael sat leaning back in his chair with his mouth open, snoring quietly. I nudged him and he woke irritated.

"Let's find a pay phone and call home. I'll give Kevin a call. He should be home now," I said.

I walked to the window. The man at the desk was reading a racing form and circling numbers. He looked slowly up at me from the paper. He was skinny with pasty skin, greasy hair and slate gray eyes. I asked him where we could find a pay phone.

"Walk out the door and head two blocks on your left," he said. "You'll find a couple of phones there. Don't wander too long. Second shift jobs will start coming up and you boys could probably do a better job than this batch of drunk-assed Mexicans."

On the street four pay phones stood lined up against a tall building. I got hold of the operator and placed a collect call to my home in Buffalo. Michael called his sister Colleen. My mother answered. I could tell she had been drinking and thought how pathetic she sounded at this time of day.

She sounded hollow and far away. "You're where?" In Texas? Good Lord, that is something. Your brother's been driving me crazy waiting for you to call. Why the hell doesn't Jimmy call? What's his problem? He says we gotta know where to meet them out in Colorado. He's driving me nuts, Jimmy."

"Is he there?"

"Do you know where he is, Jimmy? He's sleeping, that's where he is. Jesus, Mary and Joseph it's a perfectly beautiful summer afternoon and he's downstairs sleeping his life away, wasting away his god-dammed life sleeping. Then he'll wake up, eat something and go out with those friends of his until four in the morning."

"Can you wake him?"

She screamed toward the basement. "Kevin, get your ass up and come here! Jimmy's on the phone!" Then she said, "The little ones are no better, complain, complain, that's all they do. We're bored, we're bored, that's all I hear from them. They're driving me crazy, Jimmy."

I knew that scene all too well. I let her fume about everything on her mind. It was ungodly hot, the kids were driving her insane, and my father was out with every whore in town. I thought of my dad who worked his ass off while my mother berated him daily and his kids ignored him more and more.

"Things will get better, Mom," I said hoping she would get off the phone. "Just relax and enjoy the rest of the summer."

"Easy for you to say, gallivanting around like that. Hold on, your majesty's crawled out from his cave. I love you, Jimmy," she said.

She handed over the phone to Kevin and I could hear the muffled tirade continue.

"Hey, Jimmy – what's up?"

His voice was rough and groggy, like he had been chewing on sandpaper. I could still hear my mother's yelling fading in the background.

"Shut the hell up!" he yelled to her. "Jesus Jimmy, where are you? When can I get the fuck outta here?"

"Are you two ready?"

"Yeah, we're all set. I'm ready to go."

"Okay. We're in Houston working. We blew all of our money. It goes quickly, Kevin. We'll be in Denver by the thirtieth. Meet us at Johnny's brother Tommy's house. I left his address in your top dresser drawer. Tommy knows you're coming and Johnny's already there."

"How long will it take us?" he asked. "How long does it take to hitch-hike to Colorado?"

"It depends," I said. "Just get on the ramp at Main St. That's the I-90. Take it to I-79 South to Pittsburgh and then you can pick up I-70 West all the way to Denver. It's a straight shot. It'll probably take you a couple of days."

"Okay, Jimmy," he said. "I'll get a hold of McShay and we can leave in the morning."

"Be careful, Kevin. Try to get to the truck stops. If you're lucky you can sometimes catch long rides from truckers if they're willing to pick you up. Don't forget Tommy's address. Once you get into Denver look for Englewood, that's where Tommy lives. Like I said Johnny is already there waiting. We'll be up there around the thirtieth, okay?"

"Yeah, I'm excited and glad to get outta here. I'm just a little concerned for the girls. Mom has been fuckin' hammered all summer and Dad doesn't give a shit about anything. The girls though...I don't know."

I thought of my two little sisters. Twins. Ten years old, and just as sweet and pretty as can be. Them, watching my mother lounge on the couch looking at game shows with that constant sinister snarl on her face, smoking cigarettes and drinking whiskey and cokes until she became dangerous and vicious. My dad wanted nothing to do with her. He couldn't stand her any more, couldn't stand the sight of her. He would have split a long time ago except he couldn't in good conscience leave us to her, especially the girls. I thought of our house. Our house in Buffalo on that little dead end street crammed in with the others and separated only by narrow driveways and tiny slivers of lawn. The kind of driveways they built for Model A's or Model T's or whatever those early cars were. Some houses had no driveway at all and the roofs almost touched one another. Inside, my brother slept in the basement. It was dark and quiet and warm in the winter and he put some dry wall up and made a nice little room for himself. The twins shared a room on the second floor. So did my mother and father. My grandmother (my mother's mother) and I had our own rooms. My grandmother's room was pretty small. It held a bed and a dresser and not much else. She was blind and moved in with us a couple of years ago after my grandfather died. He was a good man. Smelled like butterscotch pipe tobacco. Died quickly of cancer and left Grandma nothing. It hit him in the liver. They never had anything. They lived day to day, paycheck to paycheck. They loved each other a lot. He repaired washing machines and dryers and his hands were callused and cracked and permanently blackened from the thick oil he worked with. My room was a little bigger and I still kept the bunk bed set up from when Kevin shared it with me.

"I don't want to hear that now, Kevin," I said feeling helpless standing at the damn phone booth in downtown Houston. "You talk to them. Take them to Dairy Queen for an ice cream cone. Maybe see if Grandma Rose can have them stay over there for a couple of weeks. She'd love that and the girls would be a lot better off. See if you can set that up, okay?"

"I'll do that. That's a good idea. I'll call her after I hang up. Good idea, Jimmy," he said.

I hung up, lit a Marlboro, and waited for Michael to finish his conversation.

Houston was white heat. Blazing hot. Along the streets strolled lots of pretty girls all nicely dressed. I supposed that Michael and I looked trashy to them. Some of the businessmen wore those embroidered western suits with cowboy boots, big hats and fancy belt buckles.

Back at the labor pool the Mexicans continued to doze. The guy behind the counter looked up from his racing form and waved us towards him.

"A ride will be here in about half an hour to pick you boys up and take you to work," he said.

We ended up sitting in the back of a pick-up with our packs tucked underneath our legs and heading somewhere on the outskirts of town. The sun hung fiercely in a cloudless sky. We approached a bunch of drab warehouses and loading docks with a lot of trucks and forklifts scurrying in all directions. An old timer with a slight limp greeted us at the loading dock and ushered us into the big warehouse. Inside was brightly lit and forklifts tore through the place at lightning speed.

"You boys look like we might get some work out of you," he said. "Usually that labor pool brings us a bunch of damn drunken losers."

He grabbed a forklift and took us to an area loaded with pallets thrown into a big sloppy pile. There were hundreds of them.

"The job's easy," he said. "These things have been thrown here for the last couple of days. You need to straighten them out by putting them in stacks of five. I'll get a guy with a forklift to take them away."

This was easy, mindless, and productive work. We were pretty much left to ourselves and by one in the morning the pallets were condensed and nicely stacked into piles of five just like the man asked. The forklift driver showed up every hour or so to check up on us and remove a few stacks to give us some more room. He was impressed with our diligence and speed. He was tall and skinny and black with a short cropped balding head. He wore blue coveralls and had warm easygoing eyes.

"Damn, you boys is all through?" he observed.

"How are we going to get back into Houston?" Michael asked.

The forklift driver shook his head. "You ain't. Not till six o'clock when the truck heads back down to the labor pool."

"Well, that's great," I said. "I'm beat. What should we do?"

The forklift driver reached into his coveralls, pulled out a cigarette and lit it using a blue tip wooden match that he struck on his zipper. The big flame ignited and when he sucked on the cigarette, his cheeks collapsed and folded like a dried apple. I realized then that he had no teeth.

"There's some trucks parked out in the lot. I can get y'all a ride on this here lift and you can sleep in one of the cabs. There's enough room. It ain't bad."

"Not much else we can do," Michael said pulling a Marlboro from his pocket and lighting it. "We might as well get some rest so we can work in the morning."

We each hopped onto one of the forks on the lift and the toothless driver carried us out to the lot. It was warm and breezy. Black clouds rolled in and it was getting ready to rain. The air was thick and wet. The forklift driver dropped us at an old eighteen wheeler with a sleeping cab. It was big inside with plenty of room. Before long, the rain came down hard and fast and pummeled the cab furiously with big fat drops. We listened quietly. It was loud and soothing. We were very tired and quickly fell asleep.

Michael's dead father Tasos Theotikos entered the cab and woke his son by shaking him gently.

"Hello, Michael."

"Pop?"

"How are you, Michael?"

"How did you get in here?"

"I wanted to see you. I haven't seen you in a long time and I wanted to see you. I see you are traveling with Jimmy. I remember him. You are good friends together."

"Pop, you really fucked up. I mean you really fucked us up."

"I know and I am sorry. Can you forgive me, Michael?"

Michael swung from the bed in the cab and hopped into the driver's seat behind the big steering wheel. His father sat in the passenger side with his back leaning against the door so he could get a better look at his son. His eyes were coffee brown and warm and intense. Michael lit a Marlboro and cracked open the window. He took a long drag from the cigarette and sent the smoke out the window. The rain had stopped and the air was thick and full.

"Where are you, Pop?"

"I'm nowhere, Michael. I can't get anywhere I need to get to. I'm stuck, Michael.

Michael looked at his father long and hard. "I tell people you died a long time ago," he said. "I tell them you died of a heart attack. People are

sad when they hear that and they tell me they are sorry. When I tell people
that you killed yourself they don't respond. They change the subject."

"I was foolish. I did not think it all the way through. I did not think
of you or your mother or George or Nick or Colleen. I only thought of my
own pain and I did not want to continue. And now where am I Michael? I am
nowhere."

"Mom was too hard on you."

"No she wasn't. Your mother was right. I was foolish. I wandered
aimlessly. She was not a dreamer. She was practical and she knew what she
needed. I could not give the things she wanted, the things she needed to
have."

"Pop, you could get things. I know how you came from Greece. I
know how you traveled and ended up here. You were good, Pop."

"What can I say Michael?"

"I don't understand you. Do you know that? I don't understand
how you could do what you did to us."

Tasos Theotikos' eyes softened. "I love you Michael. Do you hear
me, son? I love you."

"What are you doing sleeping on the steering wheel?" I asked.

Michael shot up. "What?" He shook his head. "How did I get
here?"

"Let's go," I said. "The pick-up truck's right outside to take us back
down to the labor pool."

We rode back in silence. The clouds cleared. The rain stopped and
it promised to be another Texas scorcher. We entered the labor pool. A new
batch of Mexicans lounged on the folding wooden chairs. The skinny guy
with the racing forms behind the counter called us up and handed us forty
dollars apiece. He said he got a good report from the warehouse. Said we
worked hard and fast and didn't give anyone shit. He said it was too bad we
had to sleep in the truck, but worse shit happens. Then he sent us right back
to work at another warehouse unloading train cars packed tightly with

diapers. Again we worked hard and at an admirable pace. We enjoyed the work and laughed our asses off the whole time. It was one of those days. We lunched on ham sandwiches and potato chips and Coke in the employee cafeteria. We laughed while watching an old timer sitting with his legs crossed over one another and eating a banana while his temples bulged in an out with each chew. He looked as if he were in a trance. I bet you he worked there fifty years.

Soon we were back at the labor pool and this time the guy behind the counter handed us fifty dollars apiece. He set us up for the next day at the same place. We told him we needed a place to sleep and he pointed us to the Salvation Army. Said there were around two hundred fifty beds and we would be sure to get one. Said there were showers and a television too. We stopped at a greasy spoon diner and ate chicken fried steak with white gravy and corn and big French fried potatoes. Then we walked to the Salvation Army and were led into a large gymnasium style room with rows and rows of cots. The room was big and brightly lit and very clean. Men lounged everywhere. Some slept, some read, others sat in clusters playing cards and telling lies. Michael and I secured two cots next to one another and then took our packs with us to the showers where we took a well needed long hot shower. The hot pulsating water felt good. We shampooed our hair and the dirty water disappeared down the drain. Later we sat in the TV room and watched an episode of *Starsky and Hutch.* We watched the one where Starsky feels pretty shitty because he accidently shot a young pretty art student.

It was lights out early at the Salvation Army. Michael and I returned and placed our packs below our cots. Michael put his hatchet underneath his pillow. You just never know. We talked with a couple of the guys for a bit. Wanderers, always with a scheme: "Here's how you can fool this dumb motherfucker and get this" or "You get yourself to California and you can live on the beach for almost nothin' by selling plasma and hanging out with the hippies." "Good women, them hippies. They go for that free-love shit all day and all night long."

In the wide hollow hall a gruff voice yelled "Lights out," and soon in the midst of darkness, two hundred and fifty men lay snoring and wheezing and coughing and farting. I listened to a steady flow of men slowly getting up in the night, their bare feet shuffling on a warm linoleum floor to and from the bathroom. A sea of lost homeless souls lay tossing and turning under the soft white light of a big, bright, pale summer moon glowing through the windows under the vast black Texas night.

Five in the morning. Lights up. Breakfast is served down the hall. Scrambled eggs, toast, and coffee. Men sit hunched over long tables eagerly eating with only the mushy sounds of jaws moving filling the big room. We are well rested and clean. It's six in the morning and we are back at the labor pool. Another tired bunch waits in blithe anticipation on the wooden folding chairs. The skinny guy with the greasy hair sits behind the counter. He is glad to see us. Does he live there? Does he live in the back with his own cot and a pile of used and marked racing forms? Again we are carted by the pick-up truck to yesterday's job site. Today we unload more diapers and work faster and harder. This is easy money unloading these trains in the scorching afternoon.

Another fifty bucks a piece and now we are good. That's one hundred and forty dollars each. We have enough to carry us for a couple of weeks as long as we don't get too crazy spending.

We returned to the Salvation Army for another shower. The grime and soot from the train yard swirled off of our bodies and down the drain again. We grabbed our packs and walked to a Laundromat where we washed our clothes, read, and wrote in our journals. The air was thick and so sickening hot inside that we sat on the sidewalk in front of the laundry. Once the clothes were done, we headed to a small grocery and stocked up on bread and canned goods. We bought beef jerky too. At five o'clock we made our way toward the highway and sat on a guardrail at the ramp where the road leads west towards Dallas. We shared a can of corn, and ate sandwiches made from a can of baked beans. We chewed on the jerky, and drank water from our canteens. It was hot. Cars passed and we did not stick our thumbs out. Finally, after finishing our dinner we put our stuff away and crushed the cans and put them into a plastic bag to get tossed into the garbage later.

Almost immediately an elderly couple pulled over and offered us a lift. They are quiet and content. They drive a new Ford. It is light blue. Michael and I sit in the back seat and I can see that the man gently cradles the woman's hand in his. They speak slowly and ask us where we are from and where we are going. They want to know a little about us. "Who are those boys, with those backpacks, standing on an exit ramp in Texas?" They are both curious and never interrupt one another. There is calmness, a comforting familiarity, a serenity they share. Simple. The man wears a straw fedora with a pin striped band around it. His shirt is white, short sleeved, and unbuttoned at the collar. A small dark brown cigar hangs from his mouth. His left hand holds the steering wheel tightly. The woman's face is kind, gentle. She turns in our direction. Her eyes are wide and friendly. Her drawl is sweet and syrupy. She wears a simple light blue summer dress with white trim. Her face is smooth and her teeth are perfect and white.

She tells us about her dead son, Sam. He was killed thirty-eight years ago in the Second World War when a torpedo hit the submarine he was in. None of the men were found. "They had a lovely memorial service for our Sam at the church, and there is a beautiful plaque in the cemetery that honors him. He's our local hero."

She tells us this story and her husband's hand never leaves hers. Her hand tightens.

"I'm reminded of Sam because he was about your age," she says. "He was very young when he left us."

"Do you have any more children?" I asked.

"Yes, we have two beautiful girls. Mary and Ellen. They're wonderful. Mary lives in Dallas with her husband. His name is William and they have two beautiful children. Two little girls. William's not from Texas. He's from up North like you. He's from Boston, but what a nice kind man and he loves Mary so. William is a dentist. I guess when he met our Mary, he just decided to stay down here and become a Texan. And Ellen lives up in Fairfield. That's where we're heading, up to see Ellen in Fairfield. She's married to a doctor, a brilliant man and they have the loveliest old house. It's an enormous home with four absolutely marvelous columns at the entrance. It is a sight to see. It's entirely terrific. We live in Houston, but we're from Huntsville. That's where Sam Houston's from, but everybody in Texas knows it because that's where the prison is. It's a big prison with some mean and evil men in there. I dare say: I would not like to make the acquaintance of any person in there."

We drove along the flat, dry Texas highway for a couple of hours. It felt good to be moving and listening to their gentle stories. I thought of my parents who rarely spoke to one another. I thought of the tension and the sarcasm. I thought of Michael's parents and their loud fights, the screaming and yelling. Maybe it was where we came from. In my neighborhood our fathers ran wild. Guys named Danny or Tommy or Jimmy or Mike or Tim. All Irish. All workers: policemen, firemen, newspaper guys, mailmen, car salesmen, bus drivers, city workers. They hung at Checker's bar, drinking beer and Irish whiskey; fighting, hugging, watching sports and betting on any game. It was a clan. "How's your mother?" "How's your wife?" "How's the family?" "You give them my best." When one died, they'd drink at Checker's until four in the morning and the next day when Father gave that same old eulogy about flaws in man and how God forgives, they'd sit in the church pews sad and hung-over and after the service they would go right back to the bar and drink to their health and the memory of their dead brother. And I knew them all. And I'd go to their homes and their kids were loud and ran wild and the mothers screamed and put big meals on the table and the mothers and the fathers and the kids ate and laughed and fought and loved. That's the way it was in my neighborhood: Loud and busy.

So we drove down the highway halfway through big Texas, and we listened with pleasure, and we noticed the calm gentleness of this man in a straw fedora, with a pin striped band around it, tenderly cradling the hand of this old woman in a blue summer dress with white trim.

Chapter 15

Moving On

It was another mercury hitting prize winner; another sticky, sweaty morning in another golden field. Again, we peeled out from our sleeping bags emerging into the hot sun. In July, the sun in Texas is a big, hot, fiery flame. It bites early.

Michael knelt in the field and rolled his sleeping bag. Crickets hummed. His upper lip held beads of sweat.

"Man, it is really hot. I'm sweating already."

He gulped water from his canteen, swished it in his mouth, and with an unpleasant grimace spit it out. He looked towards the highway and saw the golden arches of McDonald's near an entrance ramp.

"Let's go clean up, get a quick bite and get the hell out of here. I'm ready to get to Colorado," he said.

Inside McDonald's we ordered coffee and an Egg McMuffin. We took turns in the bathroom brushing our teeth, washing our faces and combing our hair. We filled our canteens with water from the sink. The water was barely cold and the bathroom walls and floors had a dirty film on them. Rivulets of grime swirled in the sink. After breakfast, we fastened our packs onto our backs, walked to the ramp, and took a series of short rides towards Dallas. We crawled. None of our rides lasted more than fifty miles and we spent a lot of time waiting on the side of the road. Flat, brown, barren, endless terrain surrounded us. The sun climbed higher. It attacked with a fury. It broke a hundred degrees. It was not a good day for rides.

Finally, we got a lift from a tall skinny cowboy who called himself Corky. Wore scuffed brown pointed cowboy boots, tight faded Levi jeans, a red and blue plaid western shirt with pearl buttons with the sleeves rolled to his elbows. His shirt was open revealing a long smooth chest. His head sat under a big fitted white Stetson with a pointed chin and nose; he looked like an Indian arrowhead with his tiny eyes sunk deep into their sockets. Talkative, friendly eyes, reminded me of a hawk or maybe an eagle. He hadn't shaved in days and blonde stubble glistened on his cheeks and chin. The three of us drove in the cab of his pick-up. It was a four speed with the shifter on the column. I sat in the middle.

Corky sang the lovesick blues, crying his eyes out over a lost girl, feeling down in the dumps, a poor heart-broken cowboy heading north on Highway 45 towards the big city: Dallas.

He had an iced six pack of PBR's in an old metal cooler and offered us one. We popped open our cans and the first taste of the ice cold malt and barley was crisp and refreshing. I was thirsty and drank that first beer quickly. We all did.

Corky motioned towards the remaining cans, "Drink up, boys. We'll stop if we need more." He was good-natured.

We took our time with the second can and drove contently down flat scorching Highway 45 listening to Bob Dylan's *John Wesley Harding* from his eight track player.

Corky told us his story, "Eight months, boys. For eight months I've been courtin' this wide-eyed little blonde girl. Fine looker with a baby doll face. Smart girl. Maybe that's the problem, smart girls think too much, too deeply. Now, I ain't sayin' this was one of them clean relationships. We both had our baggage. Hell, nothin's easy. Not in this life, no sir, ain't nothin's easy. Now, I'm a cowboy. I work a ranch. I ride rodeo. But, I'm a poet cowboy too. I got the love of words in me. I tend to think of myself as a wordsmith. I like to say things and I like to write 'em down, and most of all, I like to share them words 'specially if they's tender words and they got meaning. So, I told this pretty little bird all sorts of nice things. And I meant them. I know I did 'cause I felt them words way down deep in the pit of my gut and I told 'em to her. And I said them words 'cause I was thinkin' she wanted to hear 'em. I thought she'd like 'em.''

He finished his beer in a long slow swallow, put the can between his legs and took a pinch of Red Man chewing tobacco from a bag sitting on the dashboard. The bag had a picture of an Indian in a full headdress. *America's Best Chew* was written across the top of the bag. He dipped his thumb and index finger into the bag and pulled out a wad of fresh chew and placed it securely into his cheek. He offered some to us, but I didn't figure we wanted to learn to chew tobacco right then and there, so we politely told him "No." Corky sucked the flavor out of that tobacco occasionally spitting a stream of light brown liquid into his empty PBR can.

He was a talker and he needed to shed his woes. He continued, "Boys, I can tell you're young men and ain't got a lot of experience with women. So you don't understand them. Well, I'm forty-six years old this month and I ain't got a clue about 'em neither. That's why I'm talking to you. See, just yesterday this pretty little wide-eyed blonde I'm mentioning to you stuck a note in my mailbox. It was 9:30 in the mornin' and I was feeling damn good and I got this note and hell, boys – it just knocked my cowboy ass down. She wrote in that note that she appreciated my honesty and was flattered by my attention. Flattered. Boys from the yap of a cowboy poet the word flattered don't mean nothin'. When I say, 'that sure is a pretty dress you got on,' well that's flattering. It don't mean much. It's meant to be a compliment. I told her deep words and all she could tell me was she was flattered. While I was reading this note from her I thought about that line the Nurse says to Romeo in *Romeo and Juliet* when she warns Romeo not to treat Juliet like some poor fool. "*If ye should lead her into a fool's paradise, it were a gross ... behavior.*" That's what she says and I realized right then that I led myself to my own fool's paradise by sayin' all them nice things and her response was that she appreciated my honesty and was flattered. I felt like a fool myself; felt embarrassed with myself."

Michael and I listened without much of a clue about how to respond. Michael pointed to the bag of Red Man and asked for a chew.

"Sure thing, you grab a pinch," he said drooling another mouthful of brown liquid into the PBR can before continuing his story. "Then she wrote about staying clear of any path that would lead to regret and she wanted to maintain a strong bond as friends without compromise. I ain't makin' this up boys, that's what she wrote me and she ended with something like I hope it is all fine. And that is it my friends. That's the way it ends. Just like that. All that time, and one morning she opens her eyes and lifts her little head off her pillow and decides right then to cut me off. Ain't that somethin'? But, you want to know the craziest shit of all? Right at that particular moment when I was readin' that note I could have cared less. It is true. She's a fine woman, a real beautiful lady, but at that moment I just did not care anymore. I was embarrassed at all those nice things I said and I wanted to take them all back, but as true as a vulture tearin' in on the ass of a cow's carcass, I did not care one goddam bit and I felt like a big ol' burden was lifted. I scribbled on a piece of paper: My honesty leads to my foolishness. It's fine. And it is."

We drove silently. The air slapping at us from the open windows was dry and hot. Dylan crooned *I'll be Your Baby Tonight* like a wounded coyote. Michael broke the silence. He spit the brown liquid from his mouth into his empty PBR can and said, "She was no good for you. She just left a note; that's no good. It seems she could have told you in person. I'd be careful with that."

I chimed in, "I told a girl good things too. Things I felt. Things I thought I meant. Like you said, things I thought she wanted to hear. Then we'd go places and from the corner of my eye I'd see her checking out another guy. That lustful look made me feel bad. It happened all the time.

She'd just gush over them. 'I'm just being friendly,' she'd say, but that look did not feel right to me and it made me feel like pretty lousy, too."

"Well, boys," Corky said. "I still got the faith from above that there's a good woman out there for me and God willing maybe enough for all of us. I'm still hopin' for that right little lady, but tonight we got business to tend to. Right up on the other side of Dallas is a nice big ol' lake called Lake Dallas. We'll get ourselves a case of beer and head over to that lake and cool off. I got time."

At Lake Dallas Corky sat shirtless on a blanket strumming an old beat up guitar and singing *I'm an Old Cow Hand from the Rio Grande.* His boots and socks were off and he was drunk. We had an iced cooler filled with PBR's and were knocking them off pretty good. We devoured sandwiches made with white bread, American cheese, mustard and potato chips. It was getting late, the sun was setting and we figured we'd sleep on the beach. It was quiet. No one was around.

That night the sky was deep, endless, black, and star filled. It was magnificent.

The next morning when the sun beat us up and pulled us out of our sleeping bags, Corky was gone. Under the mustard jar was a note that read *ya'all get to where you're going safely. Pleasant travels – Corky.* Wrapped inside the note was a twenty dollar bill.

"I didn't even hear him leave," I said.

"Nice guy," Michael said. "I wonder where he was going. I never asked him. Did you?"

"No. I didn't."

We took a long swim in the lake. The water was warm and cloudy with strands of algae floating throughout. It still felt good. We knew it was going to be another hot day. Every day was. The sun down in this part of the country was relentless.

From Lake Dallas we took rides to the northern border of Decatur, Texas. We picked up U.S. Route 287 a major truck route that begins in Port

Arthur, Texas and climbs northward through the countryside and small towns on up to Choteau, Montana.

Again, rides were sparse and we spent long periods of time on the side of the road juggling, reading, singing, joking, talking, and going over the map trying to figure out a solid route to travel for the summer. Our skin was browned from being outside. Most of our rides that day came from farmers in pick-up trucks going short distances. We crawled past little towns like Bowie and Bellevue and Jolly and Iowa Park and Electra. We passed through small towns with low flat buildings and big blue or aqua-green water towers seen jutting into the open sky from miles away. We watched the hot, white, flat, dusty countryside roll by. We ate a lunch of canned corn with a can of peaches in syrup and washed it down with dull warm water from our canteens.

Our next ride came from a sunbaked brown-skinned Mexican in an old white Oldsmobile station wagon carrying three cute little girls with him. Three daughters all crammed in the front seat with the oldest being maybe ten or so. They wore t-shirts, shorts and sandals. We sat in the back seat while they stared in our direction with bashful smiles and big soft brown eyes. All with straight, fine, shiny black hair. In the back end of the station wagon five chickens rustled nervously in a tiny metal cage, their heads cocked in sharp movements keeping their eyes on us. The father did not speak English. The ten year old did most of the talking. She translated for her father. She said they got the chickens from her uncle. He had a small farm in the country. These were chickens that could lay nice eggs, big brown ones. The man questioned us and soon knew our story and was comfortable with us.

We drove quickly through Chillicothe, past a series of one story brick buildings and an abandoned old red brick feed house with massive dull grey grain elevators attached to it. The man said they were built in 1893 and had been abandoned for a long time now. Chillicothe had its own water tower too. I believe it took us about a minute to drive through town.

A mile or so up the road stood a worn white wood-planked home with a big porch and a big yard. The yard was scattered with abandoned cars, and chicken coops, and a dog house that was surrounded by a chain link fence. There were two mutts inside that seemed friendly enough. They wagged their tails and howled as the Mexican pulled the Oldsmobile in and ushered us out. With his hands he motioned that he wanted us to eat with him. He led us to his front porch. It wrapped along two sides of the house and had a lot of mismatched chairs scattered about. A worn faded sofa leaned against the house. A coffee table sat before the sofa. Michael and I were guided to the sofa and the three little girls joined us. They were shy and curious. In the center of the porch at the front of the house was a screened door. Out came the man's wife, his mother, and two more girls a little older, maybe fourteen or fifteen. They were embarrassed and thought the little girls were behaving goofy.

We sat with the family and answered their questions: Where are we from? Where are we going? Do we sleep in the fields? Are Dallas and Houston big? Can I see your map? What do you eat? Do you have girlfriends? What is inside your packs? Is it cold in New York? Where is Buffalo? Are you going to California? Where are you heading next?

They sat erect and attentive, hands on their knees, their brown faces beaming towards us friendly and curious. We showed them our backpacks and everything inside. Michael discussed the importance of each item. He showed them the map and with his finger, traced where we had been. The little girls sat on his knee and traced along with him, naming each state until they got to Texas. "Texas is so big," the youngest squealed.

The mother and grandmother excused themselves and waved the two older girls to come with them. They returned moments later with the mother carrying a big pot of black beans and setting it on the table. Steam rose from the pot. The grandmother placed a tray of warm corn tortillas next to the beans. One of the girls brought in a tray with chopped tomatoes, green onions, limes, cilantro and chili peppers. The other carried in a pot of coffee with cups and bowls. We sat around the coffee table and grabbed the tortillas and filled them with beans and the other stuff. They were hot and full of flavor. The coffee was thick and black and strong. The man showed us that it tastes best with spoonfuls of sugar. We drank the coffee and it was wonderful and rich and sweet.

Next to the house the father had planted a big garden loaded with lettuces, corn, tomatoes, chili peppers, onions, green beans, carrots, cilantro, basil, and mint all rowed and spaced nicely. The deep brown soil was rich and moist. The father had tended carefully to the garden. The freshness of the meal came from the richness of the garden. Beds of marigolds, yellow daylilies, and red and pink roses spread colorfully out in the front of the house. The sweetness from the flowers and the grass wafted into the early evening. We enjoyed the peacefulness of the evening.

The oldest girl left for a moment and went into the house and came back with a small glass bottle of bright red nail polish. She pulled the brush from the bottle, placed a small brown foot on the arm of the sofa inches from my arm and began to glide the brush from the bottle and onto her biggest toe. The grandmother saw this and cursed her furiously in Spanish. The girl ran frantically into the house and returned pouting sheepishly, her toe clean. She sat on the arm of the sofa. The other girls watched her carefully with reserved smiles. Michael gave me a look and I rolled my eyes.

We stayed on the front porch with the family and watched the sun glide across the sky and hanging silently before setting in the West. The sky was orange and pink and silver. We let the family know it was time for us to get back on the road and head toward Denver. The mother chopped some ice and put it into our canteens with water. The grandmother gave us a small brown bag filled with peaches and cut celery. We thanked the family and shook their hands. We shook each little girl's hands at least ten times and their wide smiles and big brown glowing eyes never left their faces. The older girls shook our hands gently. The oldest one looked sad. The father led us to the white station wagon and gave us a lift up the road. He motioned that this would be a good spot for us. He wore a warm smile. He shook our hands firmly and left. We watched the Oldsmobile heading back up the road to the little white house. For a moment all was silent. The air smelled sweet. Crickets hummed.

"We are in the middle of nowhere," Michael said. "We'll never get to Denver."

Not more than ten minutes later a Ryder truck pulled over. A stocky guy with round glasses, receding hair, and a wrinkled shirt stepped down from the cab and let go a long stretch, raising his tired arms high into the sky. He looked beat. Said his name was Randy. Said he was going to Denver and he would give us a ride on one condition. We had to stay awake all night to keep him from falling asleep at the wheel. So we did.

Chapter 16

Littleton

It was pure luck that Randy picked us up. We barreled up the highway, through the darkness, and into Colorado. He was driving from Dallas after picking up furniture from his parents' house. Said they were killed last month when a train pummeled their car while they sat idling on a railroad crossing. Said the engineer saw the car up ahead and pulled the whistle to send a warning. There was no stopping the train, but the whistle could be heard for miles. Said they should have heard the big train coming and they should have crossed the tracks or they should have gotten out of the car. "Had plenty of time," the conductor said later.

None of this made any sense to Randy and now he was cruising north in a Ryder truck with two hitch-hikers from Buffalo, NY and heading home with a truck full of furniture to marry his girlfriend from Littleton, Colorado. Furniture he needed; furniture that reminded him of where he came from. His parents' bedroom set. A maple dining room set with a table and eight chairs. A yellow linoleum kitchen table with chrome legs and six yellow covered matching chairs. A living room set. He took plates and glasses. He remembered using the plates, his mother's cooking, his father slouched over the table eating a pan-fried pork chop with pan fried corn and pan fried potatoes with onions. His old man smothered his food with ketchup and salt and pepper. His mother ate half of what he ate. Randy remembered his family together with his two brothers, who both moved away from Texas, talking eagerly and happily and eating many meals at the kitchen table.

By the time the Ryder got to Amarillo darkness was setting in. Randy picked up Route 385 in Vega and we headed north through Channing and Hartley, then northwest through the little towns of Bolin and Texline and crossing into New Mexico, moving steadily, until picking up Highway 25 in Raton and then moving north into Colorado. As the moon lowered, the sky lightened and from the east we watched the first colorful traces of silver and pink welcoming the morning before us. A bright sliver of sun peeked from the horizon. In the distance mountains lay stretched before us long and brown, eternally placed on the endless flat and tan plains. Further in the distance, beyond the foothills, I watched the bigger white-capped mountains resting enormously against a clear pale-blue sky. We never saw mountains like that in the East.

"Sure don't see mountains like that in Texas," Randy said.

"Or in Buffalo," Michael agreed.

We drove silently up Highway 25 and the mountains got closer and bigger and deeper. Randy had been driving a pretty long time. His eyes were puffy and red and his hair lay on his head curly and disheveled like sheep's wool. By the time we got to Littleton, traffic had picked up. We merged slowly into the morning Denver rush hour.

Randy took a joint from his shirt pocket, lit it and told us about his plans.

"My girl's name is Paula. She's a forest ranger. Good looking girl, too pretty to be a forest ranger. We're getting married next week up in Estes Park. That's a nice place. Beautiful white capped mountains, ponderosa pines that smell like fresh vanilla. It's the place to be. We're going to live up there. She'll work in the park and I'm going to commute to Boulder and finish taking my coursework for my PhD. I'm getting it in Education. I have about a year and a half to go before I write my dissertation. What a pain in the ass that is."

I sat listening because I had promised to stay awake. Michael slept with his head propped against his arm and leaning on the window. I don't know how he could sleep like that, but he did. And, he could do it for a long time. Randy took a long pull from the joint, held it, and breathed it out in a long whoosh.

"Anyway, it's all pretty exciting stuff."

He took another long hit from the joint and motioned it to me.

"No thanks; never did much for me."

"Me neither, come to think of it. It just keeps me awake; gets me ready to see Paula."

Randy's house was in one of those developments. The real confusing ones with all with the apartments the same brown color. I guess the developers figured it gave a prairie look to them. They call them townhouses. They're real nice, but hard to tell apart. The Ryder chugged into the complex, made a few turns and pulled into a driveway with a big brown garage. Randy hopped out of the Ryder and pressed a button near the side of the door. The door lifted revealing a clean garage. The floor was smooth and spotless. We could have eaten off of it.

"Finally," Randy said shutting off the motor and climbing stiffly out from the cab.

Michael opened his eyes and groaned. Inside the apartment was dark. Curtains were closed and a sour stench permeated the room. I could hear a faint whimper.

"What the hell is going on in here?" Randy said flicking on the light switch.

In the center of the room a large German Shepard sat motionless on a tall bar stool. Shit lay in piles under and around the stool. Piss soaked the carpet. The dog's eyes were glassy and brown and he pleaded for a command.

"Macht schnell," Randy said and the dog leapt to his side with an air of graceful obedience. "What the fuck is going on?"

"Is that dog alright? I mean is he okay with strangers?" Michael asked.

Randy paid no attention to us. He furiously clicked on lights and searched each room in the apartment. He called for Paula. She was not here and the place was quiet. He opened curtains letting in the western sun. It slanted inward and warmed the room. Randy gave his dog a bowl of water and the big shepherd lapped at it steadily and noisily. Off of the kitchen were sliding glass doors leading to a small patch of browned sun baked lawn. He slid open the doors and let the dog out. The dog moved about the yard sniffing cautiously and moving slowly. The dog raised his head and stretched and pissed and then settled into a worn spot under a small tree and slept.

"Where the hell is she?" Randy wondered.

He looked tired, and worried. Except for the dog shit, the place was clean. Michael and I stood awkwardly in the kitchen and watched Randy move about in confusion. He opened the refrigerator to grab us a couple of beers. Inside was a new twelve pack of Coors. Next to the beer was a pot of green chili with a note taped to the lid that read: *Sorry. I guess I'm not ready. I'm lost. Please don't be angry. I didn't mean to do it like this. I need some time. I hope to see you again. Love, Paula.*

Randy read the note a couple of times while nervously twisting the whiskers hanging in wisps from his chin. He pulled three beers from the fridge, lit a burner on the stove, and put on the pot of chili. "She makes some good fuckin' chili," he said quietly and brought out a plate of soft corn tortillas and heated them on the stove in a cast-iron pan. He chopped some fresh cilantro. We sat at his kitchen table eating the hot green chili and drinking the cold Coors beer. We spent the morning listening to stories of trout fishing in Mineral Springs, Colorado, right down past Colorado Springs where you can catch golden trout bigger than a foot long. He told us about hiking way up in the mountains to the edge of timberline where the trees had been beaten down by ravishing winds and the wind smoothed and gnarled the trees into astonishing shapes. He spoke of the mountain goats living in the rocks on the tops of the summit.

"They walk down from the steep rocks just far enough to eat the patches of sweet grass and in the springtime. They shed their hair in big patches giving them a look of an old beggar man."

<<<>>>

Kuhio Avenue stretches through the heart of Waikiki Beach between Ala Wai Boulevard and Kalakaua Avenue. It is a wide avenue laden with soaring white hotels, palm trees, restaurants, shops, and boutiques. To the north, Diamond Head looms dark and large and juts forcefully into a clear blue sea. In an upscale boutique, a pretty woman, with a sunburned back, and wearing a long sheer white cabana skirt and flowered halter-top, shops quietly. She sifts through the racks of sexy lingerie caressing the softness of each piece. She has a wad of money in her purse. Money she has saved for a wedding. Money she has put aside to cover the costs of a wedding dress, shoes, and flowers. Maybe rent the small dining room at Le Central, her favorite Denver restaurant, for a quaint reception with a few good friends and some family. They could have wine, cheese, light hors d'oeuvres. Keep it simple.

Instead, she fingers through the racks of lingerie, plays with satin chemises, sheer nighties, lace baby dolls, silk robes, plush chenille robes, bras and panties. She holds them into the light and imagines herself wearing them. A clerk bags her selection and she is back out on sunny-warm Kuhio Avenue walking delicately to her hotel. She breathes in the flowery sweetness lingering in the air. She is calm. She takes the elevator to her room. It is high on the twenty-third floor. The view from the lanai faces the ocean. She lays the lingerie on the bed and tries everything on one piece at a time. She slides into a satin chemise. It is sheer, baby blue, with lace trim and satin ties. She enjoys the soft smoothness lying delicately on her skin. She steps out onto the lanai and leans over the railing looking out at the deep blue sea. She focuses beyond the beach, beyond the deep waters and settles on the horizon. She follows it carefully squinting to see what lies beyond.

Chapter 17

Boulder

The Pearl Street Mall stretches on Pearl Street between 11th and 15th streets in Boulder, Colorado. It is four blocks long. The mall is a popular place lined with shops, cafes, and bars. At 13th and Spruce streets sits the elegant Victorian Hotel Boulderado. Street musicians, students from Colorado University, residents, tourists and a healthy handful of watery eyed vagabonds move through the red brick walkways daily. In the evening, crowds wander and large groups gather and surround street performers: jugglers, puppeteers, drummers and guitar playing singers. Some get drunk and head toward and climb the nearby towering red flat irons that surround the festivities. They drink jugs of wine and bottles of beer and smoke endless cigarettes.

We met Leo in a small, dark, grimy bar around the corner from the mall. I don't remember seeing a sign on the place. A stale-sour stench hit us as we walked in. Leo had been there for a couple of hours. He was glassy eyed and slugging beers at a dollar a draft. We drank with him until we felt loose and warm. Leo came to Boulder from Buffalo and has lasted two years without returning. Says he is going to stay in Boulder and never return. "Buffalo sucks," says Leo. Leo wears his hair long and tied back. He keeps a worn red bandana tied on his head. He wears a long ratty beard and has soft, welcoming brown eyes and crimson red lips and he smokes a lot of cigarettes. His teeth are stained like tree bark. His clothes are disheveled. He is thin and walks with a slight limp. He is friendly and intelligent and has no tolerance for hippies. He likes the underground punk rock scene. Bands like Patti Smith, Lou Reed and MC5. He say's the Grateful Dead sucks.

We left the darkness of the bar and strolled into the bright sunlight of the mall. I watched a chick guitar player pound on her battered acoustic and sing *Bobby McGee*. She looked like Karen Carpenter and sang like Janis Joplin. Leo concealed a pint of tequila in his front right pocket and we watched the chick and passed the bottle between us. The tequila burned going down. I felt a little nauseous because of it.

Leo lived in a shack on Boulder Creek. That's what it was, a shack: one room with an unpainted wooden floor and a big window that looked over the grassy bank of the slow moving creek. Leo kept his place immaculate. In one corner his sleeping bag lay flat on a thin mattress, next to that his back pack, and in the opposite corner stood an old bookcase stocked neatly with canned goods and a bag of Wonder Bread. He had a lot of books stacked tidily next to his bed. He was reading *Junkie*, by William Burroughs. It lay open on his bed. We had plenty of beer and another big bottle of cheap tequila.

It was hot outside and the shack gave us shade from the sun. We sat cross-legged on the worn floor and drank the beer and the tequila and listened to the creek ramble slowly below. Leo was happy to see us. He took pleasure in hanging out with folks from back home. He lifted the bottle of tequila to his mouth and took a long pull. That was a big swallow, I thought. We joined in.

We stayed in the shack for a couple of hours and got drunk, very drunk. A couple of Leo's buddies from New Jersey stopped by: Brad and Joel. Brad had black eyes and was a real fast talker and Joel listened and watched quietly in uncomfortable shyness. They were hitch-hiking from Jersey and heading to Mt. Rainer in Washington State and hanging in Boulder for a bit. They figured that would be a good way to spend the summer. Once they got to Mt. Rainer they would hike it. Said there's still snow on the mountain and they were both pretty excited about that. They met Leo on the mall and he let them crash in the shack for a few days. They brought a gallon of Inglenook wine with them and we worked on that too. Brad figured it would be a pretty good idea to grab our sleeping bags and hike up Boulder Canyon and sleep in the woods. We all agreed and grabbed our bags and headed out of the shack. The sun was still hot and it was very bright outside. The air was dry. The sky was deep clear blue. I tagged along behind Leo leading us to the liquor store. We bought two more gallons of Inglenook. It was cheap wine. Then, we went to the Safeway and bought a loaf of bread and a bunch of cans of Dinty Moore beef stew. We also bought a bag of oranges to take with us into the hills.

We followed the creek to the mouth of the canyon and headed up toward the granite crags. The water was shallow and cold and wandered slowly down from the mountains. Thick trees on the left side of the bank gave us shade and cooled us. The hill streamside along our right was dusty and rocky. Clumps of pine trees were gathered above. We moved further upwards until we reached the tall granite rock formations projecting high and dangerous into the clear blue sky.

Brad was drunk. He had a heavy New Jersey accent and he liked to talk. He had thick dull dreadlocks and he wore baggy shorts and sandals. He had a deep tan. His feet were dirty and he had on a navy blue t-shirt with YALE written on it. That was dirty too. He smelled sour. He stumbled up the hill until falling face first onto a cactus. Shoots stuck into his lips and he swore and moaned and pulled them out. His lips swelled and got pretty bloody. He didn't talk as much after that.

The other guy, Joel, was very thin with deep set brown eyes and a hawk like nose. He must have been about six-three. He was the quiet one. With Brad out of the picture, we ambled quietly upwards until we reached the granite crag. We climbed the rock and each of us found a place to sit. From here we could see the entire city of Boulder spread below us. We sat together casually talking, smoking cigarettes, drinking tequila and washing that nasty taste down with that Inglenook wine. The two guys from Jersey told us about New Jersey and Raceway Park and the big flea market they have every weekend in Englishtown.

"It's called an auction, but it's really a flea market," Brad said. "You can get all kinds of shit there."

That's where they were from, Englishtown, New Jersey. We told them about Buffalo and snow and steel mills and long, dark and bitterly cold gray days. They wanted to know a little bit about Niagara Falls. We told them it was quite the place and they needed to see it at least once.

We drank and the conversation grew louder as we passed the bottles between us until Leo suggested we had better move into the woods and set up a camp. It was getting dark. The air smelled clean like vanilla. We found a place under some tall, wide pines. Big, long soft pine needles lay scattered on the woods floor. We gathered rocks, stacked them and formed a ring for a fire. We gathered pine needles and twigs to get a fire going. Brad got the fire lit and Michael, the tall guy, and I ventured out a ways into the woods and brought back some bigger pieces of wood to keep the fire strong into the night. Leo opened the cans of Dinty Moore. He took out a bowie knife from his sleeping bag, laid the oranges out on a rock and quartered them. Michael carefully placed bigger pieces of wood onto the fire. He arranged them like a tee-pee and soon the fire was high and respectable. He would tend to it the rest of the evening. Leo opened the cans of beef stew and carefully placed them in the coals and we passed the bottles and watched the big bold blue and white Dinty Moore stickers burning away from the cans while the stew simmered and cooked. Leo pulled the cans from the fire using his bandana as a glove and gave us each a can of hearty stew. We let the cans cool beside us until we could hold them. The stew was thick and rich and we dipped the white bread in our cans and ate the bread and the stew and washed it down with the cheap wine and the nasty tequila. We ate the oranges too. When we were finished we smoked and drank some more.

I needed to take a piss. I got up and headed away from the fire and into an open meadow. Michael walked with me and we moved beneath a big, low hanging, brightly lit moon and a wide-open dark sky filled with glittering stars. I could see the Milky Way and some stars shot across the sky and arched and burned out before us. The fire glowed orange behind us. I could hear it hiss and crackle. I could hear Leo laugh heartily at a joke Brad made. I did not know Michael's father was with us. I stopped in the meadow and pissed under the stars. A herd of elk walked delicately before us. I counted ten of them moving slowly through the meadow.

"It is beautiful, Michael," Tasos Theotikos said.

"Pop?"

"You are in a place of great beauty, but be careful. The evil can lie in unsuspecting places."

"What do you mean?" Michael said.

The herd passed slowly under the bright moonlight. It focused forward. Heads low to the ground. Tails white above muscular haunches and thin long legs. They moved silently, steadily.

"That Brad from New Jersey, he's not real bad, but he can be bad," Tasos said.

"What are you talking about Pop?"

"I'm talking about that boy from New Jersey. The one with the cactus sticking in his lip. He can be bad. I know his story. It's not his fault, but with him you must be careful. He can turn ugly."

"So you say, Pop."

"I've seen his people. It goes back with him. It goes generations."

"What does?" Michael said.

"He had an Uncle they called Billy. A distant uncle from Romania. They lived far into the country in Romania. There were no nearby villages. Uncle Billy was a good boy. He had a good spirit and a lot of energy. They called him a rascal. He liked to play on a wood pile in the back of their shack. His father and his older brothers kept the wood pile high. They

burned a lot of wood in those days and the father insisted that the wood pile always be plentiful. Anyway, this boy Billy, he liked to play on the wood pile. He liked to climb it and jump from it, fool around on it, you know."

"Sure, Pop," Michael said.

"And he was told over and over don't play on the wood pile. You will get hurt. Don't play on the wood pile. He did not listen. He played on the wood pile as much as he liked until one cold and dreary afternoon in the Romanian countryside, the boy fell from the top of the wood pile and broke his ankle and his foot. His father cursed him and yelled, now look what you have done; you have broken your foot. What will you do now?"

"What's this got to do with anything?" Michael said.

"The father was a stubborn old goat," Tasos Theotikos said. "He punished the boy by not calling the doctor to see him. His foot healed badly. His foot became deformed and turned in badly and this little boy grew into a man and limped foolishly for the rest of his life. When the boy went to the village other boys and girls would look at him and laugh. They would mock him. This boy grew up and married and turned mean. He turned mean because he looked foolish. He beat his sons and his sons got mean and they too got married and they beat their sons and it moved along that way until it reached Brad all the way to New Jersey."

"Whatever, Pop," Michael said.

"I am only telling you, it's not his fault, but that Brad boy can be a bad one."

We walked back toward the fire. A slight wind blew smoke in our direction as we approached. Brad sat reclined with his legs in front of him and his back pressed against his rolled sleeping bag, a bottle of tequila in his hand. He was finishing a story about how he punched some asshole in the face one snowy winter day.

"I'm not sure why I punched him," he said. "I think I just wanted to know what his red blood would look like in the fresh white snow."

131

Chapter 18

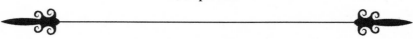

Pete's Coney Island

Pete's Coney Island is a greasy spoon in downtown Denver. By
9:00 AM the place is loaded with drunks, Mexicans, Indians, and white men
with stained yellow hands from too much Drum tobacco. Food is cheap.
Eggs smothered with green chili, fried potatoes with onions, and coffee.
Good strong coffee. Pete doesn't look any different than his clientele or his
dishwasher or his waiters. No women hovering over tables, only long, shirt
stained, brown, dark haired men who allow you no more than thirty seconds
to make up your mind to order. No menus. Coffee pot in hand, thick white
cups dropped hastily on the table and routinely filled.

We left Leo and the two guys from New Jersey up in the hills and
hitched back into Denver. We felt the sting from the tequila. My throat was
raw and swollen. We reeked of pungent smoke. Our breath was sour.

The waiter filled our cups with deep brown coffee and dropped two
orders of huevos rancheros before us. The eggs looked up at us and the
strong scent of green chilies pierced my nostrils. It was a good breakfast.
Michael devoured his eggs, attacking them like a ravenous jackal. Sweat
protruded in tiny beads from his forehead.

"This girl, Chris, works at a Subway in Englewood. She's a friend
of Michelle's. We can take the bus and be there in about half an hour," I told
him.

"How do you know she'll be there?"

"I don't."

"Then why should we go there?"

"It's not far. I feel like crap and maybe we can take a shower and get some rest. She'll let us stay there for a couple of days if we want. Michelle told me so. If she's not there we can hitch up to Breckenridge and stay with Michelle till the guys get here."

"Okay," he said. "When do you think they're gonna get here, anyway?"

"Who knows? They'll probably be here in a couple of days."

After breakfast we stood on the sidewalk outside of Pete's and could see the Capitol building perched up on a hill, its gold dome gleaming under a clear, crisp sky. The sky was pure Western sky. Bright blue, clean, endless. To the west brown mountains stretched endlessly across the horizon. Snow-caps loomed in the distance. We headed down 14th street towards Larimer Square. Michael heard about some western bar called *Soapy Smith's* that had been there forever and wanted to see what it was all about. Not that we needed another drink. I still hadn't found the cure from last night, but a walk might just help cut through the tequila that held on tight to the both of us. A few yards ahead of us a big lumbering drunk Indian staggered in our direction. His face was leather; his eyes blue and glassy. He wore a thin sparse mustache. It gave him the look of a drunken catfish. The big Indian was dazed. He was getting an earful from a tiny boy-like Mexican. The Mexican was half his size. Sinewy with black bangs curved above angry black eyes. They both stopped. The Mexican continued to argue. He paid no attention to us. We watched in curious anticipation trying to be invisible. The Mexican said something to the Indian and the Indian attempted to kick the Mexican, his big leg lumbering awkwardly and grazing the Mexican's ass. In a pugnacious crouched stance, the Mexican lunged upward and in one fast motion swiped the Indians fleshy cheek with a shiny thin steel razor. The Indian stood planted in place swaying stupidly, dumbfounded. The blade was quickly secured back into the Mexican's back pocket. The Indian put his

133

hand to his cheek and the fast blood pumping out and through his fingers frightened him. The Mexican was gone in a flash and the Indian gazed at us scared and confused. His eyes were painful like those of a small boy pleading. Our eyes met and his big drunken catfish face was pitiful.

"Jesus," Michael said. "What the hell."

We moved ahead on the sidewalk quickly and cautiously. The big Indian ploughed and weaved heavily in the other direction, blood spilling from his face to his hand down his arm and onto the sidewalk leaving a trail of big thick red droplets.

We had no intention of going to that joint on Larimer to get drunk, but we did. We drank beer mixed with tomato juice. Red eyes they called them. They really weren't bad at all, went down easy. Later we ended up at the public library. I found a book and read about Hemingway's early life in Oak Park, Illinois. I read how he hated his mother and pitied his father. We killed about three hours reading quietly in the library before we hopped onto the Broadway Street bus towards Englewood.

Chapter 19

Subway

Englewood, Colorado sits just south of Denver. Wide streets, suburban homes and strip malls. It's nothing special. It looks a lot like everywhere else. Our friend Michelle was living up in Breckenridge. She was from Buffalo. Michelle mentioned, on the phone, that she had a friend, Chris, who lived in Englewood, and worked at a *Subway*. We could stay with her for a couple of days while we waited for the others. Then we could all hitch up to Breckenridge, to her place, and camp in the mountains as long as we'd like.

I'm guessing we didn't look any better than a couple of common street urchins when we got to the Subway. I went to the counter and asked a skinny kid with a face loaded with white-headed pimples if Chris was here. He gave us a curious look and told me to wait a minute and walked back into the kitchen. Michael peeled his backpack off and propped it next to a booth. He nestled himself into the booth and raised his legs. His shirt was soaked with sweat. He pulled out a Marlboro and lit it. Smoke rose above his head mixing with bright rays of sunlight. The few people in the place gave us averted glances probably wondering who the two run down guys with backpacks were. A moment later, Chris came to the booth holding two Cokes in big yellow cups. She had a pleasant smile.

"You look thirsty," she said. A warm smile stretched across a soft pleasant face.

"Thanks, we are," I said.

"Yeah, thanks," Michael said downing half the Coke in one long pull from his straw.

She had been working with flour. She had on a blue pullover shirt with blue jeans and white sneakers. Her apron reached mid thigh; flour scattered down her legs and up and onto her breasts. Michelle told me she came from outside of Chicago. They met and quickly become good friends. She seemed happy and, for whatever reason, glad to see us.

"Michelle said you'd be stopping by," she said. "Ever been to Colorado before?"

"No, I said. "We got into Boulder a few days ago and hung up there with a buddy of ours. We camped in the woods near Boulder Creek with some of his friends."

"It's nice up there," she said.

Michael downed the rest of his Coke. "Drank too much; haven't showered in days."

"I can leave now. I'm the manager, so it's cool. I'll make you a couple of subs. You can have them later. We can go to my apartment and you can shower and take it easy," she said.

The apartment was small and comfortable. Michael took a long hot shower and I sat in the living room with Chris. A big grey cat jumped on her lap and glared at me. I felt uneasy around cats. I felt they would jump at me and scratch my eyes out at any moment. Chris kicked her sneakers into the corner, stretching her bare feet and letting out a relaxing sigh. Her face was friendly and content. Smooth as porcelain. Her eyes were a deep dark-brown with a slight laziness to them giving her a hint of sadness. Her body was full. She told me about her home and her parents and that she's so glad to finally be away from them and that Colorado is the most beautiful place she's ever lived and working at Subway was okay but her dream was to get a place up in the mountains probably near Rollinsville, a small town nestled between Nederland and Blackhawk, not too far away from here. She said

136

she'd been saving up a pretty good amount of money and could hopefully get a place in about a year. She was going to open a sandwich place with home-made chili and good beer. Nothing fancy, just stuff that mountain people would love to eat. Maybe country music on the weekends. I had no reason to doubt her.

We stayed with Chris for two days. It felt good to be clean and comfortable. Much of our time was spent listening to music, drinking beer, eating sandwiches, and playing a lot of chess together. She had this wonderful glass chess set. She beat me every time. Michael was comfortable reading Blake and Ginsburg and writing letters back home and trying to find the best words to describe places we'd rambled through like Nashville, New Orleans, Houston, and Boulder. He wrote about sleeping in fields, waiting hours for rides on the side of the highway, listening to the grumbling and choking of eighteen wheelers jamming gears, rolling down hills, and whooshing past us while churning up asphalt and blowing fields of alfalfa or wheat so that the sweet dry scent of summer wafted like spray perfume into the air. We could never get enough of that. It was that connection with the road that fueled us. The cities were fine and unique, far from what we knew in Buffalo. But, the road itself: between the towns, through the long stretches of wooded forests, of rolling hills, of endless wide open fields; golden and emerald, with brushed ginger skies fading into a black and illuminated night with stars glistening until the bright silver, pink, and yellow of dawn appeared slowly before us. It was during those times when Michael and I sat silently and contently taking in our surroundings and leaning on our back packs in the gravel near the guard rails, for hours. That's when the road was alive within us.

Chapter 20

Lake Dillon

The phone in the kitchen rang. I got out of my sleeping bag on the living room floor to answer it. Chris was gone. Michael was sleeping on the couch with his mouth slightly open. A dribble of saliva slid from the corner of his mouth. He snored quietly. He did not hear the phone. I picked up the receiver and pressed it to my ear.

"Hello?"

"Jimmy?" I heard my brother on the other end of the line. "Hey Jimmy, hey brother, is that you?"

"Kevin, where are you?"

"We're here, over at Johnny's brother's house. We're at Tommy's. We slept in his backyard, pitched the tent and slept like logs. What a trip. Took us forever, got stuck for a whole day in Manhattan, Kansas. It's a big college town with lots of chicks."

"Glad you're here," I said.

He put Tommy on the phone and Tommy gave me directions. I woke Michael and we were in Tommy's backyard about an hour later. He lived in a small white ranch style house. It had green wooden shutters. The little house sat on a sliver of a backyard surrounded by a chain fence. In the center of the yard, under the clothesline, stood Kevin's pitched orange tent. It slept two. Tommy, Johnny and Kevin gathered at the entrance of the tent passing a joint between them. Kevin held a gallon jug of Sunny Delight.

They munched on Twinkies and Ho Ho's. McShay was still in the tent. I guess he was sleeping.

"Took us forever," Kevin said carefully sucking the white filling from his Twinkie. "Rides really sucked. We got nothing longer than a hundred miles. We crawled here."

"At least you made it. Let's go to the sub shop and see Chris, get something to eat and head up into Dillon," I said.

"It's straight up 70," Tommy said. "You can't miss it. I'd shoot you up there myself, but I got to work. Pay the fucking bills."

Tommy was the manager of a Midas muffler shop. He wore a thin mustache. "We fucking do everything," he said. "Not just mufflers and brakes. Fucking you name it, we do it."

Tommy was wearing a greenish-gray long-sleeved shirt that had a Midas patch and a tag that said Thomas. He also had a pin showing he was the manager. He took another pull from the joint, bit into his Ho Ho and took a long swig of the Sunny Delight.

The sky was bright blue. Clouds stretched in the sky like sheets of gauze. The sun was climbing. The air was dry and it was going to be a hot day. We stood in the yard and gazed at Tommy's van parked in the driveway. Pictures of the seven dwarfs smoking pot from hookahs were painted on the side. Tommy took another long pull from the joint, admired the artwork sitting proudly before him, and passed the joint to his little brother Johnny. Tommy and Johnny. Tommy: slight, freckled, lazy-eyed and pleasant faced. Brown bangs hung carelessly over a rounded forehead. Johnny is a red haired version of his brother who spits continuously through his teeth leaving his mark of wet spots wherever he stands.

"Be sure to say *hey* to my sister up there in Dillon," Tommy said. "She's a good girl, gonna enjoy seeing you guys. Don't know what she's doing up there all by herself, but tell her I say hey anyway." Tommy took one more pull from the joint. "Tell her to come down when she can. I got plenty of room."

"Alright," I said.

Back at the sub shop Chris sat at a table near the counter. We kept our backpacks close to us. Chris brought us a tray of assorted subs and big Cokes. She watched us with her soft face and sad eyes. We ate the sandwiches quickly and smoked Marlboros and planned our route to Dillon. Michelle would be waiting for us.

<<<>>>

Interstate 70 turns and bends upwards to Highway 6 through Arapahoe National Forest and into Lake Dillon. Kevin, McShay, Michael and I took a shot at hitching together. We were lucky and got a ride straight up I-70, through the Eisenhower Tunnel, on the back of a pickup and got dropped off in town. Dillon sits nestled amongst pine and aspen trees. Michelle's place overlooks Lake Dillon. It is a vast lake. Buffalo Mountain towers above in the distance. It is snowcapped; postcard perfect.

Michelle: Freckled, doe-eyed, red lipped, pale skinned with soft brown hair cropped above her shoulders. She is wearing sandals, blue jean overalls and a white short sleeved cotton tee-shirt. Silver and turquoise rings are placed on her fingers. A delicate gold chain hangs loosely around her neck. Michelle smells like a warm golden field on a hot day.

"I'm so glad to see you," she says giving us all tight hugs. "I've got plenty of room. It's a great place. I really lucked out. I love it here. I miss Buffalo, but for now I love it here. You can stay as long as you want. I have a row boat. It's old and wooden, but it still floats and it has oars so you can row out into the lake. It's great. It's wonderful." She hugs us again. She smells fresh and dry. "I'm glad you're here," she says.

"We are too," we say and then she leads us into her backyard and we see her boat. It's old and beaten with dull-white painted wood. The boat lies upside down on an embankment. McShay and my brother turn it over and Michael grabs the oars from underneath. Michelle and I stand at the shore and watch them launch the boat into the placid lake. Ripples move from the hull gliding outwards smoothly and gently. Michael places himself in the middle and mans the oars. He takes long smooth strokes and they amble calmly out toward the center of the lake. We watch them. Their voices carry inaudibly over the water. We savor the smell of fresh pine, algae, warm air.

"We can sit here," Michelle says. "I have a couple of chairs and I can get us a beer. Let's relax and watch them row. It's beautiful. I can sit here for hours."

So we sit. We keep our eyes on the lake. We gaze at Buffalo Mountain. Snowcaps reflect in the water. So do the pines.

Michelle is sad. I stretch my legs in front of me. Michelle crosses hers. They are freckled. We drink a Coors beer. The can sweats in my hand. Michelle tells me about her job. She is a mountain adventure leader.

"That's a program designed for teenagers interested in wilderness exploration," she says. "We get kids interested in the natural world. Teach team working skills while learning about the Rocky Mountains' unique natural history. I plan and prepare all aspects of backcountry travel. I live with and supervise campers out in the field for week-long backpacking trips. It's really cool. I like it."

Then Michelle tells me of loneliness. She tells me of fear and anxiety, a constant fear, a fear that sits hollow in her gut, a fear that holds tightly. It doesn't let her move. She wants to know where she is supposed to be in this world. Where is her place in this wonderful land? Where does she fit amongst the blue skies, the big mountains, the deep serene, gentle lakes, the cavernous, black, endless nights, and the unhurried roads leading to nowhere? I don't have any answers, but I listen to her continue in a whisper.

"I am in the bottom of a well," she says. "I look up and it's cloudy, stormy. I cannot get out. I am in Hell. It feels normal, being in hell."

I can hear the sounds of those three in the boat. They are laughing. Oars splash in the water. The water glistens. In the distance a clump of tall sailboats rock gently buoyed near the brown shore.

"It's a visible darkness," she says, "a big wall, a big, thick glass wall between me and the rest of my world. It's tough, Jimmy."

I think quietly to myself that maybe Michelle is too alone. What is she doing here by herself? Buffalo is tough, but out here she's got nobody. Are you doing the right thing Michelle? Are you making the right moves? Should you be alone here? I wonder, but I don't ask. I let her continue.

"It's new, Jimmy. I'm going to get through this. It's tough, though. Pain is venom that penetrates with every drop. You being here is helpful, Jimmy."

"I'm glad, Michelle," and then I say, "Hey, Tommy says he wants you to come down to his place. Stay anytime you'd like. He says he's got plenty of room."

"I want to see Tommy. I just need to feel right before I see him. I will. Here I am surrounded by these beautiful mountains and I feel like I'm stuck the bottom with lead boots. I have to climb up and over them. I'll do it Jimmy. It'll just take me a little time."

I wish I could think of something comforting to say. Instead, I'm silent. Michelle is too fragile. I can't put the right words together. I do not have the wisdom, so I remain silent and watch the calmness of the shimmering water before me.

"Why are you two on the road, Jimmy?" she asks. "Where are you going and what are you looking for?"

"Adventure," I answer unsure of myself. "We're looking for adventure. It's a chance to see the country. I'm not sure how we'll see it any other way, really, and now's the time. And Michael wants to find his brother George. He hasn't seen him in a long time."

"Where is he?"

"I don't know, maybe Seattle. That's the last place we heard he might be."

"What's he doing there?"

"That's a good question. You know, he just up and left after their father died. Michael can't let him go and wants to see him. He needs to find out what's up, I guess."

"He may be gone for good," she says.

"Michael doesn't think so," I say. "He won't allow it."

The rowboat cuts across the lake. The bow is pointed in our direction. Michael pulls the oars in and out of the water, arching in a constant graceful motion. Kevin sits at the bow facing us. With long sweeps of his arms he is waving for our attention. Michelle waves back making long slow semi-circles in the air. She is smiling. The sun glistens in her hair and her eyes sparkle brown and warm. McShay sits at the stern. He waves. They inch closer.

Later Michelle prepares a meal for us. She places it on a big round wooden table. Two whole roasted chickens, pan fried corn, mashed potatoes, a big salad, and a jug of red wine. Molly picks delicately at hers. I look at McShay smacking his grease lathered lips and chewing with his mouth slightly open. Kevin inhales big bites. Slugs wine. They talk and laugh and smoke. Molly tells jokes. She tells us of her dreams.

A candle flickers in the center of the table. The flame climbs high. It is dazzling. Wax drips to the table like stalactites in a cave. It gives a warm glow to the room. The flame reflects in Michelle's eyes. It burns blue and orange and haunted in the recesses of her cheerless brown eyes.

Chapter 21

The Hike

That evening we slept soundly in our sleeping bags surrounding the hot ember glow of a dying fire. Lake Dillon gently slapped the shoreline under the endless dance of star lit skies. The air held a deep scent of pine, fresh and uplifting. Michelle lay wrapped in her sleeping bag, her mouth slightly open, breathing long and silent. McShay snored loudly and Michael slept breathing in a throaty softness. Kevin turned onto his side with his knees to his chest. All of us were temporarily in another place, another place far from here, enjoying the slumber of eternal peacefulness.

Morning came abruptly. It was cold and cloudy. A gray overcast clung to the mountains and shaded the trees and the lake. Mist hovered over an agitated dark lake. I woke first and listened to Michael turning in his sleeping bag. He yanked himself out, stood wide legged and flat footed, and reached high into a long stretch. His hair hung carelessly over his forehead. The others stayed asleep. Michael and I walked to the embankment and watched the pines sway gently in the steel-gray sky. He lit a Marlboro and continued to yawn and stretch his hands towards the sky.

"That mountain there," he said pointing in the distance, "the one with the long patch of snow above timberline. Once the others are up, we need to get ready and head to the top. We can probably make it up in a couple of hours."

"Michelle said that's called Buffalo Mountain. Looks like a good hike," I said. "It'll take us awhile, though."

"Look how long it stretches," he said pointing and letting his finger trace the long ridge.

One by one the others crawled out of their sleeping bags and prepared for the day. We all stood on the bank sleepy, disheveled and smoking.

"It got very cloudy," Michelle said.

"It sure did," Michael said. "Last night before I fell asleep there were a million stars." He continued to survey the long stretch of jagged summits on the mountain before him.

"That's Colorado weather," she said, "blink once and the weather changes."

"I hope it gets sunny later," Kevin said.

"I doubt it," Michelle said. "Today looks like it's going to be a wash out. We need the rain anyway. Sometimes it gets too dry here. Not good for the forest. Sometimes we get some real bad fires up in these hills. Idiot campers, mainly who don't cover their campfires when they break camp. The wind blows a spark into the pine needles, they catch, and the next thing you know we got a big fire going on up there. It's awful."

We busted down our gear and headed into Michelle's kitchen. Soon the big round table was alive again. Michael chopped potatoes into small pieces. Kevin chopped onions. McShay and Michelle cracked a dozen eggs into a big wooden bowl and added salt and pepper. Michelle threw a handful of parmesan cheese and oregano into the mix and McShay stirred the ingredients with a big handled wooden spoon. A black cast iron skillet sat on the stove. I oiled it and turned the flame on high. The pan heated and Kevin added the potatoes and the onions and they hit the pan with a sizzle. The room smelled wonderful. Michelle took another skillet, added butter, placed it on a burner and turned the flame on. She poured the eggs in the pan and stirred them slowly and carefully. They cooked lightly and delicately. She stirred the potatoes and soon we were back at the big round table smothering our eggs and potatoes with hot sauce and drinking big glasses of orange juice.

<<<>>>

I walked behind the others. Michael took the lead carrying a tall, gnarly walking stick. Along the way two retrievers, one golden and one black, appeared from the woods and joined us on our journey toward the mountain top. We gently climbed a worn trail through the coniferous forest. The forest was deep. The trees created a roof overhead. It was cool and the air was thick with the fresh scent of approaching rain. Dark clouds hung low. We moved steadily and silently until we were upon the remnants of an old cabin. The cabin sunk into the earth. There was nothing left but the worn, smooth, rotted wood of outside walls and a buckled floor. We rested here. Michael threw a stick prompting the dogs to run. They galloped in tandem toward the stick. Each held an end in their mouth and fought for possession.

After smoking a cigarette we continued on our hike. McShay lifted his right ass cheek high into the air and let out a long high-pitched fart. He laughed enthusiastically at his own talent. My brother called him a "fucking pig," and complained that he's been farting during the whole trip, especially when they pitch their tent and he climbs in and cuts one loose and gets the entire tent smelling like shit. McShay responded sheepishly, "It's not that bad." My brother replied, "You fuckin' stink dude," and McShay farted again, lifting his leg even higher and pushing harder. It billowed deeper and he laughed louder. "It's a ripe one," he laughed. Kevin looked at him shaking his head in disgust and said, "A fucking pig."

The trail was now very steep with deadfall scattered everywhere. I felt the muscles in the back of my calves stretching with each step. The others moved slowly ahead putting weight on crude walking sticks we picked up along the way. The dogs dug into the mountain earnestly. We climbed steadily through thick air and pines until the trees thinned and we gradually made our way out of timberline and into a field of large looming boulders. Wild grass grew scattered amongst the rocks and the huge boulders precariously balanced throughout. The land looked like the bottom of a waterless ocean floor. We rambled upwards through the rocks and underneath the low hanging clouds. We hiked straight up a long narrow rocky ridge and moved further until reaching the summit. Once we made it to the top of the mountain, each of us took our walking sticks and formed a collective bundle and plunged them together into the earth. Clouds surrounded us. The air was cold. It bit and stung at our faces. McShay farted and Kevin called him a pig and we stood looking at the vast mountain ranges before us. We could see, for miles, a remarkable display of mountains and ranges. Names like: Tenmile Peak, Grays, Torreys Peak, and Mount Bierstadt. All were mountains that beckon the fierce and wild climbers who long for excitement and adventure in the silent clamor of nature. We could see Lake Dillon sprawled far beneath us and to the south laid the town of Frisco with its streets extending like varicose veins. Beyond that we saw the towns of Dillon and Silverthorne. For a moment we stood motionless and speechless and gazed in all directions at the vast wide-open terrain below.

Finally, the wind kicked in and the sky turned a deep black and gray, and in a harried moment big drops of rain pelted furiously upon us. The dogs huddled in closer, their heads lowered, waiting for direction. We moved quickly and steadily down a steep muddy path. Rain slapped and stung at the back of our necks. Our clothes were cold and heavy. We hurried downward happily, single file, soaking wet with muddy shoes. Rivulets of wild brown water suddenly burrowed frantically along the trail. The retrievers ran ahead stopping every so often to lap at the fast moving water. They watched and waited for us. I continued moving behind Michael and Kevin and McShay through the thick black clouds, back through the boulder field and down into the deep, rich, green forest and finally onto the road leading us to Dillon and Michelle.

Chapter 22

At Chris's Once Again

Kevin and McShay got up before the sun rose, shared a dozen fried eggs, packed a loaf of bread and a pound of bologna into their packs and headed toward Rifle, Colorado, at the Western Slope, to meet up with Kevin's friend from back home, a white haired albino dude they call Strawberry. Rifle is west on Interstate 70. Michael and I stayed back with Molly and drank coffee with her until we were jittery and we had to go. The morning was cloudy and drippy. The sun was lost. A cold-gray weather pattern had hit the range.

Michelle spoke of praying. Said it gave her deep satisfaction. Michael asked, "Michelle, why do you pray? What do you pray for?"

She balled her hand into a fist absently biting her knuckles and searching thoughtfully for an answer.

"I pray because it's comforting," she said finally. "I pray for myself and I pray for strength. I pray for guidance. It's my conversation to myself and I hope someone is listening and helps me to figure things out. Things are complicated. I pray for guidance and I pray for comfort. It's pretty simple."

Michelle walked us to the road that heads out of Dillon. It was still cloudy and there was a slight chill in the air.

"I hope you two get where you're going," she said giving us each a hug.

"We will," I said and I stuck out my thumb and the first car that passed suddenly pulled off to the side. We quickly gave Michelle a hug and thanked her. She smiled and waved good-bye, watching us leave her with her sad eyes misty under the cloudy skies.

Our ride came from a skinny dude with watery eyes and nasty, sour breath. Said he was a copy machine salesman. Said he was making cold calls to businesses in downtown Denver. Said business sucked because some other company had a monopoly on everything and he said if he couldn't sell a copier today he was going to quit his job and spend a week fly fishing down at the South Platte River and bring in some big-assed trout and figure out his next move. His name was Robert and he let us off at the big white granite capitol building right downtown on Colfax Street. The Colorado State Capitol Building sits on a hill and has large pillars at each entrance with a 24 karat gold plated dome commemorating Colorado's Gold Rush days of 1859. The story goes a gold miner named John Gregory discovered *The Gregory Lode* in a gulch up in the foothills near Central City. Big ass gold score! Within two weeks, the gold rush was on and a couple of months after that the population grew to 10,000 people in search of their fortune.

We took the Broadway bus back to the Subway to see Chris again. She was dusted with flour and glad to see us. Her smile was wide and her eyes were soft. She made us each a sausage sub and we ate it at a booth inside the store. It was still early and the lunch rush had not arrived. Chris was able to take a break and sit with us. We smoked and told her of our time up in the hills with Michelle and that we were worried about her. We told her about Kevin and McShay spending time with us up in Dillon and then hitching west to Rifle and that we had planned to hook up with them in about a week in Flagstaff and then we would all go to the Grand Canyon. She listened while sipping a coke slowly through a straw.

"The weather is breaking. It's looking better," Michael said. "We can probably get out of Denver in an hour or so and make it into Colorado Springs, maybe."

149

"Stay here today and tonight," Chris said. "I'd like you to hang about a little longer." She looked at Michael and her soft eyes warmed.

So, we did. And this is how our day was spent: Chris finished sipping her coke and listening to our story until the lunch rush was upon us. Then she had to get back into the kitchen and start pumping those sandwiches out. Michael and I went to Chris's place and played chess and Michael smoked cigarettes and we both petted the cat and lazily dozed off and waited for Chris to return. She showed at around five o'clock with her friend Barbara: Tall, skinny, holding a long neck bottle of diet-coke in one hand and a super-long Virginia Slim in the other. She wore a pair of white Keds sneakers, and very short ripped and faded jeans with the whites of her pockets hanging out. She wore a purple tube top. Her hair was the color of chestnuts and it hung long and very straight. It almost touched her waist. Her arms hung gangly and moved rhythmically as she spoke and her voice emitted a strange smoky breathlessness like a forlorn jazz singer crooning in a lonely club under a dark blue light. She was fun and told good stupid jokes like: "What do you call a deer with no eyes?" "No idear," and "What do you call a deer with no eyes and no legs?" "Still…no idear." Stupid but funny. She delivered them in rapid fire with a hint of Groucho Marx in her vocal cadence.

We ended up in a dark neighborhood pub inhaling the sour stench of spilled beer and dry tobacco and sharing a pitcher of Stroh's beer. Standing hunched over a foosball table, Michael and Barbara beat Chris and me in a bunch of intense games. They beat us soundly and efficiently every time. Barbara played the front two rows and had a fast and strong hand and I could not stop her shots. Each time the ball was in her play she lined it up, held it momentarily, took a deep hit from her Virginia Slim and then forcefully pushed the little white ball past my goalie with a powerful, steady, fast, firm shot. The loud pop in my goal insured that the ball had rocketed past my little plastic goalie and landed abruptly and confidently in their point column. This went on for a couple of hours and a couple more pitchers and then we went back to Chris's apartment and I made spaghetti and Chris opened up a jug of slightly sweet red wine. I think it was Paisano by Carlo Rossi and we sat on the living room floor eating the spaghetti and sipping the wine and staying up well into the night and I watched Chris's eyes soften while she looked at Michael. She sat closely to him and their legs touched and every so often Michael clutched her knee with his hand and her slightly lazy warm eyes radiated onto his dark elegant face.

Later, Barbara asked if I would walk her home and we entered the dry, hot night and I walked her down a wide street with rows of low brick houses the color of the prairie and hardly a light on anywhere. The sky was star filled and a slight warm breeze cascaded throughout the silent street and a sweet candy scent of roses wafted into the night. I walked Barbara to her sad looking apartment building. Long, tall Barbara gave me a warm hug and disappeared into the lobby of that horrible place. When I say a sad looking apartment building I don't mean to say anything other than the building was sad in its nothingness. It was sad in its purpose to only compartmentalize people's lives. It was stale, sterile and bare. I was sad because I felt Barbara deserved more than gray-slab concrete; Barbara deserved pillars, and soft Italian marble, and an astonishing scrolled and scalloped entranceway. Instead, she slipped into the mundane hallway and disappeared.

When I returned to Chris's apartment her bedroom door was closed and Michael was in with Chris and the apartment was very quiet and on the sofa the big cat purred and waited to be petted. On the coffee table, in front of the sofa, wrapped in clear plastic, was an old Life Magazine with Ernest Hemingway on the cover and the entire story of *The Old Man and the Sea* published inside. I propped onto the sofa, petted the purring cat, poured another glass of the red wine and read the story of the old man Santiago and the fish and the sea and his struggle and his defeat and his tiredness and his great respect for strength and his admiration for the pure, simple life. Afterwards, I too, like the old man Santiago dreaming of the African white sand beaches, entered into the unconscious beauty of lonely slumber.

Chapter 23

A Park and a Bus

It was early morning and we were back on the road. We left Chris's place and thanked her for all of her warm hospitality. Both of us leaned against a guardrail outside of Littleton, Colorado at the entrance ramp to I-25 looking over the Rand McNally and planning our route: Raton, Santa Fe, Albuquerque, tracing with my finger the bold red line that is the state highway, and then the smaller, skinnier lines that show the federal highways, county highways, county boundaries, cities and towns, major waterways, and state and national parks. The Rand McNally is a good source of information and I like to look through the pages and read the names of the states and the towns and the cities. I like to look at the mountain ranges and the rivers and I like the city maps too.

Big red-brown mountains stretched for miles in the distance. The sun climbed and the sky was bright blue and yellow. It was silent. Michael leaned against the guardrail casually juggling three rocks he picked up on the side of the road. We let the map guide us knowing there was nothing telling us or suggesting where we should go. We were on a journey and going where we wanted. Places we've heard of like the Pacific Ocean, Yellowstone, the Redwoods, the Rocky Mountains, and on this day, with a feeling of luck holding on to us tightly in eager anticipation, we were making our way to the Grand Canyon because we had read and heard and seen pictures of this big red canyon that lies in the desert under the painted light blue skies of Arizona.

And so, our first ride came quickly by an old man in a clean red pick-up. He wore a long mustache and had a full head of thick white hair. He drove steadily and silently down I-25 past Colorado Springs and into Pueblo. He told us that Pueblo was his stop and asked us where we wanted to go. "Did we want to stay on the highway or go into town?" We told him we were hungry and would not mind finding a store so we could buy something to eat. He pulled off the highway and onto a tree-lined street and dropped us off in front of a small grocery, handing us a worn ten dollar bill, which he insisted we keep. We thanked him and watched as he continued down the street and disappeared.

Inside, the store was filled with Mexicans. They gave us curious looks as we strolled through the aisles with our packs slung on our backs. We bought a jar of peanut butter and a jar of jelly and a loaf of Wonder bread and a quart of milk. We also bought two apples and a Hersey candy bar and then we checked out at the counter using the worn ten dollar bill and walked out of the store and down a tree-lined street to a giant park. The park had a big lake and was shaded by enormous trees that kept the fierce sun hidden. The ground was worn with red dirt and patchy grass and we sat on a wooden bench next to one of those carousals that twirl. We watched a group of Mexican mothers spinning their kids. Their eyes were bright and happy as they whirled around and around holding tightly onto the rail and keeping focused on the secure brown faces of their mothers.

It was very hot and beads of sweat hung above Michael's lip. The air was still and the steady loud wave of humming cicadas broke through the delighted screams of the children. The mothers gathered and spoke Spanish to one another and laughed and never let their kids out of sight. We sat on the bench under a big shady tree and Michael pulled a knife out of his pack and we took turns spreading the peanut butter and jelly onto the Wonder bread and ate the sandwiches silently and peacefully. Time hung suspended in the hot, dry air. We ate the apples and shared the Hersey Bar and finished the milk and watched the kids move around and around on the carousel until, suddenly out of nowhere, a skinny Mexican man yanked a little boy off the ride and cracked him hard on the ass while shouting at him in Spanish. The boy let out a high-pitched wail and a screaming woman rushed over and tore the boy from the angry man and just like that he whacked her hard with an open palm slap.

"What the hell!" Michael said. He jumped to his feet and pushed the man hard and fast to the ground.

The skinny Mexican shook his head, rose from the red dust and stumbled toward Michael swinging wildly at him. The woman, who got slapped, pushed the boy to another Mexican woman, who was yelling at the skinny man, and then jumped quickly, like an angry vicious cat, onto the back of the man who spun her around and around to free himself from her. Her nails were long and painted red and she clawed at him and blood ran from his cheek and down his neck and onto his shoulder. They both fell hard onto the red dirt and a crowd surrounded them and watched as the woman kicked the shit out of the skinny-ass Mexican. She clawed and kicked and punched and bit him until he cried something desperately in Spanish like "I give up! Leave me alone!" She spat on him and, pulling him up by his shirt, stood him up and pushed him away from the crowd yelling stuff like "You dirty drunk," and "*Adios cabrone!*" She threw stones at his back. He staggered away uneasily and I could see by the way he was walking that he only had one leg. I figured underneath his pants he was wearing a wooden leg. He moved away awkwardly and disappeared into the park.

"Jesus," I said.

"What the hell," Michael said.

The woman stormed up to Michael huffing and puffing and trying to catch her breath. She had a red mark on her cheek and her hair was long and black and wild.

"That bastard came here earlier and tried to get money for cerveza and whiskey and wants to sit around all day and drink like a pig," she said trying to catch her breath. "I tell him, get a job you piece of shit! Cabrone! Get a job I tell him."

We didn't really know what to say so Michael said, "That's no good."

"It is no bueno," the woman said. "It is no fucking bueno. He is my husband, or he was my husband, but I won't put up with that."

"Who is the boy and why was he hitting him?" I asked.

"The boy is my son and that cabrone is the father, but he ain't lived with us in many years because he is a big piece of shit. He hits the boy when he gets drunk and angry. He knows he can't hit me, or I will beat him up, but the boy, he hits him. Some day the boy will kill him. You watch. Or maybe I will kill him first, you watch."

"That is not good," Michael said to the woman.

"I know," she said looking us over, catching her breath and calming down. "My name is Gloria Aponte. I live close by, just walking distance from the park. Thank you for helping me and for hitting that bum. I'm sorry you had to see this. I can repay you. Do you want to come over for a cerveza and some lunch?"

"No thanks, we just ate," I said.

Michael gave me a sideways look and said, "Sure, we'd love a cerveza."

She gave me a slow steady look and then she looked over Michael interested in his dark eyes and his dark hair hanging carelessly over his forehead.

"Where are you from?" she asked.

"We're from Buffalo," Michael replied. "We're heading to the Grand Canyon."

"You are not Mexican?"

"No, I'm not," he answered. "I'm Greek. You know any Greeks?"

155

"No, there are no Greeks here, maybe in Denver, but not here. Here it is all Mexican."

The little kid walked back with another woman and Gloria and the other woman said a few things in Spanish and Gloria kissed the boy and the woman and the boy walked back to the carousal. Gloria turned to us.

"She is my sister. She will keep Freddie for the afternoon. Come over to my house," she said. "We can sit in the shade and I can get you a cerveza and I can pack you a lunch to take with you to the Grand Canyon."

"What about your husband?" I asked

"No, you don't need to worry about him. He would never come back. Besides, he is drunk and ashamed and I am sure he is going back to his mama's house. She is the only woman who puts up with him and will beat if he gets crazy. No, he is sleeping at his mama's. This I am sure of."

We walked over the sunbaked red cracked dirt to Gloria's tiny house. The house is brick, a simple rectangle. The roof is brown. It sits in a neighborhood with other houses that all pretty much look the same. There is no green space only dry red dirt with meager patches of worn grass. There is a front porch with a couch and three wooden high back chairs on it. The couch is worn and beige with a colorful woven blanket draped across the back. There is a small round wooden table placed in front of the couch with an ashtray from The Sands Hotel in Las Vegas that says *A place in the sun*. There are three big candles on the table. Gloria comes from inside the house with three bottles of Stroh's beer and a bowl of cheese popcorn. She combed her hair. It is long and black and shiny. She handed us a beer and lit the candles.

"This will keep the flies away," she said stretching her legs before us. "When he is drunk he is impossible. He was a truck driver when we got married and he would drive all over Colorado and New Mexico and Arizona and he made pretty good money. I think maybe we were in love then. When I met him he was nice to me and sometimes he would take me to Denver and we would spend the weekend at a nice hotel and walk in the city. I liked the tall buildings and I liked to go to Larimer Square and stop in the shops and look at all of the sparkling jewelry. And, we would sit in the restaurants, sometimes on a patio, and have different foods. One time I had a caeser salad that had spicy shrimp on it. It was very good. I liked to look at the women who lived in the city and worked downtown. There were many pretty women and some of them were Mexican and I liked to look at them in their dresses. They walked with purpose. I imagined they were working at a big important job. I don't know, but things were good. We had money and he, Javier, had a good job and we got married and had little Freddy and we bought this house and we even talked about moving up to Denver until he went hunting with his crazy drunk brother and his brother accidently shot his leg off with a double barrel shotgun. He couldn't drive a truck no more and he couldn't work construction like some of the others around here so he got a job at the truck stop pumping gas for the big eighteen wheelers and cleaning up the property and sometimes washing dishes in the restaurant. He wasn't making good money anymore and he started to drink and he could not pay the bills and he got mean. I understood when he got mean to me, but when he got mean to Freddie, that's when I got loco."

Gloria Aponte pushed, with long slender fingers, her thick hair from her forehead. She crossed her legs and pulled a cigarette from a pack of Marlboro Reds nestled in her pants pocket. She lit the cigarette, took a long pull, lifted her head and blew the smoke high into the air. Her legs remained crossed and they were long and smooth and her feet were bare and her toes were painted the same bright red as her finger nails. She wore faded blue cut off jeans and a man's t-shirt, the kind without sleeves. The kind some people call wife beaters.

"One time he came home many hours after his shift at the truck stop and he was drunk and that was the first time he hit Freddie. I would not allow that and that was the first time I fought him back. I fought him with everything in me, with everything I had. I was not going to let him hit my boy, so I fought him and he left. The next morning I got a restraining order and he was not allowed here, but that did not stop him. I felt bad for him. I knew why he was upset. He lost everything. He did not feel like a man because he lost his leg, but I don't care. I will not put up with that. He is not a man if he beats a child. Anyway, he came over again after the restraining order and he was angry and he was drunk and he hit me and I hit him and he hit Freddie and Freddie and I hit him and he would not stop so I got a pan, a big cast iron pan and I smashed him over the head and he fell quickly to the ground. I was so mad I took off his wooden leg and I carried it next door to the old woman who was cooking beans in her fire pit in the back yard. I threw his leg in the fire pit and it burned until it was no more than ashes. He has never come back here after that. That was a long time ago."

Michael listened to her story. He ate the pop corn and his fingers were orange from the powdered cheese.

"So, why did he come to the park today?" he asked.

"I don't know. I guess he's broke and desperate, but this time I will call the sheriff. I am not going to live like this."

Tasos Theotikos shook his son by the shoulder and told him, "*Tell this Gloria Aponte to thank this Javier.*"

Michael was startled. He had not heard from his father in some time and he did not expect to hear from him now.

"Why should she thank him?" he asked. "He is no good."

"*She is presented with a choice now,*" said Tasos Theotikos. "*She can live with pain and hate or she can let him go and live with a clear conscience and a good will.*"

The candles flickered on the table. The wicks were thick and the flames were large. The flame tapered to a black smoke which rose and disappeared into the hot air. I took a final sip of the beer. It was still cold and it tasted good.

"You need to thank him," Michael said looking directly into the soft brown eyes of Gloria Aponte.

"What?"

"You need to thank him and let him go, and then you need to tell the sheriff what he did."

"Thank him for what?" Gloria said. "Thank him for hitting Freddie and hurting him? Thank him for hitting me and hurting me and scaring me, for leaving bruises on us, for breaking furniture and being mean and drunk? What am I thanking him for?"

"You are thanking him for the good things he gave you. You can thank him for Freddie, for your time in Denver, for the love he gave you. You thank him for the good things you had at one time and then you can let him go and put him out of your mind," Michael said. "And, then you move on."

Tasos Theotikos nodded in approval.

"Now you are beginning to understand," he said.

"I don't know about that," said Gloria Aponte.

"You will feel better," Michael said. "You will not put all that energy into what is bad. Thank him and let him go and then you move on. You will be happier."

Again, Tasos Theotikos nodded to his son in approval and admiration and left him sitting on this porch in Pueblo, Colorado helping a young, angry and confused single mother named Gloria Aponte make sense of a man who had changed so much during their time together. And then, Tasos Theotikos disappeared.

We drank another beer and Gloria Aponte went inside and made us a lunch and put it in a brown paper bag for us. She handed Michael the bag and said she made two sandwiches with turkey and tomato and lettuce. She put two peaches in the bag and some celery with peanut butter on them. She said that this would be good later when we were hungry. Michael and I thanked her and grabbed our packs and slung them onto our backs. Gloria shook our hands and they were strong and soft. She looked at Michael and I could tell she did not want him to leave. She told us to be careful and to have a safe trip and that she was glad that she met us and then we left. We walked for about a half an hour and got back onto the ramp that led to I-25 South.

We sat for about an hour and a half without any luck. I juggled and Michael wrote in his journal. I pulled out the Rand McNally and figured our route. We could take I-25 and head south through Colorado to Albuquerque. In Albuquerque we could pick up I-40 and head west and into Flagstaff. We would take the road north into the canyon. That was a long way off, at least that's how it felt now considering a steady stream of cars continued to pass us by without stopping. Two punks in a beat-up old rust-bucket steered off the road toward us, honked the horn long and loud and gave us the finger. Another time three girls zoomed by, honked their horn and laughed. One girl stuck her head out of the window and yelled something, but we could not make out what she said.

Another hour passed without any luck. We were bored and hungry so we ate the sandwiches Gloria Aponte made for us and they were very good. The peaches were very fresh and very sweet. Michael pulled the celery and peanut butter out of the bag and we ate that too.

Another hour passed and then another hour. It was hot and we felt cursed and we figured we would probably have to walk down the highway and find a field to sleep in and get a fresh start in the morning when people were heading to work. Our luck changed when an old school bus painted bright blue with pink trim pulled over. Down the steps came McShay with a big smile on his face and a cupcake in his hand.

"You gotta see this," he said wiping frosting on his lips. We followed him up the steps and into the bus.

In the driver seat a slender man with bleached blonde hair and thick black eye shadow extended his hand toward us and said with big wide eyes "Hi. Welcome to our home. I'm Dizzy, Dizzy Delicious." His hand was soft and his hand shake was loose. He wore a lime green silk scarf that covered his head and tied under his chin.

Inside was dimly lit in red lighting. A crystal chandelier hung in the center. The bus was decorated with orange silk curtains with silver beads draped from gold leaf curtain rods. A bright yellow stove and a refrigerator were tucked in the back. Burgundy and gold oriental rugs hugged the floors and climbing, flowing exotic plants and flowers hung everywhere. The bus smelled of incense and heavy cologne. Kevin sat at a table with two men playing cards and eating cupcakes and brownies. In the corner a long ornate birdcage hung and swayed gently with a chattering white cockatoo standing contently on a perch.

Kevin looked up at us and said to the two sitting at the table, "Believe it or not this is my brother Jimmy and that's Michael. They're from Buffalo like us. We're kinda traveling together."

The first one leaned toward us extending his hand. He introduced himself as Nicco. He was short and very dark and very muscular with a big bushy mustache. His eyes were a deep intense brown. He was barefoot and wore some very short tight blue jeans and a very tight sleeveless shirt that said Key West, Florida on it. The neckline on his shirt was cut low and a massive patch of curly black chest hair climbed out from underneath. His grip was firm and he asked us if we wanted some of his homemade brownies. He said they were fresh and delicious. The other guy was not too tall. He was slender with blonde hair and a delicate face. He said his name was *Frosting* and he wore white linen pants and an unbuttoned white linen shirt tied in a little knot above his waist. He wore soft leather glossy black loafers without socks.

"Welcome to our home on wheels," he said pushing the tray of brownies and cupcakes towards us. "You must try some. Kevin and McShay have been enjoying them."

I took one of the brownies and Michael took a cupcake. They tasted incredible.

"You need coffee to go with them," said Nicco.

"Yes they do," Frosting said and he glided gracefully toward the back of the camper to get us both a hot cup.

"Frosting will serve you," said Nicco. "He was a waiter in a beautiful hotel in Chicago called the Fairmont. He met lots of stars. He even met Liz Taylor and Richard Burton."

"She was divine," Frosting chimed in from the back. "She was lovely and Mr. Burton, what a looker and boy he sure could drink. He was fabulous. I simply loved *Who's Afraid of Virginia Woolf.* What a movie!"

Frosting floated back with two cups of black coffee in red floral pattern cups and matching saucers. We squeezed into the table and played cards and ate cupcakes and brownies while Barbara Streisand sang her heart out over the speakers of their eight-track player. We played poker betting with assorted colorful buttons from Dizzy Delicious' sewing box. Frosting was a real player and won the most buttons. He put a carrot in his mouth, like he was chomping on a cigar, and used Clint Eastwood's voice to tell us it was our bet. He had Clint's dry whisper down. Later Frosting and Nicco ran through the card game scene from *Butch Cassidy and the Sundance Kid.* The scene at the beginning of the movie where some card shark accuses Sundance of cheating and challenges him to a gun draw, but then he finds out that he just challenged the Sundance Kid, the fastest and most famous draw in those parts and that's not a good thing because if he draws on Sundance, then he's a dead man. Nicco played the card player and Butch and Frosting played Sundance and they had the lines down word for word and when they were finished they both laughed hysterically. Frosting raised his head high in the air and put his fingertips to his chest and let out a high-pitched wail that took a lot out of him. He had to capture his breath. Nicco's laugh forced him to jiggle up and finished with a long deep snort. We continued to sit around the table laughing heartily and then the bird made a funny sound and Dizzy Delicious honked the horn and we laughed even harder. We could not stop and then I figured the brownies might have had something to do with this.

That's how it was traveling south on I-25 on a bus with these three friends from Chicago who had driven to Denver so Miss Dizzy Delicious could have a special surgery and were now heading to see a friend in Raton, New Mexico to show off the new and improved Miss Delicious. After their visit in New Mexico they would journey to San Francisco to begin a new life together.

They dropped us off at a truck stop and hugged us each good-bye and told us to be careful. Frosting scribbled an address onto a cocktail napkin and gave it to me insisting that we call him if we made it to San Francisco.

It had gotten dark and the sky was wide and deep black and there was a beautiful showing of stars above. We walked about ten minutes away from the truck stop and into a field where we pulled out our sleeping bags and formed a circle. We were all very hungry and we pulled cans of Spaghetti-O's from our packs and slices of Wonder Bread and drank water from our canteens. That night we slept soundly in a field outside of Raton, New Mexico amongst the steady roar of eighteen wheelers and the shrill whistles and barks of prairie dogs scampering under the magical, deep black glistening sky.

Chapter 24

New Mexico

We slept late and when we woke the shrill barks from the prairie dogs were gone. It was August and very hot. The sky was pale blue. Not a cloud in sight. The smell of dirt hung heavy in the air. We were hungry and tired of eating canned food. McShay and Kevin offered to walk to the truck stop and pick up some eggs.

"Why don't you pull out your gas stove and use the pan hanging off my pack?" Kevin said. "It's big enough for us all. When we get back, we'll cook up some eggs."

"Alright," I said.

They moved quickly through the field and toward the store. I watched McShay light a cigarette. Dozens of funnel shaped prairie dog holes lie scattered before us. Michael frantically rifled through his back pack.

"What are you looking for?" I asked.

"I can't find my journal. Where the hell is my journal?"

"I don't know. Where did you use it last?

"Shit, I don't know. I think the last time I wrote in it was back at Michelle's. After the hike I wrote in it."

He continued to search.

"Damn," he said. "I don't want to lose that. I had good stuff in there."

"You want some paper?" I asked.

"Might as well give me some," he said taking out a pen. He leaned against his pack and began writing. He wrote with desperation trying to capture our entire trip so far. He wrote earnestly without looking up.

The other two returned about a half hour later.

"Got some good stuff," announced my brother pulling from a brown shopping bag a dozen eggs, a stick of butter, an onion, a package of Jimmy Dean link sausages, a package of sliced yellow American cheese and a half gallon of chocolate milk.

Michael kept his head buried in his journal and the other two rearranged their packs while I took care of the cooking. I threw everything in the big pan: the butter, the onions, the sausage, the eggs and finally the cheese. I had some salt and pepper and I added that too. I stirred the eggs until they were lightly scrambled. McShay had a loaf of Wonder Bread hanging from his pack and I took that, opened it and announced that breakfast was ready. We sat in a circle, leaning against our packs, and placed the eggs onto the bread and ate quietly. A delicate breeze stirred the prairie grass. McShay chewed with his mouth open and smoked a Marlboro while he ate. We wore shorts and were browned from the sun, browned from the road, bleached and browned and blended into the dirt and the soil and the earth.

After we were finished, Michael lit a cigarette and said, "Let's go to the truck stop and clean up and wash out the pan."

"Alright," I said and looked at my brother, "Should we call home, call mom, see what's going on?"

"I guess so," he said.

"Me too," Michael said. "I need to call my brother and my sister."

"Yeah, same here," agreed McShay.

The truck stop was one of those mega truck stops. A steady flow of truckers pulled their rigs up to the big diesel pumps and filled their huge tanks. The diesel smelled like oil and dirt.

We went inside to a huge bathroom where we each had our own sink to clean up in. We washed our hair and brushed our teeth and cleaned our armpits and the hot water felt very good. We left the bathroom and saw that the restaurant was full with big-bellied truckers sitting silently at the counter eating huge breakfasts of eggs and biscuits and sausage and bacon. They smoked cigarettes and drank coffee from thick white mugs. The tables were full too with more truckers and families and those who were traveling long distances on the Interstate. The waitresses were frantically moving with purpose through the dining room with lots of plates stacked on their arms.

Shiny pay phones lined the hallway between the restaurant and a store. The store was big and sold groceries and stuff truckers might use like country music eight tracks, big coffee mugs and porn magazines. Michael and McShay dialed their homes and I put a collect call in to my mother's house. The phone rang seven times and on the eighth my mother picked up. She sounded groggy and distant. The operator told her she had a collect call and she accepted the charge.

"Hello?"

"Hey Mom, it's Jimmy. Kevin's here with me too."

"Jimmy? Where the hell are ya?"

"We're in New Mexico, Mom. Heading for the Grand Canyon."

"Jesus, the Grand Canyon, imagine that."

There was a long pause. I could tell I had woken her up. She was probably drunk last night and was feeling it now. I could hear her lighting a cigarette.

"So, how are you, Mom?"

"Okay," she said. "A little tired. Your goddam father didn't come home again last night, Jimmy. He tells me he stays at work. Do you think I believe that shit? Do you think I believe that Jimmy?"

"Where are the girls?" I asked.

"They're with their grandmother. They spent the night with her."

I was glad to hear that.

166

"They're good girls, Jimmy," she said.

"I know they are," I said. We were both silent for a moment. "So, we're seeing a lot out here."

"Sure you are, Jimmy. I'm sure there's a lot to see. Are you coming back?"

"Well, yeah, of course."

"How's Kevin?"

"He's good, he's right here with me. He wants to say hello to you. He's good."

"Okay Jimmy. Let me say hello to Kevin. You be careful baby and get home safely, okay"?

"Sure mom. I will. I'll call you in a week or so."

I handed the receiver to Kevin. The others were still on the phone. I went into the store and looked around. I thought about my mother and felt hollow that I did not care much for her. I did when I was little, but that constant drinking and the sleeping in late and that hacking, gurgling cigarette cough, and the not taking care of herself, and the bitching about my father, and the way she ignored my two little sisters really got to me. She was pretty much an embarrassment.

I flipped through the magazines hanging on a rack near the checkout counter and tried to forget about her for now. I paged through the latest edition of Time magazine dated August 7, 1978. The title on the front page read *Lobbyists: Swarming over Washington*. It showed an illustration of a man's head; his head looked like the Capital Building and all of these brown suited men wearing brown hats were flying into his brain like they were airplanes stuck in a crowded landing pattern. I did not read the article but I did read that *pint sized power actor* Mickey Rooney got married for the eighth time. I read that a woman and her truck driver husband had a baby and it was the first baby conceived outside the human body. They were from England and the baby was a girl and they named her Louise. They called Louise *the first test tube baby*. I also read that President Carter's favorite musicians were Mozart, Bob Dylan and Willie Nelson and the President and his wife Rosalynn recently took a helicopter from Camp David to join 12,000 fans to listen to Willie Nelson and Emmylou Harris at some concert. When Willie finished *Georgia on My Mind*, Carter jumped onto the stage and the two of them smiled and hugged one another. I read a crummy movie review on Woody Allen's movie *Interiors* and I read a good review of Bruce Springsteen's new album *Darkness on the Edge of Town*. I was just finishing reading an article about a group of people who live in their motor homes in South Dakota when Kevin nudged me and said, "Let's get out of here."

The four of us walked to the ramp and finalized our plan to meet at the post office in Flagstaff, Arizona. We figured it would take us a couple of days so we said we would go to the post office every day at 1:00 pm until we all met. The plan was set. Michael and I walked on up the ramp about a hundred yards, while Kevin and McShay quickly got a ride and waved as they passed us by. We placed our packs against the guardrail and waited for a ride. Michael wrote in his journal and I passed the time juggling. We could see a stretch of the Rocky Mountains in the distance. Ahead the land was flat and brown. The sun climbed further into the sky.

The first to stop was from a family in a pickup truck. We stretched out in the back. They took us about twenty miles and bought us an ice cream cone at a small stand right off the highway. Our next ride came from a priest in a black air conditioned Mercury. The cool air felt good. He blessed us and said the blessing would keep us safe during our trip. Not too long after that a beat up old Datsun pickup pulled over. The driver was a skinny white guy with gnarly, dirty fingers and putrid body odor and he was drunk. I wondered why he was drunk this early in the day, but he was and I was pretty nervous as he swerved over the line and onto the shoulder of the road. After around five miles he pulled off the highway and left us on the ramp. I was relieved. Almost immediately a car pulled over with McShay sitting in the front seat and Kevin in the back. The driver, a fat Texan, took us to Santa

Fe where he dropped us off at a store and again we stocked up on some canned goods.

Inside the store we met four girls. Two of them were sisters. One of them worked in the store. Said she was a cashier. All four of them had black hair and raven eyes. The girls were pretty and laughed freely. We chatted for a bit and they told us of a park where we could hang out if we wanted to. That seemed like a pretty good idea. We decided to buy some beer and go to the park. The girl who was the cashier in the store said she had a big car and we could all squeeze in if we wanted a lift. It was tight. Three of us sat in the front and five sat in the back with our packs crammed into the trunk, but we made it to the park in a couple of minutes. The park was a stretch of shaded, tree-lined walkways and picnic tables along the Santa Fe River called Santa Fe River Park. It was quiet and serene and extended down the middle of busy downtown Santa Fe and was shaded by big cottonwood trees. We walked over a stone foot bridge, crossed the river and sat on the bank and drank beer with the four girls with the black hair and raven eyes. They stayed with us for a couple of hours until it got dark and the beer ran out. The cashier pointed to a wooded area and told us it would be safe to sleep there.

"The cops won't bother you," she said. "They won't even see you."

That was a good idea we thought. It was dark and too late to hitch and the park was quiet and we were a little drunk from the beers. Then the cashier said, "We'll come by in the morning and wake you up and drive you to the highway." And then the four girls left.

We broke out cans of Dinty Moore beef stew and Hormel chili and ate them cold. The beef stew was in thick shiny gravy. The chili had red beans in it. We mixed the stew and the chili together and ate it with white bread. We drank water from our canteens. We did not build a fire. We did not want the cops to throw us out. We slept soundly and I was the first to wake. I told the others to get up. It was later than we hoped, about ten o'clock.

"Christ," Michael said. "We slept half the day away."

McShay peeled out from his sleeping bag, his hair in all directions. "Fucking hot, that sun doesn't mess around down here." He took a drink from his canteen and spit it out. "Might as well use this water for coffee," he said with a sour look on his face.

Kevin crawled out of his bag and looked at McShay. "Quit bitchin' and let's get the show on the road."

We cleaned the area and packed quickly and began to walk from the park to the highway.

"Who knows where the highway is?" I asked.

"I don't know, but why don't we ask them," Michael said pointing to the cashier and her sister walking towards us.

"We didn't know if you'd still be here," said the cashier's sister. "We can give you a lift to the highway or we can take you to the pool. I work there. I'm a lifeguard. Anyway, you can take a shower there if you'd like. It's still early and it doesn't open until noon, so you can have the shower room to yourselves."

Michael did not hesitate, "I need a shower, badly."

Once we got there, I stood motionless under the hot water and it felt incredible. The simple pleasure of standing under a steaming shower with strong water pressure is a glorious thing. I soaped my entire body and had a small bottle of shampoo and I lathered my hair and rinsed it and watched the dirty water run down the drain. The others were equally enjoying their cleansing. We had been mostly washing in sinks at truck stops or McDonald's or washing up in creeks or lakes. This felt good and we were in no hurry to leave.

The sisters had a six pack of cold beers in a cooler in the car. We each popped the top off of the can and drank one. It was cold and refreshing. The girls looked prettier today and their black hair shined nicely in the sun. The cashier's name was Mara and I could not take my eyes off of her. I could not take my eyes off of her deep black eyes and her flat forehead and her full warm mouth. She looked tough and she looked strong. She looked nothing like the girls back home and I felt sad that I would never see her again.

They were good enough to give us a lift back to the highway and again McShay and my brother split up from Michael and me. Again, the two of us walked ahead and down the ramp closer to the Interstate while they stayed put and hitched at the entrance. It did not take long before a skinny cowboy in a pick-up truck pulled over and offered us a ride to Albuquerque. McShay and Kevin were in the back and we hopped in and the pick-up tore ass down the highway passing any car or truck in its way.

The road was long and straight. There were big puffy clouds above and the sky was bright blue and we looked out at the rugged brown desert and the low brown mountains in the distance. Wild shrubs and grasses lay scattered in tufts along the way. We took our shirts off and leaned against our packs and basked in the sun. A little over an hour later the cowboy pulled over and we were in Albuquerque. Again, we found ourselves near a park, and again, we hit a supermarket. This time we bought bologna, bread, lettuce, potato chips and chocolate milk. We walked back to the park where it was cool and shady and filled with Mexican families enjoying a perfectly sunny Sunday afternoon and taking a break from the long, hard work week. A whole lot of charcoal grills were scattered throughout, the kind that sit on top of a pole cemented into the ground. Near the grills stood picnic tables and next to the tables families laid out colorful blankets. They cooked chicken and hot dogs and hamburgers and the scent of beans cooking with hog knuckles in big black cast iron pots wafted throughout the park. Picnic tables were joined together and loaded with foods like olives and potato chips and tortillas and watermelons and all kinds of macaroni and potato salads. And on the blankets babies and little kids played with toys and some of the older girls kept an eye on them while the men formed clusters around the grills and drank beer or played horseshoes and the women sat at tables drinking their own drinks and laughing and talking loudly in rapid fire Spanish.

The day was hot and the shade from the trees kept the park cool and we were in no real hurry to go anywhere. I offered to go back to the store and get some beer and when I got back we drank the cold cans down easily while sitting on the ground propping ourselves with our packs and reading our maps and our poetry and writing in our journals and dozing on and off spending close to five lazy hours of the calm afternoon with the Mexican families. At around six o'clock we resumed our plan to head to the highway and meet at the post office in Flagstaff.

It took only a couple of minutes until Michael and I jumped into a blue Dodge and got a ride from a friendly man who took us about an hour up the road to a tiny adobe town nestled in the brown desert called Laguna. He said, "You have to see this place. You won't see anything like this back East where you come from." He took us off the highway and onto a worn dirt road leading to the village. In the center of the small village, on a slight hill, stood San Jose de Laguna Mission Church & Convento, a flat faded white adobe church with a cross on the top and two bells underneath.

"Pueblo Indians have been in the village since the 1300's and the mission dates back to 1699," the man told us.

Shabby adobe homes built on hard dirt stood crammed together. There was no grass to be seen. A few short, sickly trees were scattered here and there pitifully giving only a sliver of shade. Outside the tiny homes were hastily built stone ovens with smoke rising from many of them. Old rusted cars and car parts lay strewn throughout the village. There were a lot of other beat up things strewn about like washing machines, televisions and bicycles, too.

We walked through the village and up a steep hill to the church and stood looking at the flat façade. It was very quiet except for the frantic barking of a skinny dog chained closely to a pole. He looked like a long legged rat with pointy ears. Above, the sky was soft blue and cloudless. We watched the church and it reminded me of one of those old Clint Eastwood movies, one of those spaghetti westerns where Clint chomps on a cigar and quietly kills all those dirty Mexicans with sly smiles and toothless grins who have wronged him.

"I thought you might like this," the man who drove the Dodge said. "I thought you might like to take a snapshot of this church."

"Wish I had a camera," Michael said. He turned to me, "That's one thing we did not bring, a camera. We should have brought one."

"I'll write about it in my journal," I said. "I can describe it. It will stay there."

"You can always come back," the man said. "You can always come back and bring a camera. This church ain't going nowhere. This church's been here a long time and I imagine it will be here a long time to come. Let's get back on the road and get us a bite to eat. I'm starvin'."

Once we were back on the highway, the man pointed to a big red and yellow Stuckey's sign that said *three Stuckey Dogs 39 cents.*

"Bet you can't eat three Stuckey dogs," he said. "If you eat them, I'll buy 'em."

"Let's do it. I'm starving,'" Michael said.

We grabbed a booth inside the Stuckey's and the man ordered us both three Stuckey dogs, a basket of fries and chocolate milk shakes. He also bought us each one of those pecan log rolls wrapped in plastic. The man drank coffee with lots of cream and four or five teaspoons of sugar. He didn't eat any food.

The man handed us a log roll and said, "You eat that later when you're hungry. That's all sugar. It'll give you a bunch of energy."

I have to admit for a crappy hot dogs, they sure did taste good. Eating three was a lot, but we managed to get them down and we got the fries and the shakes down too.

"I'd like to take you further," said the man. "Hell, I'd like to take you all the way to the Grand Canyon and see it for myself. It's been awhile since I made it over there, been a while since I've done anything really fun. I haven't been on an adventure in a long time. You boys are on an adventure, a real good old fashioned adventure. Boy, I'd like to do that. Boy, I'd give my left arm to do what you're doing."

Michael stuffed the last of his Stuckey dog into his mouth and washed it down with the last of his milk shake. He noisily sucked the remaining shake through his straw, leaned back, lit a cigarette and said, "What do you do? Where do you work?"

"I have a hardware store back in Santa Fe, had it for the last twenty-two years. It's a pretty big store. We rent out stuff like carpet cleaning machines and floor washers and rototillers and things like that. And we fix small engines, lawnmowers, that kind of stuff. Of course people bring in their go-karts and mini bikes and we take care of them too. And we sharpen anything, knives, saw blades, you name it and we sharpen it."

"A pretty nice store," Michael said.

"Sounds like it," I agreed.

"It's a great store, but after twenty-two years, well, it is what it is. Got to raise a family with it. Two girls. One's twenty and the other's twenty-one. The older one's already married and living in Denver and the younger one, she's the bright one; she's in college at the University of New Mexico over in Albuquerque. She wants to be a pharmacist. She's a hard worker. They both are. And, my wife, well, we just don't get along too much. I'm not saying we fight and such, but there's just not a damn thing between us anymore. The fire's gone out. Not even a spark. Now that the girls are gone, well, it's just not the same."

Tasos Theotikos sat closely to his son and whispered into his ear, *"He has a great fear, Michael. He has a great fear of loneliness. This is a good man who fears that loneliness is all he has to look forward to."*

"That's too bad, Pop."

"What will you do for him?"

"What can I do?"

174

"You are a smart boy. You can figure it out. I'm just telling you he's a good man who has a great fear and he needs help. You figure it out, Michael."

The man continued to talk about his hardware store and when his girls were young. He spoke of when he first got married, when he and his wife lived in a separate room at her parents' house and how his wife's father did not think much of the man until years later after his store became very successful and he had out-earned his father in-law many times over. And even then he felt the old man was less than thrilled with him.

"The guy just never liked me," he said. "Never thought I was good enough for his daughter."

"You ever take any time off from your store?" asked Michael.

"Hardly ever," the man said. "Someone's got to keep her running. When it comes to business you can't trust anyone else to do it for you, got to take care of it yourself. If I had boys maybe, but the girls they didn't want anything to do with keeping a store. I can't say that I blame them."

"You gotta find someone," Michael said. "You can't work all of the time. Everyone needs a break once in a while or you'll get stuck in a damn rut and go nuts."

"Seems like that's exactly what's happening," the man said. "I reckon for some young kids you got a little bit of wisdom in you, seems like you're a bit older than you really are. I guess it's all this traveling that makes you smarter."

"We've learned and seen a lot," I said.

"And, we haven't seen anything," Michael said. "But we're looking. You've got plenty of time to get out and bail once in a while. There's a big world out there. You need to be a part of it."

"Boys, I appreciate your company today. I'm glad to have dinner with you. The business I have to take care of is at this exit. I have to update my insurance policy for the store. Kind of funny after this talk, isn't it?"

"You'll be alright; you just take some time for yourself once in a while," Michael said. "Take some time with your wife. Maybe you can remember what it was like in the beginning or maybe not. I don't know."

"Will do," the man said. "Maybe I'll take her down to the Canyon myself and we'll figure some of this stuff out. I suppose she'd like that."

He left us at the Stuckey's, but not before giving us five dollars. "You boys taught me something today. I'm glad of that. You take this and pass it on the next one who needs it. Someone always will. I hope it gets you boys a little further up the road. It's a big road and a long road. The road is open, though. That's good news. The road is always open and it will stay that way, I'm sure of that."

He was gone. It was getting dark. The clouds were darkening, and on the horizon, rain was moving our way. The land stretched wide and the air smelled fresh and clean.

The next ride was a good one. A guy in an El Camino took us all the way to Flagstaff. A six hour ride. Old Rolling Stones songs blasted from his eight track stereo, stuff from the sixties. He let us off at a campsite around midnight. Big mobile homes lined themselves endlessly in rows. Nearby, we found an area with a bunch of tents pitched. The sky was black and filled with countless stars and it was very quiet. Most everyone was asleep. We set up our tent on the fringe of the other tents and slept soundly for the night.

Chapter 25

The Grand Canyon

That morning for breakfast we opened a can of spaghetti and ate it cold. Some of the campers craned their necks in our direction and watched us curiously, probably wondering when in the middle of the night we pitched our tent and landed in their space. They kept to themselves except for one nosey guy in a Winnebago who limped over and asked if we needed anything. He had big bushy red sideburns. Wore a cap that said *Gone fishin'...following Jesus* and said he was from Ohio. Retired insurance guy, out seeing this great big ol' country. Said this was his dream. Traveling the great U.S. of A. Said the Canyon was the most incredible bit of land he had ever seen. "Understand God even better now," he said.

I had a jar of instant coffee. I heated up water in a little pan from my mess kit using my single propane burner. I put the instant coffee into my cup and drank it. We stood idly shooting the breeze with the guy in the Winnebago for a bit. His non-stop jabbering got a little annoying. He preached the ingredients to true happiness and fulfillment. Said you got to have the Lord in your life and you got to have forgiveness and optimism too. He said you got to like your work, gotta like what you do and you gotta stay away from negative stuff. You gotta have a bunch of friends, and it helps to be married too. Said the Lord taught him all that and he lived by it and suggested we live by that as well. Then he told us he was headin' towards Pikes Peak in Colorado. Said he couldn't wait to see the Rockies. He mustered up a meaningful blessing, limped bull-legged back to his big silver Winnebago, gave us a wave, and stepped up and inside and out of sight. We brushed our teeth using the remaining canteen water, combed our hair, and headed for the post office in Flagstaff. It took us about fifteen minutes to walk there.

We found my brother and McShay lounging casually on a bench in front of the post office. McShay sucked coolly on a Marlboro while Kevin sat reading the Rand McNally and writing postcards he bought inside. It was good to see them. They looked healthy and tanned. I went in a grabbed a few postcards myself. I bought Michael a few too. The four of us sat under the bright sun writing the postcards, and writing in our journals.

I wrote one to my grandfather and my grandmother who lived in a little town south of Buffalo called Springville. They owned a movie theater and my grandmother also worked in a clothing store called Simon Brothers. It was right on Main Street. Simon Brothers sold clothes for men and women and children. It had hardwood floors and big round white low hanging light fixtures. My grandmother took care of keeping the display windows current. She did a good job with that. She was clever at getting those manikins to pose in their new clothes. She liked to maneuver them and angle them so that their poses looked real. Sometimes they were at a picnic and one time, I remember, they were at the beach sporting a new line of summer bathing suits. They had those fake smiles painted on them and they looked like they enjoyed their colorful attire.

There's not much room to write on a post card so I just wrote that "I'm heading towards the Grand Canyon. It's very hot here. I miss you and I love you and I'll see you at the end of summer." Then I wrote a post card to my aunt and one to a girl in my school that I liked and one to my mother and father and my sisters. I pretty much said the same thing to all of them, but I didn't say I love you to the girl who went to my school.

The sun climbed further into the sky and it was going to be bright and clear and very hot. Thin clouds stretched delicately above. There was no hint of shade anywhere. I missed the shady maple trees and oak trees and especially elm trees back home. At least they would have helped out here in the desert, would have kept things bearable. Kevin and McShay got up, stretched, slung their packs on their shoulders and said they would walk on ahead for a bit and catch a ride. We'd meet them at the entrance to the Grand Canyon. They were picked up quickly. Michael and I hung a bit longer and finished our postcards.

It didn't take long until we got picked up by a guy in a van going into the Canyon. He said his name was Rob. Sitting next to him in the front seat holding a worn canvas sack between his legs sat a scruffy little skinny hippy who said his name was Rich. He was all brown and leathery. His hair was long and dirty and bleached from the sun. He wore it tied back behind his head and he wore a feathered ban around his head too. He smelled sour. I guess he looked to be around twenty-three years old. He carried a pouch around his neck with jewelry he made and sold to whoever would stop to look at it. Cheap silver, glass stone, and some turquoise. Not bad looking stuff. Said he's been ramblin' on the road and hitchhiking around the country for a couple of years now. Said he was hanging out with the Rainbow Family.

"Had a far-out gathering up in Umpqua National Forest east of Roseburg, Oregon," he said. "Thousands of brothers and sisters lovin' and prayin' and livin' like God wants us to live: happy, together, with music and dancing. No laws, man. It's everything under the sky. Everything happens and nothing happens, man."

Said he was from Minneapolis but didn't think he could ever go back.

Rob picked him up a few miles before Flagstaff. Both were on the road. The hippie and Rob. Rob in khaki shorts a navy blue polo shirt and hiking boots. Rob from some small town in Connecticut not far from New York City. College boy going to law school. Said he was taking two months to drive around the country then back to Connecticut to study for the bar exam.

"I'll take the bar and then, well, I may not have a whole lotta time after that to see much of this land, so now's the time. Just hope this old van makes it," he said.

We drove down US 180 a wide open black tar road cutting and snaking through red rocks and under blue skies. Not a billboard in site. Wild grass and sagebrush dotted the arid terrain. Right before US 64 we came upon the Double Eagle Trading Company, a cheesy place where they sell lots of cheap Native American crafts: moccasins, jewelry, animal skulls, raccoon tails, and things like that. Crap mainly. The store was constructed mostly out of long, wide worn wooden boards meant to look like a store in an old western town. Michael noticed McShay and Kevin sitting next to a teepee with their thumbs out. A cigarette dangled from McShay's lips.

"Hey, Rob, those two guys hitchin', they're friends of ours," Michael said.

"The one in the black tee-shirt, that's my brother Kevin," I added.

Rob pulled over and McShay and Kevin hopped excitedly into the van. Rob welcomed them. Rich turned in their direction and gave a nod. We jolted forward and Rob said, "About twenty miles up US 64 and we'll be pulling into Grand Canyon Village at the South Rim of the Canyon."

Rob threw *Who's Next* into the eight track and the crashing arrangement of *Baba O'Riley* thundered as we moved forward. Right about the time Townsend was bustin' out the chords to *Going Mobile* we hit the South Rim. We got out of the van at Mather Point and looked out. Spread wide before us was the Grand Canyon. The deep, massive crater: red, brown, and endless. The sun's rays cascading and giving the layered earth a soft gentle illumination. Tall red buttes, boundless ravines, clusters of pines unsteadily perched over rocky, jagged cliffs. The wide-open panorama spread before us without end was hypnotizing. We scanned the vista before us silently entranced by the sight... taking in the enormity of the abyss moving each of us in our own way.

McShay lit a Marlboro, took a long pull from it and exclaimed, "That's fuckin' unbelievable." I couldn't agree more. It was.

Michael gazed into the Canyon intently and silently, tracing, with his eyes, the long, winding, struggling black Colorado River. *"This is true beauty," said Tasos Theotikos standing closely to his son.* Michael, aware of his father's presence, felt intense comforting warmth enter him. He continued to stand with his feet firmly planted on the ground in contented silence. We stood together, absorbed, a bit longer until Rob suggested we go to the visitor's center and see about hiking to the bottom of the Canyon.

The Grand Canyon Village is the general destination and meeting place for those who are going to view or hike the Canyon at the South Rim. The Village contains a main visitor center, hotels, lodges, cabins, and restaurants. It's a pretty touristy place, with lots of Winnebagos and campers moving slowly along the road. It's a place you need to go if you want to hike to the bottom of the Canyon. And we wanted to do that. So we went to the back-country office and went inside. We got permits to hike down the next morning. We spoke with a ranger at the information desk. He told us to get up early, "say six o'clock or so" to begin our hike. Told us we'd be best to get down to the bottom nice and early.

"The deeper you go, the hotter it gets," he said. "Coming up's the tough part. Takes four hours or so going down, not too bad, but you need to give yourself about ten hours to get up. Better get up and on the trail by four o'clock in the morning or you'll be wiped out in that heat. I've rescued enough folks. They end up dizzy and dehydrated. Some pass out, get heat stroke. Their tongues turn white. They think they can just saunter up that canyon shooting pictures. I tell you, it ain't like that."

In order to get our permits we had to write our names on an application and write down where we lived and give a phone number so if we died someone could come to the Canyon and pick us up. I thought about my mother getting a call. I wondered if she'd bother to come at all. Pretty unlikely. I figured I'd get buried in some common grave near the Canyon with a bunch of unclaimed people who just fizzled out. If there was such a place then that's where I'd stay.

All of us got our passes and we were happy about that because the unlucky bastards behind us in line were told they would have to come back tomorrow. All the passes were given out for the day. Those in the back of the line let out a collective groan. They weren't too happy. While we were in line we met a woman named Fran. She was alone. She told us she didn't have anybody to hike with and asked if it would be okay if she dragged along with us. We must have looked like a trustworthy bunch. She had a pleasant round, sturdy face and a long braid of thick brown hair that hung down her back. Her skin was smooth and slight lines skittered under her eyes. She wore olive green hiking shorts and a plum colored shirt. It was sleeveless. Her arms were thick and muscular. She looked strong, like a Polish peasant woman hunched over a dark rocky cabbage field in Eastern Poland cramming huge heads of cabbage into a sack, or someone like that. She had on hiking boots and her legs were sturdy and tanned. I bet you she could take care of herself. I bet you she didn't take much shit from anyone. She had one of those nasally twangs, said she was from Oklahoma City. Said one of her relatives was the guy who invented the parking meter "way back in 1935," she said. "He even ran once for state senator," she added with pride.

And so that was our posse: Me and Michael, Kevin and McShay, Rob, the rainbow hippie Rich, and Fran. All of us ready to take on the grueling footpath spiraling downward into the base of the Canyon.

Michael signaled to McShay for a smoke. McShay responded reluctantly by throwing a Marlboro at him and hissing, "Get your own, fucker. I'm running out." Michael lit it and pulled the thick black bangs away from his forehead. He stood pensively. *Tasos Theotikos stood at his side studying his son, who was holding his breath. He was waiting for his son to decide.*

"Let's put our stuff in the van, find a place to park it, and go down now," Michael said.

"I don't know," I said. "The ranger said we should wait until morning, get up early. He just told us that we shouldn't go down when it's so hot."

"The hell with it, let's go down now. We'll throw our stuff in the van, fill up our canteens, take our sleeping bags, some food and water and we'll head down," he continued.

"I think we should wait," I said.

Fran spoke up, "Why not? It's not that late. We could be down there by seven. There's a place to camp at the bottom and a restaurant and we can swim in the Snake River. We should do it."

The hippie added, "That's crazy, man. We'll fry, man."

"Stay then. I'm going down. I'm going down now and sleeping on the river at the bottom of the Canyon. You want to go in the morning, fine. I'll see you when you get down there, then," Michael said with finality.

Michael was not going to give up. I knew that much. Typical. It did not matter what the ranger had just told us. It did not matter that he strongly suggested we get up early, beat the heat and head down when the sun was not so forbidding. It did not matter what the others thought. Michael wanted to do it now and I knew he would go whether we were with him or not. So I caved in, knowing full well that that would be the easiest way to go about it. Knowing full well that it would be best if I convinced the others.

Half an hour later we were standing at the precipice of the Canyon at Bright Angel Trail. We had put all of our stuff in Rob's van, filled our canteens with cold water and grabbed our sleeping bags. McShay lit a smoke while Michael discussed our journey.

"Should take us about four hours. Watch out for the donkeys, we don't want to step in any donkey shit on the way down. Let's do it," Michael said about as excited as I've ever seen him.

Chapter 26

Another Hike

Bright Angel Trail is a narrow red dirt pathway that leads from the rim of the Canyon winding downward about nine and a half miles until it ends at the sometimes brown and muddy and sometimes cool, blue-green Colorado River. Originally it was an Indian trail used by the Havasupai Indians, the only indigenous people still living in the Canyon today. They used it to commute between the rim and a small oasis now called Indian Garden where they grew vegetables, especially corn. It's right in the middle, about four miles from the rim and about five miles from the bottom of the Canyon. Later, in the 1890's, miners improved the trail and extended it to the river. Back then a pretty smart prospector named Ralph Cameron somehow cut a deal with the miners, bought the trail, changed the name to Cameron Trail and turned it into a toll road charging anyone a buck who wanted to use it. That lasted until around 1928 when the National Park Service got involved in a bunch of legal battles that took place in Coconino County, where the Grand Canyon is located, and they took ownership. They were pretty tough battles and Cameron remained bitter at the outcome. Afterwards, the trail was officially transferred to the National Park Service and renamed Bright Angel Trail.

The hippie was eager to get a move on and imagined he'd be the first to head down the trail. He figured he'd lead the way. Donned in thick wool socks, sandals, long scraggly shorts, a sleeveless shirt and reeking of sour body odor, he moved persistently downward, his hips thrust forward, shoulders leaning back with a sour trail of stench wafting in his wake. The rest of us gave him his space following quietly and happily about twenty yards behind him. McShay found a sturdy walking stick at the top of the trail. With a Marlboro between his lips and his canteen slung over his shoulder, he moved doggedly behind the hippie.

"Jesus he stinks," he muttered.

Rob followed McShay. Moving a few feet apart from one another was my brother, Michael, Fran and finally me holding the last spot. We trudged downward along the narrow footpath looking below and surveying sandstone walls and cottonwood trees. The mercury climbed past one hundred degrees. The Colorado River twisted miles below, cool and inviting. It reminded me of a serpent stretching for miles, sunning, sleeping, and watching lazily at the endless line of hikers taking the great expedition into the boiling bowels of the Grand Canyon.

An hour or so into our journey it was apparent that this was one particularly hot place. Dry: oven hot. Over a hundred degrees hot, our water was lukewarm. Red dust kicked up with every step; our skin glistened as we trudged downward. Every so often we'd stumble upon piles of brownish-green donkey shit. I was hoping we'd catch one of the mule trains that take tourists to the bottom. I figured it would not be long before we did.

We moved ahead deeper into the Canyon. The hippie kept us moving at a pretty good pace. The sun beat furiously on our backs. I could feel my shirt pressing wet against my skin. I looked at the veins running down my arm…swollen, purple, fat veins… blood flowing… everything moving.

We made it to the upper end of Indian Garden and paused to take in the vastness of the landscape. We were surrounded by cactus and cottonwoods. A small creek flowed through the oasis. I could see why the Havasupai Indians hung here. It was a fertile paradise within the hard dryness of the Canyon. A peaceful, moist, rich smelling resting spot with wild flowers scattered in every direction. A gentle stream moved serenely over smooth rocks with cool, crisp water. We stood at the bank of the creek, and took off our boots or sneakers and socks and plunged our feet into the cold water. It was refreshing. The hippie rolled a cigarette and McShay lit a Marlboro and shared it with my brother.

"It'll get hotter yet," Michael said. "I believe it could get up to one hundred twenty degrees between here and the bottom."

"I'm filling my canteen here," Fran said. Sweat trickled in mini rivulets down the sides of her flushed face. She cupped her hands and dipped them into the clear moving water. She took a long slow drink. "The water's cold and moving nicely. It's safe to drink."

The hippie dipped his ass cheeks into the creek and let out a long, happy, high-pitched yelp. He laid his whole body into the water and looked up at the sky and made those movements like you do when you're making an angel in the snow. A wide grin spread across his face like a cartoon caricature. I was glad he chose to lie in the cold water. This was probably the closest he came to taking a bath in a long time. Maybe some of that stink would wash off of him and we would get a break. He reminded me of some kind of little monkey. I'm not sure what, maybe a marmoset. We lounged along the bank of the creek filling our canteens with the cool water, taking in the sights, baking in the oven-dry heat, and watching others, who still pretty much had energy, excitedly heading down the trail. And there were those moving slowly upwards from the bottom. Those bent and slogging: worn, tired, pained, thirsty, mouths open, sweat pouring, wondering why in the hell they attempted this hike in the first place. All moving with determination and all waiting to reach the top and reveling in the accomplishment of going the distance and taking the challenge. Once they made it they could brag about it back home, that's for sure.

I could have stayed in the cool stream longer. That is until Michael jumped to his feet and announced that it was time to get a move on. Good idea. Again, our line formed and we hit the trail with renewed excitement and energy. Our formation stayed the same, but as we descended the space between us became more distant. We were all enjoying a solitary walk swathed in our own thoughts. The Canyon gave us peace and tranquility, providing a spiritual backdrop to our deepest secrets, our most precious feelings. It allowed us a chance to think alone for a change; a chance to understand ourselves with an open honesty. At least that might have explained why after a long silence, Fran found herself walking closely, and opening up widely to Michael.

I guess Fran must have been in her mid-forties or so, hard to tell. Fran: traveling the road by herself, searching. Searching for something. Searching for anything. Searching for meaning. Wondering why everything went wrong the way it did. Wondering if she could make it all right. Hoping she could make a go of it. Was there a chance? Fran hiking with passion, connecting with Michael and connecting with Tasos Theotikos who, of course, she did not know walked quietly in her shadow helping to guide her down the dusty trail. She did not feel his presence as Michael did. Michael, however, felt his presence strongly on that hot day, on that hike.

Fran spoke quietly. She spoke evenly and openly. From where her openness came she did not know. It was not in her nature to share her inner-feelings with anyone, especially someone she did not know. Fran was practical and protective. She was cautious. Speaking forbidden secrets was simply out of the question. But, under the bright blue skies and the sandstone canvas surrounding her, the honesty did come. Her voice had come. It came all the same.

"It was always late. I was so sleepy and he would appear in my room sitting on the edge of my bed. I could smell him. He smelled sour and I could smell the stale smell of cigarettes and sometimes beer and sometimes whiskey from his breath. I could feel his rough calloused hands resting gently on my shoulder or on my leg. I would wake and my feet would be cradled in his hands. It happened so much. He coaxed me and said nice things and I remember this went on for years. I was young when I went through it, five, six, seven, eight, nine years old, and then suddenly it stopped. But after it stopped, that's when I could not sleep anymore at night. I lay in my bed with a hollow nervous stomach. In the middle of the night I'd wake with my heart beating hard and fast. I could feel my heartbeat in my ears throbbing. I lay night after night and I prayed he would leave me alone and not wake me. It was the anticipation that he might appear that scared me. To calm myself down I counted things over and over: how many pencils in my desk at school or how many pictures hung on our walls at home or how many dogs lived on our street. It was unpleasant. I prayed and asked for lots of stuffed animals. They helped me. I was feeling so down. Finally, sitting at the kitchen table, eating breakfast one day, I told my mother and when I did that she wound up and slapped me hard across the face. My cheek was red and you could see where her fingers landed. It stung. My mother told me never to lie to her face again. Then she told me to get my ass to school and shut my mouth. That's what she said and that's what she did, so that was it. I never spoke about it again. It was forgotten."

It was the hottest part of the day. The hippie led us through the driest section of the trail through the endless miles of light brown sandstone. The sparse grass was dotted with tiny bushes and round bulbous barrel cacti.

"Do you still see your parents?" Michael asked.

"I've seen them all along."

"And you don't have hate for them?"

"I do. I have plenty of hate. I can't stand them. I get angry at how they behave. I get angry especially when I see them in church. My mother and my father in the front pew singing to the Lord, praising the lord, arms stretched before them, palms open, welcoming the Lord, asking for guidance while on their knees praying like subservient sheep. To everyone they appear to be good Christians, pillars of the congregation. Sometimes my father gets on the pulpit and does some of the readings and my mother helps out by working dinners and organizing church fundraisers and things like that. She even runs the annual summer talent show. The shows are pretty cute; I just have a tough time seeing her up on the stage introducing the acts. I guess I'm just bitter. I always have been."

"You're an adult now. Why don't you tell them?"

"Sometimes, especially in church, I want to shout out, right in the middle of mass. I want to shout out hey, you see those two in the front pew? You see those hypocrites? That man, right there, the one with his head bowed to the Lord, he took his daughter's virginity and at the dinner table he complains about niggers moving into the neighborhood and he bitches about faggots, and he punches his sons hard in the back or slaps them harshly across their faces if they get out of line. He's a fake! He's a goddamn fake! Don't let him pray here anymore until he confesses what he's done!"

Tasos Theotikos, who had been quietly moving down the trail, gave his son a gentle nudge. *"Keep talking to her, son,"* he said. *"Let her know it is okay to talk with you. She wants to let you know of her fears."*

We came to a blind curve along the trail and moved cautiously around the narrow bend. The drop below was sheer and endless. Looking down made my stomach a little queasy. The Colorado River meandered solemnly beneath. The river banks steep. Once around the turn, a mule train moved slowly before us. Our group moved cautiously past the snorting donkeys. They smelled sweet and hot. Their heads were bowed, their eyes big black glossy mirrors. Leading the train was an old timer in a big white straw cowboy hat. He wore a wide grin and tipped his hat in our direction and acknowledged what a fine day it was. Behind him a string of hot, irritable and uncomfortable tourists perched themselves miserably on the beasts. Red dust climbed into their eyes and noses with every movement. They were probably wondering why in the hell they chose to ride these mules to the bottom in the first place, all hot and sweaty, dropping shit along the way. It would have been more pleasant to walk. The old timer, with the straw hat, kept them moving, knowing from experience this was right about when their excitement would wane and turn to regrettable disappointment. Probably a joke all the mule train leaders shared.

Michael and Fran moved downward in tandem.

"You said you have kids," Michael said.

"I do," she replied. "Yes, two girls, beautiful girls. My oldest, her name's Nancy, she's twenty-four. She still stays with me and works as a dental hygienist. She's trying to figure out what she wants to do. Maybe go to school and be a dentist. That's what she talks about. My other daughter, Mary, she's twenty-two; she moved with her boyfriend to Las Vegas and works in one of those fancy casinos serving drinks. She's making a lot of money, more than I ever made, but I don't like her living out there. It worries me."

"Are you married?"

"I was, not anymore."

"I see."

"That's another story," Fran said.

Fran paused and thought about her twenty-one years with her husband. All that time. *Did that all really happen? Was I with him all of those years?* They recently split and were going through the bullshit process of settling a divorce.

"We're going through a divorce," she said. "What a drag that is. Who gets what? That table, that chair, some measly pittance the lawyers call assets. By the time the bastards get through with us there will be nothing. There never really was anything and now they'll get their hooks in whatever they can. We go to court. He doesn't show up or a bunch of times we go to court and his attorney and him have not responded to our proposal and nothing gets done and the judge just lets it go on and on and the lawyers make more and more money and I'm getting broke. It's a damn charade."

Michael dragged his hand across his forehead wiping away beads of sweat. "My parents should have divorced years ago. Probably should have never gotten married in the first place. I never could figure out how those two hooked up. They were sure different from one another."

Tasos Theotikos looked at his son in stale displeasure.

"His name is Rupert. He hates that name. I don't blame him. Most people don't know its Rupert, though. He goes by Rudy. Everyone calls him Rudy, his family, friends, teachers. He's named after his grandfather, so it's a family thing."

The trail was quiet. The sporadic flow of hikers moving up from the bottom ceased. It was too late to make it to the top. We could see the Colorado clearly now. We could see our destination and we were excited. Michael continued walking with Fran. They were almost shoulder to shoulder. I wavered about five feet behind them. The others moved downward spread out a short distance before us. Every now and then I could hear the hippie let go a crazy screech of excitement and every now and then I could see McShay light up a Marlboro.

Fran continued to ramble comfortably. "We got married young. I was twenty-one and he was twenty-three. I didn't know much back then and I certainly didn't know myself, still don't. He was very nice. Gentle, thoughtful, intelligent, and he had a strength that I admired. Not macho tough guy strength, but a steady optimistic control that I found desirable. We met at a rodeo in a small town outside of Oklahoma City. They have them all the time. I love going to the rodeos; its part of who we are being from Oklahoma and all. I like the bull riding and the calf roping, and I like the barrel racing too. He grew up on a farm, a cattle ranch. He was part of the rodeo, rode the bulls and roped cattle. I was pretty impressed by that. We met one night at a rodeo and from then on we just sort of hung out. We became inseparable. We took drives in the country, went to the movies, and went to the diner, stuff like that. I guess I fell in love with him. Everything was simple and we just enjoyed each other's company. Soon I was pregnant with Nancy and that was it. A couple of months later we got married and shortly after that Nancy was born and I guess we were doing what we thought we were supposed to be doing. Two years later Mary was born and we were officially a young family working and struggling to raise our kids and make ends meet."

"It's tough," Michael. "My parents struggled too."

"We didn't have money. We didn't have much, but we didn't need much. When I think about it now, it's a wonder we made it. I was taking in kids and babysitting for three bucks an hour and he was working as a cook in a steakhouse for not a whole lot more. We had our own house and a used car and we bought our clothes second hand from consignment stores and at garage sales and we were frugal with the groceries, but everything was pretty nice and when I think about it now, well, it was a pretty good time. The kids were young and we gave them baths together and read to them and told them long stories and I guess we were pretty much in love. I guess, at that time, we were in as much love as we would ever be."

The sound of the river was upon us now. I listened to the water rolling over worn, smooth rocks and figured that sound had been going on since the beginning of time. The Havasupai Indians certainly would have opened their ears to its comforting movement. It would not be long until we reached the floor of the Canyon. I looked up at the steep sandstone walls. We were wrapped by the massiveness of them.

The sun hung fiercely above. It was really hot; at least hotter than I ever felt anywhere. Wet wisps of hair stuck to the back of Fran's neck. Her cheeks were flushed deep red.

"I guess I don't really know what happened next. Everything was routine. We worked and worked. I went to school at night and did homework on the weekends and got my degree in nursing and then worked crazy hours in the hospital in Oklahoma City while the kids got older and needed more. You know, you get bogged down."

"I understand," Michael said.

"Rudy, he was burning out at the steakhouse and he went to school himself and got a degree in hotel and restaurant management and landed a job at the Marriott as a restaurant manager and later on he got promoted to banquet and a catering manager and he worked all of the time, nights, weekends and holidays. He worked every holiday. We started making money and bought a pretty good sized house and a couple of nice cars and some new furniture and it felt good not to have to worry about getting behind on the bills anymore. I worked and he worked and our kids got older and more independent and the two of us, well, we grew further and further apart hanging onto a routine that we knew had just been a cover up. We were hanging onto something we both knew was lost and neither one of us knew how to get out of. So we just stayed together. We simply existed; bored, not talking, and not sharing. Like I said, we grew further and further apart and grew more and more miserable with one another each day. I was in a relationship and yet I was lonely."

Fran stopped and took a swig from her canteen. "Yuck! It's warm," she said and continued. "You know I love him. I really do. I wish him well and I pray every day that his life will be happy and fulfilling and that he will see the good things in this world and not be so down on himself and hopefully he will see how truly good he is. He's a good person. He's misunderstood by many, but he's a good warm person and I do pray every day that his life is going to go just the way he wants it to be."

"Do you still see him or talk with him?"

"No. He hates me. I guess he feels this is entirely my fault. I left him. I'm the bad girl. Maybe he'll figure it out and move on. I don't know."

We were about two hundred yards from the floor of the canyon. The fierceness of the sun let up slightly. The air was dry.

"He'll move on," Michael said. "He'll move on. He has good things. He should be thankful."

"I feel guilty," answered Fran.

"Guilty about what?"

"I suppose it's because I damaged him. I guess in his mind we were going to stay together forever. I don't think he ever thought we wouldn't. That's what was supposed to happen. I feel guilty for hurting him."

Michael moved close to Fran almost pressing his lips to her ear. "You should not feel guilty," he whispered. "You should eliminate that word from your vocabulary. People change and when that happens they move on. I'm not saying that it's easy, and I don't even know if it's right, but it's a fact. You have to think about what is best for you. That's all you can do."

"And destroy Rudy in the meantime?"

"He'll grow and he'll learn what worked and what did not work in the relationship and he'll adjust. He'll be okay."

"How do you know? You don't know him. You don't know how fragile and how proud he is."

"This will make him stronger. It will have to. He has no choice. He'll have to learn and eventually take some responsibility for himself. He was part of the relationship too, and there are reasons why it didn't work. He'll have to take some responsibility and he'll have to take some blame too."

"Rudy doesn't think like that. He never will. I don't think he's capable. He's convinced I destroyed his life and that I made a fool of him. He's embarrassed that I had the will to leave him, that I showed some strength. He won't know what to say to his friends or our friends and he'll tear me down and throw my name around like I was some sort of monster. I know he will. That's the way Rudy is. He has to look good. He has to appear stronger. Everything has to be my fault. It's pride. He doesn't know any better."

"Then, that's too bad," Michael said looking squarely into Fran's eyes. "The worst thing in life is to not learn from mistakes. No matter how difficult they are. You have to learn what went right and what went wrong and then you need to change. When you do this it will be easier for both of you and you can move on."

Fran peered intently back into Michael's deep brown eyes. "If someone would have told me, even a month ago, that I would be by myself hiking the Grand Canyon and having a conversation with some kid from Buffalo about my life so far, well, I just wouldn't have ever thought that. But, the fact is, I realize that now more than ever, I'm on my own now. Everything is new. I'm moving ahead. I'm sad and I'm scared and I'm hollow and empty, and I do not know what is coming next, but I know I can't go back. That is the strangest feeling I have. I can't go back. It hits me deep in my gut like a dull sad ache."

"No you can't. So move forward. It's good. You'll get there, Fran."

"You're just a kid, but you're a pretty wise one. I don't think I ever met anyone quite like you."

Tasos Theotikos noticed the warm late afternoon light illuminating his son's soft eyes. He looked happily at the gentle countenance of his face, his warm thick lips, and his smooth olive skin. Tasos Theotikos was proud of his son. Proud that he was trusted and listened to. He gave advice without wavering. He gave strong, solid, practical advice, and because of that, Tasos Theotikos felt a little easier. He did not feel the turmoil or the tumultuous pressure of being trapped in between. He felt the presence and the warmth of moving closer to home. Closer to eternal rest. Sweet, gentle, brilliant, soothing...

We had arrived. Four hours later our posse stood at the bottom of the Grand Canyon with tired legs and swollen feet and happily content. A slight searing breeze gave us no refreshment. It was blistering hot. The Colorado River beckoned. We plunged into the cool, clear water. I don't believe I ever felt any better in my life. We set up camp just on the outskirts of the Bright Angel Campground near the Phantom Ranch.

Campers are supposed to pay a fee for setting up in the campground and, being that our funds were short, and against the wishes of park officials, we set up in the woods close by for free. A little later we broke out our canned goods and sat on the ground in a circle and ate Spaghetti-O's, canned corn and warm syrupy peaches. We ate slices of Wonder Bread too.

The sun slid past the high red canyon walls leaving a delicate, soft crimson sky. Near the campground we found a rustic lodge where we were able to down a couple of beers. They were cold and refreshing and they tasted real good. We met Ranger Nelson Dillon, sitting quietly by himself at the end of the bar casually sipping a ginger ale. He shared stories of how he came to being the park ranger right here in the Grand Canyon. He wasn't much of a talker at first, but the hippie needled him about his uniform, questioning who he was and what he was doing sipping ginger ale at the bottom of the Grand Canyon. Ranger Dillon opened up and told us stories of his tours in Vietnam and the Corps of Engineers and his involvement in the Special Forces. He said after he came home from 'Nam, he had to figure out his next move and it hardly took any figurin' at all. He knew what he wanted to do. He wanted to get a college degree and he wanted to work outside in the open fresh air. He got his degree up in Washington State at the University. "Got a degree in Engineering," he said.

Ranger Nelson Dillon looked like he was carved out of stone. He had a smooth slate forehead, a granite jaw and intense, lively brown-marbled eyes that peered unblinkingly when he spoke. He reminded me of one of those tough-guy actors from the forties and fifties like Robert Mitchum or, better yet, he looked like Burt Lancaster. Yes, he was the spitting image of Burt Lancaster when he played in that prison movie *Brute Force*. He sipped his ginger ale and told us stories of working on the mountain patrol up in the Wyoming backcountry, up in the Tetons rescuing people and saving lives, skiing to the stranded, liberating them and sometimes, just for comfort, giving them a snort of good whiskey to warm their innards. Now he was stationed at the bottom of the Canyon, right here on the Phantom Ranch.

"I got me a nice little cabin right down here by the river. Just me livin' with the scorpions and the rattlers," he said. Said he was hired to fix the problem of the wild burros here in the park. "Spend a lot of time trackin' 'em down in a helicopter and shootin' 'em with some high-powered darts, tryin' to round 'em up and move 'em along," he said.

Before we knew it, it was 9:00 o'clock and the lodge was closing and we were all feeling a bit drunk. We went back to our camp and skinny dipped in the moonlit Colorado River. It flowed cool and crisp, refreshing in the hot, black, bone-dry air. Back at our camp we watched an endless exhibit of shimmering stars before surrendering soundly to sleep.

The next morning we followed the advice of Ranger Nelson Dillon and got up early. By five-fifteen we were out of our sleeping bags and standing around a small fire in the still morning daylight sipping instant black coffee from our stainless steel mess-kit mugs. McShay yawned and sucked contently on a Marlboro while the hippie started his day rolling a cigarette from a pouch of Drum tobacco. We ate slices of Wonder bread with peanut butter spread over it. Figured the peanut butter would give us the energy we needed to make the long hike ahead. Fran surveyed our campsite and told us to pick up our own trash and we'd throw it out at the top. We compressed and packaged our trash, dipped and filled our canteens into the cool Colorado, and moved to the entrance of the trail.

Six o'clock in the morning. Fran took the lead this time. We moved steadily up the great incline with determined vigor. The sun climbed higher with each step. It was hot and the sun became relentless. Shade was a luxury. The Colorado River moved further away from us, shrinking, and snaking in the distance. Another mule train headed downward carrying more miserable tourists with haggard looks and sore asses. The great Grand Canyon opened wide and deep and serious before us. The sky was big and clear blue. Enormous clouds hung in the sky fat and bulging. Four hours into the hike our posse rested under a rocky ledge hanging far over the trail. We hung in the shade. The hike became physically, mentally and emotionally challenging. Our legs stung. Our tongues were heavy. Our throats were dry. The water in our canteens turned hot and lifeless and left us little refreshment. Forward again. Another mule train staggered down the canyon trail, another leader in a big white straw hat, blue-eyed, rugged and youthful led the way with a tip of his hat and a nod. Another group of tourists followed miserably behind. Moist steaming piles of donkey shit. We moved up the winding red dirt path. It was dry and dusty. The sun latched firmly in a deep blue sky. Our bodies wet and glistening. At four o'clock our group had reached the top. We all stood at the precipice exhausted.

The hippie was happy to have reached the top and he let out a weak yell and a pathetic victory dance. "Cool man. That was fuckin' awesome. I have never seen anything so beautiful before in my life, man."

Rob motioned us together. "Let's go back to the van and get a clean change of clothes. There's a campground not too far from here where they have showers. If we split up and not look too conspicuous, we can get into the place and take a long refreshing shower. I need one."

We went to the van and to our packs, got some soap, shampoo and toothpaste and headed to the campground. The showers were clean. The water pressure was strong and nothing felt better at the time than standing under the warm water watching black dirt roll off of my body and out of my hair and swirl down the drain. We used plenty of soap and shampoo and quietly reveled in this wonderfully pampering moment. I figured Fran was equally enjoying herself in the ladies' showers.

We were all sick of canned food and decided to get dinner at a restaurant in the historic village. After that long and tiring hike, we deserved a treat. The village is perched on the rim of the canyon and there are a collection of historical buildings scattered about like the Bright Angel Lodge and the El Tovar Hotel and the brown log Santa Fe Railway Depot and the adobe Hopi House and a bunch of other places. There were some newer buildings too and the place was loaded with tourists. We ended up in a huge cafeteria and ordered roasted chicken dinners with mashed potatoes and corn. The restaurant was big and bright and there were lots of long tables lined next to one another all filled with tourists. At one side of the big room was a long stainless-steel food line where you would go through with a tray and order whatever you wanted. The chicken looked good and it was surprisingly cheap so we all went for that except for the hippie who claimed that he did not have any money. Instead he watched for people to leave their tables and, when the coast was clear, he went over and ate any leftovers on their plates. He looked a little too ratty for the tourists and they stared uncomfortably at him. It didn't take long for some lady to bust him and report him to the manager. The manager, a serious looking little man with thick lips and large teeth in a white short-sleeved shirt and a black tie, led the hippie out of the cafeteria and into an office. We sat down at one of the long tables and kind of forgot about the hippie until we saw a cop car pull up front. A few moments later the hippie got into the car in handcuffs. And that was all. The hippie was gone. Problem was he left his stuff in Rob's van. I guess I felt a little bad for him.

That night we found a decent sleeping spot hidden away in the woods. Rob brought out bottle of cheap whiskey he had stashed in his van. We cut the whiskey with water, built a fire and sat around the slow burning embers in our sleeping bags sipping the whiskey, telling stories and watching the bright fiery stars gliding across the deep black sky. My legs were sore. One by one we dozed off.

As I slept, my mind raced filled with images of walking down the jagged, red, dusty trail toward the slow winding Colorado River.

Chapter 27

Charlie Bell

Fran was gone. She must have woken up and left before the sun rose while we were still sleeping. I don't know why she did not say good-bye. I guess she wasn't the type. Rob left that morning too. I gave him my address hoping to see him again. He was heading back east to Connecticut. Getting himself in the right frame of mind to take the bar exam. "Going to take back roads all the way," he said. We wished him well and thanked him for the ride and holding onto our stuff in his van when we hiked the Canyon. He was a first-rate guy. He had a gentle way about him. I wondered if he would make a good lawyer. He didn't seem to have the same hard façade as some of those cut-throat attorneys. I didn't think he'd fit in. What did I know anyway?

Again, Michael, me, McShay and Kevin were back together. The road team. We cleared the campsite, slung our packs on our backs, walked to the lodge, and washed and combed ourselves at the bathroom sinks. I felt fresh and awake, ready to get back on the road. The four of us sat on a couple of wooden benches on the porch of the lodge and plotted our next move. The morning was clear and hot and dry. The sun was bright. It glowed warm and gentle on us. Later it would, again, burn unrelentingly upon us, but now it was inviting and tender, rather pleasant.

I was glad to look at the Rand McNally, to once again glide my fingers over the map and trace the lines that would become our journey. We had come a long way. Buffalo was far off. The lines on the map had changed here in the Southwest. They were bigger and more spacious with fewer roads. All of those highways and roads in the Northeast, all of those cities crammed together, a warren of a region.

Michael looked over my shoulder and announced, "Yellowstone is the place. Not so hot, big pine trees, woods. I want to get out of the desert and into some woods."

"It'll probably take us a few days to get there," Kevin said. "What do you think?"

Michael took the map from my hands. "Here, let me see that." He traced a route with his fingers and carefully estimated how long it would take. "Looks like close to nine-hundred miles. We'll hitch through Provo and Salt Lake City and Idaho Falls. It'll take a while. I guess at least a couple of days."

"Well," my brother said. "Yellowstone is just as good as anyplace I suppose. I heard about Old Faithful, that geyser. It's right in the park. I'm sure everyone knows where that is. We can hang there everyday at noon until we meet up."

"Works for me," I said.

"Same," said McShay.

"Great," Michael said. "So that's the plan. We'll meet at Old Faithful. Check-in everyday at noon till we meet up."

Inside the lodge was a small store. We went in and each bought a can of fruit cocktail and a chocolate Hersey Bar and came back to the bench and ate. We bought a quart of orange juice and passed it between us. McShay smoked one of his Marlboros and watched tourists coming in and out of the lodge, Michael wrote in his journal, Kevin studied the map, and I read *The Killers* from my Hemingway collection of stories. It was real hard-boiled. About a couple of thugs from Chicago who went inside a diner looking for a guy they called Ole Anderson. Ole Anderson must have double-crossed them or something. In the story they waited quite a while for him. The story was tense and the dialogue was witty, quick and snappy. I would not have wanted to be in Ole Anderson's shoes. That's for sure.

<<<>>>

To get to Las Vegas from the Grand Canyon you take Highway 64 south to Interstate 40, then head west to Highway 93 and on up into Vegas. The trip takes about four and a half hours driving time. Not too long. Along the way, just below Las Vegas on Highway 93, is the Hoover Dam. We scored a ride right away from a family, in a beat up nineteen sixty-five light blue Olds 98, who were leaving the Canyon and heading to Las Vegas. Good ride. We climbed into the back seat and plopped ourselves next to a dirty, bratty, scrawny, kid who kept kicking the back of his mother's seat. He didn't say much, but he was a little pain in the ass. He must have been around ten years old or so. He shot sly mischievous smiles at us and kept kicking the seat until his mother turned around and gave him the old you'd better quit or you'll get smacked look. She wore no make-up and her face was round and her hair was straight and shiny and black as lump coal. Her lips were full and her eyes were big and brown. I figured she was an Indian. The father wore a white t-shirt covering a skinny concave chest. His hair was long and blonde and stringy. He didn't say much. In fact none of the family said much. A little while into the drive the mother opened a brown wicker basket and pulled out a bunch of crispy fried chicken legs. She passed them around with a salt shaker. We salted the chicken, ate it, and threw the bones out the window. The brat said the prairie dogs and the coyotes liked the bones so it was okay. The food got the father talking and he told us he used to hitch-hike himself. Said he hitched to Maine once. Said it was in August and he found himself in Old Orchard Beach traveling with a girl he used to know before he met his wife. Said he was about our age at the time. Couldn't get over how cold the Atlantic was even in August. Said he'd never want to live there. Nevada was better, he said but it was a dammed shame there was not much water to speak of. If there was, well Nevada would be a paradise.

After eating the fried chicken the kid leaned against the door and fell asleep with his head tilted back and his mouth slightly open. I could see caked-on dirt behind his ears. A stream of dribble slid from the corner of his mouth and he purred like a cat as he slept. Michael sat in the middle and he too fell into slumber with his head tilted back and his mouth open. I sat quietly looking out the window at the open sky and the rolling wild grass hills. I must have fallen asleep too because I seemed to be in a bit of a delirium when I heard the mother waking up the boy saying, "Get up! I want you to see this. We're at the Hoover Dam!"

It felt good to get out of the car and stretch my legs. They were a little tight from the hike earlier. The boy took off like a little jackrabbit and headed toward the dam so he could get a better look. The skinny father yelled after him to wait, but the kid paid him no mind. He was a stubborn thing. When we caught up to him, the little brat stood leaning over a wall on an overhang looking over the massive scene.

With craned necks we looked below. "Ain't it amazing what man can accomplish?" the skinny father said to nobody in particular. He placed his hands firmly on the brat's shoulder to steady him. The kid was crazy. I thought he was going to leap into the water below, leaning over the way he was. The mother followed and we all stood high on an observation deck taking in the enormous site. I have to admit, it was pretty impressive.

"Built during the Depression," the skinny man said. "I believe it was one of FDR's initiatives."

It looked to me like a gargantuan amphitheatre built into an endless brown rocky cavern. Lake Mead stretched greenish-blue far below. It was a sight, but it did not capture the brat's attention and before long we were back in the Olds 98 heading to Las Vegas.

The mother passed the wicker basket again and we ate another chicken leg and we went on like that with the mother giving the brat reminding looks on how to behave until the family dropped us off at a dismal intersection in a rundown neighborhood on the outskirts of town. This was their destination. The bright lights of Vegas were nowhere to be found here.

We stood momentarily at the intersection and watched the big blue Olds 98 disappear from sight. I think the car needed oil; I could hear the pistons knocking into the engine block as she glided away on the drab gray pavement. Michael studied the neighborhood. There really wasn't much to see. Tiny houses with chain fences sitting on brown patches of course grass and dirt. It was dusk.

"Well, shit. I thought they were taking us into Vegas," he said. "Where the hell are we?"

"Got me," I replied. "Don't see much around here."

"I'm tired anyway. I wouldn't mind a beer either. Let's head toward the city and see what we can find along the way."

It was hot. The neighborhood was dreary and grimy. A fat, dirty old beagle with a split nose surprised us by wandering out from a yard. It stood awkwardly before us growling and showing long pointed hostile teeth. I don't think either one of us felt threatened by the dog. I was pretty sure we could outrun the poor slob, even with our backpacks on, but he was a nuisance snarling motionless and firmly planted on the sidewalk refusing to let us pass. We didn't want to take a chance passing the smelly beast and giving it the opportunity of taking a bite out of one of us. So we stood there momentarily waiting and looking at the sad fat dog.

Michael reached down and picked up a stone and threw it gently toward the pathetic beast. "Get out of here. Go on," he said motioning the dog away. The dog stood its ground and bared its teeth even more.

"What the fuck?" I said.

Suddenly, we heard the cracking slam of a screen door and a tall skinny black man in a sleeveless white buttoned shirt appeared.

"Come on, Spike," he said. "You leave them two road dogs alone, now."

The old dog lowered his head, wagged his tail and nuzzled alongside of the black guy's leg. The man towered over six and a half feet, skinny as a green bean with close cropped nappy black hair, coffee black skin and washed out blue eyes. He studied us and had us figured right away.

"You boys is seein' the country ain't ya'll? You got them packs on and headin' to Vegas. The city that never sleeps."

"We're heading that way, and then up into Yellowstone," Michael said. "Hope we're going in the right direction."

"You headin' the right way, but it ain't close. You gonna get back straight up the highway till you reach East Flamingo Road, then get on that and head west a few more miles and you be in the thick of it."

"So, it's still a bit of a hike?" Michael asked.

"Sure is," he said. "You got time for a cold one? Vegas ain't goin' nowhere."

We looked down in the direction of the dog. It was calm and still nuzzling his head on the black guy's leg.

"Name's Charlie Bell," the black man said stretching his long skinny branch of an arm in our direction. "Don't worry about ol' Spike here; he won't pay you no mind."

We took our turns shaking his hand. He had a tight grip. I responded with a squeeze a bit harder than normal.

"Come on up on the porch. I'll get us a couple of cold pops," he said and returned a moment later with three short brown bottles of Budweiser and a bag of peanuts with the shells on. "Here you go. Throw them shells in the grass there, it don't matter."

He looked us over with those pale blue eyes. He told us he was from Cleveland originally, said he was a bass player and played with big time blues guys like John Lee Hooker, Bobby "Blue" Bland, Muddy Waters, Taj Mahal, B.B. King, Pinetop Perkins, and Otis Rush. He said he even played with Elvis Presley at the Las Vegas shows held on August eighteenth and nineteenth back in 1975 as part of the Las Vegas Summer Festival.

"Elvis wore that crazy blue gypsy suit," he said.

I don't think we showed any indication that we believed his story. We'd been on the road for awhile now and knew a whole bunch of people out there who stretched the truth quite a bit. Besides, why would a guy who played with Elvis only a couple of years earlier be living in this dirty run down old part of town with a big fat smelly beagle and not much more to show than that?

"You boys don't believe me now do you?" he asked.

"Well, I don't know," I said. "If you say so, then I guess it's true. I have no reason not to believe you."

"But you don't. I can see that doubt in your eyes. Step into my living room. I'll show you a couple of things."

Inside was dark. The little house smelled like stale dog and stale beer and I think maybe the dog pissed on the carpet because that stunk too. But, when our eyes adjusted and let some light in we looked at a big wall before us or rather a shrine full of pictures of him and all those mentioned earlier. There were other photographs with people we were more familiar with like the Allman Brothers Band and James Brown and Stevie Wonder and Keith Richards too and there was a picture of Charlie Bell towering next to Elvis Presley. Elvis was wearing that blue gypsy suit with big wire-rimmed sunglasses. He had a drink in one hand and a cigarette in the other. Charlie Bell had a drink in his hand and they both had their heads tilted back in laughter. It was Elvis, goddamned Elvis Presley!

"I ain't shittin' y'all," he said. "They the real deal."

"You're not kidding," Michael said. "That's really cool. You and Elvis. That's big stuff. I can't believe he's dead."

"I believe he was dying right about that time. We were scheduled to play the Vegas Hilton for two weeks and Elvis only lasted three days and five shows until he just said fuck it all and broke his contract and headed back to Memphis and checked into a dry-out hospital there. He sure was a mess, all big and fat. He couldn't keep up with the band. It was too bad. Yes, man, I think he was dying right then."

"He did lose it in the end, didn't he?" I said.

"He wasn't the same man. Like a lot of the others, he let other evils get in the way. I turned out the same way. Got hooked on them drugs. Heroin. I was on the A-list. Musicians wanted me. I was in demand. After the Elvis episode I was on the black list, too risky, did too much smack."

Michael looked into Charlie's pale blue eyes peering closely. "You still do that stuff?"

"I ain't touched nothing in over a year now. I hit bottom and lost the respect of my friends. Musicians are funny. They don't fault you for being an addict. They understand. Being on the road pulls you in crazy directions you ain't never been in before. Anyway, even if you hit bottom, they still talk about you as a great player. They say he's an in the groove guy or he's a pocket guy. They don't talk about all the shit you put 'em through while you was on the road together. They don't talk about it, but they know when you're more interested in getting high than keeping tight. They don't talk about that kind of shit, they just don't use you no more and the word gets out. You can't be a heroin addict and maintain the demands of being on the road with a group. The demands are too high, so you just stop getting calls. It happens just like that."

Michael took a nudge from Tasos Theotikos and proceeded to tell him: "You gotta call one of them and tell 'em what's up. Tell them you don't do that anymore. One road trip and maybe you can be back if you want."

"Look at this shit-hole I'm living in," Charlie Bell said narrowing his eyes. "I want to tour again. I ain't really no good at nothin' else, but I don't know if I got the courage to go on the road. It's a lot of pressure, man. It's the cause of all that shit. I don't know if I can do it."

"What are you doing now?" Michael asked. "I mean how are you making a living?"

"Giving bass and guitar lessons to kids in the neighborhood. There's a music store not far from here. The owner gives me some space to teach and charges me a couple of bucks a lesson for rent."

"And, what do you tell those kids?"

"What do you mean?"

"I mean what do you tell them? What's the point? What's the point of playing? Do you tell them to sit in their room and play or do you encourage them to join a band, maybe get good, maybe get real good and play for a living, maybe have a really cool life and travel and meet people like you did."

"Man, I don't tell them none of that shit. I show 'em scales and progressions and have 'em concentrate on their instruments. That's about it."

"Then you're a coward and a fool and probably not too much of an inspiration as a teacher. You have to get back to living it and sharing it. That's what you need to do. Make a call. You still have contacts."

Tasos Theotikos's guided his son. His heart filled with glorious admiration as he watched his son inspire Charlie Bell. He watched his son put the dead, pale-eyed bass player back into a world of hope, a world of excitement, a world of content.

"You have to face your fears and fight them straight on. Beat them or you will lose big time and that's a fuckin' tragedy."

Charlie looked at me. His face softened, his pale eyes sparkled softly erasing the furrows in his forehead.

"Your buddy here, he thinks he's a smart little fucker, don't he?"

"I believe so," I answered.

"Otis Rush is one hell of a guitar player and a hell of a singer too. I heard through some of my connections he's gearing up to do some club dates, mostly in the South. They used to call it the *chitlin' circuit:* Alabama, Mississippi, Arkansas, that scene. He knows me pretty good and he's a good man himself. Maybe I'll give him a call and see what's shakin'. You never can tell with these things."

The rest of our time with Charlie Bell went like this: he insisted we stay and have a bite to eat with him, wouldn't take no for an answer. He brought us into his kitchen. It had a big window that let in the evening sun. It was much brighter than the living room. A bookshelf taking up almost an entire wall was loaded with cookbooks from the floor to the ceiling. A wrought iron rack hung over the stove from the ceiling holding pans of all sizes. Some were those stainless steel ones that you see in restaurants and a bunch were cast iron. Tongs, spatulas, mashers and a garlic crusher invaded a large ceramic canister. A meat grinder was locked firmly at the end of a long wooden table.

"I like to grind my own pork and make sausage," Charlie Bell said. "Mine's a whole hell of a lot better than any of those fancy restaurants in Vegas."

Wooden bowls of fresh tomatoes and onions and jalapeño peppers, and potatoes, and bunches of fresh herbs like thyme, and cilantro and rosemary and basil lined a long wooden counter.

"I ain't never worked in a restaurant, but I sure like to read cookbooks and cook and maybe someday, God willing, I could open a place, home cookin', good stuff, nothing fancy," he said and then he began to immerse himself in preparing a meal and it was an orchestrated sight to see. Michael and I sat on tall stools with our beers in hand watching Charlie Bell get to work.

"I'm gonna make you pork 'n beans Charlie Bell style," he said. "Gonna make 'em the quick and easy way."

Charlie Bell pulled three cans of beans from a cupboard: one can of white beans, one can of black beans, and a can of red beans; he opened them up and put them in a colander and rinsed them and let them set in the sink. Charlie Bell liked to talk especially when he cooked, so he told us stories while he chopped garlic and tomatoes, and rosemary, and jalapeño peppers, and shallots, and he oiled a big cast-iron skillet and put that stuff in the skillet and let it sauté until the shallots turned a little brown and began to caramelize and the room opened with a powerful, warm scent of pure, fresh flavors. He told us about Chuck Berry and how Chuck used to do gig after gig and every night with a different band.

"Ol' Chuck he was a loner," he said. "Come into town all by himself and his promoter would hire some band for peanuts to play with him. I got a call from one of the cats I used to play around with when I was in Cleveland. 'Be at the club,' he said. I can't remember which one it was, but I got a call and my man told me you and me and some other cats are gonna back Chuck Berry, so be there on time. Chuck rolls up in a big ol' red Cadillac and steps out and gives us all a nod and asks, 'You boys ready for a little Chuck Berry?' and we nod and figure he's gonna lay a set list on us and we can meet and sort of figure the shit out. But, not Chuck. He just looks at us and says 'y'all just stay tight and follow me,' and we got up on that stage and the audience was hollerin' sayin' 'Chuck play this and Chuck play that,' and Chuck is laughin' and singin' and just messin' with that crowd and he played hard, and loud, and loose, and real damn good like lightning struck that mother-fucker. He kept looking back at us sayin,' 'keep up with ol' Chuck, boys!' I tell you, I ain't never played nothing like it before. When the gig ended he got off the stage and into that fine red Cadillac and drove away. Just like that."

Charlie Bell took the beans from the colander and added them to the skillet. All that other stuff simmered lightly and the beans made a hissing sound when they struck the hot skillet. He added a little chicken stock and everything blended and calmed and simmered and thickened a bit. He took a big slab of fresh pork from the fridge.

"These are boneless pork ribs, little bit of fat on them; y'all know what they say, fat is flavor, and I believe that."

He laid the pork on a cutting board and cut it into strips and placed the strips one by one into a big mixing bowl with bread crumbs and all kinds of dried herbs and plenty of cayenne pepper and he shook it real good and coated all of those pieces of pork nice and even. In another skillet he poured vegetable oil and heated it up until it got real hot and then he placed the pork strips into the skillet and the oil sputtered and splattered and the pieces of pork cooked nice and crisp and the coating turned golden-brown. When they were done he pulled them out of the skillet and laid them on paper towels and patted some of the oil off of them. "I hope you boys is hungry," Charlie Bell said placing three big bowls on the table and scooping some of those beans from the cast-iron skillet into the bowls and placing a couple of those nice pieces of pork over the top. "Now this here's pork and beans Charlie Bell style," he said. I have never had anything so damn good in all my life. That pork was crunchy on the outside and moist and juicy and tender inside and those beans were loaded with a fresh sweet flavor. Charlie Bell grabbed us a couple more beers and he calmly looked us over with those light blue eyes and we listened to his stories for another hour or so until it got dark and time to head into Las Vegas.

Chapter 28

A Park Near Vegas

It took us ten minutes to get to the highway. My belly was stretched from eating all those pork and beans Charlie Bell style. It felt good to walk in the warm, dry air with our packs hanging firmly on our backs, listening to tires whine on pavement. The highway carried a scent of diesel and oil. The two of us leaned against the guard rail and waited. Michael held his thumb out. We took a ride right away from a kid, maybe seventeen or so. He pulled over in a rusted blue Chevy pick-up. He had his girl with him, a big saggy-breasted girl wearing a halter top. Her slit eyes were encased deep in fat. She held a big bag of Lay's potato chips in one hand and a cigarette in the other. They offered to take us a couple of miles further up to East Flamingo Road. That would take us straight into Vegas the kid said. The ride was short and traffic was heavy and aggressive. The girl ate the bag of chips methodically and with determination. Every so often she licked the grease from her fat fingers. She did not share. Once we hit East Flamingo Road, we hopped out of the pick-up truck and walked west toward Vegas.

We were tired. From where we stood, Vegas didn't look all that close. Being so worn-out lessened our desire to get there. We moved slowly until we approached a house that had been turned into a business. I think it was a real estate office. At least that's what it looked like. We sat on the lawn and rested. The grass was soft and dry. Neither of us saw the cop until he shined his flashlight onto our faces and ordered us to wake up. Turned out he was pretty friendly, though. Said he got a report two drunks were sleeping on the lawn. He saw that we weren't much of a threat; we weren't drunk either. He put us into his car and drove us to a park a mile or so down the street. It was a small park with lots of trees and some wide open spaces of mowed grass. There were picnic tables and a kids' play area too. He told us to be careful. Nobody should bother us. We found a soft grassy mound near a clump of trees and spread out our sleeping bags and used our packs for pillows and fell asleep in hardly any time at all.

Suddenly, in the quiet of the night the rat-tat-tat-click-click-click of an automatic sprinkler system erupted. Water arched and spun in every direction soaking our sleeping bags and back packs.

"Christ!" Michael yelled frantically grabbing his stuff and running for dry territory. I followed. Once we were seemingly out of soaking reach, we stood sleepily searching for another place to sleep.

"Over here by the picnic tables. I don't think there are any sprinklers here," he said.

Once more we were zipped tightly in our sleeping bags with our heads resting on our packs and back to sleep until, yet again, in the stillness of the black night I heard something that pulled me from slumber: shallow breathing, then heavier, methodical. Adjusting my eyes from my sleeping bag, I looked up and, illuminated in the soft light of the bright summer moon, I focused on a large man sitting on a picnic table looking down at us and jacking off. He continued silently and intently all the while increasing in intensity. It took me a moment to figure out what's happening.

"Get the hell out of here," I yelled and Michael woke up and reached for his axe secured tightly under his pack.

"What?"

"That fucker was jacking off!" I yelled.

"Who?" Michael asked.

"Him!" I said pointing into the trees. "Some fat dude. He bolted into those trees. I'm getting out of here!

"Where?"

"I don't know, out of here! Some guy's staring at us and jacking off for God's sake. I'm not sticking around!"

We quickly packed our stuff up and walked away. As we moved through the park we noticed, under trees, on benches, on picnic tables, near grassy hills, men quietly scattered. Some were alone; some were coupled, all silently searching for someone to share at least a portion of the night with. Michael tightened his grip on his axe visible for all, as he called them, the whack-jobs to see.

"This place is fucked up. Come on, let's get the hell out of here," he said and we were off again, tired, wobbly, confused and heading, once again, into the dry, hot night, lumbering down East Flamingo Road until we stumbled upon a ratty run down trailer park with a group a trailers, all white and lined uniformly along a gravel-dirt road. In the corner of the park, in the darkness, under a tree was a patch of long grass. Tall bushes lined one side and we unrolled our sleeping bags and nestled between the grass and the bushes and quickly fell asleep.

Chapter 29

Casinos and Glam Rock

I was hovering outside of my body, astral projecting, like watching
one of those old late night movies where the main character sleeps
peacefully in a golden field and is woken by a wild old coot with a long
scraggily beard and angry eyes pointing a shotgun into his face, but that's
what happened early that morning when I opened my eyes and stared smack
into both barrels of an unsteady shotgun.

"Git the hell out of here you dirty pieces of trash! This ain't no
motel!" the old goat said pointing that thing closer to my face. I have to
admit I was pretty damn scared at that moment and I thought, "Man, I really
have to take a piss."

Michael pealed out from his bag, hair matted from sweat, yellow
crust sticking in the corners of his eyes. He rubbed them vigorously and
shook his head and focused on the old timer.

"Settle down; we're going," he said wrestling himself out of his
bag.

He stood cautiously before the old man. The old timer had a wide
toothless and lipless mouth. Thick clumps of white hairs shot from his nose
like a wart hog or maybe a wildebeest might look. I figured he hadn't shaved
in a week or so. Wore a big wide straw hat, the kind the Mexicans down in
old Mexico wear. He wore combat boots and camouflage pants and a green
t-shirt with dried white sweat stains under his arms. He adjusted his stance

and his tiny muscular body reminded me of one of those little plastic toy army soldiers I used to play with when I was a kid.

"This ain't no motel," he said again. "People live here and I aim to keep the riff raff out, so get your asses outta here, now!"

We stood motionless and I could feel the sun's heat strikingly hot even this early in the morning.

"Well, git movin'!" he said.

We figured he wasn't about to invite us in for coffee and donuts, so in a flash the two of us high-tailed out of the trailer park and plopped our asses on a bus heading into Las Vegas. It was 9:00 o'clock when we pulled right smack in the middle of the Las Vegas strip.

Big casinos and neon signs rose from the pavement and I wished it was dark outside so I could see the neon lit up instead of looking at it all in the bright blue morning light. Regardless, the streets were swarming with tourists moving in and out of busy places with names like *The Silverbird Casino*, *The Pioneer Club*, and *Del Webb's Mint Casino* with its big red and yellow sign and blue star on top climbing above a glitzy arched facade, and the *Hotel Fremont* with its sign holding two big neon horseshoes. There was a whole bunch more. Even this early in the morning the streets were bursting with those who looked like they hadn't seen sleep in a very long time, wandering in and out of the casinos, zombies on sunny, hot, white pavement.

We entered the *Golden Nugget Gambling Hall*. Spread before us on a boundless flowered red and gold carpet were never-ending black jack, craps, roulette, and baccarat tables and hundreds of glittering slot machines lined for all eternity. The casino was bright and loaded with etched glass windows and magnificent marble walls and the whole wide open flat terrain was adorned with gold and gleaming brass fixtures. I guess *The Golden Nugget* was known as one of the classier places in town. At least, at the time, it looked pretty damn ritzy to us.

What noise! Bells and buzzers and sirens triggered a cacophony of dissonant sounds. An overarching hum echoed throughout. We sauntered through, eyes wide open, in amazement, looking dirty and scruffy, not one of those gamblers even taking notice of us. They were absorbed by the dice and the cards and the noises from those one arm slot machines that roll lemons, and cherries, and dollar signs over and over and over again. Asian tourists and Americans from across the states and Canadians filled the place. I locked in on one guy who must have been a good four hundred pounds sitting on one of those motorized scooters connected to a canister of oxygen, tubes in his nose, smoking a cigarette and parked hypnotized in front of a one armed bandits sucking one coin after another from him.

Pretty girls with loads of mascara and caked-on make-up in short skirts and long legs served trays of drinks to the delirious gamblers. Some drank coffee and some wanted something with a little more kick like Bloody Mary's and screwdrivers and champagne with orange juice. Some drank beer. Everyone smoked. It was quite a scene. We attempted to fool the waitresses by looking like we were playing the slots in order to get some free drinks, but they just shook their heads and shrugged their shoulders and told us we needed to be twenty-one to gamble and get drinks. We tried a few different waitresses a few more times until we realized none of them were going to risk anything by giving us two slugs any drinks. They knew the game, so we moved on out of the glitzy room and got back on the strip and ended up in a buffet restaurant with chrome railings offering a forty-nine cent champagne breakfast.

We attacked the buffet three different times filling up on scrambled eggs and pancakes with maple syrup and sausage and bacon and cups filled with fresh strawberries and blueberries and melons. We shoved pastries in our backpacks and drank fresh squeezed orange juice and black coffee and left the place feeling pretty damn full and pretty damn good.

It was about eleven o'clock when we made it off the strip. Back in the blistering sun on the hot black pavement leaning against a scorching guardrail on Interstate 15 heading north out of Las Vegas. Our canteens hung on straps from our necks holding hot, heavy water; water that was good for nothing. It could have been good for coffee, maybe. Not good for drinking, that's for sure.

We waited miserably on the side of the road for over three hours with Michael getting increasingly more and more agitated. "Someone's gotta give us a ride out of here," he said pushing his hand through his thick black hair keeping it away from his forehead. Beads of sweat hung above his lip. We were stranded. How long can we stay here and fry? I wondered. Plenty of cars passed by, none for us. There was not much room for anyone to pull over. Michael suggested we move further down the highway, past the sign that read, *No Pedestrians, No Hitchhiking on the Highway.*

"I'm not going. We'll get picked up by the police. Do you see the sign?" I said pointing.

"The hell with it; It's too hot here. There's no luck standing in this spot. I'm not hanging here any longer," he said opening his canteen and taking a swig of hot water. He spit it out and onto the gravel.

"Shit!" he yelled. "I'm telling you, I'm not standing in this shit spot any longer!"

He tossed his pack onto his back and walked steadily ahead not looking back to see if I was following him or not. He didn't care. There was no talking him out of staying on the ramp. Reluctantly, I pulled my pack from the guardrail and put it on my back and followed about twenty yards behind him. Once we reached past the ramp where the highway merged, Michael dropped his pack and started to hitch, his thumb pointing straight up reaching high in the air, showing desperation. The temperature was pushing close to one hundred and five degrees. Cars zoomed past fast and furious; some leaned hard on their horns and the angry sound sliced and dragged across the pavement like a furious trombonist gone mad.

Finally, from the far left lane a white Volkswagen Beetle cut in and pulled over. The driver leaned from the window and asked where we're heading.

"Yellowstone," I told him.

"Heading into Montana, can give you a lift to Idaho Falls, that's the best way to get to Yellowstone," he said.

With great relief, we shoved our packs in the trunk in the front of the car. These Beetles are strange with their trunks in the front and the engine in the rear. The motor ran like a high-speed lawnmower engine as we moved on down the road heading north.

The driver said his name was Mark. He had black shaggy hair, affectionate eyes and a perpetual smirk. He wore a tight sleeveless white t-shirt, stretched black jeans, and high-black Chuck Taylor's. He told us he was from Montana and living in Los Angeles trying to make it as a screenwriter. Mark punched the Beetle forward while The New York Dolls, a gritty street version of the Rolling Stones, spewed through their song *Personality Crisis* loudly from his cassette player. Raucous glam rockers; glittering tough guys in high heels wearing lip stick and crammed into taut silver pants, their waists showing.

"These guys throw on lipstick and play pink drums and wear high-heeled women's shoes, but they're tough Brooklyn kids and they'll kick anyone's ass that gives them any shit," Mark said. "They're fucking out of control!"

Next, we listened to *Looking for a Kiss.* It was raw and snarling. He kept it blasting while he shared with us his idea for a screenplay: "See this glam-rock thing is pretty big. You got bands like The Dolls and Bowie when he was Ziggy Stardust, and Alice Cooper, and Kiss, and T-Rex. You know bands that put on make-up and wear shiny red pumps and dresses. They look like fems, but they play this raw ass-kicking music. So my idea for a killer screenplay is this: A glam rock band, loosely based on the New York Dolls, is finishing up a gig in Seattle and for some reason they have to hop into a little plane and do an afternoon show in Anchorage, Alaska the next day. I don't know maybe there was a contest or something, but nevertheless this glam-rock band needs to get to Alaska which I know is an unlikely place, but it just adds to make the story interesting. See, setting is important. So anyway, they all cram into this tiny Cessna, the whole band, all four of them with a pilot who's not too thrilled because he thinks these guys are too fuckin' weird and besides that, he likes country music and doesn't get the whole glam thing. But, you know, he's got a job to do so he takes the group anyway. Okay, so they're flying and the plane is crammed with stuff and heavy and the group is uncomfortable because they're not used to flying, so the whole scene is a little hairy. One of the guys is a junkie and he shoots up right in the plane to the disgust of the others, but they give him a break because of the crazy situation. So, he nods out and then the weather turns on them. I mean they get stuck in one scary-ass powerful rain storm and the plane is getting louder and barely chugging along and the pilot says he's losing altitude and a big bolt of lighting strikes the plane and the all of the navigation equipment goes haywire and they have to make a crash landing. And they do, right in the Alaskan wilderness! Now the whole thing turns into a classic survival story in the Alaskan wilderness and these guys can only survive using the things they packed with them on the plane which is a lot of makeup and jewelry and funky clothes."

Michael's attention was riveted at the idea. "Like, they can kill an attacking bear or wolf by stabbing it in the eye with a red pump, stuff like that."

"Exactly," Mark agreed. "And they could inject a big ass grizzly with the heroin from the junky which creates a subplot. See the junkie doesn't want to give up the junk, but the others know they can use the shit to kill wolves and bears for fur and meat. Stuff like that. It will keep them alive. That creates tension and all that conflict between characters is good in a screenplay you know."

"I like it," Michael said.

"I do too," Mark echoed. "I believe it has potential. I'm learning a lot out in California. Learning about writing, what sells and what gets thrown out. Bottom line: happy endings. This survival story has to have a positive ending. The junkie can die, but the story needs a hero and the hero needs to overcome and defeat the obstacles. That's the way it works."

Mark was pretty excited about the whole thing and not limited to only one idea. He had a bunch. He said, no matter what, he was determined to be a writer. "Just gonna keep writing and writing one after another until one of them hits. I got to keep putting in if I want to get anything out," he said and then he told us about another idea he had about a principal named Mr. Klarheit who worked in a high school. "He was one top-notch guy and everyone in town loved him and respected him for his hard work and dedication. Kids loved him, the community loved him, everyone. He was well respected for his conservative views. Most said he was a straight forward steadfast thinker, a firm member of the community, a solid guy they would say. It goes on like that for a bit; the story of an everyman in an every town. Then, one Monday morning, he does the simplest thing that confuses everyone. He paints his left pinky fingernail bright candy apple red. He just shows up to work with a painted pinky. His secretary is the first to notice it. She gives him a double take, but does not confront him about it. By the end of the school day whispers ensue and theories abound. But, nobody confronts him; see they're all so fucking confused. Then he shows up Tuesday and Wednesday and the rest of the week with that painted fingernail and it keeps going like that until the whole town is in a clamor. See the story isn't about the fact that the guy painted his pinky; it's about the collective psyche of the community. Something disturbs it; it is not quite right. It becomes a modern Salem witch trial. The pinky is insignificant. When you think about it, it's just one tiny mark, a mere brush of color, but it's significant enough to cause a stir. It's different. It's uncomfortable. They begin to question: "Who is this guy?" "Why is he doing this?"

Michael leaned from the back seat. "Cool. Where are you going to set this story?"

"Connecticut or Massachusetts. See, if I set it somewhere in the deep south, well, then it would be a different story. They'd probably confront him and say, 'What the hell's all that painted pinky shit? You'd better get rid of that right now or we'll lock you up for somethin', we ain't sure what, but we'll lock you up for somethin' that's sure enough!' So I'm going to set this up in blue blood country in the company of thinkers and intellects. They're not going to arrest him; they're going to think it through, look into the school policy, have meetings and see if he is breaking any codes of conduct or contract dress code rules. Words like appropriate attire or disruption to the educational process will have to be looked at closely. They'll shun him and his family, give him strange looks, remove themselves from his presence, keep the kids home from school, shit like that. They'll have to exile him in a more humane way. The whole thing will be a bit more psychological. I don't know where it's going exactly, but that's the gist of it."

We listened intently while the Beetle's motor kept a steady sputter northward and Mark's mouth moved in rapid fire spitting out one idea after another: a story of a deranged restaurant owner who boils the customers in big pots who have critiqued his cooking; a cross dressing football player who becomes the most famous plus-size model in the world; a king who has a fondness for goats; a mother who unknowingly falls in love with her son she gave up for adoption years earlier; a stripper who ended up as a nun, stuff like that until before we knew it we were about ten miles past Salt Lake City where we pulled over and threw our sleeping bags on the grassy shores of a tiny lake, and slept in the cool dry air under the sparkling stars of a big fine Utah sky.

Chapter 30

Idaho Falls

At seven o'clock the next morning Mark nudged us out of our sleeping bags. He aimed to get an early start. We packed our gear and got on the road. Mark dropped us off in Idaho Falls by nine-thirty and wished us a safe journey. We found a gas station and cleaned up at a filthy sink in the restroom. I had to go inside and ask the mechanic for a key. He didn't look too thrilled to give it to us. He reminded me of a weasel, all scrawny and pointy toothed. Once inside I noticed dirty walls, tile floors and the scent of oil and gasoline. Cloudy hot water sputtered slowly from a dull facet. It felt good to brush my teeth, soap up my face and wash the grime out of my hair watching the dirt swirl down the drain.

The morning was bright and the air was dry and the sky was crisp blue and the clouds were those big white puffy ones that look surreal and make you pause and wonder. It was about ten o'clock. Idaho Falls moved at small town speed. Maybe it forgot it was a city. Pleasant enough, though. We came across a Salvation Army and went inside claiming broke and hungry. A small man with small town looks, a kind face, and welcoming eyes filled a brown paper bag with corn, apple sauce, peaches and a container filled with mashed potatoes. He handed us a ticket good for three dollars at a market a few streets from here. The man preached a bit about being thankful and following the word of the Lord and being saved and stuff like that till we parted and ended up at the market buying bread, bologna, and nectarines.

After a short walk we stretched out on a grassy hill along the bank of the Snake River right next to Idaho Falls. Idaho Falls Temple, or what's known as the Church of Jesus Christ of Latter-day Saints, rose into the light blue sky escaping a cluster of surrounding pine trees. Its smooth white, stunning tower glistening in the sunlight reminded me of the top tier of a decorative wedding cake. We ate two bologna sandwiches apiece. We ate the nectarines too. They were soft and juicy and sweet. We chucked the pits into the clear moving water, then lazily put our packs onto our backs and hiked to the highway where we stood on the ramp for only a few minutes before a pick-up truck with *Big Bad and Mean* written on the back window pulled over and a tough looking girl motioned for us to throw our packs in the rear and hop into the cab.

Diane: wearing brown cowboy boots, Levis and a sleeveless navy blue t-shirt. Thick, long auburn hair, smelled like a warm summer afternoon. We peeled onto the highway, tires screeching; she was a regular hard-hitting girl, had a raspy voice and a raucous laugh; smoked a cigarette without a filter; looked at us like we were a couple of fragile, lost puppy dogs. Questions exploded in rapid fire: "Where you from? Buffalo? Boy you're a long way from home! Where you going? Trip around the country? Good for you. To see who? Your brother? In Seattle? Nice country up there. Where to next? Yellowstone? Yellowstone is a fine place. Great trees. Moose and bears and plenty of big, strong elk. Good campin' there! I go campin' there myself a lot. So you've been to Nashville? Florida? New Orleans? Texas? Colorado? The Grand Canyon? Vegas? Boy oh boy, you boys sure are movin'!"

And we were moving again, moving steadily up a long stretch of Highway 20 through towns named Rigby and Rexburg and Sugar City. We passed St. Anthony until we reached a town called Ashton where Diane called home. Ashton: Last little bit of flat land before entering the Targhee

National Forest right outside of Yellowstone. Diane cruised the pick-up down the main street all lined with beat-up American made cars and pick-up trucks. Rows of stumpy one-story buildings: a café, an auto parts store, a tavern, a bank, an auto mechanic shop with an enormous guy under the hood of a Ford Pinto (surrounded by an uneasy tourist couple that were, I figured, heading up to Yellowstone), a clothing store, a farm supply and feed store, an appliance fix-it store, and at the end of town stood a few towering silver steel cylinder grain storage tanks. At least that's what I figured was in those tanks. The town was painted dull. It looked like a place where men sweat hard at work all day for little pay. I didn't see anyone walking along the street or in and out of any of the shops. Diane turned down a narrow street just past the tanks. The sidewalks were broken and cracked and the tiny houses were set on dismal lawns: a mix of grass, dirt, dandelions and gravel. No fences separated any of these houses, only overgrown bushes and trees. I did not see any street lights, so I imagined it got pretty dark at night.

"Got a house right up here with a hot shower," she said. "Looks like you boys could use a rinsing."

Diane parked the pick-up in front of a small one story drab light brown house with beige shutters. All the houses on the street looked pretty much the same. Next door stood a dreary gray replica. Hers, like most in this neighborhood, had four wooden steps leading to a white door and no front porch. The steps were worn and unpainted. A tall thin pine tree stood firmly in the center of a tiny yard. In the driveway an old camper sat rusted and decaying.

"It's not too big, but its mine and I love it," she said.

We got out of the truck, shutting the doors with a thud, and stood on her lawn. I got a pretty good look at her and noticed a slight overbite and bright hazel eyes. She was a good two heads taller than the two of us. I'll bet she towered six feet tall.

Inside was clean and smelled like lavender. The living room had all the necessary furniture including a big stereo with hundreds of records stacked neatly in a tall bookcase. A drawing of a cowboy sitting on a wooden fence holding a Coors beer hung over an unused fireplace. The cowboy had just finished a long hard day's work and sat relaxed watching that sun set over the wide open land. Diane pulled a Bob Dylan record from the stack and carefully removed the disc and dusted it with one of those wooden record cleaners. We listened to *Blood on the Tracks,* the side with *Lily Rosemary and the Jack of Hearts.* It sounded crisp and clear.

Michael was the first to take a shower. I sat with Diane in her living room. She offered me a Squirt and I sipped it slowly.

"My boyfriend, his name's Andrew, goes by Drew though. He's a logger working up in the Targhee Forest. He does foresting and timber cutting, that kinda work. They keep him a couple of weeks at a time, so I hang on my own when he's away. When he gets back we go into the streams near Yellowstone and fish out big ol' trout, catch 'em with flies and we go into the woods and hunt elk. Shoot one of them and it lasts us nearly four months. We make steaks and sausage and stews. We use it all and it's real good. I can tell you that. We have a good time. He's a good guy, a little fucked up from 'Nam, though. He doesn't sleep much. He went in loud and rowdy and came back quiet and brooding. Sometimes I lose him. He gets lost in his thoughts and they're too deep to come back from. He comes around finally, though. I love him. Big, Bad and Mean, that's what they call him except although he's big, he's not bad or mean, never really was. Sure isn't any more."

"I know how that is when they come back," I said. "I have two cousins, twins. Big boys. Muscular Irish guys with reddish blonde hair. They're lots of fun, always laughing loudly. During the war, we had a big map of Vietnam taped to our refrigerator and I remember we had little flags stuck in places where friends and relatives were. I remember those flags very well. I used to look closely at that map, at the names of the cities and the villages and the rivers. Walter Cronkite would mention those places on the news every night. Laos, Cambodia, the Mekong Delta, Saigon, Da Nang. I watched on television the My Lai massacre and Lieutenant William Calley and thinking that Vietnam is a pretty strange place."

Diane took a cigarette from her pack, tapped it on the table, put it in her mouth and lit it.

"That Calley, he lost his mind over there. A lot of boys did. The constant presence of unknown danger lurking unseen in trees and under the ground messed them up quite a bit; little kids walking into camps with bombs strapped to them and taking our guys out. Those boys were getting ambushed constantly and some of them just snapped. Pretty fucked-up. Not a good thing."

"Those cousins of mine, they were big guys, real determined and friendly and playful. To me they were gods. We had a welcome home party for them at my aunt's house. The whole family showed up and that's a lot of aunts and uncles and cousins and brothers and sisters and grandparents crammed into one flat. I don't know how many more people could fit into those rooms. The dining room table was filled with trays of cold cuts and breads and chips and pretzels and lots of beer and it was smoky and everyone was having a good time. I looked for my cousins and when I finally made my way into the living room I saw them both sitting on the couch right next to one another and I couldn't believe how much they changed. They were real skinny and their lips were pressed tightly together and their eyes were hollow and lifeless. I thought they looked dead, but they were sitting up. That's the best way I can describe it. They did not look the same. They were somewhere else."

"It's a goddamned shame," she said.

"A real shame," I agreed taking another sip of Squirt.

Michael came out from the shower wearing shorts and a blue t-shirt. His hair was wet and combed back over his forehead, showing a white line where the sun did not reach.

"That felt great," he said. "You forget how great a shower feels when you're on the road."

"I'm sure of that," Diane said.

"You're not kidding. Can I go in now?" I asked.

"Go for it," Diane answered and then she told me to help myself to shampoo and soap and stuff.

The bathroom was tiny. Smell of fresh soap, steam on the mirror from Michael's shower. I hopped in and the water pressure was high and pressed hard on my body and it felt good to let the hot water run over me. Afterwards, I shaved with a plastic razor until my face became smooth and clean.

When I returned to the living room Michael was sitting comfortably on the sofa with a can of Coors beer in his hand. At the stereo Diane carefully dusted a new record: The Allman Brothers, *Eat a Peach*. Next to Michael sat a short shoeless girl with massive breasts and tiny toes painted bright red. She had shiny, fiery red hair, the kind of color that came from a bottle, and was crammed into a pair of tight white shorts with her creamy thighs crossing over one another. Diane introduced her as Suzie. She took a long puff from an L&M cigarette leaving a bright red lipstick mark on the filter. She took tiny sips from a can of Coors beer she apparently brought with her.

Suzie smiled brightly showing extra white teeth. She held a beer in her hand and extended it toward me. She wore rings on each finger. Some sparkled and some were silver with ornate bands and some were turquoise.

"Beer?" she asked.

"Why not?" I replied taking it and popping it open.

"I could just relax. I've got nothing to do today except take it easy," Diane said.

"Girl, all you do is take it easy," Suzie replied.

"Shoot," Diane said.

"I take it any way I can get it," Suzie squealed, humored by her own joke.

"We're not on any important schedule ourselves," Michael said taking a slug from his beer and looking at the girls. He launched into non-stop talking about our travels and Buffalo and people we've met. The girls listened to him with pure admiration. We knocked back that twelve-pack while listening to a couple of records and everyone felt pretty relaxed and Diane suggested we get some more beer and cook a big dinner.

"I'll bet you haven't had a good home cooked meal in a long time," she said.

"Not very often," I replied.

"Eating's stupid. There are better things to do than that," Suzie chuckled looking in my direction.

Diane stood up from the floor and stretched her legs. "I can run up to the A&P and pick up some more beer and something to cook up if you'd all like."

"We can all go. I could use a little air," Suzie said standing up and swaying slightly. Her breasts were huge. I mean really big, out of proportion kind of big. Like someone from a comic strip. She slipped into a pair of leather sandals and grabbed my hand and led me out the door to the front lawn. Her hand was soft and meaty. Suzie sighed pleasantly and planted herself on the lawn, inhaling deeply, and focusing on that old rusted camper as if it held some sort of precious memory. In the bright sunlight I noticed she really had the make-up caked on good and her eye lashes were loaded with thick black goopy stuff. Inside all of that eye stuff her eyes beamed clear and as blue as two shiny sapphire stones. Her perfume was nice too, fresh and powdery. She woke from her spell and squeezed my hand and looked at me as if she saw me for the first time.

"Isn't Diane the nicest girl? she said. "I'm glad she picked you boys up; it's always nice meeting new people. Not much goes on around here, mostly folks passing through, tourists heading to the Park stopping in town to pick stuff up. I was born here, been watching campers driving down our main street and through town as long as I can remember. They all come and then they all go. Those campers sure have changed; they're getting bigger and bigger and bigger. I'm talking about the vehicles they drive, not the people in them," she laughed.

"I bet it's a pretty nice town," I said.

"Well, it's not all that much. It's just a boring little town with boring little people, except for Diane, of course. That's just the way I feel. What can I tell you?" she said and gave me a slight squeeze with her soft little hand.

"I used to be married you know," Suzie said. "I used to be married to a real jerk. He's in prison now for trying to kill me. It made the papers. It made the papers as far as San Francisco."

"No kidding."

"Yep, some reporter thought it was pretty funny, the way he wanted to kill me and all. So it made a lot of papers, but I didn't think it was funny one little bit. It was pretty creepy, really."

"No kidding," I said.

"He's a hunter like every other guy around here. He'd been in the woods and got himself a big ol' bear, and that crazy coot got it in his mind that he'd pull the hide off that bear and stuff himself inside that bear's hide and walk in the paws and maul me to death with those long bear claws. They're like razors you know, would have sliced me up good. He figured, because it was winter and there was a lot of snow on the ground, the cops would suspect I got killed by a wild bear because they wouldn't see any footprints, just bear claws. Pretty smart, huh?"

She stood close to me and lifted her face and locked those deep blue eyes into mine.

"Why would he want to do something like that?" I asked.

"Because he's a wild jealous fool, that's just the way he is."

Well, that's some crazy shit," I said.

She put her little hands on my shoulders and kept her face tilted toward me. "Well, silly that obviously didn't happen or I wouldn't be standing here telling you about it. What did happened was he was working at the gas station in town as a part time mechanic. The guy who owns the garage is a big guy named Harry Ball; that's his name. He's a simple guy, not much in the brain department, but everybody knows he's a great mechanic and all the truckers or anyone around Ashton that has a problem with their cars go to Harry Ball. I don't know why his parents named him Harry; they could have named him a lot of other things, but I don't think they were too bright either and didn't figure it out till much later. Maybe they never did figure it out. I don't know."

I remembered seeing him hunched over the Ford earlier. I remembered the nervous couple who owned the car too. Probably wondering if their vacation was going to end right here in Ashton, spend all of their money just getting home. I thought Harry Ball was a pretty funny name.

"See my ex, he's dirty and conniving and he figured he could get ol' stupid Harry to do some brake work on my car, you know, rig them up so they don't work right. Harry would have done it just to be a nice guy, and he wouldn't figure all the other stuff out like me getting' killed. It would have worked too, but something deep inside of Harry stopped him. He said later that something just did not feel right. Turned out he liked me a whole lot and did not care one bit for that ol' boyfriend of mine. Harry went down to the Sheriff's office and told him his whole plan. The Sheriff told the state police and they had Harry wired up and they did some sort of sting operation where they got it all on tape, how he was going to do it and stuff and that's where they learned about the bear suit. I guess he figured the bear idea was too much effort and maybe I could have run away and he would have looked pretty stupid and suspicious inside of that thing. Might be hard to explain. Harry said later to the police that my boyfriend was a mean man and he was glad to put a mean man in jail. It was in all the papers, like I said, even as far as San Francisco."

Diane and Michael wandered out from the tiny house. Diane locked her door, looked at us and smiled warmly.

"Let's hop in the truck and head into town," she said.

"I want to sit in the back with you," Suzie said. "I haven't ridden in the back of a pick-up in a long, long time."

We were off. Suzie tilted her head back and giggled pleasantly as we picked up speed and shot down the road, her hair whipping wildly in the whooshing wind. She tucked her arm inside of mine and nudged closer. Our shoulders, hips, and ankles touched. Diane drove through town and onto a winding two lane road until we arrived at a small grocery store. It was nothing fancy, not like some of those mega-stores that were popping up all over the place, just an old-fashioned grocery with lots of canned goods on the shelves and hanging lights and hard-wood floors. Once inside, Diane insisted on paying for everything and after a strategic sweep, we left with a couple of big brown paper bags filled with a package of spaghetti, ground beef, bread, a gallon of milk and another twelve-pack of beer.

We hopped back into in the pick-up and headed back to the brown house with the beige shutters. On the steps a slender long haired mustached guy sat picking on an acoustic guitar. Near his foot was a bottle of Early Times whiskey with a couple of slugs taken from it. I don't know if he was playing anything particular, but it sure sounded good, kind of a mixed strumming and picking while tapping his fingers on the guitar's body to create a rhythm.

Diane stepped out of the truck, ran to the slender player, and gave him a big tight hug lifting him right off his feet.

"Hey, there little brother! What the hell you doin' here?"

Once the guy got his feet back on the ground, he returned her hug. His guitar slid behind his back and hit the railing causing a dissonant clank.

"Just stopped by to visit with my big sis; nothing more than that," he said.

"Well, I'm glad you did," Diane said looking a little thrown. She introduced the guitar player as her little brother Markey who came all the way from his horse farm outside of Dickinson, North Dakota where he'd been living for a bunch of years now.

"Nice to meet you," he said and after a few "how you doin's and what's new," we all piled back into Diane's house and Diane got right to it in the kitchen and started cooking up a big dinner.

The kitchen was enormous. It was the biggest room in the house, hosting a big wooden table with bench seats. Markey opened the bottle and placed it in the center of the table. Michael popped open a couple of beers and passed one to each of us and Suzie kicked off her sandals, glided into the living room and fingered through the albums until she selected *Sly and the Family Stone's Greatest Hits.* She cranked it to a good volume and came back and seated herself on the bench close to me while Diane seared onions and garlic till the room was filled with a satisfying scent. She seasoned the ground beef with dried basil and sage and thyme and salt and pepper and added some tomatoes and let it all simmer on the stove while we sipped the whiskey and let it settle warmly in our guts.

"Where's that wife of yours?" Diane asked while lugging a pot full of water to the stove and putting a high flame under it.

"Well, sis, that's a bit of a sore subject. I ain't seen her in close to a month," Markey said taking a short pull from the whiskey bottle. "Ellen's been down in Colorado learning how to train horses by talking to them; by whispering to them it's called."

"I heard about that. It's supposed to be a humane way to train," Suzie said.

"I guess you're right. It is humane at that," he said letting out a long sigh. He took another slow pull from the bottle then rubbed his chin reflectively before continuing. "She treats our horses better than she treats me. See, my wife she's got this friend of hers. Ann Dwyer, they've been pals for a couple of years now. Seems like I've been taking a back seat to whatever they do and they always seem to be doing something together without me much in mind. Like I told you, she's been gone with Ann Dwyer now close to a month and does not seem to be coming back all too soon. So, I don't really know."

"Is she married?" Michael asked. "Is this Ann Dwyer married?"

"Sure is, to a nice enough guy, hard worker, has a big spread himself, 'bout a mile from us, with a bunch of horses, likes to rodeo too. I see him down at the bar sometimes drinking a cold beer after a long day, but we don't talk too much, ain't really that much to say."

"Well it sure sounds like she's doin' the old down and dirty with that broad," Suzie chirped.

"Suzie!" Diane scolded. "We don't know that for a fact."

"Oh, I betcha. It sure sounds like that to me," Suzie added.

Markey rolled a cigarette and sipped from his can of beer. "I gotta tell you, Suzie, I believe you could be right. It ain't been much of a relationship lately, or a long time for that matter. I've been having those same thoughts."

"Well, hell. You can stay here as long as you need to little brother," Diane said. "We got an extra room and Drew won't mind. You know you're always welcome. This is your home anyway."

"I appreciate that. I got a friend of mine feeding and watering and running the horses for now, but I can't be gone too long. I might hang a day or two, though."

Diane threw the spaghetti in the pot of boiling water, "As long as you want," she said and Suzie chimed in that she had room at her place and would be delighted to have him stay too because, "He shouldn't be sittin' at home all alone while that floozy was gallivanting all over with that two-timin' dike," and Michael suggested that maybe Markey might like to sing a song on his guitar and he thought about it for a moment and launched right into *I'm An Old Cowhand from the Rio Grande* and Suzie took over the harmony vocals complete with *yippie yi yo kayah* and I must say, they both sounded real good together. Suzie could sing. She could sing real well and together they belted out some pretty cool tunes like *Swing Wide Your Gate of*

Love and *Whoa Sailor* and *A Six Pack to Go* all made popular by one of Markey's favorite entertainers: honky-tonk Western Swing singer Hank Thompson. He told us he liked him better than Hank Williams or Bob Wills for that matter.

As soon as the spaghetti was done Diane and Michael set the table and in the center placed a big bowl of the spaghetti with the meat sauce that Diane called bolognaise. We ate heartily and continued to nip from the bottle and drink the beers and listen to all of this new and wonderful music that I had not really paid attention to before. The kitchen softened and the music continued long and steadily into the still night. Markey didn't just strum or even pick at the guitar; instead he blended these incredibly soft melodious chords and played songs by people like Gershwin and Cole Porter. Markey, himself, looked like he played: soft, fragile, like fine white china. His hair was long and shiny and his skin was delicate pink and baby smooth and his mustache was long and curled at the ends. He reminded me of a pampered Westerner, maybe like General Custer might have looked like when he was primping himself before a night out at a fancy restaurant. He surely didn't look the same as one of those dirty long haired hippies sitting on the corners in the cities banging out chords and belching grizzled blues tunes.

We all slid deeper into the night feeling warm and smooth. Suzie swayed melodically into the living room and came back with a bongo-drum and Michael tapped it lightly to the guitar's rhythm while Suzie sang a sultry smooth version of *Close to You* and I remember thinking at that moment that these two could get out on the road and make some real noise. They were that good. Then the whole bunch of us sang *Yellow Submarine* and *Sweet Virginia* by the Stones and *The Weight* by The Band and then Suzie sang a slow sad version of *Heartbreak Hotel* and when she finished the song her face sunk and she cried and cried repeating over and over that she was not going to let that bastard crush her spirit or her dignity. She was drunk and had enough. Diane put Suzie in her bed. She came out and said, "She'll sleep it off and feel better in the morning." We took a couple of more nips from that bottle and cleaned up the kitchen and told stories further into the night and then Michael and I rolled our sleeping bags out on some beds in the rusted out camper parked next to the house. Markey slept soundly on the couch in the living room and Diane lay in her bed closely wrapping her arms around a deep breathing Suzie who slept peacefully in the big bed.

Chapter 31

Yellowstone

On a clear sunlit afternoon in September of eighteen-seventy, businessman, historian, explorer and vigilante Nathaniel P. Langford, a member of the Washburn-Langford-Doan Expedition exploring the northwestern region of Wyoming, that would ultimately become Yellowstone National Park, described a cone geyser in his journal that was "indeed a perfect geyser." With pleasure and astonishment, Langford and his group marveled at the sparkling boiling water glistening in the sunlight and spewing harshly upward over one hundred and twenty-five feet in the air at intervals of every hour or so. It was Henry D. Washburn, leader of the expedition who gave the geyser the name Old Faithful because of those periodic eruptions.

On a dull, rainy day one hundred and eight years later, Michael and I sat on our backpacks in front of that very same geyser feasting on sweet rolls, cookies, apples and lemonade given to us by a camper leaving the park who walked up to us and asked simply, "Do you want some food?" We must have looked like fairly pleasant road bums, and he was quite happy to chat briefly with us and give us the family leftovers before returning home from his summer vacation.

We took a couple uneventful rides out of Ashton until we got a lift to Old Faithful by two park employees. A cool misty rain filled the sky. Concrete gray clouds hung low and moved slowly overhead. The rotten egg odor of sulfur from the geyser blended with the calm vanilla scent of the ponderosa pines and the stone wet air. The cool freshness of the air felt good. It smelled wet and clean. We figured this was about as good a place as any to wait for Kevin and McShay. We hoped they wouldn't be too long.

Later we moved out from the rain and sat in the big wooden chairs in front of the mammoth fireplace in the lobby of the Old Faithful Inn: a tremendous lodge with stylized rustic wood, a log-framed cavernous lobby and gnarled, bulbous wooden railings. The room was seven stories high and illuminated in soft yellow lighting. It was crowded because of the rotten weather. We did not mind sitting, reading and carrying on idle conversations with those who chose to lounge in front of the fireplace, making the best out of a cloudy rain filled day. One camera strapped tourist, who filled us in that he was from Pennsylvania, marveled at being in the presence of such an incredible structure.

"Largest logged structure in the world," he said eagerly scanning the wide open interior. "Look at the craftsmanship…the wood… this fireplace… can you imagine what it must have taken to load and stack those boulders? It's a wonder; it's amazing," he said and his wife nodded in agreement and turned the page of her Reader's Digest getting lost in one of those stories and never saying a word further.

We spent our time that day back and forth between the Inn and Old Faithful. Watching the geyser erupt was an event that thrilled and stirred everyone around. It began in the lodge with a comment: "It should go off soon" or "Any time now, she's gonna go," and those who lounged contently in the big chairs in front of that huge fireplace jumped forth and hurried to the geyser, gathering quickly in the gentle mist. In a quiet stillness all would wait, heads up, eyes fixed in eager anticipation. When the moment arrived cameras clicked in rapid fire and tourists scampered into position so they could snap photos of one another just at the moment of the watery explosion. Those pictures would be placed like trophies on mantles all over the world. What a prize indeed!

By day's end the rain moved out, the stars showed themselves glistening in the blue-black sky, and still no sign of Kevin and McShay. Michael and I gathered our gear and figured we'd find a soft patch of grass in the woods, pitch our tent and get a good night's sleep. Hopefully, tomorrow they would likely arrive.

It was ten-thirty the next morning when we woke. It must have been the soft grass and cool night air that let us sleep as long as we did. I awoke with tremendous energy. The sun beamed brightly and the air was warm and comforting. There was a crisp freshness in the air and everything was clear and light. Every detail was outlined with minute clarity. Michael rummaged through his pack and pulled out a can of pork and beans. We sat on our packs outside the tent eating the beans with bread and drinking water from our canteens.

Michael glanced awkwardly at the giant trees arched above. Rays of sunlight cascaded upon us, bright green ferns and mosses carpeted the woods floor and purple and pink wildflowers lay scattered in every direction. He took in the surroundings, deep in thought.

"I hope they get here today," he said. "They shouldn't be too far behind us."

"Unless they aren't having any luck getting rides," I said.

"That's for sure," Michael answered slowly, almost reflectively. "They could still be stuck out somewhere in the desert for all we know."

"I don't mind hanging here, though. It's pretty comfortable," I said breathing in the fresh scent of grass and pines.

"Absolutely," Michael answered and shot a deep melancholy sigh that filled me with a cold-hollow feeling of uneasiness. *Tasos Theotikos shifted contentedly taking hold of Michael's mood.* "There's something about this place that makes me want to stay. I'm not sure, but I have this weird uneasiness about moving forward. There's comfort here. I'm not sure where we're going."

I thought about it for a moment. "We have time to choose, east or west, it doesn't really matter. I wouldn't mind swinging west into California, maybe the coast. We could go to Oregon, then onto Washington State. It's all the same for me, really. I've never been anywhere till now."

"I suppose so," he decided stuffing more bread and beans into his mouth.

Sometimes just when you are sure this world could not be a more perfect place and all is as it should be, when everything in your presence appears aligned and balanced and clear and harmonious, when nothing should be any different or more ideal than it is at that very moment, sometimes when pure bliss exists a crow flies in and disrupts that paradise and casts an evil darkness in your midst. That is what appeared to be happening at that moment, on that day when, while sitting peacefully in the sunlit woods eating a can of pork and beans, we heard the dry crack from a branch being stepped on in the near distance and a high-pitched sad scared whimpering. At first sound, I don't think we thought much of it. We figured the whimper might have been a coyote with her pups or maybe a fox until we heard more commotion, more cracking branches and a mix of high and low voices growing louder and louder. I couldn't make out what was being said, but the high voice sounded scared and I could make out *please* and *no* and *stop.* There was crying. The lower voices growled and I could make out words like *shut your mouth* and *be still.* I also heard *kill you.*

Michael froze. In slow motion he carefully set his beans down and reached for his pack pulling over the flap and retrieving his axe. No words were spoken. The cries grew louder and more desperate. Twigs and branches cracked like brittle bones. I found a strong thick tree limb; a club with a rounded head. I held it tightly in my hand. We moved slowly in the direction of the sound. Birds sang melodiously overhead. Tinder crunched lightly beneath us as we walked hunched low to the ground. Michael waved for me to hide with him behind a thick pine tree. Roughly twenty yards ahead, in a small clearing, we watched two bearded men in red flannel shirts pushing a shirtless woman between them. She pleaded and cried for them to stop and they laughed and fondled her breasts and kissed her aggressively on the mouth. One of the men theatrically tossed her to the ground and in one savage tug yanked her shorts down over her knees and past her ankles until she lay on the wooded floor spread before them naked and crying and pleading while the men roared with laughter. I noticed these guys were twins, both, with tightly cropped shoe polish-black beards and red flannel shirts. Both wore extra-tight blue jeans and brown work boots. While she struggled before them, the two, in unison, ripped off their shirts revealing hairless and extremely muscular physiques. For a split second, in smug harmony, they flexed their bulging muscles before one of the twins knelt before the fallen girl and eagerly unzipped his pants. The other grabbed her hands and positioned himself near her head and he too peeled off his tight jeans. I noticed the girl settle comfortably between her captors and at that moment Michael bolted from the tree with his axe raised before him screaming in a high-pitched guttural shrill that could have come from an ancient Cheyenne or Arapaho, someone like that. I bolted behind him holding my club high in the air. My eyes locked on him as he pounced on the muscled man at the feet of the girl and got on top of him jamming and twisting his face forcefully into the ground. I took my club and walloped the other hulk, missing his head and connecting with his shoulder in a hard dull thump. He let out a long groan and the girl screamed, "What the fuck!" and three guys appeared out of nowhere holding cameras and sound equipment scowling and shouting things like, "You fuckin' idiots," and "Are you fucking nuts?" We all froze. For a moment we stood stupidly in a circle, in the warm sunlight, breathing heavily and eying each another. The twins slowly and painfully pulled up their tight jeans. One spit dirt from his mouth. The girl, still naked, walked up to Michael and said, "We're shooting a movie! A porno you idiot."

All was silently still at that moment. Birds sang a sweet shrilling melody.

Michael said, "Hell, we thought you were getting raped; that's what it looked like to us."

The twin with the bashed shoulder grimaced in pain. "That little fuck broke my shoulder. I need to see a doctor," and I could see that the right side of his collar sunk awkwardly lower than the other. He was pale and perspiring heavily. The blood had drained from his face and his eyes grew dark and I noticed he spoke with a sweet effeminate voice.

"Oh, baby," the girl said cradling his cheeks in her palms, "we'll get you back to the lodge and find a doctor. You're going to be okay, baby. Don't you worry; you're going to be just fine."

The other twin spoke in a low gruff voice completely opposite from the other. He stood towering before us with his dirty lips and his black beard. His sweat glistened in the sun, his chest and arm muscles were smooth granite pillars. He reminded me of one of those Greek or Roman statues, bone white porcelain-marble. He covered himself with his red-flannel and handed the naked girl's clothes to her.

"Suppose it looked mighty bad," he said finally. "You fuckers must have been pretty scared yourselves."

A willow-thin greasy-haired weasel of a guy popped out of the woods holding a camera. He turned out to be the director. He said they shoot low-budget porn movies on location. Said this one was called *The Lumberjacks of Yellowstone*. Said if the officials in the park knew what the hell was going on they'd all be arrested, so we had better keep our mouths shut. Said he'd have to figure out a story to tell the rangers about his friend's collarbone that was clearly busted.

We stood awkwardly for a couple of moments longer and then Michael and I and the film crew journeyed back to the lodge. The greasy haired director took the black bearded giant with the busted collarbone and the funny voice with him to one of the park workers. She looked like a high school girl working a summer job. She led them both into a room and they did not come out for a long time after that. The others sat with us in front of the big fireplace and blended in with the tourists rather nicely. The girl, who was getting it from both ends, was very pleasant and carried herself more like a schoolteacher or a cashier than a low-budget porn queen. Her name was Janet and she moved to California from Seattle. The lumberjacks were twins who came from Seattle too. They all grew up and went to high school together and performed in their high schools production of *Grease* and everyone told them they were top-notch talent. They thought they could ride that wave and move down to LA and make it big by getting into movies or commercials or something like that. That's when they met the greasy haired director at a dingy tequila bar on the outskirts of Los Angeles. He made them a financial deal they couldn't resist. He told them, "Everybody does these little movies to get some big bucks quickly, then they go on to bigger and better things like commercials or major movies. It's the way things are done around here. You'd be surprised how many movie stars started out this way. It's the way it's done. Think about it," he told them.

Old Faithful was gearing up to make another showing, so we parted ways with the porn crew and went out. The weather was nicer and the crowd was bigger and cameras clicked faster and camper's *ooohed* and *aaahed* and clapped and whistled in delight as the watery force surged before us in spectacular climax.

We stood next to two plump girls with bright eyes and round welcoming faces. Both wore their hair long and in braids. Their skin was light and creamy. Both were friendly and laughed often. One was named Ann, the other Donna. We found out they drove all the way from some little town in Connecticut to work here in the summer. Both loved the cool, dry, sweet air. Both went to Boston College. Both were in their second year and both had known each other since they were eight years old. They worked in an employee kitchen and told us if we were hungry they could get us some food if we wanted. We did and we walked with them to the back door of a big kitchen connected to a dining hall where the park employees ate. They went inside and came back shortly with a brown paper bag full of fried chicken and some oranges. We walked back to our camp where we all sat cross-legged in a circle while Michael and I devoured the chicken and shared a bunch of our stories. The two girls shared secret glances and giggled and sneakily smoked extra-long menthol cigarettes. As for the porn crew, I imagined they were heading back to California beat-up and broke and without much of a film career after all.

The chicken was juicy and crispy and salty and we ate every piece until there was nothing but a pile of bones. Our bellies were full and slightly rounded.

"That sure was good. I don't think I can eat again for another week," Michael said pulling a Marlboro from his pack and lighting it. The two girls stole a look at one another and giggled. Their smiles were wide and their faces bright, buttery and pink in the warm Wyoming sun.

"We'd better get going," one of them suggested suddenly. "We need to scoot along and prepare dinner or we'll get the boot."

The other thought that was a cute comment and chuckled fondly at her friend.

"Yes, we'd better scoot or we'll get the boot right in the butt," she squealed.

Full, rested and happy, we slowly wandered back to the Lodge and waited for Kevin and McShay to arrive. They showed about an hour later. Both walked toward us bent and beat as beggars on a long dusty road. Road weary, like a couple of real bums, skin dirty and brown, hair greasy, black dirt under their fingernails. They spotted us and looked relieved.

"We're starvin', been stuck in the desert without any rides eating nothing but bread," Kevin complained.

"Fuckin' brutal," McShay agreed and lit a cigarette with his filthy hands. "We sat on the side of the road somewhere in the middle of Nevada for a day and a half, and then we just crawled here. Not fun."

"How about you two?" Kevin asked. "Any luck getting rides?"

"I guess we must have lucked out. We moved pretty fast," I answered. "We've been here for a while."

My brother shot me an irritated look.

"Figures," he said. "Got any food?"

"Sure, some cans of spaghetti in our packs," I replied.

Michael glanced guiltily in my direction. I could feel the savory chicken resting in my belly.

Back at the camp, Michael pulled out a can of spaghetti with little meatballs. Kevin and McShay spooned the saucy pasta on a couple of slices of bread making a big sloppy sandwich out of it. We watched them quietly fill their cheeks and take swigs from their canteens. McShay kept a dry smile and a Marlboro lit throughout the ordeal. The two devoured the sandwiches and then we were off on a short hike into the hilly wilderness to see the random small geysers and then to the grand geyser, which lasted close to fifteen minutes. What a sight it was!

Later we played basketball with a few park workers at an outdoor court, and then watched *Butch Cassidy and the Sundance Kid* at the park amphitheatre. We sat on logs under a big starry sky smoking Marlboros and watching Newman and Redford smugly stealing their share of loot. All went pretty well until they got into Bolivia. They had a few problems there.

The four of us slept at our camp in the woods near the ranger station. A hard pelting rain woke us somewhere around four-thirty in the morning. I rushed to set up my tent. We threw our packs in and brought out some plastic and rain gear to cover ourselves. McShay swore revoltingly as the rain continued popping loudly on his plastic tarp. We sat silently and tiredly in the warm moist woods waiting for daylight. That was all there was to do. Wood was too wet to start a fire and the lodge was not open, so we waited. The rain continued to pour and when daylight finally came, we trudged through the wet grass and mud to the lodge, arriving with our clothes clung to us heavy and wet. We changed into dry clothes in the bathroom and then sat in front of the big fireplace waiting for the rain to stop. It finally did a couple of hours later and the day wore on in a light cool drizzle.

McShay and my brother announced they would be heading east to Boston to see some friends. McShay needed to get back earlier. He had a job of some sort. I think he worked with his brother cleaning up construction sites, something like that. Said they wanted to get out of the park and on the road before it got too late. We said our casual good-byes. We wished them both safe travels and luck with rides. See you back in old Buffalo. I told Kevin to tell our mother I'd see her right at the beginning of September. Just in time for school to start. It was going to be a big year. I was going to be a senior in high school.

After they left, Michael and I sat a bit longer at the lodge in front of the big fireplace tracing the Rand McNalley with our fingers, tracing the highways and settling on moving west. We needed to find George. We headed down the narrow road leading us out of the park. It was cloudy and sprinkling slightly when a big 1976 Chevy Titan camper pulled over and drove us out of the park.

Chapter 32

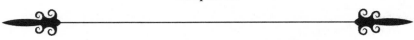

Boise

Boise is a city nestled in a vast wilderness that is called Idaho. Getting there from Yellowstone is a journey through black tarred roads, sun warmed open skies, lava rock plains, yellow wind-blown fields, brown dirt hills and slate-gray mountains. Giant pine trees stand erect and are scattered everywhere. You take Highway 20 most of the trip and head west through tiny brittle towns like Arco and Cary and Fairfield and Dixie until you push north onto a bigger highway and up into Boise. Boise: located along the Boise River and huddled against the foothills of the Rocky Mountains is a town filled with a tremendous variety of dense trees casting cool fresh shade on wide quiet streets.

When the big Titan pulled over back in Yellowstone, I figured a whole bunch would be inside, a big family with a gang of tired kids heading home from their annual trek to the state park. Instead, the door opened and an older man with white hair and a trimmed white beard waved us aboard. He was alone. Said his name was Arthur and he would take us on into Boise if we desired.

I pegged Arthur to be in his mid seventies. He wore crisp khaki pants and a powder-blue poplin shirt with sleeves rolled to his elbows. His shoes were dull brown leather tie-ups, classic. He wore a clean straw fedora with a blue and red band around it. He wore it well. Kind of what I would imagine a Cuban fisherman to look like except his skin gave off a soft powdery hue and his eyes were steel blue and I imagined a Cuban fisherman would look more like leather and coffee. Nevertheless, Arthur shared with us right away, in a smooth, calming voice, that he was seventy-six years old and married for fifty-one years to a wonderfully beautiful woman who had died only a week ago. She had been diagnosed three years earlier with a terminal cancer, a brain tumor and was given, by a number of doctors, three months to live, only to stubbornly outlast those predictions by a year and then another year and finally another until there was nothing left but the ashen skin and fragile bones of this precious woman fondly named Rose by her mother because, as he told it, when she was born in the big bedroom of her parents farmhouse on a stifling August afternoon, just as she was pushed into the firm expectant hands of the country doctor, her tiny sticky body bore a bright red glow and, at that precise moment, wafting from the open window, climbed a big full deep bed of red roses, whose sweet, rich, amorous, scent flowed abruptly into the nostrils of her mother and her husband and the country doctor and she was named at that moment without any further thought. She was to have been named Sarah, but the creamy scent, the sweetness, the freshness, the purity, intoxicated the worn out mother and, upon seeing the baby, Rose was the name that came from her lips.

The Titan was a smooth ride with big wide windshield offering us a great view of the open road. I sat in front, in the captain's chair, and watched as we cut through a small slice of Montana and back onto Highway 20 through the flowering meadows of Island Park and back toward Ashton where we left Diane and Suzie and Markey a few days earlier. Michael and Tasos Theotikos sat at a table directly behind Arthur. We continued to roll and bend through the wide country toward Idaho Falls where we caught US 20 and moved west. Arthur did not talk as much, he seemed content to have people with him. Said he'd been lonely since his wife died.

"I sat by her side for weeks," he said. "Got her one of those hospital beds and put it in our room. Had to take our bed down and I slept on the floor next to her on a pad in a sleeping bag. She didn't want to die in a hospital and I wasn't going to let her. Anyway, she just wilted, got worse and worse and faded into nothing. That cancer ate her up good. It does some awful things to the body, I can tell you that. I've never seen anybody expire as pitiful as Rose did."

Tasos Theotikos nudged his son and Michael gave him a gentle look in return.

"So, what are you doing now?" he asked.

"We bought this motor home a few months back. Figured we'd use it and take a long trip and go everywhere we wanted to, just live in it and see the country. Rose was up for it. She was feeling pretty good. We both thought maybe the doctors didn't quite have it right. Maybe it was a miracle or something. Maybe we could pull it off. Who knows?"

Michael held up a Marlboro and Arthur nodded. After a snap from a blue tip match, the dry scent of cigarette smoke filled the motor home.

"You going to take the trip?" he asked.

"That's hard to say. I'm not too sure anymore," Arthur said tightening his grip on the big steering wheel. "I took this monster up to Yellowstone just to get a feel for her. She's smooth, glides real nice. I didn't think I'd be able to handle her, but she maneuvers pretty well, kind of like a heavy car."

"It does ride nice," Michael said.

"Yellowstone was our test. We were going to work the kinks out and live on her as long as we wanted. Didn't matter, that was our plan, our dream. Rose didn't make it, but I did. Now I got this big rig; I'm retired and hell, I don't have much else to do."

Michael scooted himself up and plunked down on the edge of my seat. I slid over to give him a little room. *Tasos Theotikos stood behind him, resting his hand gently on his son's shoulder.* Michael spoke excitedly.

"I think you should take the trip. I mean it'll be a blast for you. You won't be stuck in one place thinking too long and making yourself sad. You can't stay in one spot. And when you're feeling low, you'll be on the open road heading somewhere. You'll have a destination, somewhere to go; it occupies your mind. Wouldn't she like that for you?"

"I imagine she would," he said.

"Being on the road gives you a purpose. It forces you to move from one place to the next. It gives you a reason for getting up. I'm thinking a little purpose is something you need at a time like this."

Arthur pondered this as he glided the big Titan effortlessly along Highway 20. We pulled over at Craters of the Moon National Monument and Arthur made us ham sandwiches with Swiss cheese. The ham was paper thin and the bread was fresh and chewy. He pulled out three lounge chairs from the back of the big camper and we ate the sandwiches and sat amongst the hard, ancient, blackened lava. Craters of the Moon was a strange and eerie place. Millions of years ago a bunch of volcanoes erupted and left the place a never-ending hilly lava field. Now it's a tourist stop. I could see why. It was awesome. We ate the sandwiches and gazed at Inferno Cone, a huge bare lava mound silhouetted sharply by a big bright blue Western sky.

"I believe when I get back to Boise I'll pack this rig up and head east to Maine, Bar Harbor, maybe. Never been up there and I'd really like to go. Go on a whale watch, eat lots of lobster and oysters and drink plenty of beer. That sounds good to me."

"Alone?" Michael asked.

"With Rose; she's with me. She's always with me," Arthur replied tapping his fist on his chest. I may find someone, a companion for a time along the way. I don't mind, but Rose, well, she stays with me."

Arthur had made up his mind. He sat contently in his lounge chair looking up at the dark, smooth mound of Inferno Cone. He ate his sandwich slowly and drank an ice cold Pepsi out of the bottle. Michael and I hiked to the top of Inferno Cone and stood in a sagebrush garden growing stubbornly out from the black dirt. From atop we could see without end in every direction, the black earth, the green hills and the snow-peaked mountains far in the distance.

We hopped back into the Titan and took Highway 20 to Mountain Home and then up Highway 84 and on into Boise. It was going to get dark shortly. Arthur proved to be hospitable fellow and offered to let us stay in the Titan for the night.

"There's plenty of room. You boys can pull out the beds and sleep. It won't do you any good to move on in the dark. I can cook up some dinner and we can have a party," he offered.

That sounded fine to us. We arrived in Boise at dusk. It is a city filled with trees. Arthur drove into the center of the city and gave us a tour. He cruised past the round sandstone Capitol Building poised in the center of town. Told us the sandstone came from a quarry just east of Boise. "They used inmates from the state penitentiary to cut and haul the stone, tough work." The Capitol had a fine dome sitting atop enormous pillars with a giant sandstone eagle perched at the peak. We drove north another ten minutes or so and into a neighborhood called Hyde Park. Nice place, historic and quaint with lots of trees. All kinds: mountain alders, river birch, sugar maples and the mammoth black cottonwood and English and red oaks. There were more. Arthur told us more than in most places. Arthur turned down 15th Street and glided the Titan into the driveway of a small red-brick house with a well manicured lawn. Had a good sized white ash tree in the middle of his lawn and a big silvery-blue Colorado spruce to the right. It climbed high in the sky.

Arthur turned the key and the engine coughed, shuttered and shut down. "Home," he announced letting out a long sigh. "Why don't we go in, get cleaned up and have a bite and a couple of cold ones. Sound good?"

"Sounds great," I said.

"Yes," Michael said.

For a small house, Arthur had a good sized kitchen where it looked like he and Rose spent most of their time. A big worn-wooden table butted against the wall. An oak bookcase stood in the corner filled with cook books and books about birds and flowers and trees. Arthur opened the refrigerator and pulled out three cans of PBR's.

"How are these?" he asked.

"Great, love 'em," we agreed.

"I have some cheese and bread," he said. "I could grill the cheese with tomato and bacon. It's a good sandwich."

"Sounds fine," Michael said popping a cold PBR and lighting a cigarette.

Arthur pulled the stuff out from the fridge and placed it on the table. He cooked the bacon in a cast iron skillet. Once the bacon was crisp, he made the sandwiches by placing the cheese and the tomato and the bacon together and spreading butter on both sides of the bread. He melted butter in another skillet and placed three sandwiches in over a low flame until the bread was crisp and golden brown. He flipped the sandwiches with a spatula and let them cook for a minute or two more; then, he placed the sandwiches on a cutting board, cut them in half and brought them to the table. They were good. He used Monterey jack and sharp cheddar cheeses.

Michael devoured his sandwich while Arthur chewed each bite slowly. He spoke carefully and thoughtfully and contemplated loneliness.

"Life is good," Arthur said pausing and reflecting on his point, "and life is challenging. It gives and it takes away. Life has given me many wonderful experiences and I'm fortunate because, for me, life has been comfortable. I'm a veterinarian you know, retired now, but I was at it close to fifty years. That's how I met Rose. I worked out of an office just a few blocks from here. It was my own place. After I got out of school, my father fronted me some money and I opened up a little place and it just got busier and busier. I worked on all kinds of animals, you name it and I've treated them one way or another. The office was getting too busy and difficult to run on my own so I put an ad in the paper looking for a receptionist, someone to help manage the office. Rose was the first to answer the ad. She was fresh out of college, had a degree in Business, and was looking for something to hold her over until she figured out what she was going to do. I loved her the moment she walked into the office. She was a pretty girl with a willowy figure and I was drawn to her handsome face and her bright kind eyes. Rose had a wide friendly smile and pretty teeth. She started off as a receptionist, taking phone calls, managing appointments, and then she helped more and more with the animals by giving the anesthesia, helping with suturing, stuff like that. I taught her all I knew and she read all of my school books and pretty soon she knew and understood all about being a good veterinarian. Rose was determined. She said, "Look, I've got all this knowledge, I just need to get a degree, get the paper to prove it," and that's what Rose did. All the while she managed the office, she took day classes and night classes for a couple of years and she got herself that degree and we became partners and ran a very large and very successful veterinarian business."

Arthur took a bite of his sandwich. It got stuck a little in his throat and he washed it down with some difficulty with the PBR. His eyes glistened and his lower lip quivered slightly. "Boys, you think it's going to last forever. Years and years of routine and you think nothing can touch it. I mean you know it's inevitable that it will end, but you just don't let your mind take you there until you're sitting right in the thick of it. Rose is gone. She's dead. I'm alone and she's dead. That's what I know now. She was here with me and now she's not. I've got the Titan and a whole great big country before me. She's gone and I'm alone and that's the whole reality of it. I'm going to get through it. I have to, but I just have to figure out how."

"Like I said earlier, that Titan is your key," Michael said. "That's what'll take you where you need to be. Look, you need to get a big road atlas, a Rand McNalley and you gotta open up to the page where the whole country is spread out. Look at the highways and the roads and the states and imagine going to 'em all. The map is magical."

Arthur took another slug from his can. "You have a lot of insight for a young guy and you've got a lot of enthusiasm. I admire that. You've got a good head on you."

"It's what I know," Michael said.

"What about you? What are your plans? What's this life got going for you?" Arthur asked.

"I don't really have plans," Michael said. "Not now. Today I'm enjoying the luxury of doing nothing, just moving forward from one place to the next, seeing what I can see and experiencing all the cool things there are on the road. That's all I really need right now."

"Ahh, *far niente*," Arthur said. "Pleasant idleness, it's an Italian word that roughly means the art of doing nothing. It's an admirable trait."

"It's simple," I agreed. "There's no need to take it too much further. Since we've been on the road I guess we're looking at things differently. I mean, this is such a blast, so for now it's okay to just enjoy what we're doing. There'll always be something out there for us. We'll just wait and see."

"A good plan, boys; I admire that." And that's about all Arthur had in him. He was tired from the drive and tired about wondering what lay before him. He finished his beer and we helped him clean the dishes and he offered to let us sleep in a spare bedroom with a big soft bed and we took him up on that offer.

Chapter 33

San Francisco

We woke early to the smell of Arthur preparing breakfast. Pancakes, sausage, eggs scrambled with orange juice and coffee. Pure heaven! He packed us each a peanut butter and banana sandwich and wrapped them in tin foil. He packed apples and pears too. Arthur took us to I-84, gave us twenty bucks and told us to watch out for all the lunatics in this God-forsaken world. Michael assured him we would.

Boise to San Francisco is roughly six-hundred and twenty-five miles and takes approximately eleven and a half hours to get there. Depends whose driving, I guess. Coming from Boise, the road glides and twists through wide and exposed land with brown-green hills, open fields, meadows, and clear soft blue-white skies. In some stretches the vastness of the land is limitless. On this morning the sky was clear topaz. The clouds were big and white, tinged in silver light.

While leaning against the guardrail at the entrance ramp, I made a tattered cardboard sign and held it up. It read *San Francisco*. Traffic was heavy. A steady line of cars and trucks passed. Some honked. Some waved. None stopped. Two hours went by. No luck. Michael didn't mind. He took this lull without disappointment. He was all hopped up about going to San Francisco.

"It's where all the wild stuff happened," he said. "Haight and Ashbury, all those whacked-out hippies doing whatever they wanted. I read about Golden Gate Park, about how all these crazy kids hitch-hiked from all over the country and met in the park and once they got there they camped all over the grass in sleeping bags and pup-tents and smoked pot and listened to all kinds of wild music and had sex with everyone and hung out like it was one big eternal party, which it was. They took over that park."

"What's there now?" I asked.

"I guess it's a park without all the hippies," he said. "My buddy Johnny's older brother, Jerry, you remember him, back in '67 when he was about seventeen he hitched out there right during all the shit, the Summer of Love, but it all got too nuts and they started going crazy and all the peace and love shit turned into kids just coming and stinking the place up begging for money and bothering everyone around the city."

"A lotta crime," I said.

"Yeah, a lotta crime. The politicians and the cops weren't going to deal with that for too long. It got old real quick and just ended. I bet it was pretty cool, though, at the beginning."

"I remember Jerry," I said. "He lost his mind out there that summer."

"Right," Michael said. "He hitched back to Buffalo after a bad acid trip and hasn't been right since. I think he still lives at home. I see him sometimes at the park playing pick-up basketball and eating tiger milk candy bars. He's pretty out there."

We took a bunch of short rides and inched toward Reno. Our longest came from a little old German man with a thick accent, fleshy jowls and a bald head. His countenance was perpetually miserable, but his eyes were bright and cheerful and he told good stories and was glad to have company. Said his name was Herbert Gutman. He wore a canary yellow polo shirt with white etching around the pocket. White slacks. A pack of Lucky Strikes in his pocket. Drove a plain brown Dodge of some kind. A black-balled compass attached itself to his dashboard.

"I have been driving since Chicago. For a couple of days now," he said with a guttural growl. "I stop when I want. I'm in no hurry. I'm going to the San Francisco Fairmont from the Drake. They're hotels. I'm going to work in San Francisco now. I was in Chicago, a great town."

"Are you German?" Michael asked.

"Ja, born there, but moved to Argentina during the War. Buenos Aires, with my sister. We escaped Hitler. She's still in Chicago. She won't go anywhere else. It's a good town. I guess she's all set there for now," he said.

He sat low in his seat and drove with both hands on the steering wheel. Never went a mile over sixty. He drove slow, straight and methodical, took us forward a few hours almost into Reno, never passed one car, kept the radio off. Spoke with a crunchy throaty voice. When he laughed his shoulders rose and his head sank and his eyes got shiny and teary and from deep in his gut he emitted a low raspy growl. I never heard anything like it. Michael encouraged him to tell stories so he could get him to laugh. He smoked Lucky Strike non-filters. He kept his cigarette hanging precariously on the left side of his bottom lip. Sometimes the ash would grow long and fall on his shirt, "Aah, shit," he would say brushing the ashes off.

We learned he worked in New Orleans before Chicago. Mostly in hotel restaurants, had a sister, liked to grow flowers, thought Kennedy was the greatest president and Nixon was the smartest. "But Nixon was a sneak and paranoid and couldn't run the country." Told us he liked to drink Budweiser out of a big wine glass. Told us he liked fresh green beans and he especially liked steak. Told us: "I remember nineteen sixty-one, no, nineteen sixty-two, Argentina. I got pyria. My mouth schtunk. I told the doctor pull all my teeth. He was going to give me a shot and I told him no Novocain. He pulled all my teeth, blood everywhere. I rinsed my mouth with salt-water and got up to leave. He told me no schteak for a week. You know what I ate that night? Schteak!" …and his head sank and his eyes glistened and he looked in our direction and let out that low rasping throaty laugh. I swear it sounded like a lawnmower starting up, something like that.

Herbert drove us as far as the outskirts of Reno on that hot clear afternoon. "I've had enough driving for one day," he said in a tired voice. He pulled the brown Dodge off the exit ramp letting us off at the end.

"You two take care," he said and he drove slowly off. I watched him disappear into the Reno traffic. In the rear window of his car were two little figures of brown dogs, their heads bobbing slowly up, down and side-to-side.

We decided to skip Reno and move forward toward San Francisco, hopefully get a ride right through. Maybe make it in three or four hours.

We perched ourselves on the entrance ramp taking in the endless dark green patches of pine trees spread out in the sprawling Sierra Nevada mountain range. The sun was high. The afternoon was bright and dry. I held the San Francisco sign up, my arm straight out, emphasizing the urgency that we needed a ride. Michael broke out the banana and peanut butter sandwiches.

"I'm starvin'," he said leaning against the guardrail wolfing the sandwich down. "This is good; he put honey in it too!"

We sat another two hours, juggling, reading the Rand McNalley, tracing with our fingers our journey and ready to just call it quits and head into Reno until Brodie Wilson pulled over in a flashy red El Camino with hot-rod tires and gave us a lift into San Francisco.

Brodie: sixty-five years old, youthful, thick head of shiny black hair carefully combed like Elvis. Wore a sleeveless white t-shirt, a big silver cross hung from his neck, tight blue jeans and a massive pair of mirrored silver sunglasses shielded his eyes.

"Throw them packs in the back and grab a couple of pops from the cooler," he said.

In the back an old green and white Coleman cooler held some much needed ice cold Budweiser's. I grabbed three and slid onto a vinyl benched seat next to Brodie.

"Nice to meetcha," he said popping open his Bud. "We'll be in San Fran in about three and a half hours unless all hell breaks loose, and if it does, fuck it, I've got a full cooler of Buds, so I'm a happy fuckin' camper."

Brodie, from Payson, Arizona. "Smack-ass flat in the center of Arizona," he said proudly. "You boys know anything about Payson?"

"We don't," Michael answered.

"Nobody really does," he said, "but, I'll tell ya, it's a pretty fuckin' alright place. Known for two things: bootleggin' and rodeos. Best rodeos in the world right in Payson. Ranchers, cowboys and town folks been having wild times up in that rugged mountain town for over a hundred years and that's a fact. Every August they come and rodeo and gamble and fight and drink and pretty much go wild for three days straight. And before that it was Apache land. A whole bunch of crazy shit happened up there, I'm telling you."

Brodie's words spewed fast and high and lyrical. Unlike Herbert crawling down the highway, Brodie drove fast and frantic, holding onto the left lane, whizzing past anything in his way. He had to pass any car in front of him, he just did.

Michael lit a Marlboro. He let his arm rest on the door. Wind whipped through his hair. The road was flat and rugged. Foothills stretched in the distance. Brodie told us the stories of his wives.

"My first wife was stabbed by a Mexican bitch; she jammed the knife in her gut and twisted until she was dead. Stabbed her over my kid's lunch money. The bitch tried to take my kid's lunch money on the playground before school and my wife, who had a hell of a temper, told her to get her own god-dammed money and the bitch stabbed her. Got three years in prison and then got paroled. Nobody saw it except my kid and she was so fuckin' scared she clammed up to the police and she clammed up in court so that court appointed bastard lawyer got the Mexican bitch off. My second wife gave up drinking for eighteen years then went off the wagon. Got in her car and drove into a telephone pole, killed her instantly. My third wife, she's a fucking bitch, we're in court now; she's trying to take everything I have. That's not going to happen. I ain't got much, just this El Camino, a couple of bucks saved up and a little place in the city, and she's not gettin' any of it."

"Where's your kid now?" Michael asked.

"She's in Frisco. Got through the shit pretty good. Ended up being a lawyer herself, married one too, but she doesn't protect these scumbags, she puts 'em in jail. She turned out to be a pretty tough girl."

Then Brodie told us about the Rolling Stones concert at the Altamont Speedway. "I went to the Monterey Pop Festival; I went to Altamont too. At Altamont the Stones arrived in a helicopter and I smoked two joints with Charlie Watts in his trailer, just me and him. He's the most intelligent fucking guy I've ever met, nice too. That concert turned out to be pretty fucked-up. Lots of Hell's Angles pushing people around. Between them and all the booze and drugs, it got real ugly. I was with my second wife and I said let's get the fuck outta here. We didn't even see the end of the show. It was no Woodstock, that's for sure."

It was evening when the El Camino rolled into the city. The air was cool. The streets were lively. We drove in the darkness to a narrow street with rows of apartments. Most of the buildings were two and three floor white wooden structures with a few brown-sandstone buildings here and there. Brodie lived on the third floor of a white walk-up. His apartment was small with a big window that overlooked the street. I looked out from the window and down at a corner store with a red and white neon sign that said *Toby's Grocery*. A steady stream of customers strolled in and out. Two men in jeans and tight pocket t-shirts shared a cigarette under the sign. Brodie offered to let us sleep on the floor in his living room. We figured there wasn't any better place to go so we stayed. For such a brash guy, the place was decorated in soft pink and light blue hues. He had a bunch of big exotic plants and most of his furniture was wicker. A big round white rug covered shiny hardwood floors. He was quite neat.

Brodie told us to get ourselves comfortable. "It's not a big place, but it'll do," he said. He went into the kitchen and came back with three ham and cheese sandwiches, a bag of chips and three cans of Budweiser.

"Have a little bite boys," he said. "I'm starving."

We ate the sandwiches. Brodie threw the chips on his sandwich and devoured it in a couple of bites. He slugged his beer and announced that he needed to get some sleep.

"I'm beat; you all make yourselves at home," he said and disappeared into his bedroom.

There wasn't much left to do. It was getting late and we were pretty beat as well. Michael and I sat in the living room and smoked, looking out the window at the street below. The neon sign lit the corner and a steady stream of people continued to enter and exit the store.

"Do you think about George?" I asked Michael. "Do you think we'll find him?"

"I do," Michael said. "I think we'll find him. I don't know what I'm going to tell him exactly when I do, but I have a strong feeling we'll run into him."

"We're getting close; Seattle's not too far off. He may not want to see you," I said.

"That's tough shit," Michael said. "He's going to see me. I didn't come this far for nothing."

The next morning the sun slanted into the apartment onto the floor waking the two of us from a refreshing sleep. Brodie sat in his kitchen at a yellow linoleum table reading The Chronicle and sipping from a big wide mug of coffee. His hair was combed in that fifties hard guy style and I noticed it was dyed a deep-glossy black. He looked up at us as we sleepily walked in.

"Hungry?" he said pouring coffee into two mugs and pushing them toward us. "Got milk and sugar if you want it."

"I could eat," said Michael.

"Me too," I replied.

"Help yourselves. I got this really good bread at the bakery this morning," Brodie said. "They fuckin' bake it at like 5:30 in the morning and by 6:30 it's pretty much gone, so I get my ass out of bed and get a loaf. Good stuff, ten grains, really healthy."

Brodie toasted the bread and put a slice of cheddar cheese on it. "Try this. It'll push all the shit out of you. Keep you nice and clean."

I had to admit, it was pretty good and the cheese made it even better. The coffee was thick and rich and strong and I realized Brodie was quite the food connoisseur. No Wonder Bread and Maxwell House for him.

We sat at the table and bantered over who would have a better season this year, the Bills or the 49ers. Brodie thought about it and said, "The 49ers basically suck; they're at the bottom of the standings, but they got your boy OJ Simpson over the summer, so maybe they'll get a little better, but then again, he's coming of that knee surgery so there's a good chance he'll suck too. Now the Bills, they suck as well, only winning three games last year and OJ gone and all. But maybe there's a little hope with your new coach Chuck Knox leaving the Rams and your new quarterback Ferguson. We'll see what he can do. It's gonna be tough though, your defense sucks royally."

Michael lit a Marlboro and sipped his coffee from the big mug.

"They're both crappy," he said. "Not much good is gonna happen for either team, not this year. Pittsburgh, The Pats and Miami, one of them will get to the Super bowl and probably play Dallas or maybe the Vikings or the Rams. That's my guess."

"It's Pittsburgh for sure," Brodie figured.

I listened to their conversation with half an ear and read an article in the Chronicle about bottled water being introduced to the Americans. The article said a few things about the industry in general and Perrier in particular and the writer didn't think it would fly here. At least people would not buy it in large quantities. The soft drink industry figured sales of bottled water by Perrier and others would never make an impact on sales of more traditional soda in America.

"Look," Brodie said getting up from the table and rinsing his coffee mug in the sink, "I gotta go to work. You can hang here for a day or two if you want. I got nothing going on and if you don't mind the floor, I don't give a shit if you stay. I gotta work, but if you want to hang out and see the city, it's okay with me."

"Thanks, okay, that's cool," Michael replied. "I'd like to check out San Francisco."

"Might as well while you're here. I'll be back around six or so if you want to do something," and he was off and so were we.

We spent the day crisscrossing streets, hopping trolleys, and hitting the touristy spots like Lombard Street with its red brick and hairpin turns, fancy houses and lush landscapes.

We ambled down Castro Street. Past places like *The Castro Bean Coffee Shop*, *Andy's Donuts*, and *Dino's Liquors* where an angry woman with bright orange hair, wild-pink lipstick and big black sunglasses screamed at a little man with a bald head and a bushy mustache, "You ever call me that again, you fucker, I'll kill you dead!" she yelled.

We passed *The Badlands Restaurant* and *The Corner Grocery Bar* where they played classical music and had a deli bar. Some of the places that attracted the gays included *Castro Rock Steam Baths*, a cruise bar called *The Midnight Sun*, *The Naked Grape*, a leather lesbian bar called *Scott's Pit* and a bar called *Nothing Special* that opened and started slinging drinks to an eager crowd at six in the morning. Bars and restaurants with funny names like *The Neon Chicken* and the *Purple Pickle* and the *Sausage Factory* were pouring drinks for their first customers of the day. We wandered past all of these places on a crisp, bright sunny morning watching men and boys in short shorts and tight jeans and leather pants and leather vests holding hands with one another as if it were the most natural thing in the world.

Michael insisted we go to The Haight, or better yet the corner of Haight and Ashbury. Haight Street was crowded and wide and long. We wandered past record stores and book stores and thrift shops and bars and restaurants. Drop-outs, bums, careless youths, all hung on corners aggressively accosting anyone who walked near them for spare change. Some lay sprawled in filthy doorways smoking rolled tobacco and drinking from glass bottles filled with brown booze. As wacky as Castro was, The Haight was grittier, seedier, more unpredictable and dangerous. The neighborhood seemed to have somehow lost all of that love we had read and heard about.

The smooth echo of chords flowing from an acoustic guitar drifted from the corner of Haight and Ashbury where a shoeless, tiny dark skinned girl in a tattered white dress sang to a small crowd gathered before her. She crooned a velvety rendition of *You ain't nothing but a Hound Dog* gentle and fluid like liquid honey. Before her lay a wooden crate filled with audio tapes wrapped in brown paper lunch bags with drawings of stick people saying little messages like, "Sing to the Sky" and "The Streets Breathe, Do You?" all written with different colored crayons. We joined the crowd. Michael lit a Marlboro and the tiny girl belted out a few more tunes, jazzy melodic complicated songs. Stuff like Gershwin and Cole Porter's, *Someone to Watch Over Me* and *You'd Be So Nice to Come Home To.* She sang Elton John's *Tiny Dancer* and Simon and Garfunkel's *Homeward Bound.* Then she attacked her guitar blasting chords and screaming long chants about war and hunger and death and politicians who don't give a shit about you or me, only corporations and greed and stuff like that. It was a remarkable transformation. We watched in awe.

The tiny girl belted out one last tune and put her guitar down. The crowd politely clapped; a few tossed money into her case. Delicately, she scooped the bills and the coins and, without counting, put them into a beaded leather pouch dangling from a long leather strap tied around her waist.

Michael approached her with a smile and a handshake. "Where're you heading?" he asked.

"Not really your business, but if you need to know, I'm catching some lifts and going to the Wharf to sing some more. Good money there. Whole lotta of tourists."

"You're really good," he said. "Really amazing."

The girl looked past Michael and gazed at me through small dark eyes. "How 'bout you? What do you think?"

"Awesome," I said.

"Awesome?" she repeated. "That's a funny response."

She gazed at us intently, calmly, seemingly looking deep into our soul, trying to understand something through some sort of primal telepathy. I stood awkwardly before her. Michael pushed his hair from his forehead and had nothing to say either until finally, "I like the Gershwin and the Cole Porter stuff. You don't hear much of that around, especially on street corners."

"What about the other stuff? The stuff I write," she asked.

"I like that too," he said looking back into the tiny girl's eyes.

"Which do you like better?" she asked patiently.

"You know, I know Cole Porter and Gershwin, so it's familiar, but I liked your stuff a lot. It's real and fresh," he said.

"Good answer," she smiled. "You want to come to the Wharf?"

"Sure!" we said.

She slung her guitar over her shoulder and we walked along the busy streets and hopped a trolley that took us to *Fisherman's Wharf*.

"My name's Kristen," she said. "The Wharf really sucks. It's an awful place. The food is terrible and it's over crowded, but you can see Alcatraz on the rocks in the distance. That sure was a fucked place to be. You have to be a real bad-ass to end up on the Rock. No way to get out.

266

Those waters are icy cold and rough. I'd rather be in any prison except that one."

The real money was at the Wharf. The crowds were bigger. Tourists filled the battered guitar case with a bunch of crisp bills and shiny coins. Her tapes sold and Instamatics clicked rapidly as she hammed it up and posed. She certainly was a show girl.

After singing for the tourists, her tapes were gone and her pouch was full. "Not a bad day." she said, "And still early!" Kristen sat on the sidewalk and pulled a pair of sandals from her crate. Putting them on she announced, "I'm starvin'; you boys want to join me for a bite?"

We ended up in a small grungy diner on a quiet side street. The smells of onion and bacon and coffee filled the room. A skinny hippie waitress in a long billowy dress and long hair under her armpits took our order. Michael and I went for scrambled eggs and bacon on rye toast with ketchup. Kristen ate a poached egg on wheat toast and drank a crisp beer in a tall pilsner glass. She added a little tomato juice to the beer. It looked washed-out red. We drank a couple of beers too and the tomato juice was a nice touch, kind of mellowed it out and gave it an interesting flavor. I thought of Denver and figured it must be a Western thing. The waitress returned with four shots of bourbon and the four of us toasted to all the fuck-ups in the world and slammed them down. The little singer-guitar player didn't wince a bit when it went down. Her eyes remained steadily focused on us.

"Now that's a breakfast that'll get you going," she said. "What do you want to do now?"

"City Lights," I answered quickly. "I want to go to City Lights Book Store."

"We can do that, but I need to take my guitar and crate home," she said. "I don't live too far from here. Do you want to walk with me?"

After walking about twenty minutes, we ended up on a side street with rows of white houses. It was similar to Brodie's street. Kristen also lived on the third floor, but down a narrow hallway at the back of the house. We went inside. Her apartment was tiny. A dark slender boy lounged in a big reclining chair in the living room eating corn flakes, smoking a cigarette, and watching *Let's Make a Deal*. He sat cross-legged and shirtless wearing silk pajama bottoms. Thick black eyeliner surrounded big, soft, delicate coffee-brown eyes. The television blared. Monty Hall offered a woman in a clown suit one hundred dollars if she had a ball. She rummaged feverishly in her purse searching for any kind of ball and found nothing, and then she announced, in a piercing squawk, that she had an eye ball. Monty and his sidekicks, the ever-loving Jay Stewart and Carol Merrill and the audience were buckled over roaring in laughter. Monty gave her two hundred dollars for being so clever. It was a special *Let's Make a Deal* moment. The boy eating the cornflakes looked up at us and didn't say anything. He wasn't impressed.

"That's my brother," Kristen said. "He won't talk much."

He had the same gentle round face and soft brown eyes as his sister. There wasn't much response from him so we muttered an obligatory, "Hey." Without answering, he nodded and spooned another mouthful of cornflakes.

The three of us walked out of the apartment, down the stairs and onto the street. Clouds had rolled into the city. The air was cool and gave off a scent of wet slate. It began to sprinkle lightly.

"City Lights isn't too far from here," she said. "It's down on Columbus Avenue about a fifteen minute walk."

Kristen changed out of the white dress and into tight orange jeans with a black t-shirt and white Converse sneakers. She let go of her free-form hippie look and opted for seedy street punk attire. Her hair was black and shiny and cut into a pixie. Her face was delicate, round and smooth with black fresh eyes. She was petite, built muscular and strong. She walked rapidly with determination and purpose. She talked non-stop.

Michael and I walked quickly managing to stay about a half-step behind her. I felt as if I were running to catch a bus leaving the stop without me. Michael tilted toward her and asked how long she had been playing guitar.

"I don't know," she said. "Time is too funny for me. I mean, I don't think much about it. Of course that sounds probably absolutely crazy, but I can't remember just precisely *how long* I've been singing and writing an playing the guitar, maybe always."

"You must be able to place a *time* when you began, at least approximately," Michael said. "How old you were when you began?"

Kristen contemplated briefly, "You'd think that would be easy," she said. "You'd think I'd be able to answer that flat out, but it doesn't work for me. Time doesn't matter."

She stopped suddenly and we huddled in the middle of the sidewalk on Columbus Avenue. Anyone walking down the street had to move around us. It felt good to catch my breath.

"See *time* doesn't matter for me, she said. "I know it does for some, for many, for most, but it never got hold of me. The way I see it most everyone I know lives this life doing the same thing. We're born and we die. We eat and drink and fart and fuck and fight and love and laugh and cry and hope and dream and we find work and etch out our lives and some of us are happy and some of us are sad and miserable and some of us are fulfilled and some of us are lonely and depressed and most of us hook up with someone and have kids and they're born and they do the same thing and then they die and more are born and more die and it keeps going on and on just like that."

"Well okay, but, time gives us reassurance and safety and it helps us to know when something good will happen like maybe something special that you've planned for in the future," Michael said.

"If you're talking about mechanical time, then that's exactly what I'm saying is not for me," Kristen said. "See, setting a limit on something or forcing someone to be somewhere at a certain time is too restrictive. Mechanical time squashes emotions like happiness. You have to put happiness or feeling good into a compartment or a spot. You can be doing something that makes you very happy and then you look at your watch or a clock somewhere on a city street and you know you have to stop because you have to be somewhere else or you have an appointment or you have to cook dinner or whatever, it makes no sense to me. It's really a wild scene and I don't need a schedule or a clock to tell me when I need to do any of that."

"We all need some type of schedule," Michael responded. "Time keeps us focused."

"Focused?" Kristen said peering straight into Michael's eyes like an attorney toying with a confused witness. "Focused on what? What type of schedule are you on? Where do you have to be right now? Here we are on Columbus Avenue in San Francisco. It's a beautiful day and I'm happy right now to be hanging with you two guys. Which way do you have to turn? Where do you have to go right now? It's about three in the afternoon; what does your schedule tell you to get done right now?"

I watched Michael tilt his head slightly and look back at me. He shook his hair back off his forehead. I saw in his eyes that he admired this free-spirited fire cracker and if she believed that time or schedules did not fit into her world, then so be it! I knew he could have continued this discussion and kept it going and he could have explained that we are all affected by time because it is absolute and takes hold of us all in one way or another. He would explain aging and wrinkles and baldness and sex and seasons and the circle of life or birth and death and how time connects us with past, present and future. He would explain logically the importance of the constant movement of seconds and minutes and hours and days and weeks and years and how it is rooted in all of us. Instead, he paused and simply said, "My schedule tells me we need to get a beer, right now" And he gazed at me and said, "What about you, Jimmy? What does time say of you?"

"I'm feeling parched," I said. "A beer fits nicely into my schedule."

Kristen giggled, "Now you're talkin,'" and in an instant we were off the street and standing in a dark sour smelling bar with low ceilings and a dirty floor. Towering behind a row of beer taps stood an enormous cross-eyed blonde woman with a filthy bar towel resting on her shoulder.

"What'll it be?" she barked.

A moment later she opened three cans of Budweiser and three shots of Old Grand-Dad Whiskey. The bartender went by the name Cross-eyed Heidi, a monster of a girl with massive shoulders and dark eyes that crisscrossed over the bridge of her nose giving the appearance of one who did not put up with any shit from anyone. Long, tight blonde braids hung on both sides of her wide face and flat forehead. She could have been one of those big German broads slinging armfuls of beer to drunken tourists at the Hofbräuhaus in Munich.

At the end of the bar sat an old crusty dude with a flakey scalp and uncombed white hair. He was connected to an oxygen machine smoking cigarettes, taking long, deep swallows of beer and throwing back shots of some cheap brown swill.

A guy everyone called Kenny no-arms – he only had tiny hands sprouting from his shoulders - wandered from person to person telling Henny Youngman one liners: *A bum asked me, "Give me $10 till payday?" I asked, "When's payday?" He said, "I don't know, you're the one who is working."* He'd lean into anyone in his sight and throw the joke and tilt his head back in a knee slapping guffaw. He was an irritating bastard. No one laughed much at his jokes. I figured he'd been knockin' around this place many times before. He seemed like a regular pain in the ass. Kenny no-arms gripped his Budweiser tightly with his baby hand raising his shoulder and sucking at the bottle. He had it down. It looked like he'd been doing it for years.

"You see," Kristen continued, "the main thing I want out of life, right now, is to be able to play my music and sing my songs. I'm not afraid to say it; I want to be famous like Janis Joplin or Patty Smith. I really don't care about anything except playing my guitar and writing songs and singing; that's all I want to do. Only problem is that all the music that's popular and sells is either bad disco or arena rock nonsense or fuckin' elevator music or there's the underground punk scene here in San Francisco, Dead Kennedys and stuff, but it's not my bag. I mean, I like what they say, but that three chord pounding is all crap and the kids who go to those shows are all lug-heads."

Kristen talked about combining Gershwin with Dylan, "That's what I'm talking about," she said and we ordered three more Buds and three more shots. Kenny no-arms wandered over to us, "You got a quarter for the juke?"

"Scram, Kenny," Cross-eyed Heidi warned, shooing him away. "Leave 'em alone."

"I ain't botherin' no one; I just want to hop this dump up with a little music," he said.

"Put your own damn quarter in the juke," Cross-eyed Heidi said looking in our direction. "He can be a real pain in the ass."

A skinny auto mechanic with long black hair and oil stained hands wearing a Texaco shirt chimed in, "I call Kenny PITA 'cuz that's what he is a god-dammed pain in the ass. Ain't that right Kenny?"

"Look who's talkin'," Kenny said. "You slim ass mother fucker. You're so skinny you got to run around in the shower to get wet," he said tilting his head back in laughter.

"Up yours," the mechanic said and Kenny no-arms was out of ear shot and bumming change from two dykes sitting at a table drinking a pitcher of beer.

The bar was filling up. I guessed none of these folks worked, at least not during the day, and getting drunk was the main focus. Kenny no arms bummed enough change to get the juke playing. Kenny Rogers sang *You picked a fine time to leave me Lucille*, and Cross-eyed Heidi sang along.

Kristen continued telling us about her quest for super-stardom, "You see, me and my brother moved down here from Gasquet. That's where we're from. Gasquet's a little town way up in Northern California near the Oregon border. Not many people know about it except for fishermen who come up and fish for salmon. We left last year after my parents were killed in a car crash. They got blind-sided by a semi and we ended up with a settlement, got enough to get us out of Gasquet and down here. My brother didn't like it up there. He got beat up all the time 'cuz he's gay. He can't hide it and he feels better here. Anyway, I'm going to get him through high school. He has one more year and I'm going to keep singing and writing and making money for us till I hit it big. I will and that's a fact!"

The old timer on the oxygen let out a long gurgling gasp and then lowered his head in a coughing fit. A long brown and yellow glob of phlegm slid from his lower lip and onto the bar. The old timer looked up to see Cross-eyed Heidi shooting him in the face with the soda gun.

"You dirty old fuck!" she said. "Why don't you go to the bathroom and do that!?"

"I'm sorry, I didn't know it was coming," he said taking a long gulp from his beer.

"Oh, for Christ's sake, Mel!" Cross-eyed Heidi said grabbing a bar towel and throwing it at him. "Here, you clean it up."

Kenny no-arms moved in and out of the crowd. *Why do Jewish divorces cost so much? They're worth it.* Debbie Boone crooned *You Light up my Life.* A short woman with big breasts and a tight shirt ordered a beer and Kenny no-arms took a dollar bill from his shirt pocket, stuffed it between her breasts and said, "Dance for me." The woman took a swipe at Kenny no-arms. He ducked, missing what surely would have been a heavy whack on the side of his head. The woman stormed out of the place for a moment and came back in sneering at Kenny no-arms.

"Hey, sorry," he said laughing. "Just fuckin' with ya."

We downed three more beers and three more shots. My stomach became queasy and my face burned. I moved unsteadily on my feet. Michael and Kristen leaned toward one another, deep in conversation. I put my arm around Michael's neck and said, "Gimmy a smoke."

"What the hell," he said, "you hardly smoke. I guess you're getting drunk, huh Jimmy?"

I was. The beer, the Old Grand-Dad, the smoke, the dark sourness of the room, the music, Kenny no-arms popping in and out of nowhere cracking those jokes; everything was fuzzy, tilting, swirling. My balance was off. Words slurred. I put the smoke in my mouth and Kenny no-arms came out of nowhere with a lighted blue-tip in his baby hand.

"Need a light kid?" and suddenly he was air bound, a sack tossed effortlessly over the bar, a crash of bottles, a heavy thump and a groan.

"What the fuck!" Cross-eyed Heidi yelled picking Kenny no-arms off the floor from behind the bar. In the distance I heard a loud angry voice, "You ever touch my wife again you fuckin' freak; I'll cut off your fuckin' hands!"

Later, somewhere in the blackness of time dissolved, I woke on a hard bed in a dark room with my mouth dry and rotten; my throat raw and swollen. I tried to figure out where I was. I heard faint, cloudy voices. Then, I recognized Michael's laugh and another man and girl's voice. I lied stiffly on the bed fully clothed, my stomach empty and hollow. I needed water and walked toward the voices in the other room. Michael, Brodie and Kristen sat around the kitchen table filled with beer cans and plates of spaghetti. A cloud of smoke hovered over the table.

"Sunshine!" Michael said with a great big smile. "You're awake! How are you doing, sweetheart?"

"How'd we get here?" I asked

"I or we pretty much carried and dragged your sorry ass here; people on the streets thought we were lugging a dead guy around. A cop even pulled over and wondered what the hell we were doing."

"I feel sick," I said.

"I bet you do. You sure puked enough: in the bar, on the street. You got Brodie's entranceway pretty good, too."

"That's for sure," Brodie said. "Man, it looked like Niagara Falls coming outta your mouth. I ain't seen anybody that fucked up in a long time. That's for damn sure."

"I'm sorry," I said.

Brodie dismissed me with a wave of his hand. "We got it cleaned up," he said.

Kristen motioned for me to join them at the table. "Want some spaghetti?" she asked.

"It's good," Brodie said looking at Kristen. "Boy this girl can make sauce. It's loaded with tomatoes and basil."

"Eat," Michael said. "The spaghetti will do you good."

I suddenly felt famished. "Sure," I said joining the table and downing a big glass of water. Kristen piled some spaghetti on a plate and scooped sauce and sprinkled cheese over the top.

"Eat up," she said. "You must have barfed five pounds between the bar and here."

"My sick little Jimmy boy," Michael said. "What the hell are we gonna do with such a lightweight?"

We sat at the table for a couple more hours. A light breeze flowed in from the open windows in the living room. The neon light from the corner store lit the street. My stomach felt better after eating. I even managed to down a couple of beers. Michael and Kristen were sitting closer and noticing each other more and more. Brodie had no trouble popping beers and telling stories well into the night when he finally sat back let out a long satisfying sigh and announced he was going to "hit the sack."

Michael and Kristen took the floor on the living room and I ended up back in the dark room on the hard bed. Lying and listening to the faint murmur of voices on the street below, I realized we never made it to City Lights. I hoped Ferlinghetti and Coroso and Ginsberg and Kerouac might forgive me. I hoped they would approve of our stay in San Francisco.

Chapter 34

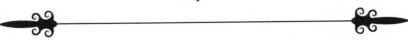

Muir Woods

The crisp wide-open, cool and refreshing Northern California Coast, known by some as the Redwood Empire or the Redwood Coast is a stretch of rocky, rugged, cliffs with hills and beaches and redwood trees. After San Francisco I was ready to get out of the city, shake off this hangover and stay away from drinking and smoking and puking. I needed a break.

After an early breakfast in a small noisy diner, we said our goodbyes to Kristen and Brodie, slung our packs over our shoulders and walked across the massive Golden Gate Bridge leaving San Francisco at our backs. Kristen told us that more people committed suicide on that bridge than in any other place in the world, said there was a ninety-eight percent chance you would reach your goal if you took the plunge. "Pretty good odds," she said.

It felt good to be on the road and heading into the inviting unknown. That was the beauty of the road. Any turn, any stop was new and fresh and different. The road has a pulse, a life. It's an uncertain ride filled with interesting and fantastic and pathetic characters. The honesty of the road is unabridged. It's wide open, clear, stark, and available for all to see. The road invites us to understand the vast human experiences of our country. It's a twisted transformation of the soul, a perpetual place to delve deeply within ourselves and understand and appreciate where we fit within the dialects of our land.

Our first ride came from an easy going skinny black kid in a bright red satin shirt and a big round afro. He was heading north on Highway 101 and sucking on a big yellow joint. He listened to some funky black morning radio program and didn't say much, but he kept a big wide smile on his face and didn't seem to have a care in the whole wide world. The kid offered us the joint and we filled the car with smoke and very quickly got very stoned. He took us into Marin City and dropped us off at the interchange connecting us to Highway 1.

"That road will take you right up along the coast," he said with a big, wide toothy grin. "I'm headin' straight up on 101, but you want to head on Highway 1 through Muir Woods and onto the coast. If you ain't from around here, check out them Redwoods, they pretty nice."

It didn't take long before two guys in a blue Chevy Malibu pulled over and offered us a ride. They were edgy and jumpy. Sweat bubbled from their foreheads. I felt uneasy at the sight of them. The road narrowed and we twisted along it slowly. The driver watched the road from beady almond brown eyes. He ground his teeth with ferocious desperation. His eyes darted frantically between the road and the passenger's penetrating stare. The passenger was a skinny runt who barked driving instructions.

"Watch out for the fuckin' trees!" he said.

"I can see them! Let me drive and shut the fuck up!" the driver said.

"You shut the fuck up," he said. "I don't want to go into the goddamn forest!"

"Shut up! We're not going into any fuckin' forest," the driver said tightening his grip on the steering wheel. "I know what I'm doing!"

"Slow down," the passenger said looking out the window and up toward the redwood trees. They suffocated him. "Those fuckin' trees," he said.

We moved slowly. The Malibu hugged the road inches from the thick forest. The forest was full with redwoods and ferns. Everything was dark, deep green. Rays of sun slanted through the trees giving the whole area a sublime dream-like quality. It reminded me of the kind of place where fairies lived fluttering and prancing deep within. A line of cars and campers hung a couple of feet behind us. They were getting impatient. The passenger looked into his side mirror.

"Pull over and let those cars pass," he said.

"There's nowhere to pull over," the driver said. "You want me to drive into the fucking woods?"

"There are too many cars. You gotta let them pass!"

"Shut up I told you! I'm driving, cool it!"

Michael gave me a look. He rolled his eyes. The driver slowed down. The driver in the car behind us laid on his horn.

"Fuck you!" the passenger yelled turning around and giving the honking horn the finger.

The horn persisted and the driver and the passenger got more aggravated and other cars and campers blasted their horns and soon a cacophony of horns filled the woods and the driver tightened his grip on the steering wheel and the passenger put both his hands on the sides of his head and squeezed and yelled, "Shut up! Shut up! Shut the fuck up, they're driving me crazy!"

Seconds later a car with flashing lights passed and pulled in front of us. The car stopped and the passenger turned in our direction and pointed a blue steel pistol in my face.

"Fuck!" I heard the driver say.

The passenger waved the gun inches from my face. His eyes were wide and his pupils were dilated. Sweat streamed down both sides of his face.

The driver leaned out of the window and shouted to the approaching officer, "You better stop right there and get out of the way and let us pass or these two fucks in the back seat are gonna get it."

The driver in the car behind us pressed harder and longer on his horn. The officer stopped. The barrel of the gun was pressed firmly onto my forehead. No one moved. The horn stopped and all was still. I could smell the rich freshness of the woods and I thought how bright and clear and dry it was. It really was a brilliant day.

The passenger said, "He's a fuckin' ranger; he ain't gotta gun."

"He's park police, he's gotta gun and he's pointing it right toward my head. Don't do anything stupid!" the driver said.

"I told you not to take Highway 1. I told you to stay on 101," the passenger said to the driver while pressing the gun harder into my forehead. "You don't fuckin' listen, do you?"

"I listen to enough of your shit. That's why we're in this mess!" the driver said.

The park policeman moved closer toward the car.

"Well, this is a fine fuckin' mess," the passenger said. "I'm not gonna sit here all day waiting to go to jail."

The passenger tightened his grip and pressed the gun harder against my forehead. "Listen to me good fucker, you and me are gonna walk outta this car and walk into those woods over there," he said pointing his eyes in the desired direction.

"What am I supposed to do?" the driver asked.

"It's your shit," the passenger said. "I don't give a fuck what you do," and he opened the car door and kept the gun on me and leaned the seat forward and yanked me out of the car while jabbing the gun into my back and pressing it firmly into my kidney. We walked into the woods through tall grass and sticks and fallen branches. I listened to the crackle and the pops with each step we took. The gigantic gnarled trunks of the redwoods stood out like prehistoric dinosaurs. The driver eased up jamming the gun in my back. We walked further. Birds skittered above singing high and melodious songs. The passenger didn't say much except once or twice, "Keep looking straight ahead and keep moving." I did and then, after a bit more walking, I had a feeling he was not with me and I said, "How long are we going to walk?" and there was no answer, so I said it again just a tad louder and I turned to look at him and he was gone.

I figured he must have stopped and once I was a good distance ahead, he high-tailed into the woods. At least that's what I figured. I also figured it was safe to head back toward the road. When I got back the trunk to the car was open and Michael and the cop were looking at an opened suitcase filled with neat rows of tightly packed clear plastic bags filled with white powder.

"That's a lot of heroin," the cop said.

"Jimmy," Michael said when he saw me. "What the hell?"

"He disappeared out there," I said. "He told me to walk ahead and after a while I realized he wasn't with me and he was gone. I don't know what direction he went in."

The driver sat handcuffed in the back of the cop car. His shoulders sagged and his head sunk low and forward. The line of campers and cars moved on, the passengers craning their necks and peering curiously as they passed. The guy who was directly behind us blasting his horn pulled his car over and stood with Michael and the cop. He was an old soldier with no neck, a square head, and a crew cut. Next to him stood a little wrinkled and tan woman with a sailor's cap and big thick purple veins crisscrossing her legs. I guess they were married. He felt, being so close and pressing his horn, that somehow he had helped capture the "piece of shit druggie crooks" as he called them.

"I figured they were trouble," he told the cop. "Told the little woman they were trouble, could smell it a mile away."

The cop was all business, carved out of rock. His massive head was all muscle and skin tightly pulled over a thick skull and hard boned face. His hair was a patch of tightly cropped bristles packed uniformly on a rugged plateau. He looked at the bags of heroin and he glanced toward the woods calculating where the passenger might be. He walked toward his car in his crisp uniform and shiny shoes, his hat tilted slightly forward as he spoke into his radio. He walked back and said that he needed to get some more information from us. Another car would arrive shortly and take us to an office in the park. The old soldier asked if he could be of assistance. The cop asked if he could identify the guy who took me out into the woods. He couldn't except to say he looked like a "shady piece of shit." The cop told him, "Thanks, I think we'll be all right. You have a good day, sir."

The tiny office was tucked behind a tourist's café. It had a desk and a phone and a typewriter. A big picture of *Smokey the Bear* hung on the wall behind the desk. Smokey wore blue jeans and a white straw hat; above the brim it read *Smokey*. He gripped a shovel in his left paw and used his right paw to point at me. Underneath Smokey's desperate stare it said *Only You* in bold black letters.

The cop who brought us to the office was another one of those park police. He was an older guy with soft white hair, and bright eyes. He had a habit of clearing his throat and he was easy and relaxed. The first cop sat behind the desk with a pad of paper and a pen in front of him. He scribbled our responses to questions like who were we and why were we in Muir Woods and how were we acquainted with the two guys in the Malibu and if we had any idea of where they were coming from or where they were going or what their names were. He asked if we knew they were *drug traffickers* and if we had any idea where they were heading. Once the interrogation was over the cops looked at one another satisfied we knew nothing that could be of any help.

The cop taking the notes said, "We've seen this before, running drugs up the coast from San Francisco to Portland and on up to Seattle. They usually don't stop in the woods here, though. They usually cut over to the beach and on up the coast."

"They were pretty high," Michael said. "Maybe the redwoods intrigued them."

"Maybe so," the white haired cop said, "but I don't like the idea of the one running around in the woods with a pistol. That could mean trouble for someone."

The other cop agreed contemplating the fugitive's next move. "My guess is he'll try to steal someone's car. He's not going to stay in the woods too long. He's not the outdoorsman type. He'll look for a break and steal a car and try to drive right out under our noses and that's when we'll nail him. I'm sure of that."

"You're probably right on that," the white haired cop said looking in our direction. "What about you two? Where are you heading?"

"Seattle," I said. "We're heading up to Seattle."

"Lot of rain up there," he said.

"My brother's living somewhere up there," Michael said. "We're going up there to tell him his mother's dead. He left a long time ago. I haven't seen him in years, since I was twelve or something."

The cop didn't react much to that. "Well, that being the case," he said, "I can give you a lift over to Muir Beach. It'll get you back up the coast highway and you can get on from there."

Chapter 35

The Junkie

It's not every day I'm wandering through the woods held captive by a paranoid, gun-lugging, junkie fugitive. That played pretty rough on my nerves. It wasn't until the white haired cop dropped us off at Muir Beach that the uneasiness left my body and I felt slightly normal again.

"The coast highway will take you straight on up," he said. "Hell of a nice road for scenery from here on in."

The white haired cop drove off. We hiked a short distance past clumps of tall wild grass and onto the shore. The air was soft and warm. Waves spread onto the shore light and easy. A dark oiled couple wearing skimpy bathing suits lay side by side on a large white blanket. A young mother happily watched her little daughter, lugging an orange pail, clumsily hauling water back and forth from the shore to a small hole next to her. An old man, in baggy shorts, stood on the shore casting a long big-reeled fishing pole out into the ocean.

"Might as well take a swim," Michael said looking out over the Pacific.

We stripped down to our shorts and waded into the water. The sand was warm and fine and the ocean was shallow and calm. Looking back onto the beach we could see flowering hills and grassy bluffs along the coast. A couple walked an excited dog along the beach. The man repeatedly threw a red ball into the ocean and the dog bolted into the water, hopping over waves to retrieve it. This went on for quite some time. The dog did not want it to end. The two of us swam and floated in the cool, salty water. Bulging white clouds hung effortlessly in the sky. The day was warm, sunny and bright. We came out of the water and lay on the sand resting our heads on our backpacks. Michael lit a Marlboro and we lay still listening to the dull rumble of the waves roll onto the shore. It was soothing and we both fell asleep until that junkie was standing over us asking where his driver buddy was.

He appeared calm and he wasn't sweating, but I detected a nervous tension in his voice. I guess he may have been scared. I noticed he did not have a gun and it didn't look like he had one shoved down his pants. In some strange way he looked likable enough.

"Where's your gun?" I asked.

"Where's the guy I was with?" he answered.

"Last we saw him, he was in the cop car," Michael said.

"They brought us into an office and questioned us," I said. "The cop said you were hauling heroin up into Seattle. They figured we weren't with you so they took us out of the park and gave us a lift down here."

"What did you tell them?" he asked.

"Not much to tell," Michael said. "We were only with you for a few minutes. We told them that."

"Cops figured you'd steal a car and try to head out," I said. "They said they'd get you then. How did you get here?"

"Doesn't matter," he answered. He looked worried. He surveyed the coast. I guess he was figuring his next move and searching for an opening. I had never seen a big time drug dealer and he didn't fit in to my expectations, whatever they were. This guy looked like a centerfold for preppy magazine. Young, clean-cut, blonde, and kind of Ivy League looking wearing a white short sleeved cotton polo with a green alligator emblem on it and a pair of khaki shorts and worn penny loafers. Looking at him, I figured those drugs can make just about anybody do shit they might not normally do. He had a bluish-yellow bruise and a deep purple wound in the vein on his arm where he shot his dope. He was real pale too, didn't seem to be getting much of the California sun.

Michael stood up and brushed sand off his back end. "Well, I don't know what happens now. I mean we're bookin' outta here and heading up the coast to Seattle. I'm not telling anyone we saw you, but we're not hanging around with you either."

"This is a fucked up mess," the passenger said. "That guy I was with is a pretty big deal. He sells a lot of shit. Me, I'm just a fuck up. Got caught up bangin' this shit and I can't stop. I was going up to Seattle with him just to keep him company and get high. I don't sell."

"You have to turn yourself in," I said. "You don't have a choice. Get cleaned up and stay off that shit."

"It's crazy," he said in a cracking voice, tears welling in his eyes.

"It is," Michael said.

"I'll figure it out," he said wiping tears from his cheeks.

"Good, I hope so," I said and we put on our shirts and sneakers and headed off the beach, past the tall grass and onto the coast road.

We propped our backpacks against one another and raised our thumbs to the passing cars. From the road I could see the passenger sitting cross-legged in the sand looking past the soft foamy silent waves spreading upon the shore and into the wide Pacific Ocean.

Michael looked at him, shook his head and said, "It's those drugs, man, they've got him hard. Not a good thing."

"No, probably not," I said.

Chapter 36

Stinson Beach

The coastal road was loaded with hitchhikers thumbing rides up the Pacific Coast and going as far as Oregon and Washington State. Some even crossed the border and headed into Vancouver and beyond. At any time as many as fifty hitchhikers could be found stretched along this section of road. Oftentimes, a pick-up truck would pull over and take as many of us that could pile into the back bed. We ran into a lot of wild people on the back of those trucks. All kinds: booze-drenched wandering losers with nowhere particular to go, with tobacco-stained hands, brown teeth, greasy stringy hair, and wild beards and wilder stories. Their breath reeked like sour garbage and they drank heavily and carried a perpetual stench of sweat, grime and booze with them. These were guys who hit the bottom, who took on day jobs at the labor pool or tore down rides at carnivals and checked into the city missions or the Salvation Army's when they hit the cities. They usually greeted you by bumming a cigarette. These guys had a tough time getting rides. You could tell they were trouble from a mile away. Others were the forlorn poetic wanderers who experienced the road while reading stuff like Nietzsche and Zen Philosophy and Ginsberg and Kerouac. Many had the look of German intellects wearing scruffy chin hairs and round wire-rimmed glasses. They smoked weed and Thai stick and hash oil and tripped on whatever crazy hallucinogens they could get their hands on. Peyote was the real prize. They scribbled verse in tattered notepads while sitting in truck stop diners or waiting for rides on the side of a desolate road. These guys always seemed to have a spacey stare and a strange laugh. I remember others too. I remember meeting a hippy couple squatting on the side of the road surrounding a beat up metal pot and eating raw carrots and celery and bean sprouts from it. The girl wore a long colorful printed skirt and had dirty sandaled feet with hair on her legs and underarms. She wore a loose fitting sleeveless t-shirt showing saggy tits and big nipples pressing against the fabric. We met college kids who had hitched from as far as Boston and Maine and every once in a while we'd run into someone who took to the road with their dog or cat.

Standing first in line at the side of the road was prime real estate; at least you were assured of being next to get a lift. I remember no one was ever in any particular hurry to get anywhere. At least it didn't seem so. I guess if you were in a hurry to get up north you would take Highway 101 or Highway 5, which was even faster. Highway 1 could take forever. No one ever said, "Look man, I really need to jump ahead of you. I've got something going on and I need to get to Eugene or Seattle or Vancouver real fast." Instead these scattered road-dogs waited patiently on the side of the road. Some standing, others sitting, some reading, some eating, all moving forward in a casual manner as if time had no holds on or importance to them.

Irritation took over when Michael saw these tattered wanderers strung casually along the road. "We'll never get a damn ride." Michael wasn't particularly in a hurry either, but knowing these crowds would slow him down got him a little wacky. He gets impatient when he's not in control. If he has to wait it doesn't fly right with him.

We got lucky coming out of Muir Beach, though. A sky blue Mustang fastback with a surfboard strapped to the roof pulled over and raced us up to Stinson Beach. We blew by a bunch of hikers raising their thumbs and holding their signs high in a desperate attempt to get a ride. No more room in this car.

The driver was a thin, tanned bleach-blonde with an intelligent face and youthful eyes. His age was impossible to tell. I figured by the leathery texture of his sun-cragged skin he was a bit older. He gunned the Mustang past the line of hikers.

"I usually don't pick anyone up anymore, but you two looked okay," he said. "Lot of freaks hanging out on the road these days and I'm not in any hurry to pick them up."

"How far are you going?" Michael asked.

"Right up this road to Stinson Beach. It's not too far. Some of the best surfin' around and I aim to hit some waves today. You boys surf?" he asked.

"I never have," Michael said.

"You in a hurry?" he asked.

"No, we're not in any big hurry," I said.

"Good, I'll take you up and give you a shot on the board if you're up for it," he said pressing the pedal a little harder. "Where are you two from?"

"Buffalo," Michael said.

"Well hell-shit," he said. "I guess you never have been surfin'... skiing maybe?"

"That we've done," I said.

"Oh, yeah, Jimmy here he's one hell of a skier. The last time we went he had his front teeth knocked out and got a bunch of stitches in his lip," he said telling him the whole story with a wide grin. "You can see the scar if you look close enough."

I remember that day well. That was another one of those adventures that I reluctantly agreed to go on. Early on a bright Saturday morning in December, after we got a good dumping of heavy snow the night before, Michael was in the backyard throwing snowballs at my window to wake me. Once inside he looked at me with those bright determined eyes and announced, "We're going skiing!"

I'd lived in Buffalo all of my life, but I'd never taken to the slopes. That was a sport for the families that had quite a hell of a lot more money than we did growing up. Skiing was expensive. All that gear and the price of lift tickets and lunch at those expensive restaurants was way too much for my family to handle. Instead, we took beat up wooden sleds or metal saucers or inner tubes or even odd pieces of plastic and slid down the hill at Delaware Park or we pulled one another on them through the snowy city streets. Sometimes we played hockey and ice skated on big puddles that froze down at the end of our street on the railroad tracks.

Some of the fathers in the neighborhood transformed their backyard into a hockey rink by shoveling the yard until there was just a thin layer of snow on the ground and bringing out the hose and spraying water evenly onto the snow until it froze, then spraying the next day and the next until a couple inches of ice formed into what we agreed was a damn good hockey rink. Only problem was, our yards were hardly more than a sliver of lawn and our houses were pulled so tightly together that they almost touched, but we managed and played hockey on those rinks for hours and hours. For the past couple of winters, when the streets were smooth sheets of ice, we'd lace up our skates and hit the bars throughout the neighborhood. Skating home in the quiet dark nights on those icy, shiny black streets sure beat walking.

Anyway, Michael was going skiing and nothing was going to hold him back and nothing was going to stop him from bringing me to the slopes with him. We got into his rusted-out orange Dodge Colt, with big holes in the floorboards allowing a nice view of the snowy streets below, and barreled toward *Kissing Bridge Ski Resort* in the South Towns about forty minutes outside of Buffalo. That's where the real deep snow falls. If we have five inches of snow in Buffalo, they have twenty inches in the South Towns. That's just the way it is. Western New Yorker's call it the Snow-Belt and from December through March the Snow-Belt gets pounded with blankets of deep heavy snow. The skiing is good and the slopes get real crowded on snowy weekends.

The day was bitterly cold and unusually bright and sunny. Michael took Route 240, a two-lane road that twists through woods and pines and fields covered in fresh white snow. We pulled into *Kissing Bridge* and the slopes climbed high into the clear cloudless sky. I watched the skiers glide effortlessly down the hills. They reminded me of ants skittering over marshmallows or vanilla ice cream as they scurried down the big hill busily moving in all directions. There was something unreal about the whole bunch of them. The two of us got ourselves a pair of long fiberglass skis with poles and boots. I put them on and could barely stand up, let alone walk in them.

"Here, watch," Michael said. "You have to get into the motion and slide with them. Don't pick up your feet, just glide like this," and he showed me how to move from one place to the next on a smooth flat snowy surface. I followed his instructions and still had a horrible time moving.

"This is a hell of lot harder than ice skating," I said.

"Once you get it, it's easy," he said. "Come on, follow me. We'll take the bunny hill for a quick run to get you used to it. Then we'll get on the chairlift and take it to the top."

I clumsily followed him toward the bunny hill. The bunny hill was pretty lame. It was filled mostly with kids who couldn't ski and resorted to sliding down the hill on their asses. To get to the top of the bunny hill you had to grab onto a rope connected to a pulley that yanked you toward the top. I grabbed it, pointed my skis forward and was dragged about a hundred yards to the crest of the hill. Michael hung behind me and gave me further instructions, "Keep your skis straight when you go down. Use your hips to turn. When you want to stop, pretend you're on ice skates; it's the same thing." Once we made it to the top he said, "follow me," and he was gone. I placed my skis together, pointed them downward and bolted down the hill moving faster and faster without any control whatsoever. Anyone that saw me barreling toward them frantically got out of my way. I could not turn. I could only race forward. In the muffled distance I heard a woman scream, "Slow down you fucking idiot!" Somehow I managed to stay up and make my way to the bottom. I realized I had no idea how to stop so I fell to my right and hit the snow. My skis and poles flew in every direction. I lay disheveled on the snow for a moment. Michael stood over me guffawing like a jack-ass and trying to catch his breath. This was one of those laughs where his mouth hangs wide open and all sound is suspended, then a deep exhale and an inhale and another exhale.

"You looked like fucking Lurch or Frankenstein barreling down that hill," he said trying to catch his breath. "You have to bend your knees and turn; you can't just go straight; you'll kill yourself!"

"This is bullshit! I can't ski! I've never done this before," I said.

"Don't worry about it," he said. "At least you stayed up. You just have to learn to turn so you can slow down. It's easy." He helped me gather my stuff and get my skis on. "Let's hop on the chair lift and take it to the top."

I took in the massive hill before me. Skiers wove effortlessly toward us. "I don't know," I said. "I don't think I'm ready right now."

"Yes you are," Michael said. "You're ready. Let's get on the chairlift."

Somehow I managed to crawl to the lift. "Let the chair hit you in the ass and lean back," Michael said. The chair swung around and bumped into the back of my legs. I lifted my ass and found myself moving up the hill sitting snug on the metal bench. Michael pointed out the skiers sliding below, "See, they flow in a sort of an *S* pattern as they go down. They don't just point straight. You need to bend your knees and move your body in and out. You have to control your speed. It's not that hard."

I had to admit they looked pretty graceful meandering down the slope as though they had not a worry in the world.

"Slide forward when I say *now*. The chair will swing around and head back down. We need to get off when it makes its turn."

I had a hollow pit deep in my stomach. Fresh snow hung on the big pine trees and when I turned to look behind me I could see a wide vista of snow draped fields and woods. Route 240 twisted and turned in the distance. I'm not a big fan of heights. I get a sick queasy feeling in my gut when I'm up high, but I felt pretty safe in this chair. The chair was ready to round the bend and Michael gave directions in quick choppy commands: "Okay, get ready...put your poles in front of you... like this... put your legs together... point your skis forward...okay...slide off." In a flash Michael was off the chair and looking at me. I tried to slide off, but hesitated just for a second and somehow found myself hanging with one hand as the chair made its turn and headed toward the bottom. "Let go!" he yelled. "Let go!" I figured I must have been about ten feet from the ground and I knew the chair would lift higher and I might be in real trouble. I let go and plummeted to the snow. Once again skis and poles flew in every direction. One of my boots came off and a crowd of skiers quickly came to my rescue.

In the dull distance a voice asked, "Are you okay?"

"Yes," I said and again Michael was bent over in laughter, eyes bright, his mouth hanging wide and gasping for air.

"Why didn't you get off with me?"

"I don't know; I just froze."

"You're unbelievable," he said. "Okay, let's do this, like I said, don't just go straight down the hill. Move your hips and turn so you have control and can slow down when you need to. We're up pretty high, so it will be a good run to the bottom."

We were off. I was a few feet in front of Michael and could hear his shouts. "Crouch! Turn! Keep steady!" I began to build speed. I was able to turn slightly and navigate myself away from a kid sprawled on his back and sliding down slope before me. I felt pretty good and a bit more in control. Michael shouted from behind, "Come on, faster, let's move!" The snow underneath my skis was packed hard and slick. The top layer was a smooth sheet of gleaming ice making the hill lightning fast. Once again, I pointed straight and wiped out all of Michael's instructions. I barreled down the hill moving faster and faster, muffled cries in the background, cold air on my face, my legs locked straight and I felt the horrible pressure that I was completely out of control. Right then, I hit a mogul and shot awkwardly into the air slamming down hard with my ski pole smashing violently into my mouth crushing teeth and tearing into my bottom lip. I rolled into a series of summersaults that tore my skis from my boots. My mouth was hot and stinging and pieces of teeth coated my tongue. Blood slid down and over my chin and onto the white snow.

Michael approached me and his eyes narrowed. "Jesus," he said.

"My mouth," I said. "It hurts."

A crowed gathered and a woman on the ski patrol appeared from nowhere and pushed a big piece of gauze onto my mouth and pressed hard. She looked seriously into my eyes and said I'd probably need a couple of stitches in my lip.

"Once the wound is cleaned and the blood stops, you'll be okay," she said.

I spit blood and pieces of teeth onto the snow and the woman on the ski patrol thought it might be better to get me into the lodge. "No need to freak people out," she said. I insisted that Michael ski some more. "Get some runs in; I'll be alright," I said.

The woman took me into first aid and cleaned me up pretty good. "You're going to need to see a doctor *and* a dentist in the next few hours," she said.

My lip stung and felt burning hot. It began to swell and I was miserable. The woman told me she couldn't give me any pain killers, not even aspirin.

"Resort policy," she said. "If you get some type of a reaction from it, then we're screwed. I suggest you get a whiskey, sit in the lodge by the fire, and sip it. That'll work."

The bleached-blonde driver took in the story. "Hell, surfin's nothing like that, although you might get bit in the ass by a shark, with your luck and all."

It was late afternoon by the time we pulled into Stinson Beach and got out of the car.

"My name's Neil," he said and shook our hands using the brotherly less formal grip. We shared our names and Neil grabbed the surfboard from the roof, tucked it under his arm and carried it as we walked on the sand toward the beach. His movements were quick and precise and he moved toward the shore like an enthused child. A few surfers were in the water cutting diagonally across the tops of the arcing waves. The wind blew offshore onto the water creating a silvery spray with each crashing wave.

"Not bad," Neil said. "The sets are coming in pretty big, about ten to fifteen feet. That's decent."

Neil walked a few feet in front of us wearing flowered board shorts with scallop-legs and snaps that kept them tight on his legs. All of the surfers had those pretty cool shorts. We sure didn't look like surfer dudes in our cut-off blue jeans. The three of us got in the water and Neil gave us some basic directions. The water was a little chilly and a light breeze blew our hair away from our faces.

"You want to paddle out a ways like this, then turn the board around and keep the front pointed toward the shore. Look for sets of waves; you'll see them. Once you hit a wave that you want to take, you paddle real fast with your arms to get on the crest of the wave then do a quick push-up and slide up onto the board by pulling your knees to your stomach and hopping to your feet. Then use your arms to balance, the way a tightrope walker does. You'll need to bend your knees and turn your waist to maneuver and you need to cut diagonally while riding the top of the wave so you don't get ahead of it and fall forward. What do you think?" he said.

"I think snow skiing is easier," I said.

"Awesome," Michael said. "Let's do it."

"I'll go out and show you," Neil said. "When I raise my hand, it means I've eyed a wave that I'm going to hit. Watch me then, okay?"

Neil grabbed the board and paddled about fifty yards into the ocean. He pointed the board toward the shore and laid belly down while looking behind him. In a moment he raised his hand then began paddling frantically toward us. I watched a big wave build under his board and in one graceful movement he crouched upwards and was standing with bent knees and riding on the crest of a huge wave. The water sprayed white, silver and blue and he crouched and leaned into the wave and shot across the water with great speed. Watching Neil, it was apparent that he had more command and control than any of the other surfers out there. He played with the waves; he tamed them; he owned them. He continued moving in our direction until reaching us. Then he simply stepped off with a wide grin.

"Not a bad wave for this place," he said.

"You looked awesome," Michael said. "You really rode that bastard."

"You want to give it a shot?" Neil asked.

"Hell yeah!" and Michael was off and paddling furiously into the silvery ocean.

A couple of the other surfers who had watched Neil on his run approached him complimenting his grace and elegance. They talked surfer stuff and were captivated when Neil gave pointers on how to attack and respect the waves. He'd been doing this a long time I figured. I watched Michael take the board further out; his brown body lay rigid on the board, his arms rowing in unison like a precise machine carrying him further into the blue water. White-caps moved toward us at an angle and Michael was about as far out as Neil had been when he turned the board back toward shore and waited for the right wave.

"He's got a nice set just behind him," Neil said and in a suspended quiet moment, we watched and wondered if Michael would grab one of the approaching waves. He took one that was building gradually underneath and began paddling his arms with great determination. The wave rose to an incredible height and for a moment he got lost behind it. "It might have got ahead of him," Neil said and then, in an instant, on the crest, Michael appeared slightly crouched on the board with his arms stretched outwards steadying himself and shooting fast toward the shore. "He's gonna over shoot the wave and crash forward. He's gotta cut or he'll get flushed like a piece of shit." We watched closely as Michael rode high on the wave's precipice, the tip of his board stretching slightly ahead of the wave. The sun brightened and the spray from the water shined blue and pink and yellow and green. In a split second he bent his knees further and leaned toward his left shooting himself brilliantly over the peak of the breaking wave. The wave arched slightly ahead and Neil shook his head, "That was fucking incredible! He tamed that fucking wave!" A moment later the wave lost its height and moved ahead of him. Michael paddled in beaming as Neil and the other surfers greeted him. "Fuckin' awesome; unbelievable ride for a first timer," Neil said.

It was a good day surfing. Neil let us take the board out a bunch of times. I wasn't so graceful or lucky and never stayed up on the board. I just didn't have the agility or the rhythm. Michael made it look easy. He clung effortlessly to the board taking the bigger waves with the skill of a life-long California surfer. At least that's what Neil said.

Later, when the sun lowered beneath the blue-black ocean and an orange glow fell softly over the warm brown sand, we lit a small fire and sat casually warming cans of Campbell's Chicken Noodle Soup and tearing into soft slices of white bread. As darkness came and the stars brightened, other small fires appeared on the beach. Neil stayed and shared dinner with us. We felt it was the least we could do, him letting us use his board and all. Surfing gave us a ferocious appetite and we devoured the soup and bread.

"It's a good day when the waves are out like they were today," Neil said. "Hell of a good day. Makes taking the afternoon off worthwhile."

"What do you do?" I asked.

"Work in an ice cream stand," he said and paused. "It's by choice, though. See, I was on a pretty important path, at least that's what I thought. I went to UCLA, studied architecture, got good grades and was told I was pretty talented. Right out of college I got hired by a firm in LA and worked on a team that designed shopping malls and apartment buildings and office buildings. We had contracts up in San Francisco and down in San Diego and then we started building in Denver and Phoenix. Things were moving quickly. I was working my ass off sixteen hours a day and I thought I loved it."

"Awesome," Michael said. "Did you make good money?"

"More than I could have imagined," Neil said. "I bought a great house on the beach and paid cash for it. I bought some cool ass cars too like my sixty-six Mustang. It's a four on the floor, sky blue with a white top. I love Mustangs. Still have it, only take it out once in a while, though. I want to hang onto it. I even bought an old rebuilt forty-seven Ford Woodie station wagon. The ultimate California surf mobile. I had all kinds of stuff and I had a good friend who knew the stock market real well and right at the end of 1974 and the beginning of 1975 the market started doing better and I started to invest in oil companies and things were looking pretty good."

Michael lit a Marlboro and stretched his legs. Small fires dotted the shoreline. The air cooled and the sand had lost most of its warmth. "Love those old Woodies'; you don't see those around Buffalo, that's for sure."

"I don't think I ever have," I said.

"They're getting harder to get around here too," Neil said. "So, like I said, things were looking good and I was in Denver on business. We were showing models to a client, going to put up an office complex downtown near their train station and after the meeting we thought we'd get a bite for dinner and then maybe see what the bars were like. We had a big dinner at a really great restaurant in a place called the *Brown Palace Hotel*, first class establishment. The Beatles even stayed there during their first tour back in the sixties. Anyway, after this incredibly fine dinner, we walked across the street to this little bar and as I was crossing the street a car swerved from the opposite lane and was heading right toward me. I didn't see it coming, but apparently some guy, I guess he was a street person, a bum, he jumped in front of me and got clocked by the car. He flew twenty feet into the air and came down on his head. I watched him go up. It was surreal. Everything was slow and disjointed and he hit the pavement with a hollow dull thump. I never forgot that sound, like a big ol' sack of flour plopping down on pavement. I heard him exhale long and deep. He let out this long sickening gurgling noise and his life just left him. He was dead instantly. The car hit him so hard that both his shoes flew off his feet. He was a mangled mess. I don't know why, but he took the blow for me. He did it on purpose.

When the cops got there they recognized him. Said he was a drunk and probably did not see the car coming, but I didn't believe them. For whatever reason, the dude got in front of that car and saved my life."

"I wonder what made him do that." I said. "That's really wild."

"No shit," Neil said, his cheek twitching and his eyes narrowing in thought. "It got me thinking about the meaning of life and all that shit. How quickly we can just be gone. It really fucked me up and then living felt different. Everything became more pronounced, more vivid. I started seeing things I'd never paid attention to before. I started not giving two shits about working my ass off long hours designing shopping malls and office buildings. I got to the point where I didn't have it in me anymore, so I quit, just like that. My bosses and the people at the office told me not to be so hasty. Take a break they said. They said I was just a little screwed up from what happened. So I did. I went to Peru for a couple of weeks and hiked the Ancascocha Trail and it was there that I made up my mind that I was going to live my life the way I want and lose the burdens of working my ass off in some shitty office every day."

Michael nodded in comfortable agreement. His eyes softened. I could see he understood immediately the need for Neil to shed his expected conformity for a freer more fulfilling life. Michael admired his decision. It was something given to him by his father.

Neil shifted contentedly in the sand, his face relaxed. A soft fire warmed in his eyes. "I had read about Peru and thought that would be as good a place as any to take a break. Ended up in Cusco, it's in the southeast near the Andes Mountain range. I was in a little place having an ice cold beer and I met this bearded dude from England who said he just got back from a hike that changed the way he viewed the world. He said he hiked 7,000 feet above sea level to a little place called Machu Picchu, a majestic city of ruins, nestled on a small hilltop above the Urabamba Valley. He said he met a shaman who hiked with him and between the shaman and the experience of the hike he found a new purpose in life and figured a better way to live the way he wanted to."

"What's a shaman?" I asked.

Michael responded quickly, "It's a spiritual leader that can reach an altered state of consciousness in order to interact with the spirit world. I read about them. They're pretty big shit, especially in Peru."

Neil was impressed, "Good description; they kind of work on you through this weird meditative ecstasy claiming they are the liaison between god and humans. They're really deep and I never really did follow too much about them, but somehow during that trip I felt all of my negative energies that had confused or polluted my soul were gone. I was awake and the life I was leading was no more. I guess my outer journey opened my inner journey and that's just the way it turned out."

"So you came back from Peru and went to work in an ice cream stand?" I asked.

"It wasn't quite like that," he said. "Actually I came back and got married, shotgun style. See, I met this little girl from Sausalito, fell for her hard. We started dating and shit happened and pretty soon a kid was on the way and we got married. Nice small wedding right on this beach here as a matter of fact. Right here on Stinson Beach. After we got married I would bring up ideas and plans and talk about our future together. Stuff like that and she never responded much. I figured she was a little quiet and shy;

maybe all of that stuff was a bit new for her to digest. But, I felt comfortable. We had a house, the stocks were doing well, we were in love, or so I thought, and a kid was on the way."

"Sounds like a good start," Michael said.

"Yes it did," Neil said. "It was a very good start. At the time it couldn't have been better. Anyway, one afternoon while we were in the house she was hunched over in pain and her water broke, so I packed her a bag and pulled out the car and we hurried to the hospital and about an hour later she delivered a little boy. I was right there in the delivery room and saw the whole thing. Afterwards, I spent a couple of hours with her and the baby. Looking back now, I can remember that she never held him. Said she was too scared, said she didn't want to drop him. Before I left I gave her a kiss and told her I'd be back in the morning and I'd have the house ready for her and the baby. We still hadn't picked a name. She liked Jason and Justin, but they didn't do much for me. When I got back to the hospital the next day she was gone. She walked right out of the hospital earlier in the night leaving the baby right there. I never saw or heard from her again. That was sixteen years ago. I could have looked for her, but I thought, what's the use? She was gone and she didn't give any indication she wanted back, so I just thought the hell with it. Life sure is funny and life sure does go on. So, I took the kid out of the hospital and I named him Lorne. That means forsaken or ditched as he likes to say, and hell, we've been living pretty good lives."

"And now you're living on investments and an ice cream stand?" I said.

"Oh yeah, that," he said. "My dad had a small burger stand over in Almonte. That's where I'm from, a little city not too far from here. He sold burgers and fries and ice cream cones, pretty simple operation. I noticed he was selling a hell of a lot more ice cream cones than burgers, so I put together a business plan for him, a proposition. I told him we'd split the business fifty-fifty. Told him we were going to lose the burgers and concentrate only on ice cream. I designed this crazy looking stand that looked like a big, tall ice cream cone and we changed the name to *Custard's Last Stand* and sold cones and shakes and sundaes and the place went crazy. We built five more in the San Francisco area and they made me and my dad rich."

"So, it's a little more than working in an ice cream stand," Michael said.

"A little bit," Neil agreed. "As weird as it sounds, I like to work the stand. I put in about four to five shifts a week just pumpin' out cones and shakes and sundaes. It's oddly fulfilling and customers are pretty nice for the most part, and I can surf anytime I want, so it's all good."

The air cooled and we added more wood to the fire. Other fires were scattered along the beach and the low murmuring sounds of talking and bright laughter filled the night. The waves lapped the shore with a dull murmur. Neil hung around a bit longer.

"You're best to sleep up in the grassy hill over there. No one will bother you," he said.

"I'm beat," Michael said. I'll have no problem sleeping tonight."

"No kidding," said Neil. "Where are you heading next?"

"Up around Seattle," I said.

"I have a brother somewhere up there," Michael said. "I think he's in a place called Vashon Island. I hear you need to take a ferry from Seattle to get there. I think you can see Mt. Rainer from there, too."

"It's nice up there. Too much rain for me, though," Neil said.

"He sent a letter back home a couple of years ago saying he was there. He still could be. I don't know. I guess I'll find out."

"Sounds like he's keeping away," Neil said.

"Been gone five years," Michael said.

"Why do you want to see him?" Neil said.

"He's my brother and he bolted. He left his family and I need to know why. It's pretty simple."

"Why is a good thing and, I suppose, it could be a not so good thing as well," Neil said. "I never did find out why. Neither did my boy. I hope you find him."

"So do I," Michael said.

Chapter 37

The Western Coast

The morning was warm and breezy. I woke before Michael and unzipped myself from my sleeping bag and sat on the grass hill looking over the sandy beach and onto the dull blue water. The waves came in low and tiny whitecaps broke at the shore. I watched the beach curve in the distance, the brown-green hills losing their height as they merged into a point far along the coast. Michael slept snoring slightly. I took out my copy of Hemingway's short stories and read *Up in Michigan*. It was short and sad. Then, I pulled the Rand McNally from my pack and traced our journey.

There was something enlightening about having traveled so far. I had a sense of understanding that only traveling long distances can provide. I realized I could go anywhere and live anyplace. I would be fine anywhere. We journeyed through the South and Texas and the Rocky Mountains and the desert and onto the California coast. Life could be adaptable anywhere, at least every town and every city had the amenities or the foundation to get yourself started and if you didn't like the way the wind blew in one city, well, then, you could pick yourself up and move on to the next. I realized it was that easy. Our land, our America was the same all over. It was a big place and anybody could carve their niche wherever they wanted. Looking at the distance between Buffalo and Stinson Beach was incredible, but in every city and every town and every hamlet, life was the same. That trepidation we had back on the first day of our journey was gone and a new confidence was planted firmly inside of me. I had learned the power of travel, the sameness of people, the comfort of knowing I would be okay, anywhere.

Sitting on that hill looking over the wide Pacific Ocean and breathing in the warm salty-breeze, I suddenly felt a kinship to where I came from: gritty, tough, steel-gray Buffalo, New York. The Queen City, or as some called it, The Nickel City. Buffalo was home and I suddenly missed her. I missed her because she was mine; she was where I came from; I had claimed her. I missed her stifling hot, heavy, sticky summers; her dark-grey, brittle, bone-chilling winters; her fragrant, rich, wet, chilly spring days, and her dry, crisp and colorful autumns. I missed her steel mills; her big smoke stacks reaching high into the dull ashen sky billowing black smoke, soot and eternal fiery flames. I missed her houses, row after row of three story houses all with big front porches crammed together on narrow car clogged streets. You can only experience that sense of pride when you have traveled to another place, when you have seen the other places people have settled in and called home. Buffalo may not impress the masses, but there is a depth that envelops its people and an understanding that, as a city, we are tough and uncompromising and there is really no need to answer to anyone who doesn't like it. You can see this on a snowy bitter cold Friday night in a warm, crowded smoky corner bar where Genesee beer flows endlessly from tap to glass; where a crispy golden haddock fish-fry with fries and coleslaw (the crust crunchy, the fish sweet and moist) is placed in front of every diner in the joint. There are hundreds of these corner taverns, and on Friday nights they are all jam-packed with loud talking, hearty, laughing folks taking a break from the busy week. It is Buffalo and Buffalo only. I figured the country was loaded with those thinking the same about their own places: Pittsburgh, Cleveland, and Knoxville, Des Moines, St. Louis, Denver or anywhere folks claim as their own.

That was how I felt and what I was thinking when Michael woke and looked at me sleepily through wandering eyes.

"We need to go," he said.

We shared a can of peaches and we brushed our teeth with toothpaste and water from our canteens and we combed our hair and we rolled our sleeping bags and secured them to the bottom of our packs and we walked to Highway 1 and took a bunch of rides. The first one got us out of Stinson Beach. We traveled through places like Bodega Bay, Jenner, Horseshoe Cove, Fisherman Bay, Gualala, Cuffey's Cove, and Navarro River. We took rides into Whitesboro Cove, Buckhorn Cove, Mendocino Bay, and Casper. We moved through Westport and inland to the Redwood Highway through Smithe Redwoods State Park and Richardson Grove State Park. We continued through Benbow, Garberville, Humbolt Redwoods State Park, Rio Dell, Fortuna, and on up into Eureka. We followed the route past Arcata Bay into Arcata to Highway101 north through Trinadad and Big Lagoon and Stone Lagoon and Freshwater Lagoon and into Crescent City and over the Oregon border into Brookings and Brandon to Coos Bay to Reedsport to Florence and along the coast through the Siuslaw Forest and into Newport. We followed Highway 101 through Lincoln City to Seaside to Astoria to Raymond to Aberdeen and then cut over through Olympia, Washington to Highway 5 and right on up into Seattle.

Chapter 38

Seattle

Our last ride into Seattle came from a couple of long-haired grungy fishermen heading to the docks to ship off into the Alaskan waters for three months of steady fishing. They'd been bumming around San Francisco on furlough and were heading back when they picked us up outside of Olympia. For pretty much the entire ride we smoked joints and passed a bottle of whiskey between us. They dropped us off on a crowded intersection in downtown Seattle.

It was early afternoon. Somber clouds slung low over dull black pavement and a misty rain kept the air cool. The streets were crowded and most everyone clutched an umbrella and had on light jackets or long sleeves. The whiskey burned a fiery knot deep in my stomach and the hits from the joints put my head upside down. I never really liked smoking that stuff.

We found ourselves senselessly standing on a busy downtown corner in front of a place called Burt's Shoes. The store windows were loaded with the latest shoe designs and big shiny leather purses. Around the corner a flashy neon sign read *Herfy's Burger Shop.*

"I can't stand here anymore. I'm getting wet. I need to get something to eat or else I'm going to puke," I said. "Let's grab a burger."

It was busy inside. We ordered two burgers, crinkle-cut fries and a couple of cokes from a cute waitress with a really big name tag. Her name was Sandy and she took our orders with a curious look. Our burgers came

loaded with sliced tomato and onion, lettuce and mayonnaise. I bit into mine
and a river of juice dribbled down my chin and onto my shirt.

Michael watched me lose all control in burger sensation, "Come on
man, you're spilling shit all over."

I snatched a wad of napkins from the holder, wiped my face and
caught my breath.

"A little messy," I said.

"I guess," Michael said shaking his head.

Sandy returned, "How are your burgers?"

"Mine's great," I said.

"I like your packs," she said looking them over. "Where are you
from?"

"We started in Buffalo," Michael said. "Been traveling for a couple
of months now."

"A long way," she said.

"It is," I said.

"Are you hiking the Mount?"

"The Mount?"

"Mount Rainier, you can see it from everywhere. We just call it the
Mount around here."

"Yes, we saw it on the way into Seattle," I said.

"I don't know," Michael said. "We hadn't thought about it. My
brother lives somewhere around here, I think."

"Where does he live?"

"That's a good question. I'm not sure. The last time he wrote he
mentioned Vashon Island and working in some bookstore in a place called
Pioneer Square. That's all I really know."

"And that was almost five years ago," I added.

"Pioneer Square's not far from here," she said. "Get your way down
to First Ave South and you go right into it. It's not far; you can walk. There's

a bookstore on First and Main called The Ellicott Bay or something like that. It's a big place. You might get lucky there."

I felt better. Sometimes a good greasy burger is all it takes to wipe away the effects of bad whiskey. The uneasiness from the pot left my brain and I could think a lot clearer now. I vowed to not smoke that stuff again. It didn't put me in the right mood that others got into when they hit on it.

Back home most of my friends couldn't get enough of smoking that stuff. They'd smoke bowls of it while we walked to school in the morning. They'd smoke joints in the bathroom between classes. A couple of times a week we'd skip out of school and head to a restaurant on Main Street called *The Red Barn*. It was a big red shiny fast food joint with a glass front and it was shaped like a barn. Their big famous burger was called *The Barnbuster*. There was another one called *The Big Barney*. We'd hop in my buddy Duane's car, a dull green nineteen sixty-eight Pontiac Tempest and he'd pull a wooden pipe with four hoses that stuck to the dashboard from his glove compartment. Duane spent the better part of his day in a pot induced haze. His hair was a helmet of thick kinky blonde hair that sat on his head and looked like the top of a corn muffin. We called him muffin head or the muffin man. A huge set of yellowed horse teeth filled his wide mouth and when he got stoned he wore this wide grin giving him the appearance of a happy albino donkey. Another one of the guys who made the great escape was Antonio, a good looking dark skinned Sicilian kid from across the street, who wore his hair down to his shoulders and donned a red bandana around his head giving him the look of a Cherokee Indian instead of a Sicilian kid from Buffalo. The last in our group was Jimmy Valley a big kid with a strong jaw, a movie star chin, and light blue eyes that crisscrossed. When he got stoned, you weren't quite sure if he was looking at you or not. The four of us would hop out of a window after first period, meet at the car and head to *The Red Barn*. Duane cranked The Allman Brothers or Robin Trower or Johnny "Guitar" Watson on the eight track player and we'd cruise down

Main Street smoking that wild snaky pipe. By the time fourth period rolled around I'd be back in one of my classes stoned and speechless in my seat.

"Thanks for the info," Michael said. "I guess after we leave here we'll head down."

Sandy told us to "forget about it" when we asked for the check. "It's on me. Welcome to Seattle," she said.

That was nice. We left *Herfy's* and the rain stopped and the clouds lifted. The sun cast a warm glow over the city. The air was fresh and clean and moist.

We made it into the old red brick neighborhood called Pioneer Square and found the bookstore right away. It was a massive cavernous store with brick walls and tall archways and hardwood floors. The store was filled with shelves and shelves of books. Books everywhere! Ten foot high shelves! Wooden spiraled stairs took you from one level to the next. We browsed through the fiction section and the war-history section and I hung in the poetry section for a long time pulling books from shelves and reading excerpts from local poets and contemporary poets and those long dead. We made our way throughout the store and up and down the stairs. There was no sign of George anywhere.

I never asked Michael what he would do when he ran into George. What should he do? What would he say? George could shut him down right on the spot and then Michael would give him hell, he'd get all fired up. That's what he'd do.

A skinny guy with pasty skin and a greasy comb-over was removing books from a cart and putting them on the shelves.

"Does a guy named George Theotikos work here?" Michael asked.

"I don't believe so," he answered in a high-pitched whisper. "I'm only here part time. You might want to ask someone else," he said continuing to shelve books.

Up the spiral stairs near the cash registers, a girl with a black bob haircut, a pudgy face and round glasses was also taking books from a cart and shelving them. "Never heard of him," she said and pointed in the direction of the manager engaged with a customer holding some gardening books in her hands.

"She's been here forever," the girl said. "If anyone would know, she would."

We stood politely a few feet away, making our presence known. Surrounded by these stacks of books opened me to all the possibilities in the world. I'd never been in a bookstore quite so big. They were all small neighborhood stores in Buffalo. We never saw the likes of this.

For a moment Michael stood nervously bursting with visible tension and anxiety. Here we were standing in Seattle, Washington, very far from home. The last bit of communication between the brothers was a simple note that said, *Working in a bookstore in Seattle and living on Vashon Island.* That was our lead, and as soon as the woman had her gardening questions answered, we were going to find out if George was anywhere to be found.

"I have a brother, George Theotikos, who may work here," Michael said approaching the woman. "I was wondering if he works here or if you know him?"

The woman's long, delicate, ivory neck became splotched in patchy pinks when she heard George's name.

"George is your brother?" she said, the pink fading before our eyes.

"Yes, I'm from Buffalo and he left a note a few years back saying he was working in a bookstore here in Seattle. I haven't seen him in a long time," Michael said. "Do you know him?"

"He hasn't worked here in a couple of years now," she said. "He did, but he left. He lives on the Island, Vashon Island. It's not too far from here."

"Do you think he's still there?" Michael asked. I mean, have you seen him?"

"He hasn't been around in a while," she said. The crimson disappeared from her neck and the soft ivory glow returned. "He used to come into Seattle maybe once a week, but lately I haven't seen him. He started writing poetry, good stuff, real gritty. He even gave a couple of readings around town and people took notice of his poetry. My guess is he's staying on the island and writing and when he's ready he'll come back into the city and maybe publish something and make the reading rounds."

"George is a poet?" I asked.

"A brilliant one," she said.

"Must have come from the old man," Michael said.

Chapter 39

Vashon Island

At thirty-seven square miles, Vashon Island, a hilly, woodsy island west of Seattle, is the largest island in the Puget Sound. There are no bridges to connect the island with the mainland. The only way to get on the island is to take one of a series of recurring ferries from downtown Seattle. It takes roughly twenty-five minutes to get from point to point. It is rural and even more laid back than Seattle. There are some pretty nice beaches too except the water is usually cold. Mt. Rainier emerges like a prodigious white dinosaur in the distance.

We slept the night before in a dingy hotel in Pioneer Square. The walls were yellowed and the room smelled of stale cigarette smoke. The bed was nothing more than a stained tattered mattress lying on big loose springs. It curved into the center and made annoying noises when we moved. I would have preferred to have slept outside, but it had gotten late and it was raining and there was really nowhere to go, so we bit it and sprung for the dump of a room. After a good breakfast of bacon and eggs and coffee in a diner that had a worn sign that said *99 cent Breakfast,* we made it down to the pier and got onboard the ferry heading to Vashon Island. We stood with our arms dangling over the railing on the deck of the ferry and smoking Marlboros as the boat churned toward the island. The day was dreary and dull. A misty rain covered us. The water pushing against the hull sprayed green and white and radiant. A fat man in bright white sneakers, khaki pants and a light blue windbreaker earnestly snapped photos of the distant Cascades and the encroaching island. He had one of those cameras with a very long lens.

After docking, we took a ride from a kid in a red pick-up who was getting off the ferry and heading into town. He let us off at an intersection with a hardware store on the corner. It looked like any rural town. A calm beauty, relaxed and friendly, low connecting buildings, a market, a coffee shop, a bank, a post office, a hardware store, a bar and a couple of small restaurants. There was no traffic to speak of. The sidewalks were dotted with those who unhurriedly wandered in and out of buildings or stopped to chat with a neighbor.

Michael gazed doubtfully about. "I can't imagine George hanging here," he said. "What the hell would he do?"

"Got me," I said.

"It's got kind of an artsy vibe," he said. "You know, these coffee shops and bookstores and stuff. People look like a bunch of hippies."

"George is no hippie," I said.

"That's for sure. George is no hippie, that's for sure," he said.

We walked past a corner bar and a gigantic man with wild red hair and a red beard tumbled from the front door and fell hard at our feet. It was if he was thrown to the sidewalk by some great force. He lay on his back looking toward the sky twisting and groaning. Michael looked at me then back at the man. He had on a plaid flannel shirt, blue jeans and worn brown construction boots. His hands were huge and gnarled and even laying on his back you could tell that he had an enormous tight gut. A moment later a wiry guy with thin scraggily hair and a tomahawk nose came busting out and landed on the redhead. The redhead received him with a grunt.

"Fucking bastards!" the little guy said. "Throwing us out like that."

"You can't cheat them like that," the Giant said. "How many fucking times do I gotta tell you?"

"Fucking bastards," the little guy said getting up brushing dirt from his sleeves with his hands. The big guy stood up slowly. He towered close to

313

six and a half feet tall. He gathered himself with a bewildered expression. I wondered who the hell could have thrown him out. He was a giant.

"What the hell are you looking at?" the little guy said in our direction.

Michael responded with a reserved smile, "Looks like a tough place to have a drink."

"If Johnny here wasn't such a cheat at darts, it wouldn't be so bad," the Giant said.

"Up yours," Johnny said. "I played it square."

"You gotta bet *before* you throw," the Giant said.

"Aw fuck," the little guy replied. "What now?"

"We gotta go back in and buy 'em a beer so they forget about it," the Giant said. "What about you two, you coming in?"

"Why not?" Michael said. "A beer will be good."

The bar was long and narrow and dark and lively. Four guys in flannel shirts and beards had control of the dartboard. They were all massive like the Giant.

A monster of a man with wide teeth and a flat forehead standing a couple of inches taller than the giant looked at him and said, "You at it again, Butch?"

"Yeah, Dan, I'm game. This time Johnny will play it fair, bets before the throw. Those are the rules," he said giving Johnny a crooked look.

"Yeah, yeah, bets before," said Johnny.

In the corner a rag-tag group of musicians with guitars, a banjo, a fiddle and one of those Irish drums you hold with one hand and hit with a mallet with the other were beltin' out Irish and hillbilly music. Butch pulled a harmonica from his shirt pocket and joined in and sang *Dirty Old Town* with a gruff voice that hit all of the notes perfectly. Everyone at the tables listened and some tapped their hands on the table tops and some sang along. Most of the tables held pitchers of beer with glasses. There were tiny shot glasses on the tables too.

The bartender spun and twisted gracefully behind a deep oak wooden bar filling pitchers of beer, cleaning ashtrays and wiping spills along the massive counter. She had long thick curly black hair and wore her sweater tight. She had a full face with round cheeks and bushy lips.

"How about a pitcher and two glasses," Michael said. "Something for you?"

"It's too early," she said. "I have a long night ahead, thanks."

It was happy hour and beer was cheap, so were shots of whiskey.

The pitcher arrived with two short beer glasses and a basket of popcorn from a machine behind the bar continuously spewing fresh batches. A comfortable, friendly, aroma drifted in the air. We sipped the beer slowly and passed on the whiskey and joined in on darts and lost a couple of bucks. This group was too good. They played with serious precision. The band kept rhythm to the drinking and the dart playing. The place was filling up and getting louder and most everyone sucked on cigarettes that sent clouds of smoke floating overhead. The Giant lost a couple more games of darts and the plaid clad players were satisfied to take his money. He gave up and joined the band for a few more tunes singing *Long Haired Country Boy* and a country version of Bob Dylan's *Maggie's Farm*. A skinny toothless old timer with combat boots, camouflage pants and an orange t-shirt danced in front of the band crouching and shooting an imaginary assault rifle throughout the room.

"Fuckin' Dudley," the Giant said. "He's wacked as hell."

The music continued. Michael ordered another pitcher and we were feeling pretty good when the Giant stumbled over and offered to continue the party at his place on the western side of the island. An announcement was made, the gang agreed and soon we were holding on tight riding in back of his pickup after stopping off to grab a couple of cases of beer and heading to his place.

The Giant owned a grey weathered clapboard house on the western shore. It had an assortment of sun-bleached antlers hanging on it. In the back yard a massive fire pit, surrounded by a group of long haired boys, crackled and spit enormous flames and orange tinder into the sky. The boys: Jack, Max and Dan were all brothers and close in age. I guessed they must have been between ten and sixteen years old or so. There was no mistaking the Giants' lineage: strong jaws, flat foreheads, red faces and pale blue eyes. They were a knockoff of the Giant. A few other boys, equally full of brawn, sat at the fire poking at the burning logs with long sticks with fire-hot tips. The Giant's wife greeted the gang with a look of reluctant reception.

"Not too late tonight," she warned the Giant. "We have to get the yard work done in the morning and you promised you'd be up for it."

The Giant planted a tender kiss on her forehead. "I'm plannin' on it, baby," he said cracking open a beer. "I'm plannin' on it."

Chairs were set up and scattered around the burning pit. Beers were taken out of cases and placed into a big old cast iron claw foot bathtub positioned against a tall shade tree. A couple of the kids helped out by opening bags of ice and covering the beers. Bottles of Old Grand-Dad made their way around the yard. The boys in the band set up a spot near the fire and broke out their acoustic guitars, banjos, fiddles, washboards, and harmonicas. Music filled the air, the fire burned brightly and the gathering grew larger.

The sun had lowered. The air was thick and moist and the sky grew dark. A sliver of moon peaked from shadowy moving clouds. Michael showed the long haired kids the Rand McNalley. He traced our journey for them, telling stories already embellished. The boys listened with quiet curiosity. More people wandered in. Couples arrived bringing chairs and adding beer to the claw-tub. Some lit joints and pipes passed between them. The long haired boys gathered to the side of a shed and engaged in a rowdy game of horseshoes. The clanking sound of iron filled the night.

A playful pack of dogs appeared out of nowhere. I counted five dodging in and out of the crowd and circling the growing game of horse shoes. We drank the cans of ice cold beer. Michael slugged from one of the bottles of Old Grand-Dad; his head tilting back and his eyes getting lost in a drunken haze. He rarely got drunk, but I could tell he was slipping into a state of sloppy uneasiness. A cigarette dangled from his lip and his face melted like hot butter before me.

An old drunken broad found her way next to me. She swayed clumsily moving her head from side to side. "Are you from far away?" she asked wiping her dirty bare feet on the grass. She wore a long flowing skirt, the kind the hippy broads wear. Her hair was pulled back into a thick long braid that hung on her back; her face was plain with dull brown eyes and when she smiled I noticed traces of yellow-brown stain in her teeth. She clutched a beer and a cigarette in one hand and she placed the other on my shoulder pushing her face closer to mine.

"I said, are you from far away?"

"Pretty far," I said. I didn't feel like getting into the whole story.

"You look like a kid I knew in Cleveland," she said. "Are you from Cleveland?"

"No," I said.

"Are you sure?" she slurred. "You look just like this kid I knew in Cleveland. You look just like 'em. Are you sure you're not from Cleveland, from Murray Hill?"

"I'm sure," I said.

"Well, you look just like this kid I knew," she said. "You remind me of sunshine and warm summer days too. You know that?"

I didn't respond. She got bored with me and swayed uneasily toward the boys playing music, placing her hands on everyone's shoulders along the way, like they were walking canes. A fat woman in very short shorts guzzled a beer and then vomited foam while a group of wild haired giants cheered her on. Michael knocked back cans of beer and smoked profusely and his buttery face melted grotesquely as he staggered from one group to the next. The amused Giant watched him and let me know it would be no problem for us to pitch the tent and sleep in his yard for the night.

"No skin off my nose," he said.

In the soft darkness someone yelled, "Look at the sky, look at the sky!" We all lifted our heads toward a brightly lit orb floating eerily on the horizon over the dark waters.

"What the hell is it?" someone asked.

"A plane!" another shouted. "It's a little plane."

"That's not a plane," another responded. "There's no sound. It's a fucking zeppelin man. It's a fucking zeppelin with a big-ass spotlight."

"It is," another agreed. "That's cool as hell!"

"I wonder what it's doing up there?" Someone asked.

"Probably some shit going on in Seattle," another answered and we watched it hang weirdly over the sound, all thinking our own wild and dooming thoughts.

There was a break in the clouds and a soft yellow light from the moon lit the swarming lawn. Everyone gathered in groups and their voices got louder. The clanking of horseshoes hitting the pole became more frequent. I figured there were some good players in the pit. Michael wandered sloppily from group to group. His posture loosened and his legs wobbled. When he spoke, he leaned closely and carelessly toward them. He reminded me of an awkward gawking bird.

It was at that moment when George and a slight girl with big round eyes and long dark bangs walked from the house and onto the lawn. George held a striking presence. His hair was thick and black and combed back from his forehead. His skin was soft and dark almond color and his eyes held the shade of the deepest roasted coffee. He wore tight faded blue jeans and a soft white cotton shirt unbuttoned at the collar. The girl, whose arm was tucked inside of his, was quiet and mysterious. She wore sandals and a light sleeveless cotton dress cut just above her knees. They looked as though they had slid out from the pages of GQ Magazine.

The Giant greeted them warmly. George responded with a firm, confident handshake. The girl extended her long delicate hand and the Giant held it gently in his big paw.

"Nice to see you, Melissa; you look fantastic," the Giant said. George scanned the yard.

"Nice get-together," he said.

"After happy hour they all end up here," the Giant said. "So, what else is new?"

George tightened his arm firmly around the girl's waist and surveyed the crowd. He glanced in my direction and when I caught sight of him my stomach flipped tightly. I raised my arm and gave a wave, but he was looking past me, into the crowd, and did not notice me. Was that George? He looked slighter and darker and better looking than I remembered.

The party flowed in calm energy and the moon cast a soft glow over the yard and the still night held suspended when suddenly everybody turned to the sound of a loud splash followed by another. Everyone raced the edge of the yard and watched Michael and a girl racing one another naked in the moonlit Puget Sound.

I found myself standing next to George. George watched the two swimming smoothly in the water. His girlfriend's eyes followed their bodies heading gracefully toward the shore, their arms pulling them in and their asses rising from the water for all to see. They moved in unison. They were neck and neck and the cheering began.

I turned to George who did not recognize me and I said, "He's very drunk now. He doesn't drink too much, but every once in a while when he gets going, he falls out."

George's girl was thrilled to watch the race. She participated in the rising chorus of cheers. Her white dress swayed gently with her movements. George lost interest in the spectacle. He looked at me with a vague familiarity.

"I guess we all get drunk once in a while and do things spontaneously," he said.

"I think he got drunk because he knew he'd run into you pretty soon," I said. "He figured once we got to Seattle it wouldn't be long."

George's eyes narrowed and his countenance suggested confusion. Michael beat the girl by only an arm's length. They emerged from the water with their naked bodies dripping in the moonlight. The girl was long and pale with small tits and wide hips. Michael's dark skin blended into the night sky and walking toward their clothes they presented an unlikely pair. George watched closely at the couple on the shore putting on pieces of clothing. Michael shook his hair vigorously to dry it and looked up at the cheering crowd gathered at the end of the yard. A wide smile broke across his face. George gazed starkly into the night at the victorious swimmer below and his face dropped.

"Jesus Christ," he said turning to Melissa. "That's my kid brother down there."

Chapter 40

Hauling Loads

George's pickup truck was a dull-white nineteen-fifty eight
International with chrome bumpers and a big steering wheel. Flecks of
brown rust spotted the bumpers. The strong axel and a sturdy bed were
meant for hauling heavy loads. George said he got it for a good price. He
used it to haul anything anyone wanted hauled on the island. After a couple
of months he had the truck paid off. He hauled furniture, rocks, fence posts,
livestock, garbage…you name it, if someone needed a truck, he was the man
they called and he stayed as busy as he wanted to and made decent enough
money at it.

After Michael got out from the water and dried off, George insisted
we stay at his place. Actually it was Melissa's house. She got it after her
divorce. The guy she was married to said a lot of shitty things to her.
Sometimes he hit her and she'd have to take off and stay with a friend until
he calmed down. She got the house in the settlement. She took out a
restraining order against him and he never came back. She heard he moved
to Olympia where he grew up. She heard he was managing a bowling alley
and had a girlfriend who used to run with some motorcycle gang. Melissa
did not think that would last too long.

The house was small and wooden and white with aqua shutters. It
was more like a country cottage. Melissa had a passion for gardening.
Flowers and big green leafy plants grew everywhere. The yard was loaded

with all kinds of odds and ends: old unpainted wooden benches and barrels and tables holding wild flower baskets and climbing wisteria. A rose pergola stood at the entrance of her front door and bright yellow, red and white roses blossomed from the tremendous structure. Big eucalyptus trees helped shade the garden and in the center of the yard stood a round white metal table with four matching chairs where she and George would have breakfast or lunch or dinner on warm calm days. Near the back screen door, an old washing machine stood brimming with pink and white impatiens.

This morning George had to pick up scrap and haul it to a dump on the other side of the island. He had a list of clients scheduled for the day. He did this every Tuesday morning which meant getting up at six o'clock, having a quick breakfast and getting on the road. Melissa woke us up and led us to the table in the yard where George was already sitting quietly reading a newspaper. He appeared awake, alert and serious. He wore blue jeans and a white western shirt with the sleeves rolled to his elbows. His hair was thick and dark and shiny. It was combed back off of his forehead and behind his ears. We sat down. On the table were four coffee mugs, a plate with toast stacked on it, and some grape jam and butter. There was also a sugar bowl shaped like a head of lettuce and a quart bottle of milk. Melissa offered us coffee from a pot. Her hair was pulled back and I noticed her dark eyebrows were thick. George put the newspaper down, buttered his toast and then spread the grape jam on it. He did this slowly and deliberately. He looked at us curiously. He spoke quietly and I couldn't help but feel that his mind was perpetually in another place.

George studied Michael and asked, "How's the noggin?"

"Cloudy, but it's okay, I deserve what I get," he said.

"I was surprised to see you coming out of that water last night," George said looking at the both of us. "I never thought I'd see that."

"I don't know what came over me," Michael said. "That girl, she said, I bet I can kick your ass in a race and I said something like I'll race you to that tree and back and she said not running, swimming. I bet I can kick your ass swimming. So we took off our clothes and plunged in."

"Her name is Andrea," George said. "She's nuts. She's getting a divorce and has been acting crazy lately. If her husband was there he would have killed you first and asked why you were swimming naked with his wife later."

Melissa gave George a cold look of warning and offered us more coffee.

"You were always a bit spontaneous and reckless," George said. "It's the kind of behavior I recall from you."

"I think everyone in our neighborhood was a bit reckless," I said.

"Agreed," said George. "You should hear this, Melissa. Jimmy is right, everyone in Buffalo is a bit reckless or at least they make brash decisions. It runs in our family doesn't it?" George said looking closely at Michael.

Michael looked at George unfazed. George glanced at Melissa. She shot him another look. Michael bit into his toast and some of the jam stayed lodged in the corner of his mouth. He licked the rest in.

"Do you want to see my paintings?" George asked. "I've been painting and I have some in the house. Would you like to see them?"

"Sure, why not," Michael said. "I didn't know you painted."

"Sure," I said.

In the back of the house was a small room. It was clearly George's. Book cases filled with all kinds of books lined the walls, and in the center of the room was a small wooden table with four spindly legs holding a typewriter. The typewriter had a sheet of paper on the roll. There was a stack of papers with writing on it. Next to the table was a wastepaper basket filled with tightly rolled balls of discarded paper. Also, on the table, was an open book about northwestern bird species. In one corner of the room stood a painter's easel with an unfinished painting of a lighted yellow figure of a woman floating in the sky into the center of a cosmic universe. There was another painting of a tall dark woman standing on a hill under a murky sky surrounded by thirteen brightly lit stars and there was another painting of an indigenous Peruvian girl peering at us with dark, inquisitive eyes. There were others. All had a spiritual mystical afterlife vibe to them.

"I just started painting," George said. "They came out of me somehow and I can't explain it. I just painted."

"I like them," Michael said.

"Me too," I agreed.

"I enjoy writing poetry," he said. "I've been writing a lot of poetry and some of it sticks, I mean some of it is pretty good. Some of its lame, though. I'm hanging onto the good stuff and when I have enough I'll see about getting it published. That would be a good thing."

"We've heard about the poetry," I said. "About your readings and stuff, that good-looking chick, the one with the pale skin, down at the bookstore in Pioneer Square told us you were up here writing. She said you wrote good stuff and when you finished you would get published and do more readings."

George hesitated; he thought about the girl in the book store, her pale blushing skin.

"So, you've been looking for me?"

"Yes, we've been looking for you," Michael said.

"And now you have found me," George said. "Do you want to do the garbage run with me?"

"Sure," we said.

The three of us crammed into the front of the International. George brought a bottle of champagne with him. He popped the cork and we drank it out of coffee mugs. Melissa gave us a brown paper bag filled with fresh cherries. We took back roads and cut east until we picked up the Vashon Highway near the town of Burton. From there we headed north. The day was bright. There were big, white inflated clouds overhead and the sky was light blue. George had all of his stops mapped out and we rode up the narrow highway passing Quartermaster Harbor and up through the dark woods and the golden meadows and the pine trees into Vashon Town and back up through the thick trees and ferns until we almost reached the northern tip of the island. Along the way we drank the champagne and ate the sweet purple cherries from the bag spitting the pits into our palms and throwing them out the window. Along the road, we picked up an old washer and dryer and gutters and indoor water pipes and other pieces of discarded scrap metal. At each stop George collected his fee and by the time the truck was loaded he had a thick wad of cash in his pocket. George dropped his load off at some guy named Bill's place who was going to salvage the metal and ship it over to Seattle in an old thirty-two foot Trojan cabin cruiser.

George was happy working. He spoke brightly of moving to Seattle and, as he put it, ending up in paradise, which is how he referred to Vashon Island. He said he met Melissa at one of the poetry readings and fell for her instantly. He was hanging with the chick at the bookstore, but she was too intense and brooding.

"Together we were tortuous poisonous souls; that's even too much for a poet," he grinned.

When we got back to the house later that afternoon, Melissa had been in the kitchen cooking a big meal. She wanted to please us and she wanted to make George comfortable.

"It's a good evening to sit outside and have dinner," she said. "We get a lot of rain here, so when it's not too cold or rainy, I like to have dinner outside. I made a green salad and baked us some chicken with corn and mashed potatoes."

"Ouzo!" George announced banging his fist on the table and opening a clear bottle and pouring a shot in each of our glasses. "Tonight's a celebration!" Let's drink Ouzo with little brother Mikey and his Irish side-kick Jimmy!"

Melissa shot George a look of warning.

"I only drank it once and I swore I'd never drink it again." I said.

"That's because you got hammered on it," Michael said turning to George. "You should have seen him, George. This past Christmas I picked him up from his house and brought him home. Uncle Herc and Aunt Rena and Uncle Tom and Aunt Talia and Uncle Johnny and Mom, they were all sitting at the table after dinner and Uncle Tom said give your friend here a little Ouzo and that's when Jimmy proceeded to get inebriated."

George listened blankly holding tightly to his glass.

"I don't even remember," I said. "I never had anything that I completely blacked out with. I just remember something about your mother's hands."

"You kept on telling her how beautiful and soft her hands were," Michael said. "You wouldn't let go of them. She sat across from you and you held her hands. You wouldn't let go."

"Jesus," I said. "She did have incredible hands."

"You kept saying over and over to everybody at the table, do you know how long Michael and I have been friends? Do you have any idea? Every time you said it Aunt Rena said, 'that's nice, that's nice.' You wouldn't let go of my mother's hands."

Melissa passed the salad and George raised his glass.

"Opa," he said.

"Slainte," Jimmy replied, and we threw back the chilled, clear, sweet anise flavored drink.

Melissa announced that it was time to eat and suggested we get started by passing everything to the left. George filled our glasses again and I watched his skin redden and his eyes turn complicated.

"You are the finest cook on the entire island, my dear," he said raising his glass and shouting "opa!"

We drank again and I could feel my ears burning. We ate busily and silently. The chicken was tender and juicy with a seasoned breadcrumb coating. The potatoes were golden and mashed with plenty of butter and sour cream and seasoned nicely with salt and pepper. Melissa fried the corn in a cast-iron skillet and added plenty of butter and salt.

"This is fantastic, Melissa," Michael said. "We haven't had home-cooked dinners as good as this."

"Thank you, Michael," she said.

"We eat a lot of bread with peanut butter and jelly and canned goods too," I said. "It's easy to carry and it lasts a long time in our packs."

"I'm sick of peanut butter and Jelly. If I never ate it again I wouldn't care at all," Michael said locking his eyes and holding his glass to George's. George poured us another and we drank it down.

Sitting closely at George's side was Tasos Theotikos. George was unaware of his presence. Michael watched his father's face smiling tenderly at both of his sons.

George filled our glasses again and returned a steady look toward Michael.

"I suppose you want answers," he said.

"That's up to you," Michael said.

"You want to play that game?" George asked.

"I'm okay with it," Michael said.

Tasos glanced affectionately toward George.

"You've come a long way to find me. What did you think you were going to find?" George asked.

"I don't know, George. I wasn't sure what you'd be doing out here. You've been gone a long time."

George paused for a moment and stretched back in his chair.

"I know Mom's gone," he said.

"Yes she is," Michael said. "I was there. I watched it."

George shifted uneasily in his seat. "What was it like?"

"Sudden and stark," Michael said. "She looked scared and lonely and pathetic dying on the floor. I don't know why I thought of you at that moment, but I did. It left me cold and angry that you were not with us. After it was all over and we buried Mom in the ground I thought about you a lot. After some time went by I knew I needed to find you and that's when I told Jimmy that we were going on a road trip and we would end up here looking for you, to let you know what things have been like for us in Buffalo without Dad and now Mom."

George held nervously onto his glass. His face was calm and his voice was matter of fact. Melissa watched him.

Tasos leaned in and listened intently.

"I know things that you never knew, Mikey. Dad was a mess. He was a pitiful worn-out out mess with nowhere to go. He didn't like himself and he couldn't see where he was going and he couldn't find where he wanted to be. Somehow I understood him Mikey."

"He was a coward, George. He killed himself," Michael said.

"He wasn't a coward, Mikey. He was very brave. He thought too much, though; it was a curse for him for him to live the way he did and he couldn't go on. He knew it. It's sad and it's pathetic, and I wish it was different, but that's the way it was."

"You were close to him," Michael said.

"I understood him and I was afraid I'd become like him so I had to leave and do things myself. If I failed, it would be on me and I wouldn't have to feel the humiliation he went through. And, I wouldn't have to hurt others like he did."

"That's bullshit," Michael said. "That doesn't do anything for us and it did nothing for Mom. It's pretty damn selfish."

"Maybe it is." George said. "Maybe its complete bullshit and maybe I'm one selfish bastard, but that is the story. That is what happened. Wrong or right, the story does not lie. Dad and I had an agreement. We understood one another. Dad finally came to realize that the truth in life is to accept what is. Dad didn't like what it was. He couldn't continue."

Tasos Theotikos moved from his seat and walked toward Michael. He placed his hand firmly on his shoulders and lowered himself to kiss his son's forehead. Michael felt the warmth from his father and realized at that moment Tasos was going to be fine. Tasos was in the place he needed to be. George helped him to see that.

I watched Michael's face soften. I guess he figured there was nothing else he could do or say and, at least, George was honest. Melissa gave George a warm look and placed her hand on his shoulder.

George averted his eyes downward and away from me. I had it figured out and George knew it. I knew right then that George pulled the trigger. I don't know how George pulled it off, but I knew he did, or *they* did. The two of them. It was a perfect plan. It was all so clear and no one was ever going to know but George and me. I wanted to shout, "You George, you pulled the trigger and you killed your father!" But, what would that do but cause a whole bunch of trouble. The old man was dead and he wanted out and he was too weak to do it for himself. He was a coward and George was not. George was an artist and he wasn't a coward and the old man was a sad case and that's the way it was, period.

I wish I could say that everything changed with this revelation, or that George came back to live in Buffalo, but that is not the case. He did visit once and then left again never to return. I guess, maybe, Michael understood George a little bit better and developed a genuine fondness for him.

Later, when the warmth of the Ouzo settled in and held us close, George read some of his poetry. His black hair glistened and his brown eyes gleamed brilliantly. He read slowly with passion and confidence. He read the poetry he was going to bring to the crowd over in Seattle. The stuff he had been working on. It was stark and stunning. I listened quietly and his words opened our lives for all to see. I saw George and Michael and Nick and Colleen and their sweet mother with her deep brown eyes and soft-white porcelain hands. I saw Buffalo and her colorless dreary skies and her tight neighborhoods and her big, full elm trees rising into arches above gray city streets. I saw warm red-brick buildings radiating under a bright summer sun. I saw tight, long, dark streets lined with steel garbage cans on gloomy chilly rainy nights and I saw big Fords and Chevys and Pontiacs stuck under mounds and mounds of deep sparkling-white heavy snow. I saw ice storms and dark rolling rain clouds and pink sunrises and bright red sunsets with silver, orange and yellow clouds glowing in the distance. And, I saw a strong dark-skinned Greek boy with soft eyes named Tasos Theotikos wiping sweat from his brow, getting off a boat, the air wet and thick, and stepping onto a wooden dock in Tarpon Springs, Florida with a quiet and peculiar dim-witted uncle and a dream of all the possibilities this new land had to offer.

Acknowledgements

Many sincere thanks to Brenden, Tara, Emily and Quinn who have always been a boundless source of inspiration for me. Thank you to Elaine Thomas for editing my manuscript, helping me through the awkward prose, and finally making the work publishable. And thank you to all of the generous folks who gave us lifts, took care of us and shared their stories.

Made in the USA
Middletown, DE
23 April 2015